PRAISE

NOI

Selected as one of the ... Roberts' DARK WITCH and Julia Quinn's SUM OF ALL KISSES. USA Today Contributor, Becky Lower, Happily Ever After

"Ava's story is witty and charming." Barbara Freethy #1 NYT bestselling author

FRENCH ROAST
"An entertaining ride...{and) a full-bodied romance." Readers' Favorite

THE GRAND OPENING
"Ava Miles is fast becoming one of my favorite light contemporary romance writers." Tome Tender

THE HOLIDAY SERENADE
"This story is all romance, steam, and humor with a touch of the holiday spirit..." The Book Nympho

THE TOWN SQUARE
"Ms. Miles' words melted into each page until the world receded around me..." Tome Tender

COUNTRY HEAVEN
"If ever there was a contemporary romance that rated a 10 on a scale of 1 to 5 for me, this one is it!" The Romance Reviews

THE PARK OF SUNSET DREAMS
"Ava has done it again. I love the whole community of Dare Valley..." Travel Through The Pages Blog

THE CHOCOLATE GARDEN
"On par with Nicholas Sparks' love stories." Jennifer's Corner Blog

Also by Ava Miles

The Dare Valley Series:
NORA ROBERTS LAND
FRENCH ROAST
THE GRAND OPENING
THE HOLIDAY SERENADE
THE TOWN SQUARE
THE PARK OF SUNSET DREAMS
THE PERFECT INGREDIENT

DARING DECLARATIONS:
An Anthology including THE HOLIDAY SERENADE AND THE TOWN SQUARE

The Dare River Series:
COUNTRY HEAVEN
COUNTRY HEAVEN SONG BOOK
COUNTRY HEAVEN COOKBOOK
THE CHOCOLATE GARDEN

THE
Perfect
INGREDIENT
AVA MILES

This is a work of fiction. All of the characters, organizations, and events portrayed in this novel are either the products of the author's imagination or are used fictionally.

ISBN-13: 978-1-940565-15-6
www.avamiles.com
Ava Miles

To my brother, Brandon, the youngest in our family of six, who used to draw magical desserts as a little kid and ask me to make them. You were the perfect ingredient to our family, and I love and cherish you so much.

To all women who have experienced violence at the hands of a man. You are not alone.

And to my divine entourage, who keeps cheering me on and helps me move forward always.

Acknowledgements

My eternal thanks to Team Ava, especially Sienna for bringing joy as well as organization into our partnership; to Greg for every piece of support he gives me visually; to Kristen for always going the extra mile; and for a bunch of others who make this journey so much easier and fun.

Janet Geary for again always being at the ready to answer police-oriented questions.

Matt Mattery for being my go-to on investment banking in the Big Apple.

T.F. For being the part of me that I hold with faith, love, and trust.

And last but not least, all of you wonderful readers, who spread the word about our amazing Dare family, of which you are all members. Thank you from the biggest part of my heart for being you!

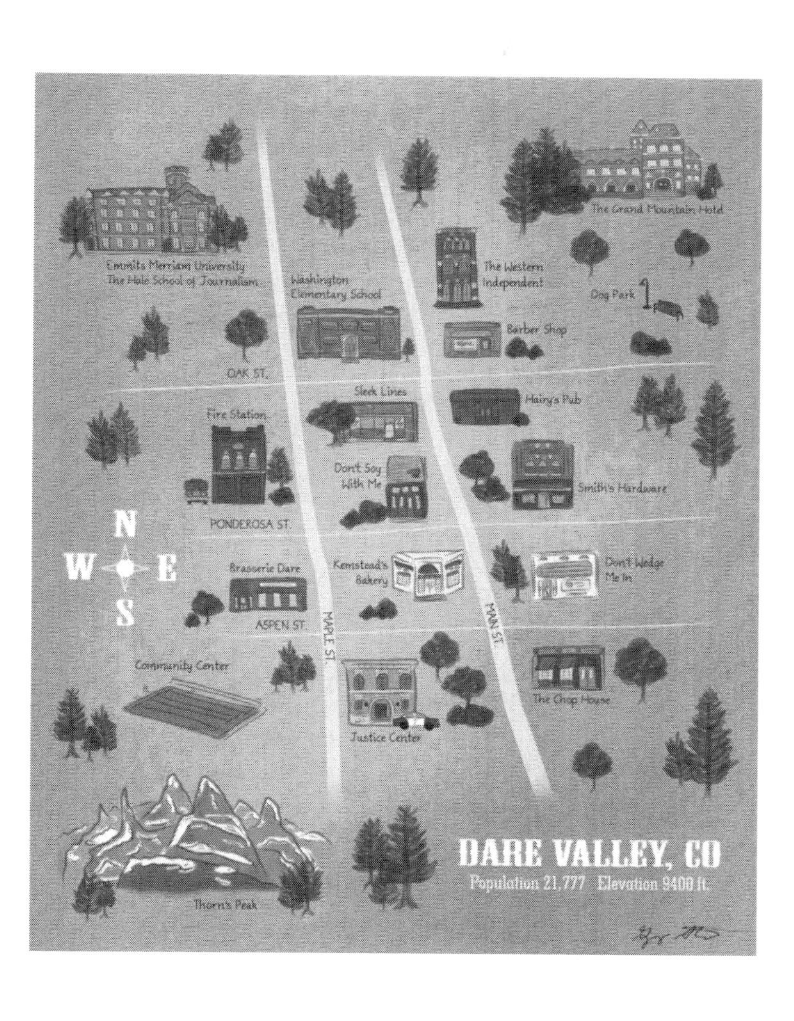
The Grand Mountain Hotel
Emmits Merriam University
The Hale School of Journalism
Washington
Elementary School
The Western
Independent
Dog Park
Barber Shop
OAK ST.
Sleek Lines
Hairy's Pub
Fire Station
Don't Soy
With Me
Smith's Hardware
PONDEROSA ST.
N
W
E
S
Brasserie Dare
Kemstead's
Bakery
Don't Wedge
Me In.
ASPEN ST.
MAPLE ST.
MAIN ST.
Community Center
The Chop House
Justice Center
Thorn's Peak
DARE VALLEY, CO
Population 21,777 Elevation 9400 ft.

Prologue

Two years ago...

It was the last time between them.

She knew it.

He didn't.

As Terrance's body trembled against her own, Elizabeth closed her eyes to savor his smell, the feel of him—so she could remember everything about him when she was gone.

She loved him.

But it wasn't enough.

She forced her eyes open to gaze at the bruised, swollen knuckles on his hands, those hands that had caressed her skin so softly, so sweetly tonight after punching a guy flat for looking at her wrong, for calling her horrible names.

Dressed in a form-fitting sequined Armani gown, wearing six-inch stilettos as Vixen, Rhett Butler Blaylock's poker babe, she'd heard worse.

Only the people she worked with knew her real name—Elizabeth Saunders—and that Vixen was a mirage. She was Rhett's poker scout, and being the gaudy, ditzy Vixen allowed her to conduct her duties under the radar. Heck, she was really a Harvard graduate, a numbers geek, who adored poker.

Terrance stirred and kissed her shoulder. "Hey. Are you sure you're okay about what happened earlier?" he asked softly, tracing her neck. "You seem more...emotional tonight. I was only trying to defend you from that asshole."

"I'm fine," she made herself say.

But she wasn't.

She waited for him to fall asleep.

As she lay next to him, listening to his breathing grow more even, she cursed herself for being a foolish girl. She'd wanted to unmask herself and tell Terrance everything. She had rehearsed her speech to him in front of the mirror earlier as she put on her wig and stage makeup.

Something that would never happen now. The wounds of her past were deep. She could not be in love with a violent man. Certainly not one who made her feel this vulnerable.

Her chest filled with unshed tears as she slid out of bed and dressed.

Terrance turned onto his side and hugged a pillow to his chest like he already missed her. His griffin tattoos appeared to fly across his forearms, as if urging her not to flee.

She crossed the room and scrawled a hasty note on the hotel stationery, laid it on the desk, and turned around to gaze at him one last time.

Terrance Waters would never know Elizabeth Saunders. It was for the best.

She shut the door on him—and her heart.

Chapter 1

Terrance Waters had turned into a lovesick head case.

He was on his way to confront the first and only woman who had broken his heart. Elizabeth Saunders, formerly known as Vixen. The odometer on his new gun-metal gray SUV turned over to 333 miles, and he wondered if it was an omen. Having been the chef at The Peacock Hotel & Casino in Atlantic City, he knew a thing or two about lucky numbers.

Right now he didn't feel so lucky. His stomach felt like he'd just made an appearance on his good friend's show, *Dangerous Dishes*, where the guests ate things like rotten shark steak wrapped in a seaweed aspic.

He'd met Elizabeth two years ago at The Peacock and spent the most erotic and emotional summer of his life with her. She'd left him high and dry when September rolled around. The note had been short, but less than sweet: *It was fun. All my best, Vixen.*

Vixen.

It was the only name she'd given him at the time. He had respected her desire not to talk about the past because he hated to talk about it too. No one wanted to hear about the poor New York City street rat, Terrance Waters. People liked success stories, but they didn't like to hear about the unseemliness that had come before. People called him Chef T now, and that suited him just fine.

His temporary home of Dare Valley glowed like a picturesque town in a Thomas Kinkade painting off in the distance as he turned too fast onto the road that would lead him to her house on the bench. With thirty thousand people, this town was too small for him—so different from New York City. He often didn't know what to do with himself when he left The Grand Mountain Hotel, where he was the new head chef. Granted, he'd only been in Dare Valley a few weeks, but still...

Tonight, the kitchen had come to a halt at about ten thirty, and since he didn't clean the grill anymore unless he was pissed off, he didn't have anything else to do. There was an Irish bar in town called Hairy's, but it closed at eleven on weeknights like this one. *Eleven!* So he'd decided it was finally time to face Elizabeth.

Rhett Butler Blaylock had settled in Dare Valley, and Elizabeth was here too, working as his publicist now. Terrance hadn't recognized her at first—she looked so different without all the heavy makeup and flair of Vixen. But he'd quickly worked it out. The shock of seeing her again, of realizing they'd be living in the same small town, had made his gut quiver, something he didn't have time for anymore. He'd planned to be gracious about it, but she'd lied to his face when they ran into each other at The Grand Mountain Hotel and he called her Vixen. What was it she'd said? Oh, yes. *You must have me confused with someone else.* To add insult to injury, she'd gone public with the information about her dual identity not long after.

Terrance could tolerate a lot, but there were two

things he couldn't stomach: running away and lying. A confrontation was overdue.

Since Vixen—heck, Elizabeth—had struck him as an experienced partner who was straightforward in what she wanted, her behavior was puzzling.

It was time to find out why she'd run and why she'd lied to him weeks ago.

Her house was set down a long, snaky driveway lined with discreet lights in one of Dare Valley's newer developments. She'd been a night owl like him, so he had no qualms about showing up this late. Plus, all the better if it set her teeth on edge.

Pissing her off would make him feel better since she'd pissed him off plenty.

He exited the car, grateful the snow had melted earlier. Snow in late April. Nothing fun about that. New York was cold, but this was something else. The wind was brisk coming down the mountain, and he could see the pines sway in the eerie light of the half moon nestled in a sky exploding with stars. The silence was eerie, too, when he was so used to big city noise. Nothing disguised his footsteps as he walked to her two-story craftsman home, jogging up the porch steps. When he reached her door, he simply rapped on the wood and waited for her to answer.

And he waited a long while, his ears growing cold in the frigid air. "Elizabeth," he finally said, "I know you're home. Your lights are on. Open up. It's time we talked."

Silence.

His P.O. factor was growing. "You're being childish. Open the goddamn door." Great, now she'd made him swear, something off his daily menu now. That meant he owed another hundred to his Cuss Fund. Since he'd forget if he waited, he fished a crisp bill out of his wallet.

The door swung open, and there she stood in all her natural glory, her blond curls soft around her face, wearing boring red flannel pajamas. Okay, his Y chromosome had been hoping for a silk peignoir and robe.

Seeing her like this, like a normal woman, was still a shock. Vixen had dressed to be every man's fantasy in her form-fitting designer dresses and high heels. With her face devoid of makeup, her skin glowed, and the force of her natural beauty stole over him. Then he realized her breathing was rapid, like she'd been working out, and her pulse beat strongly in her neck.

The powder blue eyes he used to drown in during their time together fell to the money he hadn't yet stuffed into his pocket. "If you're looking for a hooker, you've come to the wrong place."

Well, that was a nice way to start. "You made me swear, so I had to dole out my punishment."

"What? I thought that's what your fans loved about you," she said, and he heard the quiver in her voice.

Were her lips trembling too? What was going on? Was she afraid of him?

His fans loved his badass attitude, but the president of the television channel that was supposed to air his dream primetime network show was a different story. Lane Adams had chewed him out like he was a bad kid in grade school after seeing his interview on a cable network. Admittedly, it had been an off day...or an on one, depending on how you looked at it. Terrance had cussed through much of the spot, stringing together one innuendo after another. Then, rather than accepting Lane's medicine like a good boy, he'd sworn a blue streak in their follow-up meeting. He was paying for his brief loss of control. He'd been put on probation by the network, and if he didn't clean up his act in two months, his show was toast.

"I'm giving up swearing for a while. Now are you going to let me come in? I'm freezing my ass... Jeez, you have no idea how hard it is to talk without using bad words." He pulled another bill from his wallet and tucked both of them into his pocket.

Her inhalation was stark, like she was gasping for breath. "You're different from how I remembered."

The last two years and all the secrets between them rose up in his throat. He swallowed thickly. "So are you."

"You shouldn't have come to my house late at night like this, Terrance." She exhaled jaggedly as she said it, making him wonder again what was wrong, why she seemed afraid.

"Just because I'm pissed at you, doesn't mean I would hurt you. Ever. I only want to talk. Don't you think it's time? Your secret is out to the world now, and I deserve an explanation."

"You think so, huh?" Her eyes narrowed. "It was two years ago."

"Well, it cut me in two." He hadn't planned on revealing the truth to her, but perhaps it would ease the fear hovering around her, something he hated himself for causing.

Her mouth parted, and she took another tortured breath before stepping back to let him inside. He entered and reached down to pull off his wet hiking boots, which was when he noticed a baseball bat resting against the wall beside the door.

So this was more than a simple fear of him.

When he stood, he gestured to the Louisville Slugger. "What's going on? Have you formed a newfound appreciation for baseball, or is there something you're afraid of right now?"

She shoved the bat into the nearby closet as he shed his jacket. "I told you that you shouldn't have come here at this hour. It scared me, hearing you come up the drive, not knowing who it was."

Vixen hadn't ever seemed afraid. "I'm sorry. I hadn't thought about that." And now he felt like the world's biggest jerk.

Her house was a revelation, a window into who she was. They'd both had suites in The Peacock, but even the best hotel room was impersonal and cold. There had been no insights into her character there.

This place was different.

There was a sense of comfort, elegance even, but he hadn't expected the simplicity. Cool tones and clean lines defined the space, from her cream leather couches resting in a U in front of a waning fire to the seascape portrait resting above the mantle. Other café scenes of a woman drinking coffee or a martini hung around the room. The walls were powder blue, like her eyes, and he cursed himself again as he remembered telling her how much they reminded him of the ocean.

What a fool he'd been.

Now he was a fool who'd lost two hundred dollars already, and he hadn't even been in her presence ten minutes. At least the money was going to charity at the end of his probationary term, and at the rate he was going, he would likely be on their board of directors for all the money he'd be donating.

"I like your house," he said, and she jumped at the sound of his voice.

Now he knew something was really wrong. This wasn't just a momentary flash of fear. Something had her spooked. And her reaction told him she wasn't used to men showing up here at night. A primal satisfaction streaked through him that there was no one else right now, even though he knew it was ridiculous. She was right. Two years was a long time, but he couldn't control how he felt.

"Terrance, just say what you need to say and go," she said softly, and without her usual fire.

This wasn't how he'd imagined it. He was a passionate person, and from what he remembered, so was she. He'd thought they would yell. Now he wondered how much of an illusion Vixen had been.

There was a poker tournament paused on the big screen in the corner of her den, but it was the only outward sign of Vixen. Did the woman he'd fallen for really exist, or had she been another one of Vegas' mirages? He had to know.

"I'd like to fix you something special to make up for coming here and scaring you," he said with new determination. "You always loved late-night desserts. Where's your kitchen?"

Her eyes fell to the floor, and he could all but feel her remembering him coming back to her suite with a special dessert he'd concocted just for her and then feeding it to her in bed. His own body tightened with lust.

"I didn't come here for that, Vix...Elizabeth. What should I call you?"

"Elizabeth is fine. And you don't need to make me anything."

"Without all that makeup and girly stuff, Elizabeth suits you. And I *will* make you something."

He could be stubborn too, and he headed into the hallway. Their floor plans were pretty similar—her front room was a combination den and dining room just like his—so he figured he could find the kitchen on his own.

"Stop this, Terrance, really," she said from behind him. "Just say what you want to say and leave."

The kitchen was in the same part of the house as his, but he'd replaced all of the appliances to make room for his Viking range and walk-in cooler. Her walls were sage green, the cabinets white, and the Silestone counters a tan shot through with chocolate brown lines. He pulled open her refrigerator and clucked his tongue.

"Your pantry sucks," he told her, eyeing the single quart of almond milk, the low-cal dressing, the nonfat yogurt—horror—and a couple of take-out containers showcasing a limp Cobb salad and a cloudy chicken noodle soup with the worst noodles on the planet. "And your taste in food hasn't improved much."

She'd savored his food but complained about it adding to her curves. He'd always bandied back that he loved her curves.

"Are you going to insult my food choices all night?"

Her voice, all soft and smoky and *familiar*, shot pure lust through his system again. Yeah, those had been the days. His body apparently didn't care about the history between them. It wanted her as much as it always had.

"Nope. I'm done."

He opened some vegetable bins and could at least approve of the kale and Swiss chard. But there was nothing he could work with for dessert. "You don't even have eggs?"

"You sound appalled," she replied. "I told you that I don't need dessert, and you should just—"

"Bananas!" he cried out at last as he looked around her kitchen and spotted some in a wooden bowl in the corner. "Please tell me you have ice cream."

"Of course," she said as he pulled out real butter, *thank God,* from the fridge.

"And bourbon?"

"Yes, Rhett loves it. What in the world are you planning to make?"

"Bananas Foster. Where are your spices? Please tell me you at least have cinnamon." If she didn't, he might just have to walk out the door right now and fetch his own.

"Yes, I have cinnamon."

Funny how she'd always smelled like cinnamon to him—even though her Chanel perfume ran more exotic than that. He always thought of her when he used the spice, even now. For a long time, those thoughts had been wrapped up in longing—a feeling he pretty much hated.

"Sauce pan? Cutting board?" he fired off, expecting

her to produce them like a good sous chef.

"What about a monkey to eat the banana?" she quipped, and this time he heard the fire in her voice and was glad for it. The vulnerability of that other voice, the one belonging to this new woman named Elizabeth, made him unsteady.

"You know, I've eaten monkey brains before. They're not bad."

She made a gagging sound. "That is so gross. I can't believe you'd eat something like that," she said, stacking the items he'd asked for on the counter.

"You can blame a friend of mine for daring me. Your knives suck," he commented as he drew one out of the block and ran his finger over the blade. "I can't cut shi—"

Okay, he'd caught that one. A minor victory.

"How sweet of you to say," she replied, vinegar in her voice this time, making him smile. "Anything else you want to insult around here?"

When she leaned on the counter, gazing at him like that with her big baby blues, he was glad he was no longer holding the knife. He might have cut himself like a first-year at the Culinary Institute of America. "Nope."

With that, he busied himself with slicing the bananas, heating the pan, dropping in the butter, and then adding the bananas. At least her stove was gas. If it had been electric, he would have refused to cook on it. She handed him the cinnamon, which he knew was likely as old as a used car, but he dusted the bananas with it anyway, inhaling deeply. Even old cinnamon had an alluring scent, and when a vision of a naked Vixen sitting on his lap as she fed him cinnamon rolls popped into his head, he almost burned his finger on the side of the pan.

"Where's your sugar?" he asked finally, pleased with the way it was coming together. He wouldn't even dare hope she had simple brown sugar, not after seeing the sparseness of her refrigerator.

"I don't have any," she told him, and it was hard to miss the glee in her voice.

"You don't have sugar? What kind of human being are you, anyway? You mystify me," he told her, and it wasn't just because she didn't buy sugar.

Silence reigned for a minute as the bananas sizzled on the stove. Yeah, she knew there was a deeper meaning to his words. They might have pressed pause on their conversation, but this *was* a conversation—the things said and unsaid, the meaning behind their gestures and glances.

"I have honey," she finally said, opening the cabinet and setting a half-filled smiling bear—dear God—beside him.

"Even the bees are embarrassed by this honey, but at least you have something sweet. Now I won't have to report you to the Basic Ingredients Police."

Her mouth twitched, and he felt it sparking between them again.

That explosive connection. The simple joy of being in her presence. Something he'd never felt with another woman.

"Feel free. I've always loved a man in uniform."

It was an old joke between them, and he stilled at her casual use of it. She'd said his chef uniform was a turn-on, which he hadn't heard too often. It wasn't like an armed services uniform or anything, and it always smelled like an assortment of food.

Was she feeling it between them too? Did she want them to act on their old passion? Hell, he wasn't ready for that. Okay, his body was ready, but...

"Bourbon?" he rasped out, drizzling the honey over the bananas and watching it bubble golden brown.

"In the liquor cabinet. I'll get it."

After she left the room, he kicked the stove and yelped since he'd forgotten he was barefoot.

Elizabeth was as beautiful and intriguing as Vixen had been. More so. And the old feelings were as fresh as his dinner special had been tonight.

He'd wanted closure, but he'd gotten anything but.

Coming here had been a bad idea.

CHAPTER 2

As Elizabeth headed to the 1930s Art Deco bar cabinet, she rubbed her hands over her arms, trying to banish the goosebumps. She'd worried her late-night visitor was Ryan James, who hadn't stopped pestering her about going out with him again after one bad date. But the muted porch light had illuminated Terrance's handsome face instead, and her trembling had changed into something else.

She was still afraid of what he would say to her, of what he would ask, but there was also the white-hot anticipation of being in his presence again. The sight of his lean, rock-hard body in that black leather jacket and those faded designer jeans that hugged his muscular legs made her mouth water. Add in his military-cut black hair, bottle green eyes, and the wicked scar on the right side of his mouth, and it was all she could do not to jump him.

It didn't help that she was on a Man Fast, her first since she'd left him.

And he was cooking for her. Right here in her kitchen.

Her heart squeezed.

And this no swearing thing? She must have lived in Dare Valley too long because she thought it was as cute as a greeting card.

Selecting Rhett's most expensive bourbon, she smoothed her hair down with her free hand and walked back into the kitchen, deciding not to fuss about the flannel pajamas—so sexy—and her lack of makeup.

"At least someone has taste," Terrance commented when she handed the bottle to him.

"Rhett can drink the good stuff or rotgut," she told him like he didn't know. He'd been friends with Rhett and Mac Maven, the owner of The Grand Mountain Hotel where he was working as head chef, going on ten years now, three years longer than her friendship with the two men.

"Well, I don't let him drink the rotgut around me," he said, stepping away from the stove and trickling some bourbon over the concoction.

It caught fire, the wall of orange licking at the bottom of her microwave right above the stove, making her worry about the plastic melting, but since he didn't seem concerned, she kept her mouth shut. He set the bottle aside and shook the pan, making the fire blaze to life again. When it died out, he searched in her cabinets for a spoon, and upon finding one, tasted the sauce.

"How is it?" she asked.

"Your cinnamon isn't as intense as my special blend from Ceylon, but it does the job."

"I'm so glad you can suck it up down here in food purgatory," she said dryly, producing the ice cream without him asking for it and reached into a cabinet for two blue bowls.

"Salted caramel gelato," he murmured. "I remember you liking ice cream."

"It's one of my favorite indulgences."

"How can you eat this and nonfat yogurt?"

She laughed at his playful shudder. "Eating nonfat yogurt gives me more leeway to eat fully loaded ice cream. It's all about balancing out the calories."

"That diet logic is a load of bull— Aha, I caught myself again."

And when he smiled, the expression full of pride, her heart simply flew out of her chest and fell onto the floor in front of him. Like, here I am again. Remember me?

Her heart had always gotten her into trouble.

He spooned the ice cream out, making sure it resembled the most perfect sphere ever fashioned. Then he deftly slid the bananas onto the side and trickled the sauce over it. Even she could smell the cinnamon now, and her mouth watered.

Dammit. Terrance had always known how to get to her.

She took the bowl he handed her and led him to the small table in her dining nook, not wanting the formality of the dining room. He sat across from her, and as if on cue, they both took their first bite together. Caramel soaked into her tongue, followed by the coolness of cream, the punch of cinnamon, and the warm banana.

"Yum," she managed.

Another one of Chef T's famous mega-watt smiles, which she'd seen on TV more times than she cared to admit. Yes, she watched his show...she couldn't help herself.

He'd left the Peacock a scant month after their breakup. She couldn't help but wonder if he'd returned to New York City because of her. Soon after, he'd landed his own cable show, *The Tattooed Chef,* on her favorite food channel, and she'd been glued to the screen ever since.

As a viewer, she could feed her addiction to his smile, his badass attitude, and lust over his rock-hard body. Even laugh as he made innuendos about food—something he was famous for. Along with the swearing.

"So tell me what really made you so afraid earlier?" he asked, something she hadn't been expecting.

"It's nothing," she said, shoving another bite in her mouth. No way she was talking about it with him. First, it was personal, and second, he was alpha enough to handle it for her, which she didn't want or need. As she'd told Rhett, she was dealing with it.

After her violent past, she needed to be strong enough to handle it on her own.

"I might not have known your real name until a few weeks ago, but I know you don't scare easy. At least not so much that you'd keep a Louisville Slugger by the door."

Well, she didn't keep it by the door. She kept it by the bed, and she'd run for it the minute she heard the car in the driveway. Terrance was wrong. She might put up a brave front, but she scared way too easily after being stalked by an ex-boyfriend while in her M.B.A. program at Harvard.

"I don't want to talk about it," she fired back. "And it's not why you came over anyway. Aren't you going to ask me what you came here to ask?"

He set his spoon aside, and she watched his ice cream continue to melt under the heat of the bananas. "Why did you leave like you did? Was it because I punched that guy who put his hands on you and called you a slut? You told me you weren't upset about it."

"I don't have a very good reason." At least not one she could share. His violence hadn't been directed at her, but it had horrified her nonetheless.

"I deserved better than that note, dammit."

When he drew another hundred out of his wallet, she had to stop from reaching for his hand to comfort him.

"We both knew our time together would end."

Except she hadn't wanted that, which had only scared her more, giving her another reason to flee.

His mouth quirked up. "Did we? It might have started out that way, but I thought..."

Her heart thudded in her chest, and she set her spoon aside too, her appetite gone. He'd thought they had a future? Mr. No Commitment Chef T himself?

"I'm sorry."

His eyes flicked up to hers, and inside their green depths she saw the hurt and vulnerability he never showed to the world. "Me too. Why didn't you tell me about Elizabeth? I would have kept your real name secret. Rhett's my friend too. I mean, I understand why you wanted to keep it quiet that you and your friend, Raven...ah, Jane, were his poker scouts and not just hot babes. The whole masquerade was pretty genius if you ask me. But I deserved to know."

Their disguise had been genius. The three of them had concocted the plan together after Rhett offered them jobs as his scouts. Elizabeth and Jane, both Harvard M.B.A. graduates, had been eager to escape their lives—Elizabeth, because of Vince, the man who'd stalked her and told her he would kill her if she went out with another man and Jane, because of her controlling parents, who wanted her to work on her father's political campaign. The arrangement had served them all well.

"Until last month, no one knew but our small circle. I couldn't tell you because it would have endangered the people I love most in the world."

He picked his spoon back up and made circles in the melting ice cream. "I suppose we didn't talk much about the past when we were together."

No, but she'd wanted to, and it had been a first. Relationships didn't work, at least not in her experience. Certainly her parents hadn't been happy. She'd sworn never to make herself vulnerable to another man after the disaster with Vince.

Yet Terrance had threatened to peel back all her barriers.

Which was, of course, part of the reason she'd left.

"Why are you here, Terrance?" she finally asked.

"At your house or in Dare Valley?"

"Dare Valley."

He clicked the spoon against the side of the bowl and then let it fall. "Only Mac and a few other people I work with know, so I'm trusting you."

Okay, that scared her. "Maybe you shouldn't—"

"I'm on probation of sorts. I've been given a primetime cooking show that's a mix of cooking and reality TV. The deal was set in place before the new president took over, and he's trying to undo it, saying I'm a loud-mouthed, no-good SOB, who... Well it doesn't matter. I fired back, living up to my reputation, and now he's delaying my show. I have two months to prove I can clean up my act for primetime. No swearing. No innuendos. No fun. It sucks, Vix."

That nickname, the one he'd always used for her, made her throat squeeze.

"Sorry, it's going to take some time for me to remember to call you Elizabeth." His smile came and left his face, like he was just as awash in old memories as she was.

"Anyway, I want this show. Badly. So when Mac called me to ask me for some recommendations for a new head chef, I asked him how he'd feel about me taking the job for a while since I wasn't working. Then Mac threw back some ideas about me not only heading up the kitchen here, but having final say over all the menus for his four other hotels and the new one he's building in Vegas...not to mention the top catering jobs. Of course, he also promised me the flexibility to do the show once it starts up and travel back and forth. It was an offer I couldn't refuse."

"That's Mac. He might be a World Series of Poker winner, but his business acumen is second to none."

"I couldn't agree more. To sweeten the deal, we made an agreement for his hotel chain to become an exclusive vendor of my new gourmet food products, which are just launching. We're also planning to launch niche gourmet products with my picture on them and the name of Mac's hotel chain, but we need to work out the details before securing financing."

"Congratulations, Terrance."

"Not bad for a New York City street rat," he mused and shoved back his chair to stretch his long legs out.

His rough upbringing had always been a touchy subject with him.

"And the whole hundred-dollars-a-word thing?"

"I was having a hard time controlling my language, so I decided only one thing would incentivize me. Money. Something I never had growing up and something I don't ever want to be without again."

That she understood, having grown up in a trailer park.

"Now let's talk about you. Are you still happy with your job?"

She took another bite of melting ice cream and nodded. "Jane...uh, Raven...decided she wanted to play poker professionally after winning the big tournament last month, so now I'm Rhett's main scout. We have to recast my proximity to him at tournaments since the ruse is up, and everyone on the circuit knows what I do, but I think we'll find a balance. Jane still plans to help out here and there when there's no conflict because she loves the work as much as I do, but now that she's engaged to Matt Hale, she has a lot going on."

"I've met him through his cousin Jill at the hotel. He seems like a nice guy. I'm happy for her, but I have to admit it's an adjustment to see her as she is now. You...have more of a resemblance to Vixen than she does to Raven."

Well, that was diplomatic. Her curves were natural, but Jane was reed thin and had been padded into a new shape to become Raven.

"Matt's great. All of the Hales are." And she was happy her best friend had found the happily ever after she'd always wanted and believed in. Not so with Elizabeth.

Something inside her had frozen after Vince.

"I've had a chance to meet Mac's wife," he continued. "She's a pistol, but I have to say I didn't see Mac marrying a cop."

"None of us did, but she suits him perfectly, just like Abbie does Rhett."

"Yeah. I'm glad it worked out between them. Rhett was devastated when she broke things off before."

The two had dated in secret for a while—a fact not many people knew. Well, well. Rhett must have told him. She'd file that away for later.

"It's weird to see Mac and Rhett settled down after all the fun we used to have together."

Boy fun, he meant. "I imagine it is." Yes, it was different for her too, and her best friend's engagement was another big change. But she was finding her way, making new friends. Keeping active.

"How has it been for you, coming here?" he asked, crossing his arms across the chest she knew to be muscular and mouth-watering.

Part of her couldn't believe he was sitting across from her at her kitchen table, talking casually as the clock ticked toward midnight. There was so much left unsaid between them, but she was surprised to realize he was one of those old friends with whom the passage of time held no meaning.

Becoming friends with him had been a surprise before, and in some ways, it had scared her as much as their passionate sexual connection. She preferred to keep things simple and unemotional with men. Easy. Maybe she and Terrance could be friends now, setting aside their emotional baggage.

Except she also wanted him to sweep the plates off the table and lift her onto him so he could kiss her senseless and rock her world. Not exactly friend-like.

"Dare Valley is different than Vegas, there's no denying it. But it's growing on me. I love being here with Jane and Rhett, and there are more wonderful people they're bringing into my life. I...have a family here," she finished and looked down at her lap.

She'd never had a real family growing up, so Jane and Rhett had become one. Even the town's famous family, the Hales, was making room for her, and all because she was the best friend of Matt Hale's fiancée.

"I'm glad you found people you could belong to," Terrance murmured, and his voice was so gentle, she couldn't help but meet his eyes.

Yes, he knew about that desire to belong. Both of them had lived on the outside for most of their lives before finding the passion that transformed them—his home was in the kitchen, hers in the poker dens where fortunes were made and lost.

For a while, she'd wanted to belong to him and ignore everything she'd ever come to know about betrayal and loss and fear at the hands of a man. But her fear had proved too powerful.

"I should go," he finally said and stood.

She rose and walked him to the front door. Her hands seemed to hang awkwardly by her sides as she watched him pull on his hiking boots. Part of her wanted to reach out and embrace him, just one more time, so she could feel the hard muscles of his chest against her cheek, smell his scent of spicy, erotic cologne mixed with the aromatic smells from his kitchen.

But she couldn't.

When he touched his finger to her cheek, doing what she could not, her heart rapped hard in her chest, and she had to clench her fists at her sides not to reach for him.

"I was so mad at you," he whispered, tracing her cheek. "I thought for sure we were going to go eight rounds tonight, but seeing you scared—whether it was me or someone who frightened you— made all of that disappear. I don't know Elizabeth Saunders like I did Vixen, but I want to. I hope we can at least be friends. We have plenty of friends in common, and it's a small town. We did pretty well at that before."

Her regrets hung heavy in her belly. "I like the idea of us becoming friends again."

"Friends it is."

He held out his hand to seal the pact with her, but when their hands met, he held hers longer than necessary. When he released her, she rubbed her palm on her pajama pants to erase the tingling sensation there.

"I'm sorry I left you like I did, Terrance. You're right. You deserved more from me."

The side of his mouth tipped up, his scar wicked sexy. "Well, it seems we're going to begin anew. I'll see you around. *Elizabeth.*"

The way he said her name with his sin-chewing-marbles voice, one she'd never imagined to hear cross his lips in person, made her sway forward.

A special light came into his eyes. "Good night."

When he walked out, she closed the door and slumped against it.

Vixen might have come to terms with never being with Terrance again, but Elizabeth Saunders clearly hadn't.

Chapter 3

The town's most popular coffee shop, Don't Soy with Me, was Elizabeth's favorite place to meet up with Jane these days. Her friend's fiancée was running for mayor, so Jane was often downtown helping Matt's campaign staff. The primary election for mayor was on May 1, less than a week away. The coffee shop, owned by Matt's cousin Jill Hale who now worked for Mac with Terrance at The Grand, was the perfect place for them to rendezvous. Like usual, it was bustling with locals, students from Emmits Merriam University, and transplants like herself. The music playing over the speakers was bluesy, the atmosphere vibrant with its red and yellow accented walls, and the coffee and food were downright decadent.

"Hey," Jane said as she gave Elizabeth a half hug and dropped down in the empty chair at the table Elizabeth had been lucky enough to snag.

"Hey, back," she replied, not wanting to burst out the news that Terrance *freaking* Waters had finally come by her place last night. If she did, they'd never get coffee and food. "Let's leave our stuff here and get in line to order."

They hung their jackets on the chairs and took their place in the long line. Elizabeth smiled at a few college boys who were staring at them. They were attracting a new kind of attention now that the whole town knew they'd been Raven and Vixen.

"So, how's the campaign going?" Elizabeth asked.

"We've pulled far enough ahead of the competition to feel cautiously optimistic." The grin on her face suggested more than that.

"Good! Telling the truth about Vixen and Raven is working out for all of us." There had been some concern that Jane's secret identity would ruin Matt's chances at winning the election, but they'd come clean with the information before the competition could, giving him the upper hand.

Jane grabbed her hand. "Don't you feel freer? I mean, except for when people stare at us like those boys over there. Did I tell you one of the kids at Emmits Merriam actually had the gall to tell me there was no way he believed I was Raven?"

"You're kidding." At least Terrance had said it more diplomatically. "If only men had to dress up with padded bras and six-inch high heels."

"I know! The world would be a much better place. I'm sure of it."

They reached the front of the line. "Hey, Margie," Elizabeth said. "How are you?"

"Great! How are you two? Jane, everyone's so happy to see Matt pulling ahead in the election."

Don't Soy With Me's barista was sweet and knew every local's name by heart—the coffee shop's trademark service. Margie also exchanged pleasantries with everyone who came to the counter. It usually created a long line, but the barista's genuine warmth was one of the things Elizabeth loved about Dare Valley. People here knew her and cared about her. She was no longer anonymous.

"This is on me," Elizabeth told Jane, since they took turns paying. "I'll have a nonfat caramel macchiato, and my friend here will have..."

"A double chocolate mocha," Jane added. "And can I have the special crepe with ham, mushrooms, and parmesan?"

"It's awesome," Margie said. "Had it for breakfast myself."

"Okay, I'll have one too." It sounded too good to resist.

After she paid, they edged to the side to wait for their drinks.

"Jill told me she had to work on Brian big-time to get him to let her use his crepe recipe here for breakfast," Jane said. "They agreed she could only serve crepes for breakfast since Brian has them on the lunch and dinner menus at Brasserie Dare."

Jill was married to the chef-owner of the best restaurant in town. Well, maybe Terrance would change that. Seeing him go head-to-head with Brian McConnell was going to be interesting. She'd already heard the temporary menu at The Grand was impressive.

They took their coffees to their table, and Elizabeth knew she couldn't hold it in any longer.

"Okay, I have to spill the beans. Prepare yourself. Terrance came to my house last night."

Jane spewed out the sip of mocha she'd just drank, and Elizabeth angled to the right to elude the spray.

"He *what?*"

"Hold it together, Wilcox. People are staring, and as much as I love you, I don't want your germs."

Her best friend dabbed at her mouth with a napkin and cleaned up the table, her eyes huge in her face. "How could you *not* have called me?"

"It was close to midnight when he left. You were probably having sex."

Her mouth twitched. "Yep. Most assuredly."

It was a joke between them. Jane had lived like a nun before meeting Matt, whereas Elizabeth had been involved with lots of men. Now the tide had turned, and she was glad for her friend, who liked to flaunt it now that she had something to flaunt. She just wasn't glad for herself. Man Fasts sucked. Especially now that a certain someone was dangling in front of her nose like Tantalus' grapes.

"Back to Terrance." She leaned forward and Jane did the same, like they were sharing a secret. "He said he was mad at me, but I got all scared when I heard his car pull up late, thinking it was Ryan—"

"Is he still bothering you? Dammit, Liz. I told you—"

"He's harmless," she said, praying it was true. So far Ryan only called and texted her every once in a while. There had been an uncomfortable encounter on the street one day, but he'd backed off. "Doesn't matter, though, he still triggers me. Anyway, I got my baseball bat before opening the door. When Terrance realized I was scared and noticed the bat by the door, he said the fight went out of him. He made Bananas Foster to make it up to me, and then we just sat in the kitchen and talked about...oh crap, just *stuff*, like two old friends who hadn't seen each other in a while. It felt good."

"Oh crap," Jane repeated. "Is the spark still there?"

Elizabeth raised an eyebrow she'd plucked just this morning, realizing she wanted to be better groomed now that Terrance was around. Lord, when a woman started worrying about a thing like that, she knew she was in trouble. She was so in trouble. "Is the pope still Catholic?"

"Meaning you wanted to jump his bones? Ewww, it seems sacrilegious to talk about that after your pope comment."

Now that made her laugh. "Yes, I wanted to jump his bones and dump my dessert on his rock-hard abs and lick it off."

"Hey! TMI."

Her best friend might flaunt her new love life, but she still blushed like a college freshman. Elizabeth knew from experience—they'd met in their first year at Harvard. "Like you and Matt don't do the same thing."

Jane leveled her a glance. *"Anyway.* How did you leave things?"

Sleep hadn't come easy since her brain had kept cycling through their conversation. "I apologized, and he said he wanted to be friends, and I agreed."

"You're kidding!"

"Oh, and get this. He's trying to stop swearing. He's even charging himself a hundred dollars a word."

Jane set her mocha down with a thud. "Are you sure the man who came to your house was Terrance Waters and not some shape shifter?"

The thought of Terrance changing into a wolf at night made Elizabeth laugh out loud, but it wasn't too far off. There had always been an edge of danger around him. "I know! I was as shocked as you are."

"Did he tell you why he's working for Mac?" Jane asked.

As she filled Jane in, Elizabeth could only marvel at how much of a sucker she still was for Terrance's sweetness. Yes, he could be a badass, but with her, he had always been so much more. After they'd gotten past the crazy, erotic first weeks of their...relationship, they'd started talking afterward and sleeping in the same bed and hanging out in the mornings. His defenses had come down, and so had hers.

"Primetime, huh? That's huge. I mean I knew his show was pulling in serious ratings, but wow."

"And he's got that gourmet food and kitchen product line too," she added. "I'm happy for him. He didn't have it easy growing up."

"I remember you telling me," Jane said. Their food

order had arrived in the middle of Elizabeth's spiel, and Jane took a big bite of her crepe. "Every time I eat one of these, I swear if I close my eyes I'm back in Paris."

"We should go," Elizabeth said automatically, then bit her lip. "Sorry. Here you are, newly engaged, and I'm talking about girl trips."

Jane grabbed her hand. "Stop. I told you. My engagement to Matt doesn't change our friendship. Right now I can't fly off to Paris with you, but we will."

Some day. She took a bite of her own crepe and made herself smile.

Just then, she caught sight of Rhett walking into the coffee shop. Even though he no longer wore his trademark cowboy hat now that he was married to Abbie, he was still a head taller than most of the men in Don't Soy With Me. His mouth broke into a huge grin when he spotted them, and he sauntered over like an old gaucho crossing a saloon.

"Hey, Margie," he called out to the barista, who was drinking her own cup of coffee now that the line had finally cleared up. "How are you doing, honey?"

"Great. Good to see you, Rhett. Do you want your usual or something special?"

He stroked his chin. "Let's go with my regular, but be a sweetheart and add some Tabasco to my eggs."

"Sure thing, *honey,*" she bandied back easily.

Yeah, that was Rhett. Everyone in town loved him even though he stuck out in Dare Valley like an albatross in the desert.

"How's my girls?" he asked in his typical Southern fashion as he bussed their cheeks.

They both gave him the thumbs up, which made him chuckle.

"Ma'am, do you mind if I take this chair over to my friends here?" he asked the woman at the table next to them. She blinked rapidly, no doubt caught off guard by his drawl and his handsomeness. "Not at all."

"Thanks, you're a darlin'," he said with a wink, dragging it across the short distance to their table and plopping down in it.

"So the rumors are true," Jane said to Rhett. "Matt told me you were coming in today to pick up some flyers to spread around town."

"No way," Elizabeth echoed.

If there was one thing Rhett was not, it was political. Something she had always liked about him.

"Yes, way," Rhett replied. "I need to stand up for my girls now that everyone knows who you are. That, and I want to continue to make peace with Young Matthew by supporting him."

Elizabeth snickered. "Matt hates it when you call him that, doesn't he?"

"It's what Uncle Arthur calls him from time to time," Jane said.

Rhett waggled his eyebrows. "I'm just needling Matt a little bit since he's managed to take away my poker scout and my sweet little dog."

Now Jane rolled her eyes. "You *gave* Annie as a present, and you told me I had your blessing to pursue my own poker career."

"I know, but there's not much I can get into trouble for anymore being married and living in Dare Valley, so I have to get creative with my carousing."

Carousing. Now that was a Rhett word if she'd ever heard one. He'd certainly done some carousing in the old days, and in some ways, so had she. Perhaps she was settling down too, and funny how it hadn't taken marriage to do it. Just moving to this small town.

"Oh, we feel so bad for you, Rhett," Elizabeth said, her voice teasing.

"I know. Everybody feels sorry for me. Some days it's simply too much." He pretended to wipe a tear from his eye. "But I have a surprise for you, Janey, and I've been bursting with excitement to share it."

Rhett's surprises could be wonderfully sweet or outrageously flamboyant. She and Jane shared a look.

"What is it?" her friend asked cautiously.

"I'm throwing your boy a private party at The Grand on election night to celebrate his impending win. It'll be fun. Plus, I want to make the competition pea green with envy."

"Rhett," Jane said softly. "That's really sweet. But Matt and I were going to spend election night with his family—"

"And what are we?" he asked, gesturing to Elizabeth and himself. "Chopped liver?"

"Of course not," Jane protested, and Elizabeth could feel the growing pains of their little trio adjusting to new circumstances.

Margie brought over a steaming cup of coffee and an omelet dotted with hot sauce and took the credit card Rhett handed her. "Thanks, darlin'." Turning back to Jane, he said, "All the Hales can come on up to Mac's hotel, and anyone else you want to invite. I've arranged it with Mac so the restaurant will be closed for the night, and Terrance is going to cook up a feast. That boy sure knows how to cook, no offense to Brian."

Rhett had always loved to throw parties. Heck, that's how Elizabeth had met Terrance in the first place.

"What do you say, Jane? Let me do this for you two. Everyone will have a ball, I promise."

Jane fished out her phone. "Okay, let me call Matt."

When she stood and headed over to a corner for some privacy, Elizabeth almost rolled her eyes. She missed making impulsive plans with her friend.

Rhett dug into his omelet and made a humming noise with the first bite. "Checking in. Compromise. She's not married yet, but it's already beginning. I hope Young Matthew accepts my gift."

"You're only calling him that because he punched you in the face."

Rhett sighed. "Probably, but he had his reasons, which is why I didn't punch him back. It was hard on him, learning about Jane being Raven, but he's surprised me. No one could have stepped up to the plate better. They make a good pair."

Elizabeth thought so too, even though it was changing her friendship with Jane. "That they do."

"So how you handling Terrance being in town?" Rhett asked, taking a sip of his coffee, his poker face in full force now.

His directness rendered her speechless for a moment, and she fussed with the napkin in her lap to give her time to muster some impassivity of her own. "You knew?"

Not wanting to cause friction between Rhett and Terrance in case things went sour, she'd never breathed a word about their relationship.

He snorted. "Please. I was afraid I'd have to hose you two off at a couple of the parties I had in my suite."

"But we never kissed in front—"

"Honey, you didn't have to. You smoldered around each other like a gator being cooked up at an LSU tailgate."

Dear God. Now that was an image.

Rhett chewed, moaned a little more, and then took a drink of his coffee. "Rye has to try this omelet the next time he comes to Dare. I swear, that boy is going to think he's died and gone to heaven. It's as light and fluffy as a feather."

Their dear friend, country singer Rye Crenshaw, loved food more than anyone they'd ever met. It was no accident he was marrying his private chef in a few weeks.

"You're acting like a mother hen."

Rhett held out his knife. "Why don't you just castrate me right here and now? A hen? I'm the biggest rooster in this joint."

At least he hadn't said cock. Pushing the knife aside, she laughed. "That blade is way too dull. And as for Terrance, you have nothing to worry about."

"We'll see," he mused as Jane returned.

Elizabeth didn't like the prophetic tone in his voice. Everything would be fine. Especially if Terrance agreed to wear a paper sack over his head in her presence so she wouldn't notice how handsome he was. Oh, and he'd have to wear a burlap bag too, so she could forget how fabulous his body was.

Who was she kidding?

She was doomed.

When Jane returned, her smile was like the sunshine beaming through the coffee shop's windows. "Matt says it's very nice of you to throw the party, and we happily accept."

"Good. I'll talk to my boy, Terrance, about the food. Maybe he could do a tasting for us so we can sample some of his ideas for the party." Rhett put his finger to his mouth. "Elizabeth, I'll need your help picking out the food since Jane is so busy with the campaign."

A kick under the table would be too good for him. She picked up the knife he'd discarded moments ago. "Stop meddling, you old *hen.*"

"I'm sure I can find some time—"

"Don't make a fuss, Janey," Rhett said with a slow drawl. "Elizabeth here assures me she can handle being around Terrance, so I'm sure everything will be as smooth as greased shit through a goose. I'll text you when I've scheduled the tasting, Elizabeth."

His wink was pure mischief.

"You're a scoundrel," she said, digging into her crepe again.

He held up his hands like a preacher channeling the Almighty. "Finally! Someone around here remembers who I am. I rather miss being called that, I must admit, although don't tell the missus that."

Scoundrel that he was, Rhett was calling *her* out.
Was she bluffing about Terrance?
They were about to find out.

Chapter 4

Natalie Hale couldn't suppress her excitement at meeting the famous Chef T in person. As a fan of his witty and mouth-watering TV show, she was like every other full-blooded American woman—she thought the man was insanely gorgeous.

Of course, as a professional caterer, she appreciated his brilliance with food too. But that was only icing on the cake.

Matt had asked her to come up from Denver early Friday morning for the tasting. He'd only given her a day's notice, but being a good sister, she wouldn't have refused even if Chef T hadn't been in the mix. Her brother's election was on Tuesday, and everyone in the family was doing their part to support him.

Even though he'd recently wreaked his revenge for the two bumper stickers she'd put on his SUV: *I'm a Sensitive Guy* and *I Sleep With My Dog*. Now her bumper proudly proclaimed: *I'm A Trekkie. Live Long and Prosper*. He darn well knew how much she disliked that show. Matt was going down. Though hopefully by her hands, and not in the mayoral race.

When she arrived at The Grand Mountain Hotel, the majesty of the restored three-story hotel awed her, the effect only slight ruined when she left her car with the valet and he gave her that weird V sign Trekkies do to each other.

She'd spent most of her childhood in Dare Valley, so she remembered how this place used to be. It had been abandoned long ago, after the owner lost his shirt during the Great Depression. Back then, only the bravest of souls had visited the site, which was rumored to be haunted. Of course, she'd checked it out with her first boyfriend in high school. No ghosts that night, just her soon-to-be ex-boyfriend's unwelcome attempt to cop a feel.

Mac Maven had done such a fantastic job of bringing the hotel back to life, leaving the natural gas lighting on the outside and preserving the stonework. She and her two sisters, Moira and Caroline, had only made one visit to the swanky club, Ante Up, nestled on the right side of the hotel, but they'd loved the old wood siding and natural gas lamps. The intimate atmosphere encouraged reluctant patrons to feel comfortable enough to let loose on the dance floor at the end of the room.

Today she was headed to the hotel's restaurant, aptly called High Stakes, and as she entered the hotel, one of the liveried men opened the door for her and tipped his hand to his head, something her soon-to-be sister-in-law said was done at all of Mac's five boutique poker hotels in deference to the ladies.

Mac was coming down a massive staircase, and he gave her a big smile when he saw her. "Natalie," he said, taking her hand for a shake. "It's good to see you. I heard Matt asked you to come for the tasting today. I hope you enjoy it."

"I'm sure I will," she responded. "You managed to snag one of the hottest chefs out there. How in the world did you lure him to Dare Valley?"

"Terrance and I have been friends a long time," he said smoothly, not answering her question.

From what she knew of Mac Maven, he was pretty much a smooth operator all around. "Tell Peggy and Keith hello for me."

Since Peggy's brother, Tanner, was married to her cousin, Meredith, they were part of the Hales' extended family.

"Will do. We'll see you at Arthur's this weekend. I understand he's invited his Bingo friends to the barbecue he and April are hosting for Matt. Should be fun."

"I love that old man," she said. Her uncle, Arthur Hale, was one of the pillars of Dare Valley society, having successfully launched a national newspaper.

"Well have fun today." He kissed her cheek and headed toward reception.

When she walked into High Stakes, the panoramic view of the mountains through the large windows took her breath away. She might be a Colorado native, but she never took the beauty around her for granted.

Of course, the restaurant's décor blended beautifully with the rest of the restored hotel. The single-plank, original wood tables were rustic in the best possible sense, and the walls were painted gold and decorated with an intriguing combination of thick-framed wood mirrors and metal sculptures. The lighting, a marriage of old bronze gas sconces and wrought-iron chandeliers, added to the effect, but the biggest showstopper was the wall of fire behind thick glass by the bar. It gave off heat in the winter and then changed into a wall of water in the warmer months. A custom job like that must have cost a fortune, but she wasn't responsible for the bill, so she could just enjoy it.

"Natalie, honey, there you are," she heard in a thick drawl that couldn't belong to anyone but Rhett Butler

Blaylock. As far as she was concerned, he might be the most fun man in Dare Valley, nothing against the men in her family. She'd met some people from the South, but Rhett was like dramatic, eccentric Southern theater on crack minus the tragedy of a Tennessee Williams play.

"Hi, Rhett," she said, a husky drawl coming out of her own mouth, and didn't she feel like Scarlett O'Hara for just one moment?

"You ready to eat until your buttons pop?" he asked her, winking.

"Well, this dress doesn't have any, so I should be okay." She gestured to her navy wool outfit, which ended at the knee, right where her tan, high-heeled boots started. "But usually you don't end up eating enough to pop anything at a tasting."

She'd made sure to eat a good breakfast before leaving Denver for just that reason. At her last tasting, her stomach had growled right at the end. It was an embarrassment she didn't want to duplicate today.

He shook his finger at her. "You haven't eaten with Chef T yet. Trust me. He knows I'm coming, and he knows I have a big appetite, tasting or not."

"Big appetites are my specialty," Natalie heard a man say in a rough voice she instantly recognized.

Turning around, she beheld Chef T in all his culinary glory, dressed in the designer chef attire he was known for. Today he wore a chef jacket in denim with black pants. Ridiculously hot. Any woman would think so.

But he didn't *do it* for her, and dammit, she was disappointed. No one had *done it* for her since her ex-husband Blake, and she feared if a prime specimen like Terrance couldn't fire her engines, nothing would. She was in big trouble on the man front.

"Chef T," she said, holding out her hand and trying not to act like some adoring fan. "I'm Natalie Hale, Matt's older sister. And a big fan of yours."

Okay, she'd busted that one up.

"Lucky me," he said and lifted her hand to his lips, shocking the hell out of her.

Rhett nudged Chef T with an elbow. "You're playing with fire, man."

And who knew what he meant by that. She let the hand he'd kissed curl at her side, telling herself to take a chill pill. Her sisters Moira and Caroline were going to have a heart attack when she told them.

Elizabeth walked in beside them. "Hello, everyone. Natalie, great to see you again."

Natalie didn't know Jane's best friend well, but she loved Jane, so that was enough for her. She pulled her in for a hug. "Hi!"

"Terrance," Elizabeth said, rather stiffly to Natalie's ears. When she gave the woman a second look, she saw narrow eyes and a tight mouth.

Huh.

"Aren't you gonna kiss her hand too?" Rhett drawled.

Elizabeth gave him a playful shove, making him theatrically stagger back. "Do you want him to kiss *your* hand, Rhett? I'm sure he'd be much obliged. Now, are we ready to start the tasting or what?"

The edge to her voice was sharp enough to cut a ribeye, and Natalie tried to keep her face impassive since she had no idea what the back story was here. But she knew one thing: there *was* a story. Maybe it was Uncle Arthur's journalistic blood expressing itself, but she wanted to know.

"Damn, so serious, Elizabeth," Rhett said. "I was rather hoping we'd start with a drink and then mosey our way on to some yummies. After all, I don't get to imbibe at lunch much anymore. Abbie doesn't approve."

Natalie laughed at the regret in his tone. "I wouldn't mind a cocktail, either. Chef T, can you recommend something that won't ruin our palate for the tasting?"

The wicked-hot scar on the right side of his mouth tipped up. "I can always cleanse your palate."

Now there was the innuendo for which he was famous. Even though she knew there was nothing there, she almost sighed. Whew!

"Oh, get a grip, Terrance," Elizabeth told him. "There aren't any cameras filming you right now. You don't need to kiss anyone's hands or make rude jokes."

The look he gave her was hot enough to melt butter. "Take a chill pill, Vix."

They glared at each other, and Natalie looked at Rhett, who winked at her. So Elizabeth was jealous... Well. Hard to miss the sparks pinging back and forth between them. They had a history, Natalie realized. Rhett had been warning Terrance about kissing her hand in front of Elizabeth. Chef T had probably done it on purpose.

"Well, let's have those drinks," Rhett said, "since you and Terrance are old friends, and everything is *fine* between the two of you."

Elizabeth kicked him in the shin, making him yelp and hop on one foot. "Fine. You've gotten me good and ready for that drink."

Even Chef T's mouth twitched at that. "I think I'll make you a Shady Lady."

"What's in it?" Elizabeth asked, crossing her arms.

"Trust me," he said like a snake charmer.

"Not for a sec," she responded and shrugged out of her white winter coat on the way to the curvy bar.

"This is going to be fun," Rhett drawled in an undertone meant only for Natalie's ears as Chef T stalked after Elizabeth, the fire wall illuminating the angles of his tense face.

She couldn't agree more.

CHAPTER 5

Their friendship pact seemed dead in the water. Terrance had been a fool to think he could stop wanting her, feeling something for her. As it was, he struggled not to grab Elizabeth's arm and lead her into his kitchen.

He wanted nothing more than to press her against the stainless steel door of his walk-in cooler and kiss her until she stopped sniping at him.

She was acting like she was as mad at him as he was at her. "Shit, I don't know what you're so pissed off about," he told her as she hung her coat over her chair. "I'm the one you left without barely a word, dammit."

"That's two hundred dollars," she said.

He withdrew his wallet and took out two crisp bills. "I fucking know that." And tugged out another hundred.

"Shady Lady," she scoffed, pulling on the hem of her scoop-neck cashmere red sweater, only bringing attention to her perfect breasts, leaving him breathless with wanting.

"That was rude. It's a dig at my past as Vixen."

Was it? "Look, I wasn't trying to insult you. I'll make

you another goddamn drink. What do you want?" He withdrew another Benjamin Franklin. At this rate, he might as well upend his wallet. His cursing was on the rise, like the stock market on a break-out day.

"I'll have a white wine," she said, softer now. "Thank you."

Great, now she says thank you. He stalked off to the wine cellar and pulled out one of her favorite wines, the one he'd introduced her to at The Peacock. Domaine de la Romanée-Conti from Burgundy, made from the most excellent Chardonnay grapes in the world, in his opinion.

They'd all taken their seats when he returned with the bottle. He'd dismissed his sommelier, saying he'd serve them. This was Rhett, after all, and when he'd heard Elizabeth was coming too, he'd been...heck, elated. Like some stupid schoolboy. And that made him resentful. Why should he be so happy to see her after everything?

"Terrance!" Elizabeth gasped when she caught sight of the bottle. "Please don't open that."

"It's my restaurant. Don't tell me what to do." Even though he wanted to rip the cork out with his teeth, he made himself go slowly. If he broke the cork, being angry at her...

"I'll have a glass of that too," Natalie said with an almost diplomatic tone, as though she was afraid to get into the cross-fire between the West and East over something as ludicrous as wine.

"Not me," Rhett said. "Bourbon. If it won't ruin my palate."

"Like you give a rat's ass about your palate, Rhett," Terrance said, pouring the ladies an ounce.

Elizabeth didn't pick up her glass. "This is...one of my favorites."

And the way she said it made him clutch the bottle. How many nights had he sipped this same wine off her belly as she moaned and laughed, those blue eyes shining with happiness?

The wine had been a mistake.

He'd meant it as a peace offering. Okay, that was a lie. He'd wanted her to remember too, to feel some of what he'd been feeling since they'd talked like old times over dessert in her kitchen.

"This is incredible," Natalie declared, setting her glass down for a full pour.

Smiling at her, Terrance topped off her glass. Natalie was handling their volatility like a pro, and under other circumstances, he would have made a move on her. Easy on the eyes, with thick, curly brown hair hanging past her shoulder blades and curves in all the right places, she unfortunately did nothing for him. Unlike the Shady Lady glaring at him as he topped off her wine next.

When he poured Rhett a glass of Pappy Van Winkle, his friend laughed as he threw back the first shot. "Damn, if I don't love the name of this bourbon. Makes me feel all warm inside."

"And unlike most kitschy-named liquor, this one actually delivers in flavor," Terrance said and splashed more bourbon in Rhett's glass before pouring one for himself. He hadn't planned on drinking, but the way things were going with Elizabeth, he was going to need one.

"Glad you're joining me, T," Rhett said.

"I'll bring out the first course," he told them. Maybe if he gave Vix—*Elizabeth*—some time to cool off, they could resume the pleasantries.

Right now small talk was out of the question.

"May I help?" Natalie asked, sliding out of her chair. "I'm a professional caterer in Denver, and I adore food. It would be an honor to watch you in the back of the house."

Elizabeth's mouth twisted. Was she actually jealous?

Well, that cut through his ire like a serrated knife through Angel Food cake.

"I love being watched," he said huskily, laughing out loud when Elizabeth's mouth pinched shut.

So she *was* jealous.

Okay, this could be fun.

He wrapped an arm around Natalie and led her to the kitchen. When the door closed behind them, she disengaged from his hold.

"There's no need to use me to make her jealous. I have too much respect for myself and other women."

A forthcoming female? He didn't come across that every day, not when his fame had women throwing themselves at him. "I'm sorry. I didn't mean any disrespect. It won't happen again."

She smiled then. "Good. Now show me what you have in mind."

Natalie's questions were as insightful as they were straightforward as he introduced her to his staff and gave her a tour of the kitchen. She knew food, and she understood portions and price points.

When she sampled their newest dessert, an apricot semifreddo with salted almond brittle, she suggested adding a slice of wildflower honeycomb from Dare Valley's finest honey producer to give it a local touch. It was a genius idea and just the kind of thing he was looking to do at High Stakes. What a pleasure it was to speak with someone who understood his vision.

Soon he forgot about Elizabeth and was showing Natalie his new shipment of Gorau Glas, a blue cheese from Great Britain that had redefined blue cheese for him.

Too bad it wasn't the perfect ingredient, the one he sought like the Holy Grail.

The first time he'd heard the phrase was from Manny Caruthers, his childhood mentor. The head chef at a small restaurant in Hell's Kitchen, Manny had caught Terrance trying to steal food from his kitchen. Rather than turning the punk kid in to the cops, he'd taken him under his wing, giving him a second chance. Terrance's mom had died of a drug overdose a few years later, not long after his seventeenth birthday, and Manny had taken him into the restaurant's walk-in cooler and gestured to the food.

"When my grandma passed, there was this huge hole inside me. She taught me how to cook, and she said that those of us who love to feed people are obsessed with finding the perfect ingredient—the one thing that fills the emptiness inside us with peace.

"My grandma's perfect ingredient was having a glass of honey water and sitting on the back porch steps. Mine is the chipotle hot sauce from New Orleans that I add to the butter I use on my sourdough bread every morning as I watch the sun rise. Terrance, you need to search for your own perfect ingredient. Once you find it, you'll have the peace you don't have now, the peace you never had with the woman who gave birth to you and then threw her life away."

Terrance hadn't been ready to listen at the time, but Manny's words had stayed with him. He'd been searching for his own perfect ingredient for a long while now, but he still hadn't found the peace his friend had described to him—no matter how special or exotic or unusual the ingredients he'd sampled.

"Oh, my God," Natalie said after her first taste of the cheese, interrupting his reverie. "I think I might have an orgasm. Right here in your kitchen."

At forty dollars a pound, it warranted an orgasm. Thank goodness the high rollers coming to The Grand didn't blink at the prices on the menu, so Mac gave him tremendous leeway when it came to ordering the best.

Usually he never missed the opportunity to make a wicked comment, but she'd put him in his place, and he respected that. "It's life changing, isn't it?"

"I don't think I will ever buy blue cheese crumbles ever again."

"Not in the plastic container?" he asked, aghast.

"Yes. We normal people can't always afford this stuff or don't have access to it. I would go broke if I served this at an event."

Terrance shaved off a taste of the cheese for himself and slid it in his mouth. Sweet mother of... "Depends on the event. Who's your biggest client?"

She made a face like the cheese had gone sour in her mouth. "The Denver Raiders."

"And that's a bad thing?"

"My ex-husband plays for them. It's been...complicated since our divorce last year."

"I see." When she turned away, he covered the cheese and stored it. "We should join the others."

"Yes," she murmured, and something about her downcast expression told Terrance he had met a kindred spirit.

"Come on. I expect the appetizers will cheer you up."

Maybe they would cheer him up too.

Chapter 6

Rhett wasn't saying a word—he just sat there, humming into his bourbon. Of course, Elizabeth knew she was being a bitch. And Rhett always said he would never call a spade a spade when it was as obvious as a wart on someone's face.

"Fine," she huffed finally. "I'm not exactly cool with Terrance being here."

Again, no word from her adopted brother and boss.

"Why don't you say something?"

"Are you going to admit you became a green-eyed monster when he kissed Natalie's hand?" he asked in that slow drawl of his.

"Hmm..." No way in hell she was going to do that.

"Then I don't have anything to say except try and keep it clean around the kids."

"Funny."

When Terrance came out with Natalie after taking *way* too long for a mere tour—not that she'd been eyeing her watch or anything—her gaze clashed with his. He was pushing her buttons; there was no mistaking it. He'd never had eyes for anyone else during their time together, even though plenty of women had run their fingers over his arm in invitation at the parties in Rhett's hotel suite.

And Natalie was gorgeous, dammit, so here she was pea green with envy, and not liking it one bit. Who could blame the woman for finding Terrance attractive? He radiated sexuality just as surely as the raging wall of fiery heat next to her.

"Sorry it took us so long," Natalie said by way of an excuse. "Chef T ended up showing me around the kitchen, which made me drool."

Drool was an appropriate phrase to use around Terrance, but it wasn't because of his stainless steel appliances.

"Who's ready to eat?" he asked softly.

God, the way his gravel and spice voice said that made her thighs clench. *Food*, she told herself. *He was talking about food.*

"Let's see what you cooked up for us," Rhett declared, rubbing her shoulder in comfort.

"Why don't we head to the tasting room?"

Terrance led the way to a special room accented in buttery wood planks, with one glass wall showcasing The Grand's impressive wine cellar. The feel was cozy yet elegant, dominated by a rustic iron barrel hoop chandelier hanging from six thick rope cords above a ten-person, live-edge trestle farm table.

"My God," Natalie gasped. "How many bottles does your cellar have?"

"About a thousand, but I'm already planning on expanding it. I have access to some wines Mac's former chef didn't."

"What about your bourbon selection?" Rhett asked. "We poker players aren't big on wine."

"You'd be surprised what the high rollers order after they've left the tables," Terrance told him, "but you're right. A lot of them prefer hard liquor. We have about two hundred bottles of bourbon, and again, I am going to be adding to Mac's inventory."

"We should have a bourbon tasting at the next poker game," Rhett mused, plopping down in the leather high-backed chair at the head. "You need to get High Stakes running as smooth as a baby's bottom so you can join us, T. It blows that you only have one night off a week now."

Elizabeth wanted to grind her teeth. Of course, Terrance had been asked to join the weekly poker game. Mac had started the tradition, and now it included the Hales and their growing family.

"It still pisses me off your poker night is for boys only," Elizabeth mused, taking a seat on Rhett's right. "Jane and I would kick your butts."

"I expect you would," Terrance murmured from behind her, his mouth close to her ear, under the pretext of helping her into her seat like a gentleman.

Something he definitely wasn't.

To torture him, she leaned back just a fraction and angled her neck to the left, exposing her nape, which he'd loved to kiss and use his teeth on. Hearing him clear his throat put the first smile on her face since she'd arrived.

"I'll have my staff bring in the appetizers."

"You know," Rhett drawled, "my mama always says 'don't start a fire you can't put out.' My mama is a wise woman, Natalie."

Everyone knew whom he was really addressing, but Natalie nodded gamely and said, "My mom always tells us not to bite off more than we can chew. What did your mom tell you, Elizabeth?"

"My mom wasn't into sayings like that when I was growing up."

Elizabeth's mom had never given her words of wisdom, only cruel taunts. How she had delighted in proving her wrong over and over.

Pretty girls aren't smart. By fifteen, she'd won the North American Open Chess Championship and came away with sixty thousand in winnings, adding to her college fund.

You'll never amount to anything. She'd been accepted into Harvard after vowing to attend the best university in the United States.

Better land a rich Harvard boy fast and get pregnant so he'll take care of you. She'd made her own millions as Rhett's poker scout and invested it wisely, using all she'd learned at Harvard.

Elizabeth had remade herself at Harvard.

In the beginning, she hadn't fit in. She was a sexy blond, and some people couldn't see past her looks and lack of polish. But someone had been looking out for her, because the conservative Jane Wilcox had been assigned as her roommate. Under her new friend's guidance, Elizabeth cultivated her manners, dyed her hair brown to counter all the dumb blond comments, and bought more conservative clothing.

Ultimately, becoming Vixen had simply been a matter of putting on a new mask, one she welcomed, enjoyed, and sometimes exploited. If men were stupid enough to underestimate her, she was all too willing to play them.

But then Terrance came along and upended her world, making her want to unmask herself.

Until the night he punched someone.

Vince hadn't seemed possessive or scary in the beginning, even though she'd sensed an air of violence in him. Terrance possessed that same volatile air. He was jealous of the men who leered at her, the ones she played by batting her eyelashes as she carefully deconstructed their poker strategies.

His show of violence had been enough to send the dark part of her, perpetually scared and wounded from Vince, running as if her life still depended on it.

As Terrance strolled in with two assistants, the air of danger around him was still tangible. He was angry with her, and their impromptu connection over dessert the other night, a momentary truce, seemed to have dissolved like meringue dropped in water.

Terrance stood behind her again, but she didn't know if it was because he couldn't stand to see her face, or if he wanted to smell the Chanel perfume she wore—the one that used to drive him crazy.

"I spoke to Jane and Matt about their favorite dishes—" Terrance told them, handing out card stock embossed with The Grand's logo, "—so I created selections that I think will suit them. Rhett suggested we do tasting cards, so everyone can rate the dishes and leave any comments. That way, everyone can enjoy the food without debating the choices. He figured it would save you some heartburn."

Rhett was probably worried she'd tear one of the dishes apart out of frustration. He wasn't necessarily wrong. She wanted to either fight with Terrance or tear off his chef jacket and pants and make love to him until she screamed—she wasn't sure which.

"Beef skewers served with horseradish cream," he said in a silky tone as he pointed to the first platter. "I understand Matt is an all-American man when it comes to meat."

"All of us Hales love meat," Natalie said. "Except Caroline, who likes salad. We're thinking about disowning her."

Terrance and Rhett laughed, but Elizabeth couldn't even muster a smile. She was too aware of his husky voice, which seemed to wrap around her.

"Then we have shrimp wrapped in one of my all-time favorite bacons. It's cob-smoked, a rare and remarkable flavor, coming to us from the Native American tradition back East."

"Like a corn cob?" Rhett asked, plopping one of the

appetizers off the tray without waiting for anyone to serve him. "Holy heck! This is amazing. Rye would love it."

"Yes, he would," Terrance agreed, since he also knew their country singer friend well.

"I *heard* you knew Rye Crenshaw," Natalie said, clapping her hands. "Please tell me he's coming to visit. Jill couldn't stop talking about the impromptu concert he gave for your wife before you became engaged."

"That boy is about ready to get himself hitched to the sweetest chef you've ever met. He's coming here for a bachelor weekend in the near future, isn't he, T?"

"I'm already planning the menu," Terrance said.

"I don't expect he's going to sing here, but who knows."

"I'll keep my fingers crossed," Natalie said.

"Okay, T. What else do you have for us?"

"Crab cake sliders for Jane. And finally pizza, since they told me it was their first meal together."

"Oh how romantic," Natalie breathed out.

Elizabeth had to fight against rolling her eyes. It would be romantic if she wasn't so upset at Terrance. Who knew he had a nostalgic side? Okay, that wasn't fair. Hadn't he served her favorite white wine?

"I made them mini meat-lovers calzones," he said. "Easier to munch on than pizza slices at a party."

"But much harder to make," Natalie said, snaking out a hand like she wanted to snag one off the plate. "Wow! I love this idea. I might have to steal it."

"Steal away," Terrance said, and even Elizabeth could hear the smile in his voice. His profession always lit him up inside. Like her, he was one of the rare people who loved what he did. "Enjoy."

She was so sensitive to Terrance's presence, she knew the moment he left the room. Funny how when she'd agreed to do this, she hadn't considered how hard it would be to eat. Terrance had a way of filling her belly with girly butterflies.

Rhett and Natalie made up for her lack of enjoyment by moaning their way through the appetizers all the way to the desserts. By the time everyone had finished writing down their scores and comments, Terrance was standing behind her again, crowding her personal space and all her senses.

She forcibly pushed back from the table, hoping to run over his toes or smack him in the shins. But he'd always been light on his feet, and he easily ducked out of her way, a knowing look in his eyes.

Rhett stood and pounded him on the back. Terrance didn't move a muscle—a feat few men could muster.

"Man, I can't wait until the party. I'm going to gobble like a hog, eating those babies all over again."

Natalie patted her stomach. "I'm not going to be able to eat any of my mom's dinner tonight, but it was worth it. Chef T, everything was incredible. Thank you."

He held her hand a fraction too long, just to piss Elizabeth off, she suspected.

"My pleasure, Natalie. I'm glad you enjoyed it."

Then it came time for her to say something. Her mind fumbled for a minute. "I'm sure Jane and Matt will be happy with your final selections." It was the most gracious she could be at the moment.

He must have known because his smile turned secretive, his bottle green eyes filled with a challenge. "I'll see you soon, Elizabeth."

As they left the restaurant, she linked her arm through Rhett's and said, "How about we play some poker?"

Now that Jane had outted them, she had the freedom to play in public, and while it wasn't something she usually did, she felt the urge to battle the hand of fate and see how she could play the cards she was dealt.

Anything to get her mind off Terrance.

CHAPTER 7

Election day spirits were high, and early exit polling indicated Matt was winning in a landslide. Even his election consultant from Denver, a brooding, serious man, was smiling when Elizabeth arrived at the restaurant for the party.

She'd purposely arrived late since Jane had texted her to say she and Matt were having a celebratory dinner alone. If that wasn't code for election-win sex, Elizabeth didn't know what was.

Her one-shoulder gold Armani dress had been purposefully selected to tantalize Terrance, who would undoubtedly be making the rounds. He had been in charge of the food at all of Rhett's formal parties at The Peacock, and he'd always come out to mingle midway through the evening, once everything was under control in the kitchen. He would share a bourbon with Rhett and Mac before angling his way through the crowd—being stopped by woman after woman and his buddies—until he reached her. Then he would sweep his eyes down from the top of her dress to the tips of her high heels and pretty much lick his chops, knowing he was going to peel her out of that dress in short order.

Tonight the only peeling he was going to do was for the potatoes in the leek potato patties he was serving oozing with goat cheese. But he was going to look. And she was going to torture him.

As much as she tried to tell herself to ignore him and play it safe, she couldn't. He was here, and she had to push back at him like he was pushing at her.

Even though she had no idea where that would lead.

Okay, that was a lie. The greedy, lust-filled goddess inside her wanted him in her bed. The scared woman who'd run from him wanted to give him another chance to show her that he could be her non-violent Prince Charming.

Maybe the two sides could compromise, and she and Terrance could have a sex-only agreement while he was in town?

When she caught sight of him already mingling with the crowd at the party, her heart leaped into her throat, and she knew it was impossible. No man had ever opened her up to so much emotion, good and bad. He'd taught her the difference between sex and making love without even meaning to. The intimacy between them had been there from the start, like it had been ordained.

No, there would never be anything no-strings with Terrance.

Darn it all.

His head turned then, as if sensing her, and those bottle-green eyes seemed to glow like sea glass on a moonlit beach as they made that seductive trek down her body. But instead of excusing himself from talking to Jill and her husband, Brian, and coming to her, he returned his attention to their conversation.

"Girl, you need a drink," Natalie said, snagging her arm. "If you don't stop staring at Terrance, I'm afraid he might haul you over his shoulder and carry you upstairs to a hotel room."

Her belly fluttered at the thought.

"I'm not after him, by the way," Natalie added, shoving a glass of white wine into her hand from a nearby waiter's tray. "He's gorgeous and interesting and tantalizing, but I'm done with chest-beating alphas."

Now that got Elizabeth's attention. "Why?"

"Carpet burns. On my butt and my heart."

Elizabeth laughed. "Jane said I would like you, and she was right. I'm sorry I acted like a bitch the other day."

Natalie led the way to High Stakes' curvy bar past the fire wall, which always dazzled her senses, and signaled the bartender for a Manhattan. "Please. You were acting like a bitch to *him*. I was just in the way. I told him to stop trying to make you jealous when we went into the kitchen."

Her wine went down the wrong pipe, and Natalie had to pound her back. "Really?" she finally choked out.

"Really. Come on. The guests of honor might not be here yet, but my sisters are, and we'll protect you from doing something stupid."

Soon they were standing with Moira and Caroline Hale, drinking wine and moaning over the food.

"I'm going to have to eat salads for the rest of the week," Caroline said.

"Oh, for heaven's sake, you're a size six. What in the world are you worried about?" Jill said, slinging her arm around her cousin as she joined the group. "I'm up to a size eight after the twins, and you don't see me complaining."

"It's because your boobs are like milk jugs now," Natalie told her.

Elizabeth almost spewed out her white wine. This was the second time Natalie's directness had thrown her for a loop.

Moira peered at Jill's awesome breasts. "You don't need a padded bra right now, that's for sure."

"Like I ever did." Jill socked her. "Stop staring at my chest, Mo."

"I'm just jealous. How can we even be related?" She pointed to her own flat chest.

Terrance had to have special male hearing, the kind able to signal that women were talking about breasts, because he made a beeline for their group.

Natalie grabbed her hand. "Let's go talk to my Uncle Arthur for a while."

"Okay," Elizabeth said, letting Natalie drag her over to Arthur Hale, who sat at the head of a table with Natalie's mom and the women Matt had dubbed his Easter Brigade, three sweet elderly ladies who dressed only in pastels and were the first volunteers on his campaign.

Arthur leaned back in his chair. "Well, if it's not the other Harvard Smarty Pants."

She leaned down and kissed his weathered cheek. It was his nickname for Jane, chosen to send a message to everyone in town that he approved of his future great niece-in-law. Elizabeth was grateful he'd extended the honor to her. Even though he was in his late seventies, the Pulitzer-Prize winning journalist still ran his legendary newspaper, *The Western Independent*, with help from his granddaughter, Meredith, and her husband, Tanner.

"Hello, Arthur," she said and nodded to everyone else with a soft smile.

"Young Matthew had better show up soon, or I'll be dozing off through his acceptance speech. We old people have earlier bed times, right, Joanie?" Arthur asked the woman sitting beside him, who was dressed in a lovely pale pink.

"Speak for yourself, old man," she told him.

"Amen," the other women chimed in.

"Matt had a special surprise for Jane," April told them. "He knows her dad's old election parties were hard on her. He didn't want her to get caught up in bad memories, so he took her and the dogs for a walk at their park at sunset, and since the day was nice and warm, he brought a picnic for them to enjoy."

"Is my brother the best man in the world or what?" Natalie asked, and Elizabeth had to agree.

At that moment, the guests started to clap and whistle, and Elizabeth saw Jane and Matt jog in together through the crowd, holding hands and grinning like the world lay at their feet.

She joined in the revelry as the couple climbed the raised dais at the back of the restaurant. Matt kissed Jane sweetly and looked into her eyes a moment before he picked up the mike.

"I just heard the news from my campaign manager," Matt told the audience. "It's official. We won the primary! Get ready for November, folks!"

Everyone broke into applause, and this time, people shouted their happiness from the crowd, including Natalie, who now had her arms wrapped around her mom.

"This primary wasn't what anyone in Dare Valley was expecting. Heck, even I didn't know how it would go when I decided to run for mayor. Then I met my beautiful, talented, and awe-inspiring fiancé, Jane Wilcox. We weathered a pretty serious storm together, and I'm so proud she stood beside me. I'm even prouder that we never once lowered ourselves to the opposition's negative campaign tactics."

The cheers were so loud, Elizabeth's eardrums shook.

Then he flashed that all-American smile that made him so likable. "Well, except for my mother, who confessed she took down some nasty campaign signs on Main Street."

People around her chuckled, but Elizabeth did not. The signs had targeted Jane, showing pictures of her as

Raven.

"The Hales have deep roots in this town, but never once have we *ever* held the honorable seat of mayor. Right, Uncle Arthur?"

Elizabeth looked over to see Arthur raise a hand in the air in response.

"My campaign manager tells me I will likely run unopposed for mayor. The other party doesn't think anyone can beat me, but we'll see if that holds true. November is a long time away. I've told you what I stand for, and I'm not planning to talk your ear off tonight. We're going to have fun and party and enjoy this moment. I want to thank everyone who believed in me and voted for me, but I especially want to thank my campaign volunteers and election consultant, Rob, who made this happen. Have fun and thank you again!"

Matt and Jane left the stage and were immediately surrounded by well wishers.

Then the hairs on the back of her neck rose, and Elizabeth knew Terrance was staring at her. Her eyes swept across the crowd until she found him, looking so damn sexy in that denim chef jacket he'd worn at the tasting.

Her eyes met his, and in them, she could see the same confusion and lust she felt.

Her whole body tingled in response.

They both wanted, *needed* this longing to end.

But it wasn't that simple.

What in the world were they going to do?

CHAPTER 8

Terrance had never cared for politics, since the system had failed him before he was old enough to vote. Still, Matt Hale seemed to be one of those rare candidates with integrity and a solid vision.

Not that politics could distract him from covertly watching Vixen. Correction. Elizabeth.

Not even coming across the perfect ingredient, something he'd traveled the world to find, could prevent him from staring at her. And that was significant. In Istanbul's famous Spice Market, he'd once spent ten days going from vendor to vendor in search of it.

He'd set aside his pursuit for the perfect ingredient only once—for the summer he and Vixen had spent together—and he had a sinking feeling she was going to distract him again.

Even though he could purchase saffron at two thousand dollars a pound, nothing satisfied the hollowness at his core, the emptiness that stretched back to his early childhood, spent with a resentful mother and the specter of an absent father. Cooking was more than food to Terrance. It had filled a void in his bones, saving him from God knows what kind of life on the streets, but it hadn't completed him. The perfect ingredient would do that. He only had to find it.

When Elizabeth left him, he'd redoubled his efforts, traveling to the world's most illustrious food markets. In Brazil at Kauppatori Market, he'd sampled smoked reindeer. In India at Khari Baoli, he'd bought the most delicate cardamom in existence. And still he'd ventured to China to the Kreta Ayer Wet Market to taste the most innovative curry blend to ever cross his palate.

But none were the perfect ingredient.

Looking at Elizabeth, even without all the sequins and makeup, created an odd warmth in his belly, like the comforting simmer of a fragrant stew on a winter's day. Her slender right arm was bare in the slinky gold number she'd chosen. All he wanted to do was kiss his way up the inside of her wrist. And then there were her legs... The dress ended a few inches shy of her knees, and well, he wanted to kiss his way up her smooth thighs too. She was a sexy siren tonight, and no woman could compete with her. Not that any ever had in his mind.

His heart warned him to be careful. The Dear John letter she'd given him had left a permanent dagger in that mysterious organ. But he could not stop himself from trying to corner her again. She'd successfully eluded him all night.

Running meant fear. He knew because the same restlessness raced through his blood.

Along with lust and curiosity and a whole bunch of other uncomfortable emotions.

"I didn't realize how deep things ran between you two," Rhett drawled, settling a hand on his shoulder. Fixated on Elizabeth, Terrance hadn't even heard his approach.

Terrance took the bourbon his friend shoved at him and downed it in one swallow. "Leave it alone."

His friend's sigh was long-suffering. "You know how much I love her, and God knows you and I have been friends quite a spell. Just be careful. She's more tender-hearted than she lets on, and even though you're a tough guy like the rest of us, I have a feeling the right woman turns you into pudding on the inside."

No one used more colorful language than Rhett, and Terrance couldn't help but smile. "Pudding? Never been fond of the stuff."

"You know what I mean."

Terrance's eyes were still pinned to Elizabeth. Her movements were less bold and assertive now, he realized. Perhaps the hooker heels had given her hips a more pronounced sway, or she'd been hamming up her role. Either way, there was still a sensual rhythm to her movements, but it was all her.

"She's more beautiful as herself than I ever imagined," he told Rhett, not fearing anyone would overhear them in the corner of the restaurant.

"You never saw her in her...all together?" his friend asked in shock.

Laughter tickled the back of his throat. "I saw her naked plenty, but never without her makeup on." Naked, her beauty had stolen his breath, and his blood beat hot at the thought of seeing all of that curvy, soft flesh again. "I didn't even realize she wore a wig. Explains why she told me not to touch her hair."

"Shit."

"Shit is right." Terrance withdrew a hundred and waved it in front of Rhett's face. "Giving up swearing is an expensive proposition."

"I should start charging myself per word too. Dustin needs a good role model, even though my mouth is as pristine as white sheets on a clothesline compared to what it used to be."

Terrance handed him a hundred. "Here's my donation to your Cuss Fund. You can pick your favorite charity."

"What's yours?" Rhett asked as one of Terrance's hand-picked servers stopped and offered them some of the excellent chocolate chip cookies they'd baked as a nod to Dare Valley's small town community.

Terrance and his staff had chuckled about baking something so simple and wholesome, but it was Matt's favorite, and the secret to catering events was catering to the hosts' taste. The cookies were moist, the chocolate decadent—as only a special dark chocolate from Belgium could be—and the hint of coconut oil instead of butter set them apart. Terrance made everything with his special touch, even chocolate chip cookies.

"The Children's Aid Society in New York," he said.

"Sounds nice. I'll probably donate it to a charity that helps women who've experienced violence."

"That's a great cause."

As a kid, Terrance had seen plenty of defenseless women get preyed upon. As a teenager, he'd started intervening. He might be a violent man—he'd been told as much—but he abhorred violence against women.

And it made him wonder for the hundredth time what Elizabeth had been scared of the other night.

"Why does Elizabeth keep a baseball bat by her front door?" he asked his friend.

Rhett's mouth turned grim. "I'll let her tell you that, but it's another reason for you to take care with her."

That comment punched into his system, like a bruising upper cut to the jaw. And he wondered again if she'd run from him because of his fight with that asshole poker player who'd disrespected her and put his hands on her. It made more sense now. She'd been hurt before, and God help him, the anger and rage that rose inside him at the thought of *anyone* hurting her only confirmed what he already knew.

He had to be with her again.

Yes, they would have to wade through the old anger

and mistrust, but he wanted her, needed her. He was old enough to stop questioning why.

"I'll be careful," he promised.

Rhett waved at Mac, who was talking with his wife, Peggy, by the bar. "Not too long ago, Mac and I had the same conversation about Abbie. I'll tell you the same thing he told me. We'll always be friends, regardless of what happens between you two."

This time Terrance slapped him on the back. "I appreciate that, man. Time for me to make my move."

The center of his attraction broke away from her group and headed to the bathroom. He increased his pace, and when she reached the hallway, he snagged her arm and pulled her into the empty side room, where his staff kept their things.

"Hi," he said softly, seeing the pulse pound in her neck. "We haven't talked yet."

"You're not interested in talking," she told him in a flat tone.

"Now that's not true. I talk with you more than I've ever talked to a woman."

As if she'd been holding her breath, it expelled in a rush, and he felt it across every inch of his skin.

"God, you're beautiful."

Vulnerability shone in her eyes. "More so than Vixen?"

He finally touched her, pushing a strand of her blond hair back from her face. "Yes. But in a different way. You're more approachable like this."

"You never had any trouble *approaching* me before."

Going for honesty, he stroked her cheek. "When I first met you, I didn't expect much more than hot sex. And then—"

"We talked," she finished for him. "I know. I didn't expect anything more either."

"I guess that's why we both ended up being

surprised with each other. Elizabeth, I still want you."

She swallowed but said nothing.

"I want you. *Again.*"

"Is that all?" she quipped, looking over his shoulder, her body heat calling to him like a hearth fire in a snowstorm.

"Why are you fighting it? Yes, we have some shit to sort through, but we still know how to talk to each other, and God knows there's plenty of heat between us."

Her mouth quirked up. "Made you swear." It was said like a gloat.

"You're costing me a fortune," he admitted. "This torture has to end, Elizabeth."

She pushed against his chest, and he stepped back. "I'm not so sure. It's not going to be just about sex if we get together, Terrance."

"It wasn't before," he admitted. "Is that why you left without saying goodbye?"

Her hand rested on the doorknob. "I had my reasons. Anyway, if I hadn't ended it, you would have. Eventually. I wish you'd stop being angry about it."

"Don't fucking tell me how I should feel."

His angry words seemed to shake the air between them, making her shiver.

"I need to get back," she said and opened the door.

Taking out two hundred dollars, he deposited the bills in his pocket and stood there for ten seconds before following her.

As he headed toward Elizabeth, Natalie stepped into his path. *"Chef T."*

"You're not going to stop me from getting to her," he told her.

She studied him and braced her hands on her hips. "I am tonight."

His eyes flicked over her shoulder to where Elizabeth now stood, surrounded again by Natalie's sisters and Jane, whose gaze held a clear warning.

"Fine. I don't want to ruin the party, but you can tell her that this isn't over."

His gaze clashed with Elizabeth's. Her pulse still beat strong in her throat. He let his mouth curve to convey he was only slightly amused.

"I'm not your messenger. You can tell her yourself," Natalie said. Then her gaze caught on someone or something to the right, and her face seemed to freeze.

He looked over. A distinguished man with silver hair in a suit stood on the outskirts of the party. A man came up and hugged him, joined by a young boy.

"Who is he?" he asked.

She shook herself and regained her composure. "My father. We didn't know he was coming tonight. He had a surgery scheduled."

Her sisters locked arms and went over, leaving Elizabeth to wander over to the Mavens and the Butlers. He kept his eyes on the Hales. Natalie's sisters awkwardly hugged their father. He realized the other man was their brother, and the kid could only be his son. The family resemblance was unmistakable. Then Matt Hale came over with Jane, and the tense family greeting continued.

"I don't want to keep you," he said, wondering what the older man had done to create such a rift between him and his children. Terrance didn't know much about the Hales, but he knew they were close.

Her smile had teeth. "Please do. In fact, why don't I introduce you to my mother? She won't admit it, but she'd appreciate a little moral support tonight. It's the first time she's seen my dad since she left him in the fall."

Now he had a good picture in his mind.

"I'd enjoy meeting her, and since you're both from Dare Valley, you can tell me what you think this place's perfect ingredient is. I love to hear about what a place has to offer and how I might use it in my cooking." Her suggestion to add the honeycomb from a local Dare Valley producer to the dessert on his new menu only made him want to hear what else she had to offer him.

The sparkle returned to her eyes. "That would be fresh-picked huckleberries from the mountains. My mom used to make them into jam, but our neighbor used them on venison. I felt bad for Bambi, but I pretty much gobbled it up."

Huckleberries.

"Do they taste like blueberries?" he asked, feeling that familiar excitement. "I had some in New Hampshire once."

"No, ours here in the Rockies are different. They're ruby red and translucent. Tastier. I've had ones both sweet and tart. Their flavor is intense because they grow in the wild."

"When can you pick them?"

She threaded her arm through his and led him in the opposite direction of the woman who was captivating his thoughts. "July. I know a place in the mountains. If you'd like, I'll take you, but you have to cook for me."

"Deal."

His heart started to beat faster like it always did when he learned about a possible new contender, but he couldn't stop from looking back over his shoulder at Elizabeth.

His pulse tripled, and for a minute he forgot about the huckleberries. He cursed under his breath and drew out another hundred.

Natalie only raised an eyebrow. "You're going to lose all your money if you continue on like this."

"I have plenty of money," he growled.

When they arrived at the table clustered with people in their golden years, he had no trouble picking out Natalie's mother. She had the same lovely cheekbones as her daughter.

"Mom, this is Chef T."

When he took April's hand, he made sure to hold it while he talked to her. Even he could see the valiant effort she was making not to look past him at her estranged husband.

"It's good to meet you. We're big fans of your show."

"Please call me Terrance. Natalie was just telling me about your huckleberry jam. I'm always looking for what a place has to offer. Huckleberries sound like just the thing for me to use on our summer menu."

"The huckleberries around here are quite special," she said. Her hand was relaxing now, so he finally let go.

"And let me introduce you to my wonderful uncle, Arthur Hale, and some of Matt's incredible campaign volunteers."

The trio of older woman looked like they ate Charlotte Royale for dessert every day with rose hip tea. He was charmed since he didn't have contact with any of his own elderly relatives. His mother had burned every bridge to her family with her drug habit.

"It's great to meet everyone. I hope you enjoyed the food."

"Especially the chocolate chip cookies," Joanie said, "but there was something a little different about them. In a good way, of course."

Ah, she was too cute with her round face and soft hair. "I used coconut oil instead of butter."

Arthur snorted. "Something wrong with butter?"

Natalie put her hand on his arm like she was trying to soften her uncle's bluster. "Uncle Arthur likes to complain about Jill's coffee, especially the ones he insists are crazy concoctions, like her raspberry mocha latte."

Her uncle crossed his arms, his intelligent blue gaze raking over Terrance. "If people want to have dessert, why don't they eat it instead of drinking it?"

Terrance felt his mouth twitch. "People eat the

darndest things. Now me, I'm the kind of guy who will try anything once."

"Somehow that doesn't surprise me," Arthur said.

Joanie hit him gently. "Oh, ignore him. He's all bluster. What's the strangest thing you've ever eaten, Terrance?"

There were many, so he picked the first one that came to mind. "Grasshoppers. They're considered a delicacy in the Congo."

All of the women shivered.

Arthur snorted. "And what did you expect them to taste like? A steak?"

Laughter shook his chest. "I guess it's like climbing a mountain. If it's in front of me, I'm going to give it a go."

"You're braver than I am," April said. "And speaking of being brave, it's time I say hello to my hus...my ex-husband."

Arthur stood with her and took her arm. "We'll both go say hello to that moron."

"Now, Arthur..." she said as they walked away.

The frown on Natalie's face spoke volumes. "I supposed I should go too. It was good to see you, Chef T."

"Please call me Terrance. If you're going to keep me away from Elizabeth, you might as well use my full name. Not too many people have the balls to get between me and what I want."

She laughed like he'd hoped. "Ask my siblings. I have balls as big as any man."

As she walked away, he headed to the kitchen, the only place on earth he had ever felt at home until waking up in Elizabeth's arms.

Chapter 9

Even though her two brothers had plenty of space in their houses, Natalie and her sisters always stayed with their mom when they were visiting Dare Valley. The older house where April lived certainly wasn't grand, but its contents felt delightfully familiar, like the music box resting on the mantle. Natalie used to crank it on snowy days, twirling the models around to "Somewhere Over the Rainbow" from her favorite childhood movie, *The Wizard of Oz*.

And then there was the family farmer's table boasting nicks and scratches from its long years of watching them grow. Their mom hadn't taken everything from her house in Denver with their dad, but this table... Well, it had been more hers than his anyway. Their mom had sat with them at this table while they did their homework. She'd set cakes blazing with candles in front of them on their birthdays, as the lucky kid sat in the prized head of the table position, the guest of honor for a day. And this was where the Hale children had sat to talk over a problem with their mom—or sometimes even a sister or brother.

Right now, Natalie and her sisters were huddled around it, drinking vodka shots. Not the wisest thing perhaps, but seeing Dad tonight had shaken everyone. Including mom, which was why she was taking longer in the shower than usual.

"I still can't believe his nerve," Caroline said, kicking back in her chair. "It was hard enough for Matt to invite dad, but what does he do? He says he probably can't make it because of surgery."

"And then he goes and shows up without telling any of us," Moira added, sweeping a dramatic hand through the air like a symphony conductor before fumbling to shove her brown hair behind her ear.

Despite her Irish name, Moira couldn't hold her liquor.

"He could have given Mom a warning," Caroline continued. "Heck, all of us could have used one. Even Danny was reserved." Natalie had noticed too, and their brother Andy's son was the type of kid who would give anyone a hug.

Caroline hiccupped. She didn't hold her liquor much better than their other sister.

"You're not saying anything, Nat," Moira said, pouring another shot.

Natalie grabbed the bottle and set it on the floor beside her, causing Moira to stick out her tongue and giggle.

"Spoil sport."

"Nat's pissed," Caroline said, and Natalie glared at her even though it was true.

"Dad didn't tell anyone he was coming because he never thinks about being kind to other people," she said "It wouldn't surprise me one bit to learn he's clueless about how upset we are."

"He's a cold fish," Moira said, sipping her vodka more slowly now.

"That's why he can cut up people on the surgery

table for a living," Caroline declared.

Natalie winced at the image and downed her shot. Picking up the bottle, she poured herself another.

"Why do you get more?" Caroline complained.

"Because I can hold my liquor."

Her phone vibrated on the table and started to skip across it like it had a life of its own.

"It's Andy," she announced and hit speaker.

"Hey, Andy cakes," Moira called out first.

There was an audible sigh on the line. "I knew you guys were drinking. What's your poison tonight? Tequila?"

"No, vodka," Caroline said. "The liquor store was closed, so we had to make do with mom's pathetic stash."

"Where is she?" Andy asked.

"In the shower," Natalie told him, "but it's been almost an hour. Seeing Dad really upset her."

"Of course it did. Hell, it upset everyone. Even Danny asked me why Grandpa didn't seem happy to see him. I had to lie to my kid and say he had an off day at the hospital."

Clenching the drink in her hand, Natalie fought back the harsh words she wanted to spout back. "I had hoped he'd changed."

Her sisters teared up when she said that, and silence descended around the table.

"I had hoped he'd changed too," her mom said from behind her.

Natalie swung around in time to see her mom dash a few tears off her cheeks. "I'm going to bed for good now. I love you—all of you."

"Oh, mom," Moira said, rising out of her chair and rushing over to wrap her in a big hug.

Caroline and Natalie joined her, and the warmth of everyone embracing lightened her heart some. Their dad might not be around—heck he never really had been—but they had each other, and that was what mattered.

"Don't drink all of my vodka. I need it for the cosmos I'm making for my book club."

"We'll buy you more, Mom," Caroline said, giving her another kiss on the cheek.

"You girls," her mom said, shaking her head. "And Andy, good night to you and Danny."

"Love you, Mom," he said over the phone.

"Love you too."

When she left, the sisters lowered themselves to the table. No one reached for another drink.

"Mom's the bravest woman I've ever known," Moira said, sliding her chair close so she could lean against Caroline and rest her head on her shoulder like they used to do when they were younger.

"Does anyone know where Dad is staying?" Natalie asked finally.

"He told Matt he was staying at The Grand," Andy piped in from the phone on the table. "He needed to leave early to get back to the hospital, you see."

"I'm glad he didn't expect anyone to put him up," Caroline said.

"It's sad, don't you think? None of us even wanted him to stay with us." Moira wiped the tears streaming down her face.

"I just hope it didn't ruin Matt's night," Natalie said, rising and filling water glasses for everyone. "He deserves to be happy. He's worked hard for this, and with his new engagement..."

For a moment, she allowed herself to think about how happy she'd been during her engagement to Blake. Nothing had been strong enough to burst that bubble.

But the happiness hadn't lasted.

She hoped it would for Matt and Jane. They seemed the perfect match.

"Jane knows how to deal with tense parental

situations," Andy said. "She's a pro. Matt's a lucky man, and so are we to have her join our family. Okay, I'm going to bed. If the little guy wasn't asleep, I would sneak over and drink with you. Love you."

"Love you too. Night, Andy," Natalie and her sisters said in chorus.

After his call ended, Caroline drained her water. "So, Chef T is pretty hot. You into him?" She waggled her eyebrows at Natalie.

It was easy to answer. They didn't need to know *why* she wasn't interested. "No. He only has eyes for Elizabeth."

"She has the hots for him too," Moira said. "They could have flambéed one of the passing canapés with the looks they were shooting back and forth."

Wouldn't that have been hilarious? The poor server wouldn't have known what to do when his tray of cookies burst into flames.

"They were together for a while and then broke up, I think," she told them.

"Oh," Moira said. "I love thinking about people getting back together."

Of course, Moira hadn't meant to make her feel bad. She was talking about their mom and dad, but Natalie's mind had immediately gone to Blake. They'd been so happy, so perfect for each other. And then everything had gone horribly wrong.

She rose, determined to put those thoughts away. They were only creeping into her subconscious so much lately because she was planning the annual Denver Raiders Spring Training dinner.

"All right, girls. Let's get to bed. We have to get up at the butt crack of dawn in the morning and head back to the big city. And if we're not hungover, we're finding Matt's SUV. I have a new bumper sticker for him."

"What is it?" Moira said, weaving a little in place when she got up.

"I Dance A Mean Polka."

"Uncle Arthur will love that," Caroline said with an uncharacteristic snort, and Moira hiccupped out a laugh.

"We'll definitely help you plant that one on Matty Ice."

Maybe it would improve her mood tomorrow. When she got back to Denver, she had to meet with her point of contact at the Raiders to go over the final preparation for the menu. God, please don't let her run into Blake.

Not that she was afraid of him.

She just didn't want to see him ever again.

Running into one man she loved who'd let her down was enough for one week.

Chapter 10

Parking on Main Street was sometimes a challenge, and this evening was no exception. With the weather warming, people were out in droves. Dare Valley's quaint shops were seeing a nice bit of business today, and the line for Don't Soy with Me was out the door. When Elizabeth finally found a spot, she grabbed her gym bag and exited her car five blocks down from Sleek Lines, the new studio where she taught her Latin fusion exercise class. She was running a little late, but she already had her music cued on her smart phone, so she'd be okay. Hurrying down the street, her feet faltered a step when she spotted Ryan James waving to her on the street, having just come out of a nearby store.

Dammit. Why wouldn't the guy leave her alone?

She forced a smile and picked up her pace. Being nice hadn't worked, but neither had being rude. What was left? Ignoring him?

The temptation to cross the street was strong. But she couldn't just back down like that, even though memories of Vince made her blood run cold.

As she neared him, she gave a fake smile and

barreled by.

"Hey!" he called out as she passed him in a blur, weaving around other patrons on the street. "Wait! Elizabeth!"

She kept going, her head down. There were plenty of people around, so she was going to be fine. Safe. Ryan's footsteps thundered behind her, and she picked up her pace.

"Elizabeth!" Ryan shouted again. When she didn't answer, he reached out and grabbed her arm.

Spinning around, she glared at him and yanked away. *Don't touch me,* she wanted to scream. "Ryan, I'm late for class."

His breath was puffing out some from his run, and his face fell. If she'd known he'd be this hard to shake, she wouldn't have agreed to go out with him, regardless of how handsome and fit he was. And they had only been out on *one* date.

"I was only trying to say hi. It was good to see you. I was hoping we could talk."

She shifted her bag in front of her body like a shield, her heart rate hammering in her chest. "Ryan, I've tried to be nice about this, but I don't want to talk to you anymore. We went out months ago. It didn't work for me. Please stop following me."

"But Elizabeth—"

She took off before he could finish his sentence. If she hadn't been holding her bag, her hands would be trembling. Dammit. Why was he so dense? Vince had been more methodical about staking out where she'd be and confronting her. Always touching her. Her hair. Her cheek. Her arm. She'd been too terrified to knock his hands away and tell him to step back.

Her breath heaved, and she realized she was gasping.

A hand touched her arm again, and thinking it was Ryan, she shoved at him with all her might. The action put her off balance, causing her to stumble, and she looked up to see Terrance holding his hands up.

"I know you want to avoid me, but there's no reason to act like that."

She bit her lip so it wouldn't quiver. "Sorry. I'm late for my Latin exercise class. I'm the teacher."

"Remind me not to say hello to you next time you're on your way to your Latin thingee. I didn't realize you were into the Latin exercise movement, but it suits you. I know you move well."

Those bottle green eyes measured her body, and his mouth quirked up. Fear started to slide away, replaced with lust. Damn, why did he still have to look so ridiculously hot? His white T-shirt covered his tattoos, but it did little to hide his muscular chest. He was wearing some kind of a symbol on a leather chain around his neck—something that looked like the Chinese letters tattooed on his body.

Over his shoulder, Elizabeth saw Ryan watching them on the street. Maybe he would get the hint. All the single women in Dare Valley were pining over Terrance, if the talk in her dance class was to be trusted.

"I need to go," she said because she had no idea what else to say. Standing here with her body betraying her wasn't getting her anywhere.

"This can't continue, you know," he said. "Running away again isn't going to work, not now that we both live here. Let's have dinner. We had a good time at your house the other night."

People were walking around them on the sidewalk, and she was aware of their interest. Yes, she was chatting with Mr. Hotness himself, Chef T.

"We almost tore each other's throats out at the tasting," she fired back. "No, I think not."

She turned to leave, but he reached for her again. Her body jerked in surprise, still jumpy from Ryan.

"What's it going to take to get you to go out with

me?" he asked, standing there like a badass, unconcerned they were in people's way.

The stubborn set of his jaw told her he wasn't going to give up, so she decided to make it hard for him. "You have to come to my dance class and work out with us for the whole time."

Laughter rolled out of him. "You mean dance to some zippy beat with a bunch of women while doing the cha-cha? Shit. You're out of your mind."

Immediately he took out a hundred dollar bill from his wallet.

Gotcha. Chef T was way too cool for that. "Too bad then," she said and took off.

He walked next to her. "You're serious?"

"As a preacher on Sunday. Now, if you'll excuse me."

His gorgeous body faded from her peripheral vision. Had her crazy suggestion rooted him to the ground? She hoped so. Every time she saw him, the earth moved—and not in a good way. It was the kind of shaking that toppled cities and led to rampant destruction.

When she reached Sleek Lines, a couple of students were waiting at the door—Jill Hale, who was now a regular, and her pregnant sister, Meredith. Elizabeth's classes had started out small, but they were already nearing full capacity. Mostly because Jill was her own Paul Revere in Dare Valley.

"Was that Terrance?" she asked.

Elizabeth finally looked back. He was heading in the opposite direction on Main Street with that brawler's walk of his.

"Yes. How are you? Ready to shake it?"

"He looked like he wanted to gobble you up at Matt's party. If I wasn't a happily married woman with twins..."

Thank God Natalie hadn't told her cousin anything about Elizabeth and Terrance having history. Jill was fun, but she had a rep for not being able to keep a secret.

They headed into the studio together, and Elizabeth smiled at the twenty women already lined up.

"I shake it daily," Jill answered her original question as she shrugged out of her jacket and hung it on the wall. "Have you thought about choreographing a number to Abba? Maybe you could use 'Gimme, Gimme, Gimme A Man After Midnight' as a cool-down song. The ladies would love it."

"I love Abba as much as everybody, but their music is hardly Latin."

Jill bumped her. "Live a little. Who said there had to be rules?"

As an argument, it was compelling. Rules did suck a big one. "I'll think about it."

Jill took a spot next to Meredith, who Elizabeth kept a special eye on since she was the only pregnant woman in the class tonight. Putting her smart phone in the docking station, she called up her playlist. Hot salsa music pumped out of the speakers as she took her position facing the mirrored wall, the class lined up behind her.

"Everyone ready?" she asked.

Some of the women were still struggling with the steps, a few didn't have a lick of rhythm, but the ones who always made her smile were Mr. and Mrs. Larkin, a geriatric couple who never missed a class. Mr. Larkin wiggled his arthritic hips as best as he could to the Merengue. He and his wife were always a couple of beats behind, but they both grinned throughout class, having fun.

When she got to be their age, she wanted to be just like them. Dancing. Not caring what anyone else thought.

Jill was throwing her hair around, working the music. Of all the women she taught, the redhead was one of the most fun to watch. Her rhythm was natural, her timing perfect, and she was very comfortable strutting her stuff. Often, she signaled for Jill to come to the front of the class, and they added a little extra wiggle into their motions, making the other women laugh.

A few men had come at first, thinking it was a hot place to pick up women, but they had easily been weeded out. This was a place where women could be free from having to deal with men—men other than Mr. Larkin, at least.

After sixty minutes, Elizabeth's body was flushed with sweat, but she felt marvelous. She loved coming up with the choreography for class almost as much as she loved studying poker tape on Rhett's opponents, something she would be doing tonight.

For so long, her whole identity had revolved around poker and Rhett and Jane. This class was special because she felt like it was a new facet of the emerging Elizabeth Saunders. Her mom might have worked the pole when she was growing up, and it had soured Elizabeth for a while, but her love of dance had never left her. This class allowed her to enjoy something she loved in her own way, without all the baggage.

People mingled after class, sharing information about their kids or community gossip. It was nice to connect with her students, to feel included, like a real part of Dare Valley.

"Nice moves as always, Elizabeth," Jill said. "Meredith finally admitted she's glad I talked her into coming."

Her sister rested her hands on her ever-expanding belly. "I love to swim, but Jill was right for once. It's fun to mix it up."

Swinging an arm around her sister, Jill said, "I'm always right. Okay, let's go and grab a treat at Brasserie Dare. Brian will fix us something special."

"Tanner is expecting me home," Meredith said, checking her watch.

"So is my babysitter, but we won't be too long.

Elizabeth, do you want to come? We can talk more about that Abba song you're going to use."

Jill was as funny as she was tenacious. It was no wonder Mac said she was a dream to work with at the hotel.

"Sure. Why not?" Her social calendar wasn't super full these days now that Jane and Rhett were coupled up.

When Elizabeth left the studio with the women, she skidded to a halt. Terrance was leaning against a car—not his own—waiting for her. His stance was casual, but his eyes lasered in on her like she was the prey and he the hunter.

Jill cast a sly glance at Elizabeth before grabbing Meredith's arm. "Hey, Chef T. You missed the class. Didn't know this was your thing, or I would have told you about it earlier."

Those wicked-as-sin lips curved. "There are worse ways to spend your only night off."

Elizabeth locked the door to the studio to give herself time to regain her composure.

"I'm sure you and Elizabeth have a lot to talk about," Jill sang out like she was a crazy matchmaker. Of course, no successful matchmaker would have suggested two people meet when one had sweat drying at her temples and in other delicate places.

Of course, Terrance had already seen her sweaty.

Dammit, that wasn't something she needed to remember just now.

"See you later, Chef T. Elizabeth, feel free to take your time."

"I'll catch up to you in a jiffy," she told Jill with a pointed glance.

"Don't hurry," Meredith said with a smile. "We'll keep your seat warm."

When they left, Terrance didn't move. He kept his body angled against the car like he was a model for *Bad*

Boy & Cars magazine.

"I'll keep your seat warm too," he said in a husky voice, finally shoving off the car.

Yes, his calloused chef hands could do that and more.

"What do you want, Terrance?"

"Other than the obvious, I want to go out with you. So I guess that means I'll have to come to your class next time."

Oh, shit.

He was calling her bluff and winning the hand outright. Rhett would have told her not to box herself into a corner like some first-timer on the poker circuit.

"What changed your mind?" she asked softly.

He stepped forward, and reaching for her hair, he drew out a strand and rubbed it between his fingers. Her breath caught in her throat.

"You."

Everything inside her clenched. *You.*

"So, when's your next class?"

His voice was as dark as the night falling around them, and she had to firm her feet to not lean into him and take what she wanted. A kiss. Right there on Main Street—the kind that would shock the locals.

"I teach on Monday, Wednesday, and Friday at six and noon on Saturdays."

He dropped her hair. "Dammit. I'll have to wait a week then. This is my only night off until I have the kitchen running like I want."

When he drew out another hundred from his wallet and stuffed it into his pocket, she almost laughed. Every time he was around her, he seemed to lose money. But laughter was the furthest thing from her mind.

"I'll see you in a week then." The urge to shiver was strong.

"If not before," he said. "You could always change your mind and just have dinner with me. I'd rather not embarrass myself in front of a bunch of women to be with you again."

And yet it was sweet and dear and oh so surprising.

"Not in your wildest dreams."

He skimmed a hand down her arm, like he used to, igniting nerve endings all the way to her toes. "Trust me, my dreams have been pretty wild lately."

This time her mouth curved, and she felt like a goddess again—like Vixen—the most desirable woman in the world. "I hope you're enjoying them."

The sound he made was part laugh, part groan. "Of course, being with you in the flesh was always better than my dreams, so I'll just have to remember that."

She almost gulped.

"I'll see you later, Terrance."

As she took off toward Brasserie Dare, he called out, "You'd better make it an easy class."

Not on your life. And an idea bloomed as she passed Dare Valley's well-lit shops on Main Street. What if she added non-Latin music for a few classes? Rubbing her hands together, other tunes popped into her head. Shania Twain's "Man, I Feel Like a Woman" and Beyonce's "All The Single Ladies," rounded out by "It's Raining Men." Oh, this was good.

Her ladies would love it, and if Terrance did show up next Monday, he would probably storm out before class was over. Then she wouldn't have to go out with him.

She slowed to a halt as her giddiness faded. The truth was she *wanted* to go out with him, and oh, how the truth hurt.

Chapter 11

Jill Hale might be a wild card, but Terrance knew she was the key to not embarrassing himself in Elizabeth's class. As a bribe, he'd baked one of her favorite desserts, according to her Facebook page, which was filled with photos of her adorable twin girls, Brian's culinary efforts, and anything coffee-related. He was heading to her office with a still-warm chocolate lava cake, complete with table service.

Mac's executive suite was on the second floor of the hotel in the west wing. The Grand Mountain Hotel might be smaller than The Peacock, but the lushness of the design appealed to him. Some of his chef friends had thought he was crazy for taking this job, so far away from New York's bright lights. Well, he was going to turn this restaurant and Mac's others into James Beard award winners. Of that he had no doubt.

Jill had been helping him understand the balance the hotel needed to strike between appealing to its high-roller clients while maintaining its attraction to Dare Valley locals. She was a fun and vivacious co-worker, with a passion for life he admired. She was the perfect person to help him.

Now all he needed was for her to keep his request secret.

When he reached the suite, Mac's receptionist, Casey, grinned at him. He'd already called her to make sure Jill was in her office. Lava cakes were notorious for being either under-cooked or over-cooked if you served them at the wrong time. This one was perfect.

"Chef T. Good to see you."

"One of my guys is sending up a special basket of pastries for you as a thank you." Greasing the palms of the staff through cooking was something he'd done at The Peacock too. People liked people who fed them. And when people liked you, they looked out for you. It was a rule of the universe.

"That's sweet," she said, and in her eyes, he could see the admiration he saw from most women.

The street kid still thought it was too weird for words, but the man in him didn't mind the attention.

"Thanks again. Hey, Jill," he called out from her doorway.

Her office made him wish he were color blind. Every wall was bold red, and the one behind her desk had a turquoise streak across the center. And the purple ceiling? Dear God. He almost felt bad for her husband. Had she painted the ceiling above their bed lime green or something? He could easily imagine it.

"Terrance!" she cried out, shooting out of her chair. "Is that for me?"

Her eyes zeroed in on the cake in his hands, and she looked like the cranes hanging from her crazy chandelier—ready to swoop down to fill their bellies.

"After our talk about the new menu, I wanted to see what you thought of this. It's—"

"Chocolate, and that's all that counts. Gimme."

Sexist cliché or not, women and chocolate could be a fearsome combination. He once cooked dark chocolate soufflés for a private bachelorette party at The Peacock.

The women had actually shoved him aside to get to the white ramekins.

"How about I set it down at your nice table over there?" Like Mac, she had a meeting table to the right of her desk. If he was going to ask her for help, he wanted her cozy.

And in a chocolate stupor.

"I can't wait," she said, dragging the napkin and silverware out of his hand. Pulling the fork out, she stabbed it into the center of the cake, which he was still holding. The lava flowed out, and she moaned.

He'd heard a lot of women moan, but somehow it felt weird with her. They worked together and...

"Oh my God," she breathed as she took the first bite, eyes closing in sheer ecstasy.

The cake was perfect, of course. "You should try some of the passion fruit sauce and the clove glaze on the sides."

Terrance didn't believe in over-saucing anything, but the delicate touch of a few different flavors added nuance to a dish.

She did as he'd suggested. Her moan was louder this time. Maybe it was a good thing they weren't sitting on her hideous purple Italian sofa.

"Yes. This. Menu."

Since he was used to people speaking in monosyllables when they tried his food, he didn't say anything. Just stood there and held the plate while she polished off the cake in record time.

When she finally dabbed at her mouth, she asked, "Do you have another?"

"I can easily call down and have another made," he said.

"I was up with Violet for three hours last night. I needed that more than you can imagine."

"I'm glad."

She sighed and then walked over to the purple

couch, flopping onto it like she'd just experienced a Chocolate O, which of course, she had.

He believed in the Chocolate O. Might have even had one himself over a prize blend of dark chocolate in a chalet on the outskirts of Brussels.

But chocolate wasn't his perfect ingredient.

It was too easy.

For a minute, he thought she was taking a nap. He set the plate on the only clear space on her desk—the corner—and walked over to the couch.

When her eyes popped open, the chocolate glassiness was gone.

"You had me at chocolate," Jill breathed out. "I know you want something."

"I need your help."

"This is about Elizabeth, isn't it?" she asked as she sat up straighter.

Her directness was a relief. "In a roundabout way. I need you to teach me your Latin dance routines before Monday."

Silence hung between them for a second as she stared at him with wide eyes. Finally she said, "I'm sorry. That chocolate must have made me deaf. Did you say teach you my Latin moves?"

He'd never blushed, not once in his whole life. When he was eight and riding the metro by himself, he used to boldly tell older girls he liked anything from their shoes to their lip gloss.

Yet now there was an odd burning sensation on his face. He cursed softly, "Shit."

He dug out a hundred and another for earlier.

"I heard you were trying to quit swearing. I told Brian we need to start charging ourselves too. Mia and Violet have been great deterrents, but at work..."

"Restaurant people have filthy mouths," he finished. Of course, he'd been using every single swear word well before he got his first job as a dishwasher.

Manny Caruthers had given Terrance that first job after catching him in the kitchen of his restaurant. The biker-looking dude with a half-moon knife scar carved into his right cheek, who looked like he could break a man in two, had been one of the first adults in Terrance's life to show him compassion. To give the thirteen-year-old a chance rather than judging him for his failures.

From there, it had only been onward and upward. At sixteen, he'd become a busboy. At seventeen, Manny had let him make some dishes one slow Sunday afternoon, and discovering he had a knack for combining ingredients without using a recipe, gave him a job as a line cook. With Manny's help and recommendation, Terrance had applied for a scholarship at The Culinary Institute of America.

The rest was, as they say, history.

"Back to Elizabeth's class," Jill said, clapping her hands to regain his attention. "Why do you want to go?"

His face was heating like a stove set to broil. Jill struck him as a romantic, so he went with the truth. "I don't want to make a fool of myself in front of Elizabeth, and she said it was the only way she would go out with me."

"That's so sweet," she said softly, pressing her hand to her heart.

"Shit."

He drew out another hundred.

"Ah, you're embarrassed," she cooed like he was one of her baby twins.

That caused him to curse more fluently under his breath. He drew out a few more bills.

"Sorry. Didn't mean to hurt your masculine pride or cost you a bundle."

Her knowing glance said different. "Sure you did."

She leaped off the couch and sashayed over to him like a giddy schoolgirl. If she agreed to teach him, it was going to be pure torture.

"So Elizabeth agreed to go on a date with you if you went to her dance class?" Laughter bubbled out of her mouth, a force that grew stronger until she was guffawing so hard she had to hold her stomach. "I love that girl. She makes you work for it."

Funny, but she hadn't before. Everything had been straight-forward and consensual.

"I bet you never have to work to get a woman to go out with you."

He met her gaze, and his blush faded, thank God.

"Okay, I'll help you. I just can't resist. I'm actually a good choice. I taught Brian how to dance."

"This has to be a secret between us," he told her. "She can never know how I learned the moves."

"That's going to cost you extra," she said, crossing her arms.

Terrance leaned against her desk. "Mac said you were a fierce negotiator. Fine. What do you want?"

Her finger rubbed her lips for exactly thirty seconds, according to the frightening monkey clock on the back desk.

"I want lunch brought to my office every day for a month. Chef's choice. And a chocolate lava cake at four o'clock when all I want to do is take a nap."

Talk about negotiating. "I'm only asking for a few lessons. Two weeks."

"Done. And I want you to promise me that you won't quit our training, no matter what."

Now that surprised him. "What do you mean?"

Her face went all wistful and soft. "Brian hated learning how to dance at first. All he did was complain and want to give up. You have to promise you won't, or I'll tell everyone I know. I may even tweet about it."

His stomach curdled at the thought.

The women in her class might tweet about it anyway. And wouldn't that go over like a fart in church.

Chef T, the badass, dancing Latin. The kids in his old neighborhood would laugh their asses off—not that he hung around that crowd anymore.

"Fine."

"Good," she said, bouncing up and down. "Now how do you feel about Abba?"

"*Why?*"

"Because I suggested Elizabeth use it for a new routine, and she's thinking about it."

Did he even want to ask which song she'd suggested for Elizabeth to include?

He was a man. He could take it.

"Which one? 'Dancing Queen'?" Women loved that song.

Her smile was feral, the kind women used when they knew a man was about to be flayed alive for their entertainment.

"No. Too obvious. It's 'Gimme, Gimme, Gimme A Man After Midnight.'"

He was doomed.

Chapter 12

Every morning when Elizabeth woke, she couldn't help but count down the days until her Monday dance class.

Until she would see Terrance again.

God, she needed a distraction. Thank goodness she was meeting Jane for lunch today. Now that the primary was over, her friend had more free time. She pulled on some designer jeans with a rhinestone fleur de lis on the back pocket and threw on a fitted gray cashmere sweater. The day was already in the fifties, and she was happy to leave her coat at home.

Main Street was busy with people enjoying the nice weather, and she had to park a couple of blocks from Brasserie Dare. Her black knee-length boots didn't slide on the snowy street like they usually did, since all of the white stuff was thankfully gone.

Jane was already at the restaurant when she arrived, talking to her fellow wine connoisseur, Chef Brian McConnell. Three glasses with one-ounce pours were arranged in front of her friend, and she was sipping a fourth glass when Elizabeth joined them.

"I see he has you doing blind tastings again," she commented as she slid into the chair. "Hi, Brian."

"Hey, Elizabeth," he said, shoving back some of the

brown curls around his ears. "This will be the highlight of my day. I've never met someone who's so good at identifying wine."

"I should come here for lunch every day," Jane mused, twirling the ruby red liquid around in the glass and inhaling its nose again. "Wonderful vintage. Château Destieux. Ah...2010, I would guess."

"Incredible!" Brian cried. "If you didn't already have a job, I would lure you into being my new sommelier."

Jane smiled that million-dollar Audrey Hepburn smile of hers. "You're going to hire one?"

Brian puffed out his chest. "Business is good. Real good."

"I'm so glad," Jane said. "You know it's my favorite place."

Brian made room for the server who set down water glasses with lemon, no ice, just the way they preferred it. "I'm not sure if that will change now that Chef T has taken over The Grand, but we'll see. Right now, I'm focusing on what I can control."

"A place like Dare can handle two gourmet restaurants, I think," Jane said.

Brian picked up the wine glasses. "I know he's tight with Rhett and Mac, and since he's going to start coming to our poker nights when his schedule changes, I'm sure I'll get to know him. Heck, we might have to start a drink night after one of our shifts, like I did with some of my buddies in New York City. There aren't a lot of chefs in Dare, and it's fun to talk shop with other people in the biz—even if they're competitors."

"That sounds like a healthy attitude," Jane said.

"Now that Elizabeth is here, I was going to tell you about something special I had in mind for you two. I know how you love quiche."

It had been a favorite ever since their first vacation together in France. "Tell us," Elizabeth said, rubbing her hands together, her taste buds already watering.

"Well, I have some morel mushrooms that just came in fresh, and I wanted to add some Gruyere and finish it with black truffle oil."

"Yes, please," Jane said, holding up her hand. "Elizabeth?"

"Does it come with a wheel barrow? Because I'm likely to ask for a second piece."

"How about I send you both home with whatever you don't finish?"

"That works," Jane said. "Thanks, Brian."

"Absolutely. Now, I'll serve you up your favorite appetizer to share and bring you salad with the quiche."

"You know how we like it," Jane said. "You're the best."

"Don't tell anyone, but you may be my favorite customers." He winked and walked back to the kitchen.

"He really is too cute," Elizabeth said. "Jill scored herself a prize when she married him."

"Matt told me they'd known each other since childhood. They've had some rough patches, but it's nice to see how happy they are together." Jane downed her water in a couple of lusty swallows.

That kind of thirst only came from one thing. "So how's the winning-the-primary sex?"

Jane waggled her eyebrows. "Pretty ridiculous."

Her smugness had Elizabeth laughing. "You're too much."

"Of course, Matt was pretty upset for a while about his dad showing up at the party. His brothers and sisters were rattled too, and I've never seen April look so vulnerable. Uncle Arthur stood by her like a knight in shining armor. I was afraid he was going to dress down his nephew in front of everyone, but April took hold of him and sent him a silent message to keep the peace. It was hard to see them like that. Especially Danny. That kid looked like he'd lost his best friend when his grandpa barely hugged him."

"Families, right?" Elizabeth said.

Jane nodded. "I tried to tell Matt that at least his dad came, but he wasn't feeling too open-minded. I had to backpedal a bit. It's hard to image how awkward it must have been for Mr. Hale. You know, he hasn't seen April *or* his kids since the breakup. Not that I'm excusing the way he let April walk out without a word. Apparently Matt's sisters ended up drinking all of April's vodka. They left for Denver later than they'd planned the next day."

Unlike the Hales, there was no soft landing in her family. Her parents sucked, and she had no siblings. "I like Matt's sister a lot. Natalie ran interference with Terrance for me."

"She did? That raises her to a whole new status of cool. She gets having history with a man. She and her ex, Blake, were apparently pretty volatile when things went bad between them. Speaking of volatile, what's going on with Terrance anyway? You haven't said much about him, and I know you..." Her finger lifted and she pointed it straight at Elizabeth. "What are you hiding?"

Their appetizers arrived before Elizabeth could answer. Brian's decadent homemade foie gras with a golden, crispy baguette and the best cornichon pickles this side of the Atlantic. Delicious, but not enough to distract Jane, who gave her a *don't bullshit me* look.

"Well, if you must know, Terrance asked me out, and I told him the only way that was happening was if he came to my dance class."

Jane's laughter burst out, causing nearby patrons to glance over. "You're kidding! He'd never do that."

Elizabeth spread the mixture on the sliced baguette and added a cornichon on top. "That's what I thought, but he says he's coming. We'll see. He might wimp out or *storm* out once he hears my new dance music."

An evil smile spread across her face as she told Jane about her plan. They had a laugh over it, and then she popped the bite she'd prepared into her mouth. "Seriously," she said through a moan, "nothing that spreads like this should taste this good."

"If Rhett was here, he would no doubt make up some dirty joke about that."

"So would Terrance," she said. And yes, she missed that part of him. The sexy, playful flirt.

"You still want him," Jane said as she made up a slice of baguette with foie gras.

"Of course I do. He's still sexy beyond words, funny, and ridiculously sweet at times. But I can't keep things casual with him."

Jane bit into her baguette slice. Her eyes fluttered, and she moaned too. "Brian is a genius with foie gras. Okay, give me a moment to let my brain return to normal."

"Eat away."

They both feasted on the appetizer, and pretty soon all that was left were crumbs. The server came and swept everything away.

"You were never casual with Terrance, Liz. I was there at The Peacock." She folded her hands on the table. "I saw the way you looked at him. The way you acted. You've never done that with anyone else."

Girlfriends always spoke the truth. "I don't like feeling that way. Unhinged."

"Good for you, love is," her friend said in the worst Yoda imitation of all time.

"You're using Star Wars now?" Elizabeth burst out laughing. "This has to be Matt's influence."

The waitress set their salads and quiche in front of them. They both thanked her, but neither made a move for the decadent-looking quiche.

"Liz, what I'm trying to say is that Terrance was never a jerk to you."

She picked at her salad and dropped her fork. "No, he wasn't."

"Maybe you're underestimating him...and yourself."

Elizabeth's hand clutched the edge of the table. Could a serious relationship between them really work? Terrance wasn't Vince, but he did have violent streak. Plus he liked women—a lot of women—and that wouldn't change. He might want her now, but after a while, he'd want someone new. Wouldn't he?

"Brian's special quiche is getting cold," she finally said and reached for a slice, serving Jane first and then herself.

The quiche was luscious, but they didn't eat with their normal gusto.

"What if he actually stays for your dance class and you have to go out with him?" Jane finally asked.

Her thighs clenched.

Her brain might not know what to do, but her body clearly had its own ideas.

Chapter 13

Terrance was in dance hell. Those were the only words for it.

And Jill Hale... Well, she was devious, mean, and unrelenting. He'd named her Dr. Evil after their first lesson.

"Dammit, Jill, I am not some fuc...Rockette."

Jill picked up the notepad she had on her desk. "That's four hundred dollars, Terrance, and we've only been at this for ten minutes. For crying out loud, you men are such babies. You could never give birth."

Give birth? What man had ever envied that? "I just can't wiggle my hips like you want, Jill. I swear."

"Yes, you do swear. Loud and often."

She jumped off the corner of her desk where she was sitting. Her director's perch, as she called it. Jill had been helping him for two days during her lunch hour. So far, he was sure he'd pulled a groin muscle and possibly a butt muscle from all of the wiggling and hip thrusting she'd thrown at him.

"For a man who's supposedly good with the ladies, I thought you'd be a master of the bump and grind."

The bump and grind was the most embarrassing

move on the planet *outside* of the bedroom, especially when Jill was playing Cher's "Do You Believe In Love?'"

Elizabeth had upped the ante by changing her music to songs guaranteed to castrate any man.

Someone shoot him now.

"I prefer to be naked when I'm doing that move," he said, putting his hands on his hips as he gave the motion another try.

"Oh, it's the clothes part that's the problem, eh? Brian forgot to use that one on me. Well, feel free to strip down to whatever you feel is necessary. Everyone knows I'm a happily married woman, but that doesn't mean I don't enjoy a good show."

He growled at her.

"Good! Now tuck in your tummy like I showed you and curl your hips up. It's like a pelvic tilt. You learn it in pre-natal Pilates. Maybe we should sign you up."

Her pregnancy and breast feeding allusions were making him nauseous. "Sign up yourself," he muttered under his breath.

"What was that?" Had her eyes turned red?

"Nothing."

"Okay, let's try it again. Watch me."

She thrust her hips out and then curled them back in, and just to show off, executed another move that could have won her first prize at the World Pole Dancing competition.

He started to sweat. All of the moves Elizabeth had in the class were like that. And the class was an *hour* long. He would have to dance like he was in some porn version of *Flashdance* if he wasn't going to look like a fool.

"Men aren't supposed to dance like this," he finally admitted, ready to throw in the towel.

"Oh, no. Remember your promise. If you quit, I'm going to tell the world about our sessions."

He put his hands on his hips, trying to intimidate

her like she was a new line cook in his kitchen. "You wouldn't."

"Try me."

Right. Dr. Evil didn't intimidate.

"Okay, let's try something different," she said. "I was trying to show you the easy parts before moving on to the dance steps."

The easy parts?

He was screwed.

"What do you know about salsa?"

"It's a Latin condiment of tomatoes, peppers, and spices best served with tortilla chips."

"Funny."

He thought so.

Dr. Evil came and stood beside him. "Salsa is all about rhythm. Here's the basic move. Start on the right foot. Back. Together. Forward. Together."

He tried to match her movements, and after they did it ten times, he was feeling a little lighter. "Hey, I got it."

"Not so fast, Pit Bull," she told him. "Now you have to add the hips."

The hips? Crap. He might as well try and dance with his feet tied together.

"Come on. Like this," she said, shaking her booty.

"I'm never going to get this."

She popped him in the arm, something she wasn't the slightest bit shy about doing whenever the mood struck. "Stop with the whining. I expect more from you. Tell me. What's the hardest dish you ever learned to make?"

He chose the first one that came to mind. "St. Honoré cake. I went through dozens of batches before I learned to make the puff pastry and cream puffs like a French baker...and then you have to dip the cream puffs in caramelized sugar without getting the pastry wet. It's a b—. And then attaching them to the puff pastry base without ruining the pâte à choux... You can see why the dessert is named after a saint. You have to have the patience of one to get it right."

"And how long did it take you to master it?" she asked.

"Three weeks." He'd thrown one ruined batch at the wall.

"If you can do that, you can dance for an hour. Remember, all you have to do is show up and struggle through an hour-long dance class to make Elizabeth go out with you. Isn't that worthwhile?" She flung a hand at his arm, and for a second he thought she was going to sock him again. "Don't answer me right now. It's like asking a woman giving birth if she's willing to get pregnant again."

A knock sounded on the door, and it opened before either of them could react.

"Jill?" his boss and good friend asked, standing in the doorway in a navy suit. "*Terrance*. Are you two having a party? Without inviting me?"

Right. Cher wasn't exactly normal background music for a professional meeting.

"I'm teaching him how to dance," Dr. Evil proudly announced, her eyes like twin saucers of doom. His doom.

"*Really...*"

"You weren't supposed to say anything," he hissed for her ears only.

She shrugged.

Was it possible for the ground to open up and swallow you when you were on the second floor? "What Jill means is that she's showing me the music she likes to dance to."

Mac's mouth twitched. "I see. And you have a new fascination with Cher? Funny, somehow I missed that, knowing you all these years."

Oh, the curses he wanted to unleash. His wallet couldn't handle it.

"It's a dare of sorts," Jill told their boss, who was enjoying this moment way too much.

Terrance gave her a withering look, which only made her smile wider. She locked her arm through his. "Want to see some of his moves?"

"Another time perhaps. I'll just...leave these papers for you to go over and sign." He crossed over to her desk, his shoulders shaking with silent laughter. "Enjoy your lesson, Terrance."

Great. Now his boss and friend knew his secret. Pretty soon Rhett would know too, and while Mac might refrain from teasing, Rhett wouldn't.

"What possessed you?" he asked when the door closed.

"It's going to be all over town that you showed up at Elizabeth's dance class. Might as well start getting used to the attention. Plus, maybe your guy friends can help you in your off time."

Sometimes Jill made him want to hurl himself out of a window.

"But no one is supposed to know I'm practicing."

She leveled him a glance. "You're whining again." Glancing at her watch, she tapped the hideous purple, rhinestone face. Where did she find those things anyway? "Our time has come to a close for today, and since you're not coming along as fast as I'd hoped, I'm going to give you homework. I brought in some of my favorite dancing movies. I want you to watch them."

Homework? What was he? Some kid in middle school?

When she presented him with *Dirty Dancing* like it was the Queen Mother's favorite crown, he groaned.

"You're kidding, right?"

"You need some inspiration. Trust me. This movie is going to help."

He was working on the new menu at the Grand and Mac's other hotels now. And she expected him to watch this chick flick?

"Then there's *Step Up* and *Footloose*." She shoved them at his chest.

Shoot him. Right now.

The door burst open again, and in swaggered Rhett Butler Blaylock, a grin as mile-wide as the Mile High stadium on his face. "Heard somebody's getting dance lessons."

Well, that had been quick. The glee in Rhett's voice was unmistakable. Dr. Evil had just met Mr. Evil.

"Somebody was supposed to keep her mouth shut, and I'm so outta here."

Rhett snagged him with a meaty hand and clucked under his tongue. "Mac told me your taste in music had changed, and I just had to pull myself away from the poker tables to see for myself. Cher, *mon ami?*"

"Shit."

That hundred was the best money he'd spent all day.

"And now I see your taste in movies has changed too," his friend drawled. "Jill, since you're being more forthcoming than my friend here, tell your old pal what's going on."

Dr. Evil would never rule the world with that mouth. She spilled the whole sordid story to his friend in under a minute. Rhett settled back against Jill's desk, crossing his cowboy boots at the ankle.

"Looks like a pretty nice dance movie marathon you have there, bubba."

"You can laugh all you want, but I'm not doing it." He threw the movies down on Jill's desk. "No woman is worth this shit, and no man is supposed to parade around in front of a bunch of women wiggling his hips like some jackass while they laugh at him."

"That's two hundred dollars, T," Rhett said, stroking his chin.

"I damn well know how much it is." He was losing his cool, and he knew it. Taking out three hundred, he took a deep breath.

"Our friend, Rye, has made a career out of taking his shirt off and wiggling his hips in front of the ladies, if you recall."

"I'm not Rye."

"No, but I've never seen you back down from a challenge."

Rhett re-stacked the movies and handed them back to Dr. Evil, who was trying her best not to laugh out loud.

"You're not thinking straight," Rhett finally told him. "No one is going to expect you to know all the moves. Right, Jill?"

Dr. Evil sat on her desk. "Nope. Most of the women don't, even the regulars, and certainly not the new routines."

"See! When I used to play against players better than me, what did I do?" He pointed to his massive chest.

"I don't know. You brayed like a jackass."

Dr. Evil laughed, and Rhett patted her thigh.

"Sort of. I turned the tables on them. Threw them off their game. Did something outlandish, something guaranteed to upset their rhythm."

Jill started to hum. "I see where you're going with this."

Terrance slashed his hand through the air. "Well, I don't. I have to get back to the kitchen."

"And who's coming to town this weekend for his bachelor party who knows how to strut his stuff in front of a whole bunch of women?"

"Oh, shit," he said, "Rye." And out came another hundred for his Cuss Fund.

"That man sure knows how to move," Dr. Evil commented, bouncing up and down now. "You could learn from him, Terrance."

Pointers from one of country music's biggest stars?

For a second he was intrigued, and then he said, "No way. I don't want this disaster leaving this room. I'll go to Elizabeth's class on Monday night and hole up in the corner. Do my best to get through."

Rhett stood up and crossed the short distance between them, towering over him. "You need to man up. One rooster in a flock full of hens never goes unnoticed."

Terrance slapped a hand to his forehead. "Where do you get such lines? Is Popular Hick Sayings for the Day a daily email blast I'm not signed up for?"

"Be nice, bubba," Rhett said. "We're only trying to help."

Deep down, Terrance knew that. But he still wanted to get the hell out of Dr. Evil's office. The next song in the routine had come on. How was he supposed to hold up his head after gyrating to "Man! I Feel Like a Woman?"

"Okay, I'll keep practicing with my lovely choreographer at lunch and see how it goes." But he wasn't doing the movie homework. No freaking way. "As for Rye, all he wants to do this weekend is hang with his boys, eat, and play poker. I know. He's already sent me a list of things he wants to eat."

No one appreciated food like Rye Crenshaw.

"You might be surprised by what Rye wants to do once he knows all the options. And if you feed him, of course."

"I'll kill you if you tell him."

Rhett's laugh was like a movie villain's. "Then prepare yourself to be charged for first degree, since I have a witness right here." He slung an arm around Dr. Evil herself.

Rhett was so going to tell their friends.

Chapter 14

Instead of playing poker at Rye's bachelor party, what were they doing? Talking about Terrance's upcoming dance class.

Clustered together in the large salon in The Grand's penthouse, the guys were reclining on a massive sectional, beers in their hands. Rye had arrived with his friends from Dare River: Clayton Chandler, who helped manage his career, and John Parker McGuiness, who served as his lawyer and sometimes songwriter. The trio had known each other since college, and Terrance had met them through Rhett and Mac over a game of poker.

Rhett had sold him out to the guys without pity. Clayton laughed so hard, he had to wipe tears from his eyes.

"You're dancing for a date?" he wheezed out. "I know Vixen is—was—hot, but seriously, T, have you gone plumb crazy?"

Their Southernisms never failed to amuse him. He knew the term was different than the plums that grew on trees, but Terrance had no idea how anyone had come up with such a phrase. Still, he wasn't about to crack a smile anytime soon.

"I think it's romantic," John Parker said, the only

one who wasn't laughing uproariously.

"You would, preacher kid," Clayton said.

"Now you all can see why I insisted Terrance turn the kitchens over to his sous chef for lunch so he could join us," Mac said with a knowing glance at Rhett.

"Exactly! Rye is the perfect man to help you, T," Rhett said, his lips twitching. "He's made a fortune wiggling and shaking on the stage."

"Good God, Rhett, you make me sound like a jellyfish. What you're referring to are professional moves." With that, he stood and rolled his hips from right to left with a wink.

This only brought on another wave of laughter.

"Rhett," Terrance said, "I swear I might not murder you—who wants to rot in prison?—but I will slip a diuretic into one of your drinks at the hotel while you're playing poker. You'll have to leave the table and forfeit the game to go to the bathroom."

"That's just plain evil."

Apparently he'd learned something other than dance moves from Dr. Evil.

Clayton lifted his glass. "I love it. Even Mac's laughing, and it's his hotel."

Mac settled back against his Italian leather sofa. "When you do slip Rhett a mickey, I want you to let me know. We might have to close the men's room for cleaning."

"Now that's just mean," Rhett drawled.

Rye was being oddly quiet, stroking his chin and staring at Terrance in a way that made the hairs on the back of his neck stand at attention.

"What do your female fans love about you the most?" Rye asked. "Besides your ability to cook?"

"My wicked sense of humor," he responded dryly.

"Try again. Your *body,* my friend. Don't women ask to see your tattoos when they run into you in real life?"

He so didn't like the way this was going.

"I'll bet some of them have even gotten griffin tattoos just like yours, right?"

When Terrance got the tats in high school, he'd chosen the griffin—a mythical creature that was half eagle, half lion—for two reasons. The lion had kick-ass courage, and the eagle could soar. They represented his plan to fly out of his bad neighborhood and land in a better place.

"Yes, some have," he said, "but it embarrasses the shit out of me."

He fished out another hundred and placed it in the crystal bowl Rhett had appointed the Cussing Jar. Being around his friends had made his mouth revert back to its old ways. His Cuss Fund had definitely put him in the red this weekend.

"You need to turn the tables on Elizabeth. Take your shirt off and move like you know what you're doing—even when you don't."

"No f-ing way." Parade around shirtless in front of a bunch of women? His friend was nuts.

"Stand up," Rye said like a drill sergeant, giving him an assessing glance. He added insult to injury by circling him. "You need to wear something designed to drive the women wild. If they're so hot for your body, none of them are going to match the beat. How about no shirt and some tight bike pants?"

His ears were growing hot. "No way I'm parading around like that in front of a bunch of women."

"You sound like a choir boy," Clayton drawled. "Come on, T, where's that badass attitude now?"

Dammit, he'd never been able to pass up a dare. "Fine." He tore his shirt off. "Satisfied?"

The men whistled, and he had the urge to cross his arms over his chest.

"Cut it out," he yelled.

"I think you have a plan," Rhett drawled.

Terrance rounded on his friend. "No way am I

dancing without a shirt on in front of a bunch of women."

"Afraid to start a stampede?" Mac joked.

"Shut it, Maven."

Rye drew off his own shirt. "Okay, now you're not alone, T. Show us the dance moves. We'll practice with you. Clayton? You game?"

"Why not?" He shrugged and tossed his shirt aside, then ran his hands over his chest in a flirty pantomime. "Who wants me?"

The other guys started to laugh, and even Terrance felt his mouth twitch. "You're all nuts."

Rhett rose to his feet and set his beer aside. Moving his arms and hips like he was a human choo-choo train, he strolled toward Terrance and scared the crap out of him by lifting his shirt up inch by inch. "Come on, now, you know you want to see it."

The playful shove he gave his friend only made everyone laugh harder. Soon they were all snorting and holding their bellies.

"Mac Maven, it's your turn to show us what you've got," Rhett cat-called.

"No way in hell. And if you try and undress me, which only a crazy bastard like you would, I'll have my wife arrest you for sexual harassment."

Rhett clucked his tongue. "Since I know you mean that, consider yourself a bystander. J.P.?"

"My mama might lose her job at the church if word gets out that I participated. Consider me another bystander, but *please*...feel free to show Mac and me what y'all got."

If they were on reality TV right now, their ratings would be through the roof. Here Terrance was, standing shirtless with one of country music's biggest stars and two other men who were wearing only cowboy hats and tight jeans.

"He has the video Jill took of the class," Rhett told

everyone.

Dr. Evil could have been a spy. She'd used her smart phone to capture the routines so he could practice them in secret.

"Can't you keep your mouth shut for once?" he fired back.

"Give it up, T," Rye said. "I need to see what kind of moves we're talking about here. Hand over your phone, or we'll go digging for it."

They would too. He held it out without a fight.

Mac rose and took it. "I'm going to call our audio expert for the hotel up here to hook the video up to the big screen TV. He's discreet, although I can't imagine what he'll think when he walks in on this crowd of shirtless wonders."

Never let anyone say Mac didn't run a tight ship because five minutes later, Jerry had everything hooked up. Terrance almost felt bad for the guy. His eyes had nearly popped out of his head when he walked through the door.

When the video started to play, Terrance was reminded of the reason he was going to all this trouble.

Elizabeth.

She was so beautiful, laughing as she started to warm up the class with a sway here, a twist there. Her moves were so sensual his mouth went dry.

"Holy hell," Clayton drawled. "She's even more beautiful than I remembered."

"Let's keep it clean," Rhett replied. "She's like my sister."

Rye stepped closer to the big screen. "She sure can move. Come on guys, let's line up and nail this even though the music is going to give me a migraine."

The Grammy-winning singer stumbled through the steps just like the rest of them. After seeing how much some of the men were struggling with the hip movements, Terrance felt better. He wasn't the only one who sucked at Latin dancing.

After fifteen minutes, Rye paused the video and turned to look at the other men. "T, you're going to need help. No way you can learn to move like that in a few days. If we all go with you, the focus won't all be on you. You're right. You don't want to look like an ass in front of your woman."

"Go with him?" Clayton drawled. "We're leaving on Monday, Rye."

"We can leave after the class." He nudged Terrance with an elbow. "Our friend here needs some wingmen. Who's with me?"

Clayton groaned. "I guess. Rhett?"

"Is my name Butler?"

"Yessah. Now we really need to learn these moves," Rye said. "Maybe I can use some of these steps in my upcoming tour, but dear sweet baby Jesus, who picked the music? I love Shania Twain, but this is like party music for a rabid women's group."

"Apparently Elizabeth created a bunch of new routines just in case I decided to show." Devious little hellion that she was.

"She's got sass," Rye said. "My fiancée has the same quality."

"Tory would do something like that too," Rhett mused.

"That's why I'm marrying her." He grinned like the lovesick fool he was. "Now call your teacher and see if she can come in for a lesson today. We're going to need her help."

Unleash Dr. Evil on four shirtless men? He might as well call in a hurricane. Or a missile strike.

"Not a good—"

"I'll call her," Mac said, interrupting him. "I have her on speed dial."

Was that glee in Maven's voice?

"She's the mother of baby twins," Terrance

protested, desperately wanting to put a shirt on now. Dr. Evil was going to have a field day with them.

"Hi, Jill," Mac said and headed out of the room.

Uh-oh. What in the world was his friend saying to her?

Thirty minutes later, a knock sounded on the door to the suite. When Rye opened it shirtless and stepped aside, he had his answer.

Dr. Evil had brought friends. Mac's wife and Rhett's, Natalie Hale and her sisters, and Meredith Hale. Now there were more than half a dozen witnesses to his disgrace.

His evil dance instructor picked a few kernels of popcorn from the bag in her hand and popped them in her mouth. "We heard there was a show."

Leave it to Jill to bring her own popcorn. He wasn't even going to ask where she'd gotten it.

"Come on in, ladies," Rye said grandly, bowing at the waist. He made introductions all around, even though some of the men and women were well acquainted, as in *married*.

The ladies hustled in, some blushing, some drooling, and only one keeping a straight face. That would be Peggy, Dare's deputy sheriff.

"Thinking about quitting your day job to start stripping, Chef T?" she asked, and even he saw her mouth twitch. "That's illegal in this state. I'll have to bust you. Just a warning."

"He's going to need *a lot* more practice if he's going to make a living on tips," Dr. Evil commented.

"That's pretty low," Natalie said to her cousin. "Are you as bad as she thinks, Terrance?"

Great. Now the women were going to judge him. "Maybe we can order up some score cards like the ones you used at the tasting."

"We were all at lunch when Mac called," Natalie told him. "Girl chat. Then we got a better offer to come watch all you studs."

Her sisters nodded, and he knew what it felt like to be a piece of meat.

"Okay, boy wonders," Dr. Evil said, walking to the head of the room like the dictator she was. "I see you've been watching the video of Elizabeth's class. I'll rewind a bit, and you can show me what you've learned so far."

Their backs were to the other women—except for when they had to do those embarrassing turns where they slapped their butts like they were riding ponies—and Terrance could tell most of the women were fighting the urge to laugh. Well, except for Abbie, Rhett's wife, who was blushing, sweet lady that she was.

Dr. Evil could learn a thing or two from her.

When she stopped the video, Dr. Evil put her hands on her hips and narrowed her eyes. "Crenshaw, you have moves, but your salsa needs work. Chandler, your hips have the thrust move down pat, but you need to circle them more. Butler, you look like a chicken trying to stoop when you throw your hands out."

The men groaned. Yeah, they'd laughed at him before, but now they understood her nickname.

Terrance held his breath when she finally stared him down. "Waters. You're looking a lot better. You must have watched *Dirty Dancing*. Keep up the good work."

And with that, she turned the video back on and dragged her sister to the front. Meredith's pregnant body moved a heck of a lot better than Terrance would have thought, given the basketball she was carrying in front.

His Chippendale brothers in crime glanced over with a snort and mouthed, *Dirty Dancing?*

Dr. Evil needed a new name. Something worse...much worse.

Abbie and Peggy sat with Mac and John Parker as Dr. Evil continued to walk them through the new steps.

When Natalie and her sisters got their fill of

gawking, they joined them in the routine. Natalie bumped Terrance with her hip. "I used to be a big fan, but now I think I'm an admirer. I've never seen any man do something this romantic."

He grimaced. "She may still turn me down."

His new friend only shook her head. "Not a chance. And by the way, I'm going to stay at my mom's house on Monday night. Wild horses couldn't keep me away from this class. I have a feeling my sisters will do the same."

At the rate they were going, they should sell tickets.

CHAPTER 15

Jane was coming to Elizabeth's Monday night class. Latin dancing wasn't her favorite workout, but she'd agreed to make an exception in case Terrance made good on his word.

One of the women leaving the previous class opened the door to the studio, but Jane stopped Elizabeth from going in by tugging on her arm.

"Isn't that Rhett's SUV?"

Elizabeth looked up the street, and sure enough, she spotted his car. The doors swung open, and her gasp rang out in tandem with Jane's.

Rhett, Rye, Clayton, and Terrance got out of the car and swaggered down the block. In workout gear no less.

Chef T had brought an entourage. And holy hell. Her boss notwithstanding, the group was every woman's fantasy come true. A bunch of red-blooded all-American alpha males.

Clayton even had on his black cowboy hat.

Why were Rye and Clayton still in town? They were supposed to have left yesterday after the bachelor party.

"Ladies," Rye drawled when they reached them. "We've come for your class, Vix...I mean Elizabeth. Jane, good to see you."

All of the men grinned, except for Terrance, who looked like he was still considering bolting.

"Congratulations on the engagement, Jane," Clayton drawled. "Rhett's been catching us up on all of your recent exploits. The both of you."

"Thanks," Jane responded and kissed each man on the cheek. "Are you dropping Terrance off for class?"

Like a mommy and daddy for a kid's first day of kindergarten, Elizabeth almost said but didn't.

Rhett puffed out his chest. "Nope. We're *all* taking your class today."

And when he fished into his lightweight workout jacket and pressed an envelope of cash into her hands, she could only stand there and pretty much blink, like an alien ship was hovering overhead.

"You're all taking the class?" she squeaked.

Terrance just nodded as Rhett slung an arm around her shoulder, shaking her out of her reverie.

"It's going to be fun," Rye drawled.

"It *sure* is," Jane breathed out and started laughing. "I'll have to hang with you guys. It's my first class too, and I don't know the steps."

"Great," Clayton said, hooking his arm through Jane's. "Come on, bubbas. We need to carve out a space for ourselves among the female folk."

Rye held the door for everyone, but when Elizabeth and Terrance didn't budge, he winked at them and made his way inside, leaving them alone.

"Are you auditioning for a new TV show called The Dancing Chef?" she teased.

His growl would have scared little children. "Just don't back out on your end of the bargain."

He yanked the door open, let her enter, and then followed her inside.

When she scanned the space, more surprises awaited her. Jill was already inside with an expanded posse of ladies, all of whom were talking to the guys.

But what made her smell a rat was the presence of Peggy—she *never* came to class—and Matt Hale's sisters, who should have left for Denver yesterday like they usually did when they came to town for the weekend.

She took off her jacket with renewed determination. Someone had sung like a canary.

Her money was on Rhett. Terrance had probably told him, and God love him, the man couldn't keep a secret unless he was at the poker table.

Other students strolled in and gasped when they spotted the four gorgeous additions to the class.

Time to take control, she decided, and fired up her new music—what she called an all-girl special—and clapped her hands. Terrance was going to earn every minute of their date.

"Let's get started," she said and turned to face the mirror to begin the warm up. This was going to be fun. She couldn't wait to see these four gorgeous men struggle to keep up.

Then, as if choreographed, all the guys in class—except for poor Mr. Larkin, of course—took off their T-shirts and flung them to the right. All they had on were tight bicycle pants showing every curve of their tight asses and...well, how substantial they were in other areas.

Her mouth dropped open in pure shock.

Jill Hale and a few other women cheered.

"Holy shit," she heard Jane say.

Laney Smithins mouthed, "Oh my," to Dare Valley's second grade elementary teacher, who was clutching her chest like she was in danger of imminent cardiac arrest. A few of the other women started fanning themselves, and old Mr. Larkin started clapping.

"I used to look just like that," his old wizened voice said.

"Not when I knew you," Alma fired back. "You over

there, I like your cowboy hat, son."

Yeah, Clayton had plopped that right back on his head once his shirt was off.

"Nice to not be the only man around here," Mr. Larkin added over the sultry beat.

"Come over here and join us," Rye, ever the performer, said to him.

And that's how her class went from being dignified to dirty in the space of a heartbeat.

Shakira's "Hips Don't Lie" had seemed like a reasonable selection until she saw Chef T's Chippendale Posse move their hips right along with the ladies. Rhett and Clayton sure put their energy into it, even going so far as to run their hands down their chests in a move her stripper mother would have applauded. Not something she'd ever wanted to see her boss and adopted brother do.

Rye had a natural rhythm that spoke of years on the stage.

And then there was Terrance, whose eyes latched onto her like a grappling hook and just wouldn't let go.

She'd thought her memory of his ripped chest had done him justice. It hadn't. His griffin tattoos seemed to fly across his skin as he made the sexy arm movements of her dance routine. His washboard abs still made her melt, and the two Chinese character tattoos fanning down his ribs made her miss a step. How many times had she traced those foreign black letters with a finger, marveling at how well they suited him?

Intensity.

Passion.

If she had to describe Terrance Waters in two words, those were the ones she'd choose.

Especially as he stared her down and did his best to follow her sensual movements.

Which he was doing shockingly well. Especially the forward and backward thrusts. Not to mention the turns.

Her heart rate spiked for a whole new reason, and an ache of unfulfilled desire gathered in her belly.

By the time the second song pumped out, "On the Floor" by Jennifer Lopez, she was able to break Terrance's gaze and give her attention to the rest of her class.

Brandi, the mother of five, was pretty much drooling over the newcomers, while Carrie, a divorced retiree, was making eyes at Rye.

Then she noticed how smooth *all* of the men's movements were. Yeah, Rhett and Clayton were a few beats behind at times, especially on the sensual sashay turns, but Rye and Terrance were following her beat for beat.

The truth hit her like a flash.

They'd been coached.

By the time they reached the third song, "All the Single Ladies," by Beyonce, she was sure of it. No man could have put one hand on the ground and twerked his butt like that without forewarning.

There was only one person in her class who could have sided with the enemy like this.

Jill Hale.

She danced over to the side of the room, summoning Jill to step forward and take the front with her. They both ran their hands down their chests, their hips moving in figure eights.

"I know you coached them," she hissed so only Jill could hear.

The devious redhead just gave her a saucy Mae West wink and shuffled back to her spot, pausing to pat Rhett's behind as she passed him, which made him laugh—along with Natalie, whose moves were also a little too spot on given that she'd never been to a class.

What had the redhead done? Given dance lessons on the side to everyone who was interested?

Well, if they thought she was going to go down easy, they were in for a surprise. After they finished "It's Raining Men," during which the men laughed themselves silly from beginning to end—except for Terrance, who still had that intent look on his face—she switched the music up. It was a song with an old routine.

The regulars would know it.

But not these first-timers.

Now they were really going to separate the men from the boys.

When the hot Latin number with a fast salsa beat came on, much faster than any of the other dances on her list, she executed the first few basic steps and then made a quick quarter turn.

None of the men got it, and she could almost hear Terrance grind his teeth as he fumbled.

"Girlfriend has teeth," Jill called out.

She looked over her shoulder and said, "You betcha."

Rhett chortled, totally lost now, and ran into Clayton. Then he decided it would be fun to get down and dirty with his boy, Rye, and the two of them faced each other and wiggled their hips, totally disregarding the music.

Her regulars stopped their dance moves, enthralled by the Alpha Show of Wonder.

The whole routine broke down.

She'd lost control.

Terrance grinned at her as he shoved Rhett, who'd bumped him playfully with his hips.

Resigned, she returned to the regularly scheduled program.

When Shania Twain's "Man! I Feel Like A Woman" came on, Clayton waggled his eyebrows at Terrance.

"You feeling it?" the odious cowboy asked.

Terrance ran his hands down his chest, laughing like

a nutcase. “Definitely.”

Chef T was in the groove now.

Faced with the choice of losing total control of her class again by changing up the music or sticking to the routine Terrance and his Chippendale Posse knew, she decided to settle in and watch her upcoming date strut his stuff.

No reason the foreplay couldn’t start now.

It was time to make him drool.

And “Buttons” by the Pussycat Dolls would do just the trick. The song was pure sin, and dancing to it seductively was the perfect way to make a man grovel.

Closing her eyes, she started to weave her body like the most exotic belly dancer, running her hands up her torso just outside the zone of her breasts.

“No way,” she heard someone say, only to open her eyes and see Jill Hale trying to force Dare’s deputy sheriff to hold her girls.

“Cut that out, Jill,” Peggy cried, “or I swear I’ll shoot you.”

When Elizabeth executed a model walk forward, then bent over and swept her hips from right to left, she was sure she heard Terrance mutter, “Holy Christ.”

And there went another hundred dollars into his Cuss Fund.

By the time the song finished—Elizabeth’s last move was to run both hands through her blond hair—both she and Terrance were breathing hard, and his bicycle shorts looked uncomfortable. Poor guy.

But she wasn’t done with him yet.

Fergie’s “London Bridge” was going to destroy him.

Sure enough, halfway through the song when she slid down the mirror, moving her hips while facing the class, which usually made the women laugh uproariously, Terrance’s nostrils flared—a sure sign of arousal.

Yeah, she remembered.

Jill joined her against the mirror. “Come on, Nat! I know you want to be up here.”

Her cousin danced her way to the front, and all three of them did Fergie proud.

When Terrance swiped an arm across his head to wipe the sweat trailing into his eyes, Elizabeth’s inner glow spread throughout her belly.

Yeah, he wanted her. Bad.

When the cool-down rolled around, led by the diva herself, Cher, the men’s chests were dripping. Part of her wanted to towel Terrance off, but that would be unprofessional.

She could towel him off later.

Because she knew where their date would lead: to the hottest, screaming sex she’d ever had with anyone.

Her heart wouldn’t stay silent, but she simply couldn’t resist him anymore.

When the music faded, she faced the class again. “Thanks for coming. Especially our visitors. Feel free to come again.”

“I just might,” her boss drawled. “Great workout.”

“I could watch the view all day,” Terrance added in a husky voice.

Rye came up and hugged her, lifting her off the floor. “It was fun, Elizabeth. No hard feelings, I hope. We were only supporting our boy.”

“Never,” she told the country singer, noticing a cluster of women hovering behind them with their phones. “I think your fans want pictures.”

He laughed. “Good thing Tory isn’t the jealous type.”

As he strolled off to greet his fans, Terrance approached her. Any moisture left in her mouth dried up, and her gaze zoomed in on the trail of sweat winding its way down the center of his chest.

“I’ll pick you up at seven tomorrow night,” he said, his voice hoarse with arousal.

She gulped. “But I thought you worked on

Tuesdays."

When he leaned closer to whisper in her ear, every hair on her body rose up in pure, wicked delight.

"If you think Mac would refuse to give me a night off after seeing me practice my ass off, you have another thing coming."

Coming. Her mind totally went to the gutter.

"I might get Wednesday off too," he whispered, trailing his finger down her neck.

Her eyes locked with his. "You're pretty sure of yourself."

Silence spanned a heartbeat. "I know you were dancing for me."

She fought the urge to lick her lips.

"And we're not done dancing," he told her. "I'll see you tomorrow night. *Elizabeth.*"

Just the way he said her name—like he was caressing her in an intimate place—had her breath seizing in her chest.

"Come on, T," Rhett called out. "Jill wants a picture with us."

That sexy scar shifted when his mouth kicked up. "Dr. Evil herself. If I'd known what a taskmaster she'd be, I'd have never asked her to teach me your routines."

"Why did you ask her?"

He cocked his head to the right. "Isn't it obvious? I didn't want to make a fool of myself in front of the girl I like."

Cupid's arrow speared her heart but good at that admission. Rooted in place, she watched him walk off, admiring the chiseled muscles of his back and the sexy infinity symbol on his right shoulder.

Most of her regular students had left, but the men were hamming it up with Jill, who was laughing and cracking jokes. When they picked her up like she was a fallen tree, holding her across their chests, she shrieked.

"I'm in shock," Jane said, coming to stand beside

her. "Did that just happen?"

Having no words, Elizabeth only nodded.

Natalie approached them, Caroline and Moira behind her. "He's really into you. I'm not usually a romantic, but I have to tell you...you're a lucky woman. Not too many men would have the balls to show up here and dance like that in front of a bunch of women."

No, not many would.

"Terrance's balls have never been in question," she responded.

"*Elizabeth*," Jane gasped.

"Oh, stop. You know it's true. Not like Matt's are either. Now, if you'll excuse me, I'm going to go home and eat a pint of dark chocolate espresso ice cream." Maybe that would curb her arousal for Terrance.

Right now she wanted nothing more than to rip his remaining clothes off.

Tomorrow night was too far away.

"Want company?" Natalie asked. "My sisters and I are going to leave for Denver early tomorrow morning. We could make it a girls' night."

"Why not? Let's order pizza. And Jane, I'll leave the wine to you."

"Ah...I was kinda going to head home and umm...see Matt."

"No doubt you're planning to rip his clothes off," she mused.

Jane socked her in the arm.

"Ouch."

"Yes, I am, but there's no need to say so in front of his sisters."

Moira put her hands over her ears. "Please, we know you have sex with my brother. We just don't want to think about it."

"Right. Totally understood. So, I'll be going." Jane kissed her on the cheek. "Call me tomorrow."

As Jane said her goodbyes to the Hale sisters,

Elizabeth heard Rhett call out her name.

"Come on over, darlin'. We want to take a picture with our sweet teacher."

Natalie smothered a laugh and clapped her on the back. "Go get 'em, tiger."

She sauntered over to where the four men stood, all of them still shirtless. Rye motioned for her to stand in the middle between him and Terrance—of course. Jill's red curls were bobbing up and down from convulsive laughter as she positioned the phone for the picture.

"Closer," she fairly sang out, enjoying every minute.

Terrance slid an arm around Elizabeth's waist, causing her to jump. She glared at him.

"Closer," Jill repeated.

Terrance ran his finger underneath her workout top and rubbed her bare skin, lighting a fire like a match to a matchbook. Her thighs clenched, and she fought a moan.

"Oh, take the freaking picture, you devious woman!" Elizabeth fired back.

"Hey! Just doing my part for the good of mankind." Jill took a few pictures and promised to send them to everyone.

Rye and Clayton kissed her on the cheek before taking their leave, and Rhett chucked her under the chin.

Terrance only stood there, the pulse in his neck hammering. *"Tomorrow."*

"Yes," she answered breathily.

A smile flashed across his face. "Get used to saying that word. It's about to become your favorite."

And that's what really scared her. When it boiled down to it, she'd never been able to say anything else to Terrance.

Chapter 16

Terrance and his friends were trending on Twitter the next day. A few photos of them at the dance class had gotten out, and given Rye and Terrance's fame, they'd spread like wildfire. His publicist gave him a gleeful call and asked if they could put the picture on his new line of designer aprons.

He told her "No way in hell" and hung up while she was still cackling like a crone.

Thank God no one knew the real story. So far, it was only being attributed to Rye's wild bachelor weekend in Dare Valley.

Let's hope it stays that way.

His thoughts turned to his date with Elizabeth as he picked up what little there was to arrange in his house. Since he wasn't here much, the place was pretty clean. And after being raised in a one-room studio apartment in New York City with a messy mother, he liked order.

It had taken him hours to get to sleep last night, restless time he'd spent thinking about what to cook for her tonight. Cooking for her in his home was the best date idea he could come up with. He didn't want to take her to High Stakes, and Brasserie Dare was out. When he visited Dare Valley's other gourmet restaurant for the first time, he and Chef Brian would have to chat and show each other the proper respect—and he didn't want anything to eat into his time with Elizabeth.

He'd already told himself not to assume she'd make love with him and spend the night. If she was of a different mindset, he wouldn't pressure her. He didn't pressure women.

But that didn't mean he wasn't going to pull out all the stops, remembering all the foods she'd loved in their time together at The Peacock.

His phone rang, and he frowned when he saw it was the president of the television network. Lane Adams was a pain in the butt—the reason he was losing a fortune to his Cuss Fund. The last thing he needed right now was a lecture. Or to lose his temper again, which is how he'd landed himself with the two-month probation period in the first place.

Lane was no doubt unhappy about the shirtless pictures of Terrance and his buddies making the rounds. It didn't suit the family vision he had of the network, even though plenty of the shows they aired had sex. People even cussed.

He hated being singled out. Still, he wanted his television show to move forward, so he picked up.

"Lane? Good to hear from you. How are things in New York?"

"Apparently not as wild as they are in Dare Valley. Would you care to explain these obscene pictures? The ones where you're shirtless with a bunch of guys, including Rye Crenshaw and that poker player friend of yours?"

"There's nothing to it," he deflected. "We were only having some fun for Rye's bachelor party."

"It looks like you had a homosexual orgy."

What? Terrance's hand tightened on the phone. So Lane was a homophobe? No surprise, really—the guy seemed to hate everything. But Terrance had a number of friends who were gay, and prejudice in any form pissed him off. He took a deep breath to keep his cool.

"That's a pretty interesting statement given that all of the men in those photos are straight. Rye's getting married to a *woman,* after all, and Rhett's married too. Not that there's anything wrong with homosexuals."

"Never make a statement like that," Lane said, like he had a burr up his butt. "This network might not have a public policy on that abomination, but we run clean programming. As a representative of this network, you will be expected to toe that line. How many times have we been through this?"

The urge to hurl the phone against the wall was overwhelming, but he resisted. "You mentioned curbing the cussing and any wild antics with women for two months. I'm doing that. If you have more stipulations, I suggest you call my agent and have them written down so I can make sure I understand the full picture."

Silence descended between them. Lane was pissed. Good. It was as close as he'd come to challenging him since their original altercation. And he was proud of himself. He hadn't used a single curse word in their conversation. The Cuss Fund was working.

"I told you that you'd have to clean up your image to make it in the big leagues, Waters, and this just doesn't cut it. Cable shows starring chefs from the gutter are a dime a dozen, but primetime..."

He ground his teeth. No one liked being reminded they were from the gutter, but he knew he had to pick his battles with Lane.

"I don't know how the photos got out, but it was certainly not our intention to cause trouble. It won't happen again."

Because no way he was shaking it shirtless in front of a bunch of women ever again. Even if Dr. Evil *had* asked him if he wanted to come with her to Elizabeth's Wednesday class.

"You're walking a fine line, Waters. Be careful."

Lane hung up, and since Terrance liked his smart phone too much to hurl it across the room, he jogged to his home gym, strapped on some boxing gloves, and went a few rounds with the bag. Punching it gave him release. Lane was a prick, but he was a necessary evil if Terrance wanted to make it to primetime.

Compromise was a must.

It was the strategy that had propelled him out of the gutter. He couldn't always have what he wanted, but God knew, when he set his mind to something and worked hard, he usually got it—even if it took a few adjustments.

Now if only it would work with Elizabeth.

Chapter 17

Elizabeth surveyed herself in the mirror. Her stomach was a ball of knots—both with fear and lingering arousal. She'd chosen a navy silk shirt and a black skirt with her Manolo Blahnik high-heel boots in midnight black. Casual, yet sexy and sophisticated. She'd applied expert smoky eyes—cream on the brow bones and charcoal on the lids—and a pink nude lipstick. Her blond hair hung in waves down her shoulders, and she'd decided to wear the diamond necklace and earrings Rhett had bought her as a thank you after he had won his first World Series of Poker tournament. The diamond winked above her neckline like starlight.

Vixen had always dressed boldly.

Nothing said Elizabeth couldn't sparkle too.

Her phone rang, and Jane's picture flashed on her home screen. "Hey," she said, picking up the call.

"Hey. Are you sure you don't want me to come over and give final approval on your outfit? I can be there in five."

"No, let's not make a big deal out of this. It's only a date."

"*With Terrance.*"

Right. Like she needed the reminder. "It's fine."

"Are you taking an overnight bag?"

"*Jane.*"

"*Elizabeth.*"

They both knew what she was asking. "I haven't decided, okay? Can we please talk about something else?"

"Fine, but if you need me, call. I can come over tonight—or in the morning."

Her belly quivered. If she stayed over, there would be no going back. She'd be lost in this, in him...

"I appreciate that, Jane. You know I do."

"Ah...I love you, Liz."

Elizabeth traced the diamond necklace, making sure it nestled directly between her décolletage. It would draw his gaze exactly where she wanted it. Nothing said she couldn't tantalize him while she was making up her mind.

"You've become such a sap since getting engaged. But you know I love you too. Okay, I have to run. He'll be here any second."

"Tell him Matt laughed so hard he fell off the couch when he heard about the dance class. I showed him the pictures on the Internet so he wouldn't feel left out. I wish someone had recorded it so we could watch it whenever we have a bad day."

Until she dealt with this hunger inside, she wouldn't be able to laugh at the sight of Terrance moving his body so seductively without a shirt on. There was only so much dark chocolate espresso ice cream a girl could eat.

"Okay, I'm hanging up now. I'll call you...when I call you. Bye."

She ended their call, checked herself in the mirror one last time, and strode out to her den. Sure enough, she heard his tires crunching on the gravel of her drive.

Terrance was always on time. That she remembered.

Telling herself to take a chill pill, she grabbed her Kate Spade purse and then stopped. What had she told Jane? Always allow a man to see you when he comes to pick you up. Never grab your purse and coat like you're raring to go.

Take your time. Enjoy the moment his eyes rest on you.

God, had she turned up the heat or something? She fanned herself, feeling her body flush.

When he knocked, she smoothed her hands down her front and walked to the door, her heels clicking on the hardwood.

The crisp night air cooled her cheeks somewhat, but the rest of her body went nuclear when she saw him. He was wearing tan chinos and a white linen shirt, unbuttoned at the top to reveal his muscular chest. A black and white paisley pocket square was tucked into the pocket of his blue, black, and white checkered blazer—an artistic touch perhaps, but it made him all the more masculine.

No one could say Terrance didn't have an eye for fashion.

"You look ready to grace the streets of New York City tonight," she commented. "Very chic."

"Not in my old neighborhood. You, on the other hand. Well, you'd stop traffic in any city on the globe."

"Thank you," she said softly, feeling that familiar pull in her belly—and her heart. "I'll just get my purse and wrap."

"Allow me."

She knew it was an excuse to touch her, but it was gentlemanly *and* arousing.

And she honestly didn't need to feel any more aroused right now or she might combust right in front of him.

Still she turned her back to him when he took her

cream-colored pashmina. Biting her lip, she tensed her muscles as his hands slid the silky wrap over her shoulders. Of course his fingers also slid down her forearms, and she was unable to stop herself from shivering.

"You smell divine. I'm glad your perfume hasn't changed."

Funny how her heart squeezed at that. "Nothing more classic than Chanel."

"Indeed," he said, his warm breath on her neck.

Spinning around, she walked the few steps to her purse. "Shall we?"

"After you."

When he opened the door to the passenger side of his car, she almost tripped. He'd been solicitous before, but never like this...

"We never really had a date like this before," he said when he came around to the driver's seat and started the car.

Was she so easy to read? What in the heck had happened to her poker face? Right, she'd never mastered one with him, something that had scared her to death...and still did.

"Where are we going?"

"My house," his sex and spice voice told her.

"What?" They were eating alone at his place? She wouldn't survive the night.

"Did you really think I would take you to a place where the food wasn't up to snuff?"

"I understand why you don't want to take me to High Stakes, but there's Brasserie Dare."

"We can't go to Brasserie Dare. It's a professional thing."

When he finished explaining how things worked between chefs, her hands were clenched in her lap. All she kept thinking about was the unimpeded ability to jump him at any time during the meal.

She needed to get a hold of herself.

"You don't have to stay the night if that's what you're so worried about."

Now that surprised her. And a point to him for directness. "I don't?"

His sexy scar looked downright wicked when he smiled. "No. Of course, I'm hoping you will. I have something special in mind for breakfast too."

He would. He always did. When they were together, it had usually involved him waking her up by licking his way up her body and then sliding into her while the sleep cleared from her eyes. Then they'd make love again when they were all wet and warm in the shower. Followed by a large breakfast of things like pancakes stuffed with mascarpone cheese flavored with maple syrup and cinnamon or a full Irish breakfast with black pudding—which was actually delicious despite its ingredients—and cardamom-spiced oatmeal with a side of eggs.

"You're remembering how it used to be between us, aren't you?" His voice was razor soft.

"I was thinking about the food."

"Uh-huh."

She looked out the window as sunset crested across Dare Valley in brilliant orange and turquoise. The mountains were still dotted with snow, but soon all that would be visible were the trees and rocks. Growing up in a trailer park, there hadn't been a lot of beauty. Here it was everywhere.

And no more in evidence than in the man she was having dinner with tonight.

As they cruised through a swath of pine trees and pulled into his driveway, she found herself getting excited. This was where he lived—and it was a chance to learn something new about him. And she wanted that. He still fascinated her in so many ways, from how he managed to wear Armani so casually after growing up in a rough neighborhood to the innovative way he created to-die-for food after going hungry as a kid.

His two-story house was a craftsman-style home very similar to her own. The gray rock walls blended nicely with the plain navy ones. The front porch had been stained a warm, inviting honey brown.

"Are you renting?" she asked when he turned off the car.

"No, I decided to buy. Mac said the real estate market is growing here. It will be a good long-term investment."

When he leaves. The words were unspoken between them. She couldn't imagine him staying in Dare Valley, no matter how good the job was. He was too used to the carbon dioxide in New York's streets to stay here forever. And now that Mac was building a new hotel in Vegas, he'd likely migrate to that plum position when it was completed. Many famous chefs worked in Sin City.

He came around and helped her out. "Come on. I'll give you a tour."

When they entered the house, her taste buds executed a dance of joy in her mouth. "My God! It smells heavenly. What did you make?"

"Cajun. I remembered how much you love it. And there aren't any places that serve it around here."

Another pinch in her heart. No, there wasn't any Cajun food in Dare.

"And I've made a cocktail you've probably never had," he said, crossing the open floor plan. "It's called a Sazerac. It dates back to the Civil War and is considered America's first cocktail."

"What's in it?" she asked, surveying the surroundings.

There was one big room that served as both den and dining room. His staircase was nestled in the middle, showing off a fabulous window seat at the top dotted with navy and white pillows. The massive fireplace had a fire going, something he must have started before he picked her up. His leather sofa was caramel-colored and looked inviting. His art was mostly café scenes or landscapes.

"The ingredients are a ridiculous cognac from France and bitters from The Grand, which I made myself."

"A man who makes his own bitters? I might faint. Who decorated for you?" she asked, noticing the table was set with gleaming white china and crystal on top of an immaculate white tablecloth.

"Abbie. She loves to do it, and she knows me some. I figured it would be nicer than hiring a stranger."

"She did a great job," she said, noting the small feminine touches that softened the masculine space, like the Irish merino wool throw in blue, white, and Kelly green folded over the arm of the sofa and the trio of beeswax candles on a curvy candelabra.

"Come. The kitchen is this way."

When he held out his hand, she hesitated. Touching him this early in the night wouldn't be a good idea.

"You never were afraid before."

That cinched it. She put her hand in his, feeling the familiar jolt of attraction fan out inside her, then explode like fireworks.

His kitchen's industrial perfection didn't surprise her one bit, from its Viking range to the selection of copper pots hanging on the wall. Even his knives gleamed from their perch on a magnetic strip, looking menacing—ready to slice any vegetable or fruit that dared cross their path.

"So what's for dinner specifically?" she asked as he made their cocktails.

Everything he needed was already prepped on the counter. Watching Terrance cook had always been arousing to her, almost as much as having him caress her. He brought the same intensity and passion to cooking as he did to sex.

"I didn't think you'd go for crayfish pie, although Rye could have brought me some from Dare River." He dropped a sugar cube and a splash of water into a glass and swirled it around until the sugar dissolved, then added ice chips.

Crayfish? Thank God he'd refrained. She winced at the thought of those squirming bottom feeders. Rhett loved to suck their heads, which made her queasy every time.

"So my chef friend, Beauregard Boudin—"

"God bless you," she quipped.

His easy laugh made her smile, and she knew they had found their old rhythm again. Or was it their new rhythm? Oh hell, who cared?

He added the cognac, bitters, Pernod—an anise-flavored liquor—and more crushed ice. After stirring, he strained the mixture into an Old-Fashioned glass and then impressed the heck out of her by grabbing a cigarette lighter and lighting a lemon peel on fire to release the oil. He slid the cocktail to her.

"I won't tell Beauregard that. He's wicked with a knife."

He made himself a drink next, giving it his full attention. As she watched him become lost in the art of mixology, she sipped the Sazerac. It was potent and sweet and spicy—just like her host.

"I made a combination of Cajun and Creole food to be more specific," he said as he finished preparing his drink, "but I expect you're not that interested in the difference, right?"

"Not when the food smells so good that I want to start eating right away. I didn't eat lunch." She could tell he was being purposefully vague, but she was going to call him on it.

"Saving yourself for me, were you?"

The double meaning had her thighs clenching. "Are

you going to feed me or what?"

"You always did have a one track mind."

They both remembered she had never been able to wait for anything with him.

"Cheers," he said and held out his glass, which she touched with her own. "To new memories with old friends."

Oh, the things she wanted to do for him when he was sweet like this. "Cheers."

"How does Oysters Rockefeller sound for starters?" he asked after taking a sip. "That sure hits the spot."

"I love oysters." Of course, he already knew that.

She'd fed him raw oysters one night after a super long day in the kitchen. The jokes he had cracked about oysters' supposed aphrodisiac powers had made her laugh—at least until he had proven them all correct.

He brought out a platter of already prepared Oysters Rockefeller. "I fired up the grill before I picked you up. This will just take a moment. Why don't you bring your drink out to the deck, and you can watch me?"

Oh, the way he said that...

"I might just stay in here."

His mouth twitched. "Too bad. It's a pretty good show."

Yes, this is why *The Tattooed Chef* garnered big ratings.

Her laughter sputtered out. "You're incorrigible."

"Absolutely. Can you bring my drink too?"

With both hands holding their drinks, she followed him out onto his massive deck. Terrance was already laying the oysters on the grill, shell down, in a straight line.

"About dance class last night..."

"I was hoping you weren't going to mention it," he said as he closed the lid and picked up his drink.

"Are you kidding? You show up with Rhett, Rye, and Clayton, and take off your shirts in my class... And as for

Jill teaching you, that girl is in big trouble."

"I wanted to show you how much I want to be with you again. You never thought I'd come, did you?"

She took a drink, taking her time with her answer. "I thought you might welsh or walk out early. And I wasn't sure how I felt about it."

"You threw down the gauntlet, and trust me, part of me thinks it would have been easier to whirl chainsaw blades over fire than dance like that in front of a bunch of women."

"Hence your boys."

"You know them. They weren't going to let me go into the den alone."

Now that the sun had set, the night was all around them. She saw the first star over his right shoulder and made a wish.

Please don't let me get scared again.

"What were you all thinking, taking your shirts off like that?" She already suspected, but she wanted to hear his side.

His laugh was more of a snort. "We hoped to throw off either you or your class. As you could tell, we weren't experts. Especially when you got sneaky and changed the music on us."

He checked the oysters and fished out some tongs from under the grill cabinet to remove them and nestle them back onto the platter.

"That didn't work so well for me," she commented, grabbing his drink as they headed back inside.

"Thank God. I had this horrible vision of being emasculated in front of Dare's female population."

Emasculate *him*? There wasn't a girly enough song on the planet to make that happen.

"You guys did really great for your first time, but don't you *dare* tell the other guys I said so."

He set the tray down on the counter and made the motion of zipping up his lips. "I promise. Hearing you say it is enough to rebalance my testosterone."

Her laughter bubbled out. "I have a hard time imagining it's deficient."

Their gazes locked, and his hands stilled on the counter. Like he wanted to touch her and was fighting the urge.

"Come on," he said, his voice husky now. "We need to eat these while they're warm."

Arranging them on a serving dish, he carried them to the dining room table. "Hang on. I forgot to light the candles."

Candles? Oh boy. He was going all out, and her chest was growing tighter by the minute. Arousal and romance were an impossible combo to fight. She sat down and put her white napkin in her lap. The flames danced on those twin pillars after he lit them. When he finally took his seat, he extended the platter to her.

"Ladies first."

It was another joke between them, and heat flashed through her body.

"Thank you."

"*My pleasure*."

Yep, no way she was going to last the night. Maybe she could text Jane in the bathroom to call her with a fake emergency. But that would be wimping out, standing down out of fear, and she wasn't going to do it.

The soft, delicate oyster slid into her mouth, and as she chewed, her tongue danced with the flavor of bread crumbs, melted parmesan cheese, chopped spinach, and other spices followed off by the tartness of the lemon he must have squeezed when she wasn't looking.

"Oh, these are so good. It makes me miss New Orleans."

"When is Rhett playing there again?" Terrance asked, making his own sound of appreciation when he sampled the first oyster.

"We don't have anything planned yet. He and Rye

are talking about taking Abbie and Tory there sometime in the fall after Rye's summer tour is over. We'll see. If that's the case, I may not go with him. He won't need me to play recreationally in the casinos there."

"What's it like being his publicist now?" Then he wiped his mouth. "Is it okay to talk about you being Vixen?"

She wasn't sure what he planned on asking. Nor was she sure if she was ready to answer all his questions, but this one seemed harmless enough.

"I love it, honestly. It's been fun interacting with his fans and thinking up inventive ways to promote him. Now that he's given Annie to Jane, we don't have the dog to add to his flamboyance, but he's fine with that. With Rhett's colorful way of speaking, I usually have plenty of things to tweet about or supply to the media."

He chewed thoughtfully, and she knew what was coming.

"Do you miss being Vixen?"

"Sometimes. You didn't tell me what you made for the entrée."

For a long moment, he only sipped his cocktail. Like he was waiting her out. Well, she wasn't going to bite. If she started talking about Vixen, it would only dredge up the past and other questions she wasn't sure she wanted to answer tonight.

"I made Shrimp Creole," he said finally. "Another one of your favorites."

He'd kept an eclectic menu at The Peacock, developing regional specials to suit the various poker players. Cajun had been on the menu as a special for a week during their summer together, and she'd been in seventh heaven.

When the last oyster was gone, he rose and grabbed the platter. "I just need to finish our dinner."

This time he didn't ask her to come into the kitchen with him, and it seemed as though the earlier spell between them, the one where everything was easy and light, had been broken. Now the heaviness of the past and her secrets hung between them.

She pushed back from her chair and headed to the kitchen, determined to restore it. He was flipping shrimp in that spectacular move chefs make, jerking the pan from front to back to somersault the food through the air like a circus performer.

"I didn't tell you who I really was before because no one but Rhett and Jane knew," she said in a hushed voice.

Even through his jacket she could tell the muscles in his back were tense. He set the pan down and turned to look at her.

"I don't want to go into everything," she continued, "but Jane and I both had our reasons for becoming Raven and Vixen. Can we leave it at that for now?" She reached for her diamond necklace to anchor herself. "I don't want to spoil tonight."

He turned down the flame on the stove and approached her. "If there's one thing I thought you knew, it was that you could trust me."

She shook her head. "We never trusted anyone with the information. Well, except for Mac... Rhett told him in strict confidence. I wanted to tell you..."

"But you didn't," he said softly.

"But I didn't." And there was regret in her voice.

His progress back to the stove was slow, even though he finished off the entrée with his trademark efficiency. He took another platter out of the refrigerator and set a pan on the burner, adding olive oil. As it warmed, he slid the circular cake-like objects from the platter into the pan. That done, he drew out another platter, this one filled with sliced okra.

She fiddled with her clothing as he cooked—he was either totally immersed in cooking, or he was gathering himself.

It wouldn't surprise her one bit to hear him constructing a new wall of plaster and brick between them.

And she wouldn't blame him if he did.

Not one bit.

When he brought the food to the table, her appetite had disappeared, but she pointed to the cakes anyway and asked, "What are these?"

"Andouille sausage and goat cheese cakes made out of grits. I hope you like them. Unlike creamy grits, they have a nice crunch to them. I like the structure it gives to the meal."

She served herself a small portion of food. The silence grew heavier between them as they started to eat.

"This is really good." As a compliment, she knew it was weak, but it was becoming more difficult to speak.

She knew she had two choices.

Tell him some of her past.

Or remain guarded and leave as soon as she pushed around the food on her plate.

"I forgot the wine," he said and made a motion to rise.

Didn't that speak volumes as to how tense things were between them now?

"No need. The cocktail was enough for me."

His jaw tightened, but he said nothing as he sat back down. Only speared a large tiger shrimp and chewed.

The awkwardness between them was like a heavy fog descending from the mountains, obscuring the way forward. As she took small bites of the delicacies he'd created especially for her liking, she could feel herself drawing away.

If she told him why she became Vixen, it would mean something. And she was so afraid of going back to that place with him, of making herself vulnerable.

She was afraid to care about him again. To have him

show her that there could be so much more than simple fun and sex. To trust a man was the biggest gamble of all, as Vince had taught her. What if the violence was still in Terrance, and it resurfaced again, destroying her faith in him?

"You're not eating much," he finally commented, and truth be told, he hadn't cleared his plate either.

Her mouth lifted at the corners. "The food is excellent. I guess I'm not as hungry as I thought. Perhaps you should take me home." The words made her want to cry as she said them, but she forced them out anyway.

He wiped his mouth and rested the napkin on the table. "All right."

Why wasn't he arguing with her? Why wasn't he pressing her to tell him? Just yesterday, he'd shown up at her dance class and danced—actually danced—to a series of embarrassing songs just to go out with her again.

Would Terrance Waters ever make sense to her, and would she ever want to stop running away from him when her heart asked for more? Her earlier wish on the star rising in the sky had amounted to nothing.

Rising from the table, he strode to the front door without further comment and grabbed his keys. She set her napkin aside and picked up her purse and shawl on the way out. This time he didn't open her car door. They drove in silence back to her house.

When they arrived, he didn't even put the car in park. Only turned to her, running his gaze over her face.

"Goodnight, Elizabeth."

"Goodnight." Her chest hurt, and she could barely breathe out the word.

He didn't wait until she was inside before tearing out of her driveway—the only indication he was angry.

When she closed the door and leaned back against it, her eyes started to burn. Her vision wavered.

She didn't want to feel *this* with him again.

Sharing the full story of her past was something she'd never done directly with anyone outside of Rhett and Jane, and heck, she'd only filled Rhett in on certain details last month. Matt, Mac, and Abbie knew she'd been stalked—she'd shared that information with their tight circle before she and Jane were unmasked as Vixen and Raven—but they didn't know the specifics.

Only Jane and now Rhett knew Elizabeth Saunders wasn't her real name. Liz Parenti had died long ago, but she was like a ghost who haunted Elizabeth wherever she went: the poor girl from the trailer park whose mother sometimes stripped in two-bit dance clubs and whose father ran a broken-down dusty patch of mobile homes, drinking all day.

Terrance wouldn't settle for less than the full truth. There was no way she could tell him, "I needed a change, so I became Vixen."

But how was she supposed to tell him about Vince? Especially since he possessed his own violent temper.

She'd run from Terrance out of fear, but not just the fear he'd turn out to be like Vince. He was the only man who'd made her want to wash all the makeup off, remove the wig, and let him see Elizabeth.

Well, now he could see her for who she was, and he wanted to learn more.

He *cared* about her.

Other than Jane and Rhett and their growing circle, no one had ever cared about her.

She still wasn't sure anyone other than her new family could, but Terrance was offering her that chance.

Could she take it?

She clenched her eyes shut and listened to the silence in her home. It was deafening. She didn't want to be here. Not when she could be with Terrance again—laughing and joking, making love.

He wasn't like Vince. *He wasn't.*

Pushing off from the door, she ran to the garage before she could lose her courage and turned on her car. Backing out, she realized she didn't want to be lonely anymore.

She wanted to be Terrance's, regardless of how it turned out.

If things went bad, she could always run again.

Chapter 18

Terrance's fists were already swelling and bruised from hitting the bag, but he had been too pissed to put on boxing gloves or change into work-out clothes. He'd just stripped down to his briefs and started pounding. He switched to the jab, straight right, left hook boxing combination he'd been taught by a celebrity boxing friend and felt sweat gather across his bare chest.

She'd closed him out.

Again.

The hurt had been too monumental for him to do anything but sit there, barely tasting his meal, his gut twisting. He'd hoped to finally get to know the real Elizabeth.

But she hadn't dropped her mask.

No, she was more mysterious now than ever. He punched the bag again, adding some footwork, needing to burn off his anger and the devastation under it.

She had her secrets—he knew that much—and he wondered again why she'd had the bat by her door. Did she have some crazy ex he didn't know about? Is that why she'd become Vixen?

His mother had been a woman of secrets, and he'd

come to hate her for it. All her lies about where she spent her days, how she spent the paltry sums of money that crossed their threshold, who his real father was.

By the time he was ten, she'd named five different men. He'd stopped asking.

His breath was wheezing out. He didn't need Elizabeth and her complications. And he certainly didn't need to feel like shit over her.

He'd been crazy to think they could rediscover the good times between them without lifting up the doormat and seeing all the grubs crawling beneath it.

He finally cursed like he wanted to, punching the bag once for each word that echoed in the empty room.

"Fuck. Shit. Damn..." He kept a mental count as his knuckles cracked and bled. He lost one thousand dollars to his Cuss Fund by the time he was done.

When he rested his head against the bag, defeat rained down on him like lead.

The doorbell rang, and he straightened. Were his ears playing tricks on him? A moment later, he heard it again.

What the hell? If some pizza delivery man was lost, he was about to become the convenient target of Terrance's rage. His kitchen staff scattered when he got this pissed.

Wiping the blood from his knuckles on his briefs, he decided he didn't give a crap if his unexpected visitor saw him like this. Hell, he'd been this exposed at Elizabeth's f-ing dance class.

As he ripped the door open, he shouted, "What in the hell do you want?"

When he noticed it was Elizabeth standing there, he had to brace his hand against the frame.

"I'm sorry," she said, her face white. "I...became Vixen because I was running from something, and other than Jane and Rhett, I've never told anyone the whole story. Rhett didn't even know until recently..."

His hand slid down the frame, as an emotion slid through him, something violent and hot. "We can't do this. I thought we could, but we can't. I...goddammit, Vix, you hurt me again, and I just can't take it."

She stepped forward and raised a shaking hand to his jaw, caressing it. Her blue eyes were like the ocean at midnight. "Do you think you're the only one? It hurts me too, and I don't like it either. That's why I...left you without anything but a note before. I was so scared."

"Oh, babe," he whispered and lifted his hand to cup her cheek.

"I missed you," she whispered, "and I can't handle seeing you again. Remembering how things were between us. How they still are."

Her skin was like velvet without the heavy makeup she used to wear, and the tears in her eyes made his belly quiver.

"I missed you too."

"Then," she said softly, brushing her body against him, and he wasn't sure if it was a question or a request.

He only knew he couldn't refuse it.

Yanking her mouth to his, he fused them together, devouring her. All of the time spent apart made his hands impatient as he pulled her inside the house and slammed the door behind them.

She grabbed his head and opened her lips to him, and God yes, it was just as he remembered it. The hottest kissing he'd ever experienced. Her tongue slid inside his mouth, and he groaned as his stroked hers. One hand slid down her hip and cupped her sweet round butt, pulling her to him. She moved her body against him in that slow sensual way of hers, the one that had tortured him at the dance class, the one that always drove him to the edge of madness.

Soon she was yanking down his briefs and grabbing a hold of him. His hips jerked in response. *Slow down,* part of him thought, but there was no way. He'd been without her for too long, and yesterday had aroused him to a fever pitch.

His hands tore off her silk shirt, sending buttons flying and pinging off the hardwood floor. She reached behind and took off her bra, then pushed her skirt and hose down her thighs.

Her boots were in the way, but he didn't care right now. He kept their mouths fused together and cupped her breasts, so warm and soft and heavy in his hands. She moaned deep and long in her throat, then pushed him back, sinking to the floor, sitting on her backside as she dispensed with the boots and the rest of her clothes.

"Hang on. We need a condom." His voice was raspy, like he'd gone all night without water.

She dove for her purse, which was thankfully on the floor, and pulled out a few packages, throwing them his way. "Put one on. I need you. Right. Now."

He understood. He burned for her too.

"We'll take it slow next time," he said, sheathing himself and sinking to the floor as she leaned back, radiant in her feminine glory.

His hand sought the place between her thighs, and it was too much. She was more than ready, and so was he. Resting his hands beside her shoulders, he sank into her and arched his back.

God, it was so good.

It had never been this good with anyone else.

Her legs wrapped around his hips, and their dance turned primal, instinctive, out of control. He set his mouth to that place where her neck and shoulders met and bit her lightly, coming into her hard and deep.

She started keening, and he knew she was there.

When she exploded around him, he couldn't hold back. He emptied himself, shaking from the force. Sinking onto her, he tried not to crush her, but he just couldn't leave her yet. Not when everything in him said he had found his way back to something special.

Something perfect.

She nuzzled his neck, humming, and he angled back to kiss her sweetly and softly on the mouth. He gathered his strength and rested his weight on one arm, wanting...no *needing* to caress her cheek. Gaze into her eyes.

They were open and wary, like she was as swept away as he was, and not completely happy about it.

"Hey," he whispered.

"Hey," she whispered back.

He didn't know what else to say. His brain still wasn't working. His body felt like an empty husk. And his heart...well, it was throbbing, and not because it was beating crazy fast.

So he kissed her again. And again and again, until her legs relaxed around his waist and her hands gently crept around his back. This time, he took his time and rediscovered the luscious curve of her bottom lip. Ran his tongue along the bow in the center of her mouth. And sunk even further into the deep pleasure of kissing this woman.

Vixen.

Elizabeth.

Whoever she was, he knew her completely like this. She'd never been able to hide from him here.

She finally turned her face away and pressed her cheek to his. "I did miss you. So much."

He clenched his eyes shut, his hand finally tangling in her real hair, which was as soft as corn silk. "Me too, babe. Me too."

And as he took her mouth again, he pulled her up with him and awkwardly lifted her up until she straddled his waist.

"I want to make love to you in a bed this time," he told her as he crossed the room.

She only fitted her mouth to his in response, and this time when they made love, it was sweet and slow, and it leveled all the walls he'd erected in his heart after she had left him.

Chapter 19

Part of Elizabeth felt like she was floating high above the ground in a hot air balloon. But the other part shook a little, as if walking along the ledge of a twenty-story building.

Everything she'd ever felt for him was back, and almost a thousand times larger because she knew what it was to live without him. She didn't want to feel that again.

Her head rested on his chest, and her leg was curled over his body. He was stroking her hair softly as if he couldn't get enough of this part of her real self she'd always denied him. Yet there existed a new awareness between them, and it had the teeth of their earlier silence.

He was waiting for her to explain.

"I don't know where you want me to start," she finally whispered.

He shifted until he was facing her and leaned in to kiss her again, that mere brush of lips so sweet, so undemanding, that it made tears burn her eyes again. If he didn't stop this, she was going to make a mess of herself.

"How about you tell me where you were born?" he asked when he settled back, his arm still stroking her waist.

Where better to begin than the beginning? "I was born in a trailer park outside Albuquerque, New Mexico. We didn't have health insurance, so a neighbor helped my mom."

Those bottle-green eyes seemed as if they were staring into her soul, but she made herself hold his gaze.

"We didn't have a lot of money. My mom sometimes stripped, and my dad took care of the trailer park when he wasn't drinking."

"So the dance stuff..." he mused.

"I've always loved it, but I used to be ashamed of feeling that way. I forced myself to get over it. Dancing's...magical. There's nothing dirty about the way I do it."

"The way you do it is perfect," he said, taking her hand and kissing it.

After that lovely touch, it took her a moment to decide what to share next. "I was good at school. I had a few teachers who knew...my situation, and they told me college was the way out for me. I'm...well, I'm really smart, which might surprise you because of Vixen."

She held her breath, hoping he wasn't going to be one of those guys who didn't like learning he was with a smart woman. Vince hadn't liked that she had ranked higher in their class at Harvard than he did.

"That doesn't surprise me at all."

The tightness in her chest eased. "I managed to win some scholarships and get into Harvard, and that's where I met—"

"Wait a minute. You went to Harvard? Just how smart are we talking here?"

This time she shrugged her shoulder and looked down at his chest. "Smart."

"*Elizabeth.*"

"Okay, I have an IQ of 160."

His mouth closed with an audible pop. "But that's genius level."

"Yes. So, as I was saying, I met Jane at Harvard."

He was shaking his head now and reached for a strand of her hair again, caressing it between his thumb and forefinger. "No wonder you have such a strong bond. You've been friends for a long time. You never would tell me how old you were."

No, Vixen wasn't the kind of woman who shared her age. "I'm thirty-one."

"I didn't know I was with a younger woman," he said with a teasing smile.

She gave him a playful shove. "Are you implying I look older than you?"

"Never." He gave her a soft kiss. "Back to your story. So, you ended up rooming with a prominent politician's daughter. Nice twist of fate."

No doubt someone was looking out for her that day. "It was a mistake, and her father tried to correct it, but we just knew we were sisters when we met. There was this click. Jane refused to change to a more 'appropriate' roommate."

"Her dad sounds like a major prick."

Her first easy smile appeared on her face, and it felt good. "He is, and does 'prick' constitute a swear word?"

"Probably, but I think I'm just going to donate two grand to the Cuss Fund since I pretty much swore a blue-streak after I dropped you off."

She could feel her eyebrows rise to her hairline. "That's a lot of cursing."

His eyes dimmed, and his smile faded. "I was pretty upset."

It did something to her, knowing he'd been upset, knowing she could hurt him. Again. "You didn't tell me how you bloodied your hands. I finally...ah...noticed them when we slowed things down the second time."

Seeing his hands, she'd had a flash of Vince breaking her car window in a rage, his knuckles bleeding from the cuts. Then her mind had conjured up the image of Terrance's knuckles all bruised and swollen after punching the guy at The Peacock.

"I didn't put my boxing gloves on. I was too impatient to hit something, but let's not detour from your story."

Right. No need to talk about what had happened between them earlier. At least not yet. And she didn't need to see this violent part of Terrance right now, because that timid little part of her was still scared of what he was capable of.

"Jane and I became inseparable," she continued, smoothing the sheet over herself. "Jane had immaculate manners, of course, which helped this girl from the trailer park who didn't know where a shrimp fork went. Heck, I didn't even know there was a shrimp fork."

"Sorry, I forgot to use them tonight," he said dryly, his mouth curving into a smile.

She forced her gaze away from his bloody knuckles, trying not to think about whether she had dried blood in her hair. "I'm glad. I never saw the point, but anyway, Jane helped me fit in...and I helped her loosen up. You can't imagine what her life was like, being a politician's daughter."

"I'm glad you two found each other."

Jane was one of the greatest gifts of her life. She didn't know what would have happened to her if they hadn't met. "Me too."

"What did you study at Harvard?" he asked in a upper crust accent.

"You need to roll your Rs more," she suggested. "Jane and I majored in finance."

"*Finance...*"

"They don't have poker degrees there."

"No, of course not." His eyes narrowed, studying

her. "I'm trying to imagine how you could go from finance to poker."

What he was really saying was he couldn't imagine how she'd gone from majoring in finance to becoming Vixen, and that knowledge squeezed her chest. God, this was going to be so hard. She hated to talk about Vince, and she felt more vulnerable now than when they'd been making love so slow and sweet—and she'd felt plenty vulnerable then.

Her hand fisted in the sheet. "It's hard for me to talk about this."

He traced her face and then leaned forward to kiss her again, all whisper-soft, soothing the dark edges inside her.

"You can trust me," he said against her lips. "I swear to you I'll never tell another soul."

Her in-breath didn't quite fill her chest, but it released some tension. "There was a...man...a guy I dated who went to Harvard. We went out a few times, but I broke things off."

Her out-breath came out in a rush and then she couldn't get more air. Suddenly all she could see was Vince's face.

"I can't breathe," she said, sitting up and trying to gulp in oxygen. At this rate, she was going to hyperventilate.

His hands stroked her shoulders. "Shit. What can I do?"

She shook her head and closed her eyes, focusing on her breathing and Terrance's gentle caresses until her panic subsided. She could do this. She wasn't a victim.

"Okay, I think..." God, she was tired—all the emotions of the day were draining her. "I'm okay."

"No, you're not," Terrance said, pulling her into his arms. "I'm sorry. You don't need to tell me if it's going to do this to you."

She pressed her forehead to his chest, hearing the

hoarseness in his voice. "That's why I don't like to talk about it, but I'm going to finish."

"Let me at least get you a glass of water or something. Tea? Bourbon? I'll give you anything."

Oh, how that pledge was enough to help her firm up her resolve. She pushed away slightly. "He didn't like me breaking things off, and he got violent. He started stalking me. Jane and I tried to stop him legally, but he had good lawyers. His family is big money, bigger than Jane's. Right before graduation, he threatened to kill me if I went out with another man."

"Jesus Christ," he swore, his jaw hard now.

Everything in her shivered from the memories, her body shaking too, and Terrance reached for the comforter and wrapped it around her. Then he wrapped his arms around her.

"I'm here. He can't hurt you. Not ever again."

His pledge made her want to weep. "I...I told Jane that we needed...to get out of town. We went to Atlantic City to gamble. It always cleared our heads. That's where we met Rhett."

His hands made a gentle glide up and down her back. "Keep going."

"We...ah...impressed him with our ability to see the players' strategies. We might have been able to know who had what card, but I'm not admitting that."

"Because you're a freaking genius," he tried to tease, but his voice was as hoarse as hers.

"Right. We're poker geniuses." The memories were getting better now, like the first patch of dawn's rays shining in the dark night sky. "Rhett thought I was cute at first and tried to pick me up. You know Rhett, but all we wanted to do was talk poker once he told us he was a professional player. That's when we knocked his socks off. We might have been trying to impress him, but don't tell him that."

She was finally able to fill her lungs with air, and it

was oh so sweet. "Rhett offered us jobs as his scouts on the spot, and after Jane and I thought about it, we decided it would be a perfect escape for us. But we needed an act to...hide out." Oh, how she hated that word, hated admitting that a man had made her hide. "That's how Raven and Vixen were born. And Liz Parenti died. I...changed my legal name to Elizabeth Saunders."

"Like two phoenixes rising from the ashes," he mused as he edged back to gaze into her eyes. "I'm in awe of you. Of both of you." He took her hand and drew it to his mouth, kissing the back of it.

The gesture was so gentle. How it warmed her heart. "Jane wanted to embarrass her family so she could be freed from their demands for her to join her father's political machine, and Vixen was my chance to escape..."

She didn't want to say his name, and her gaze rested on the bloody knuckles of the hands that held her. Part of her didn't know if she could trust Terrance with that detail. It was the same reason she'd feared telling Rhett, who believed in old-fashioned justice—an eye for an eye, a tooth for a tooth. Terrance had been raised on the streets. He'd already gotten into a fight over her for something minor compared to this.

"I understand why you were afraid to tell me now," he said, and his jaw tensed. "You were trying to keep yourself safe."

Safe. Yes, that's the one thing she valued more than anything.

"So now that your real face is out there in the public as Rhett's poker babe, are you worried this guy will recognize you? Is that why you had a bat by the door when I came by the other night?"

There was no way she was telling him about Ryan. He was only a trigger for her bigger fears. She still had nightmares about Vince, but the likelihood of Vince ever coming across her picture and recognizing her—unless he followed poker circles, which was unlikely—was a thousand to one. Plus her hair was so different from the dishwater brown she'd dyed it at Harvard, not to mention her clothes.

Jane was the only thing that tied her to that life, and so far, nothing had come from that.

"It's still a fear, I won't deny that, but it's been a long time."

He was silent a minute. "But you're not sure. Otherwise, you wouldn't have a bat by the door."

Again, her eyes flicked to his bloody knuckles. "The bat just makes me feel better. The thing at Harvard...really messed me up." Her voice broke.

He rubbed the hand he was still holding. "Of course it would. It would mess up anyone. Elizabeth, you have nothing to be ashamed of."

She hung her head. Shame. Yes, she still felt that. Shame that she'd somehow done something to make Vince act like that. Shame that she couldn't let it go and stop being afraid.

"I've been...edgier than usual since the Raven and Vixen thing came out. It was hard...but Jane needed to do it because she loved Matt, and I finally came around."

Not that she'd jumped up and down about it or anything. Hard was a tame word for what her best friend had asked of her, but she would do anything for Jane.

"You're one hell of a brave woman. I cared about you before, but right now... Come here."

She rose on her knees in the center of the bed like he did. When he cupped her face between his hands, his green eyes glowing now, she felt her heart burst into a million pieces.

"I thought I might have loved Vixen. Before. But Elizabeth...well, she's captured my heart in one evening."

His words shocked her to the core.

"You...you...you...thought you loved me?"

"It was the only thing that made sense when you left." This time he blew out a long breath. "I'd never been more upset in my life, which was saying a lot. When I came to Dare Valley to talk with Mac about the job last month, I went kinda crazy again when I realized you were the woman I'd run into at the coffee shop."

She'd been really upset too, if crying a lot and eating tons of ice cream were any indication.

"I...loved you too," she admitted in a whisper. "That's one of the reasons why I left you like I did."

He grew silent. His hands sneaked around his back, like he was hiding them, and then he held them up. "These...make you afraid, don't they?"

Her eyes flew to his face.

"I should have washed them off earlier, but I didn't want to interrupt your story."

No, it would have been awkward. She might not have been able to finish.

"You *were* scared of me after I got into it with that guy." His out-breath sounded like it was forced from his lungs. "That's the other reason why you left, wasn't it?"

Who said honesty was easy? Her throat was laced with barb wire now. "Yes."

He squeezed his eyes shut for a moment, like he was gathering himself. When he opened them, they shone with shame and vulnerability. "I would never hurt you. *Ever.*"

"I know that." When he tried to speak, she pressed her hand to his mouth. "I do. But violence scares me. It triggers something inside me. I'm working on it, but it's still there."

He lowered his head. "Let me go wash up."

He took off for the bathroom, and she tucked the comforter around her more securely.

When he came back in, his body movements were much stiffer. He sat on the edge of the bed, like he was afraid to be close to her.

"I don't want to trigger you. I'm sorry. More than I can say."

The harshness in his voice had her reaching out her hand. "I know you are."

"When you left, I told myself that I'd misread you. That it had only been fun for you."

"No, it was more than fun. So much more."

His hand squeezed hers. "For me too."

"What are we going to do?" she asked. Even after making love to him again and telling him her story, she wasn't sure what lay ahead.

"How about we just try and be together again—as we are—and see where it goes?"

As we are. Those words gave her the peace she so rarely found. "I've...never really tried that before. My parents were...a disaster. I'm not sure I'll be good at it."

He nodded. "My mother was a wreck too. She died of a drug overdose when I was seventeen, and I don't even know who my father was. Why don't we just do what we've done with our lives?"

Her brow knit. "What do you mean?"

"Rise from the ashes of where we came from. Imagine something better and make it happen."

"I like the sound of that."

"This time let's not hold anything back." His smile came and went on his face like a flash of lightning. "I won't bring any bloody knuckles to the party."

She felt a smile tickle the corners of her mouth. "That would be nice and much easier on your hands."

"I want this to work, Elizabeth. But I don't want there to be any more secrets between us. If we're going to do this, we need to be honest with each other."

No secrets? They're what had kept her going, what had kept her alive. "I'll try, okay? Just be patient with me. Being...outted has been pretty hard for me, and I'm still adopting new ways to handle that."

He kissed her softly on the lips. "How about this? Any secrets you can't live without, you entrust to me. I'll help you keep them safe. Keep you safe."

That undid her. A tear streaked down her cheek suddenly. "Oh, Terrance."

"Hey, now," he said, kissing her tear away. "I didn't mean to make you cry."

Being with him again, making love with him again, had opened her emotionally like the rivers running through the mountains, cutting away rock and earth until nothing stood in their way. The power of it scared her.

"You didn't make me cry in a bad way. You're making me think anything is possible."

And that his feelings for her—their feelings for each other—were big enough to carry them through whatever might lie ahead.

His hand caressed the hair lying on her shoulder. "We're both here again. *Together*. Doesn't that tell you anything is possible?"

Yes, it did. And it made her wonder what else could evolve between them now that her secrets were out in the open.

Chapter 20

Terrance cut into the bison brisket he'd smoked with Colorado's native cottonwood trees. His new menu for The Grand was coming together, and he was still exploring how to incorporate local flavors while being innovative. He'd added some pecan wood to the cottonwood to give the smoke a bit more flavor. Cottonwood alone was too light and delicate for the bison.

His staff clustered around him as he shaved off thin pieces for everyone to sample. When he tasted that paper-thin slice of meat, his eyes closed. "Sh—heck yeah. Now that's going to sell like crazy."

"Incredible, Chef," Jeremy Painters, his sous chef, said, his eyes closing in ecstasy. "Another killer entrée for the menu."

His night with Elizabeth had given him a fresh spark of creativity, inspiring him to try a few of the items he'd been thinking about adding to the new menu.

The rest of his staff hummed their appreciation as he shifted to the steaming hot venison on his other side. He'd chosen to grill it using only olive oil, sea salt, and pepper. The sauce would enhance the dish, and he'd settled on one made with wild cherries reminiscent of the Armenian cooking he'd sampled in Beirut. The addition of sage, hand-picked from the mountains surrounding Dare Valley, was yet another nod to Dare's local flavor. A splash of bourbon whiskey from nearby Breckenridge roasted the cherries when it caught fire, adding yet another power punch to the taste buds.

"Yes," he uttered in total rapture as he sampled it. Cooked to perfection, the meat melted in his mouth while the tart fruit blended beautifully with the exotic sage flavor.

He gestured to Jeremy to cut samples for everyone else, and moments later, they were all chewing and making happy sounds over his creations—just the way he liked it.

Now, he only needed to figure out what he wanted to do with the rabbit and concoct a vegetarian option. He'd already settled on a duck recipe, and it was crazy good. Mac claimed it was the best thing he'd ever tasted.

Since Terrance was still building rapport with his staff, he decided to be magnanimous. "I'm willing to take ideas for the rabbit. If you have any, put them on my desk by the end of the week."

Nothing said he had to implement their ideas, but who knew, he might be surprised. So far, he was slowly testing his sous chef and a few of the more seasoned chefs, having them suggest daily specials so he could evaluate their talent. He'd kept the restaurant's original staff so far. He would let people go if needed, but not without giving them a chance to show him what they could do.

"Okay, people, let's start prep for tonight," he announced and nodded to Jeremy, who oversaw it for him. He would make his final check an hour before the restaurant opened for dinner.

As he left the kitchen and headed down the hall to his office, he thought about going home for a cat nap. He and Elizabeth had been up until dawn, talking and making love. His Turkish coffees would get him through, but he knew tonight was going to be a bitch.

As always, she'd both invigorated and exhausted him mentally, emotionally, and physically. And she was all he could think about.

His office held his favorite cookbooks, some even signed by the chefs who wrote them. There was one by Wolfgang Puck, one of his early favorites. He was an excellent example of how a chef could develop a multi-tiered business empire. Terrance admired what the Austrian chef had accomplished, and he was now adding the finishing touches to his own culinary empire.

The primetime TV show was a crucial part. His cookware and cooking products were just being launched, thanks to the investment he'd garnered in New York from Harwick & Taylor. Soon he'd have his face on specialty items co-branded with Mac's hotel chain.

Life was good.

And now there was Elizabeth.

He missed her already, and because he could, he texted her.

Hey! Can't wait to see you again. Tonight? I'll bring by something I made today, and we can savor it together.

He almost wrote *like old times,* but reminded himself, these were new times. No need to dwell in the past. They hadn't talked about getting together tonight after he'd made her breakfast—her favorite: French toast stuffed with maple cream and fresh strawberries. She'd straddled him in the chair, and they'd fed each other the rest of the meal before making love with her sitting on the edge of the table.

Hey back. When are you coming by? I'll have the hot tub ready for you.

Now that was what he was talking about.

Can't wait to see you wet—again.

It was a bad pun, even though he was referring to the shower, but he didn't need to start sexting her. Even he wasn't that stupid. He knew smart phones could be hacked, and wouldn't Lane's underwear get in a wad if he saw messages like that on the Internet?

You are so bad. I'll see you tonight.

Yes, yes he was.

Bye.

He was in over his head again, but right now, he didn't care. When she didn't respond, he pocketed his phone and dialed up his work emails, scanning the ones from the hotel's head of catering services. Alice Rollins wasn't the most innovative person in the world or the easiest colleague. She'd told him the former chef hadn't interfered with her menus, and Terrance had told her that was changing. She didn't like it.

Not one bit.

Her bitchy reply to his suggestions on changing the menu for the group from a Fortune Five Hundred company combining poker with executive strategy sessions was the last straw. All of the food served at The Grand should reflect the hotel's standards. His.

Alice wasn't going to play ball.

Worse, she was resisting his idea of offering their catering services commercially. Terrance thought there was business potential with Emmits Merriam University for some of their bigger, more notable events. Who wanted to eat a rubber chicken dinner at a gala? Not the president of the university and his august board of directors, he'd bet. He also thought it would be possible to cater high-level events in Denver to expand the reach of the hotel. Terrance knew he was in demand, and he wanted to cook for people who were willing to shell out big money to eat his food.

Closing out the email, he decided it was time to see his boss. Since he was pretty damn pleased with his new additions to the menu, he detoured to the kitchen to make up two plates first.

"And send up a plate of the chocolate truffles to Jill," he told Jeremy as he finished plating the cherry sauce on the venison.

He'd sent Dr. Evil chocolate truffles yesterday, even though their dance lessons were finished and he was still making her lunch. He was feeling generous today. Jill loved chocolate the same way some women loved diamonds, and he laughed, wondering if that could be a funny addition to his TV show. How many women would choose diamonds over chocolate if they could only possess them for ten minutes? Hmm...something to think about.

Of course, that was assuming Lane Stick-Up-His-Ass Adams was going to release the show for production after the probation.

With the plates prepared to perfection, he set them on a teak tray and added a table service. Since Mac had beverages in his office, he wouldn't need to bring them. He took the staff elevator and cruised to the executive wing. Abbie was coming out of her office, and she smiled immediately when she saw him.

"Hello, Terrance," she said, eyes zeroing in on the tray he carried. "It's probably too much to hope that you're bringing me lunch."

He winked at her. "I can have something sent up. Just call Jeremy and tell him what you'd like. I wanted Mac to try these new additions to the menu over some business. There's more in the kitchen if you like venison and bison."

Her hand rose to her neck. "Deer and buffalo? Ah, you know me. I'm not all that adventurous when it comes to the meat department. Chicken and fish are pretty much my go-to meats even though Rhett manages to persuade me to eat a hamburger or steak every once in a while."

He remembered that about her. "I'm still deciding

how to serve the chicken. It's my least favorite meat, so it gets my attention last. Okay, and the vegetarian entrée."

She laughed. "That doesn't surprise me. I'll let you get to Mac before your entrees grow cold. Good to see you."

"You too, Abbie," he told her and nodded to Casey when he came to the end of the hall. "Is he available?"

"For you? Always."

He knocked on the door, and heard Mac call out, "Enter."

When his boss caught sight of him, he rubbed his hands together. "Exactly what I needed. A break from some unpleasant folks. I sometimes hate being charming to assholes."

"I know the feeling," Terrance said. "Since I wanted to talk to you about something, I decided to bring you the two additions I've settled on for the new menu. I know you said you didn't need to sample anything, but they're too incredible not to share."

"What are they?" Mac said, rising from his desk and gesturing to the seating area in the corner.

When he told him, his boss quickly unrolled the napkin from the silverware and got to business. After tasting the bison, he leaned back.

"My God man, I know I've told you this before, but you've got skills."

"Wait until you try the venison," Terrance added, enjoying his friend's praise. Nothing made him happier than people appreciating and enjoying his creations.

The venison was enough to elicit a moan. "My God. That's incredible. Too bad Rye missed these. He would have gone crazy."

"He'll be back," he said in a horrible impersonation of Arnold Schwarzenegger.

"Stick to your day job, T. I think we have a couple of hits on our hands," Mac said, gesturing to the plates.

"Yes, and I expect the critics are going to like them too. A few of the big ones are coming to The Grand to check out my new menu. We'll have a Michelin star before you know it."

"I never doubted it. Now, what did you want to talk to me about? Must be pretty serious for you to bring me food."

Terrance crossed his arms. Nothing got past Mac. "I don't think I need to butter you up for this. I want you to fire Alice." And he proceeded to lay out his case.

As he spoke, Mac finished eating the samples he'd brought, but Terrance never doubted he had his friend's full attention.

"Fine," Mac said. "I'll tell her. Abbie's the sweetest woman on the planet, and she mentioned feeling some friction with Alice, so I suspected there might be a big problem between you two. If she's not playing ball, then she's not a team member at The Grand."

Good. Part one was in his hands. "I also want her replacement to be in charge of the catering menus for all your other hotels. That way my brand of cooking flows down to all food served by or from your hotels. I don't see any other way to make that happen. Right now, I can work with all the individual chefs on their menus, but I can't do that on the catering side too."

Mac fished out his lucky piece, a canary yellow poker chip, and rubbed it between his fingers. "You want complete control. Okay, I can see why, and I think it's a good idea. I hadn't thought it was possible before. Do you have anyone in mind to take over the position?"

The idea had been brewing for weeks, and after checking her credentials, he knew she could handle the scope and then some. Plus, they'd work great together.

"Natalie Hale," he told him. "She has a successful catering business in Denver, as you know, with some A-list clients like the Denver Raiders. She already has a terrific way of bringing food together, something I can add to. The only problem is that I'm not sure if she'd be willing to consider coming here, but her family is here, so who knows? Maybe you could buy her business if she wants to keep it."

Mac stroked his chin. "That way we'd get her A-list clients and expand The Grand's catering services in Denver faster than we could on our own."

"I think it's the way to go."

"And since I have a celebrity chef overseeing the menus..." Mac added.

"I'm almost finished with The Grand's menu, and then I'm going to get started on finalizing the menus for the other hotels." Though he would be overseeing the menu creation in all the Four Aces hotels, the other hotels already had head chefs. Kitchen egos were a delicate matter, so he was asking for input and treading lightly. For now.

"You're going to be a busy man once the TV show starts," Mac commented. "Is that TV guy being any less of a dick to you?"

Terrance kicked back in his chair. "He got all preachy with me about the dance pictures. Being bare-chested with other men means we were having an orgy or something."

"You're kidding me," Mac shot back with a bark of laughter.

"No, but I promised you I could manage it all, and I will. Jeremy is a solid sous chef here, eager to learn. He'll do fine when I'm gone."

"Good to hear. Okay, talk to Natalie and find out what her conditions are. When I want something—or someone who works for me wants something—I do everything in my power to get it. Of course, we'll have to advertise internally first and then go out as part of our standard policy."

"I realize that. I was planning on asking Natalie if I could see her in action at her upcoming Denver Raiders event."

"I like the idea. A lot of their players come to the hotel to play poker in the off season, and I want to keep them happy."

Like he didn't know that. "So I noticed from my research when you offered me this job."

His boss' mouth quirked. "That's what I like about you. You're more than a pretty cook."

"Haha," he responded.

"At least that's what my wife said, seeing you shirtless and all."

He doubted Peggy had ever referred to him as pretty. "She got an eyeful, and I can promise it will *never* be repeated."

"You look tired," his boss finally said with a grin, rising from his seat. "Looks like your date with Elizabeth went well."

Mac usually wasn't into prurient prodding, but apparently he hadn't gotten his fill of teasing him.

"I don't kiss and tell," he said holding his hands up.

"Good idea. Rhett is feeling pretty awkward about you two. Don't give him a reason to punch you."

His friendship with Rhett was too important for him to let that happen. Plus, it would frighten Elizabeth—something he never wanted to do again. "I'd never dream of it. With those hands, he'd clock me good."

Mac laughed. "I'll call Alice now and give her a good severance. Can you handle June Ikado as the interim head of catering?"

He thought of Alice's passive deputy. "We'll manage. She won't challenge me." That's why Alice had hired her, after all.

"Sounds like you might want another change there too," Mac said, reading between the lines like usual. "We'll leave that for Alice's replacement. Thanks again for bringing up the food. It was a treat."

As he left, he deposited the tray outside Jill's office

and knocked. She looked up when he strolled in.

"Oh, it's the man of my dreams," she said, popping another truffle in her mouth and moaning. "The one who sent up chocolate with my lunch. Feel free to send chocolate anytime."

"I didn't have a chance to thank you in person yesterday for your help with the dancing gig, but I appreciate it. It will *never* be repeated, though, so you can stop the email invites to dance class."

She snorted and wiped her mouth. "Ah, and you were getting so good. I could see you as one of the celebrities on *Dancing with the Stars*. Imagine...my protégé, up on that stage."

"No way in he...heck," he responded. "I need to get back to the kitchen."

She pushed out of her chair like she was trying to be some crazy mountain lion on the prowl. "Aren't you going to tell me about your date? After all, I did make it come together."

"No way," he told her.

Circling him, she ran a finger around his chest, and he shoved it down.

"You're looking a little tired today," she nearly sang.

"Enough. Or you won't get any more food from the kitchen."

She gasped. "You wouldn't cut me off."

"Try me."

"Fine. I'll let you go, but are you sure you don't want to come to Elizabeth's class with me tonight to watch her moves? I think you have talent—really, you could be one of Rye's backup dancers."

He strode out the door with a wave. Jill would never stop talking if he didn't leave. And he didn't need to go to Elizabeth's class when he could see her moves in private.

Something he definitely planned to do more of now that she was back in his life.

Chapter 21

Natalie was having a really bad day. Blake had texted her, then called and left her a message. She hadn't listened to it.

He did this every few months, so she wasn't exactly surprised. It was their anniversary today. Every time he called he said he wanted to talk about what had happened between them.

And every time, it threw her for a loop.

Why wouldn't he just let her go?

As far as she was concerned, if it weren't for her ongoing association with the Raiders, she'd never see him again.

As it was, she was girding her loins—literally and figuratively—to be around him at the upcoming dinner. And, dammit, his rock-hard body and handsome face never became less hotalicious. Heck, he practically glowed like the crazy superstar he was. What she would give to be one of those lucky divorcees whose exes got fat and went bald.

She couldn't even watch the Raiders anymore because her body still responded to him, even in those ridiculous gold tights she used to tease him about. And she'd been a Raiders fan all her life. It was almost sacrilegious to give it up.

He'd ruined one of her favorite pastimes. Raiders football. She now had to make herself scarce on Sundays around her family since they still rooted for the team. Just not for Blake. On that topic, they were silent, respecting—if not understanding—her wishes.

Her business line rang. "Natalie Hale."

"Hi, it's Terrance Waters."

Well, this was a nice surprise and totally unexpected. "Chef T. How are the Latin moves coming along?"

"Please call me Terrance, and I can assure you the Latin moves have been retired."

"Not completely though, huh?" she asked with some mischief in her voice.

Everyone knew he'd won his date with Elizabeth, and she wondered how it had gone. She'd always had a lot of guy friends, so she settled back in her office chair, prepared to give him shit.

"Wouldn't you love to know? Listen, I was wondering if you could have lunch with me this week. I want to talk to you about something. Pick your favorite place. I haven't enjoyed much of Denver's culinary scene."

Wow. She sat up straighter in her chair. "Hang on. You're driving to Denver to have lunch with *me?"* It almost came out as a squeak. Something had to be up. He was a celebrity chef, after all.

"Yep." His smugness was kinda charming.

"Care to tell me what you want to talk about?" Oh, how her mind was racing.

He laughed. "You know, I would have given you a hint, but after your gleeful attendance at my Latin dance debut, I'm not going to tell you. I'll only say you're gonna love what I have in mind." His voice was so seductive, a nun might have broken her vows.

"You totally suck."

"That's one of the reasons I like you so much. You speak your mind, something I appreciate."

"Fine, since I'm terrible at waiting, how about tomorrow?" she asked, looking at her calendar. She could jiggle around a few meetings with other clients. "I won't last more than a day now that you've put it like *that.*"

And she was so calling her sisters the minute they got off the phone. They wouldn't believe it, and they could help her brainstorm about what he wanted.

"You don't want me to be your next Latin dance teacher do you? I know you call Jill Dr. Evil."

"Sh—don't you dare tell her. She'll find a way to punish me. You Hale women are pretty fearsome."

She twirled a pen around because that's what she felt like doing. "Something to remember. Are you sure you won't tell me?"

"Nope. I'll see you tomorrow. Text me the time and address. I'll meet you there."

That was probably better. If he met her at the office, her staff would act like a herd of heifers sighting their first bull. It would be ugly. She almost laughed at the crazy stuff that popped into her head.

"Okay. See you then."

"Later, Natalie."

When the line went dead, she stared at her phone and jumped up and down in her seat like a kid. Then she called Caroline and Moira, but only got their voicemails. Bummer.

Well, they would call back.

Her voicemail box stared at her with the number one in the corner reminding her of Blake's message. Even though she knew she shouldn't, she played it. She always did.

Hey! How's everything? Hope you're doing great. Can't wait to see you at the dinner. I still miss your cooking. Don't hit me. I can't help it. Call me back for once so we can talk. I have to bribe the Raiders' events director to give me news about you. I miss you, Nat. Please call me.

Then there was a silence over the line, so profound, she had to squeeze her eyes shut, imagining him standing in their old house—the one she still missed—trying to decide how much more awkwardness he could take and how much more he should say. Blake Cunningham at his most vulnerable destroyed her every time.

Okay, I know you won't call me back. You never do, Nat, but dammit, don't ignore me at the dinner, okay? I hated it when you did it last year, and it...fucking hurt. We used to be married. We used to be...well you know what we used to be. And we need to talk...

He paused again, and this time her throat thickened. Why wouldn't he stop this?

Okay, I'll let you go. Happy anniversary, babe.

The phone fell limply from her hand to her desk, and she hung her head as old memories washed over her. There had been sparks from the moment they had met, which she hadn't acknowledged—at first. They'd started out as friends because she had refused to go out with him. Instead of resenting the way she didn't allow him to be a playboy, he'd liked it, respected it. Not that he didn't try to sweet talk her into doing the horizontal mambo jambo, but he'd never made a move when they were just hanging out. And he'd stopped dating other women, something she hadn't failed to notice. The strength of their friendship had finally made her give into the passion between them. He'd shown his faithfulness, that he wasn't some ego-centric, promiscuous quarterback like so many in the league.

Blake Cunningham had a heart, and for a while, it had been hers.

She pushed out of her chair. Well, he wasn't hers

anymore, and she wasn't his, and it pissed her off when he called her like that.

But it didn't stop her from putting her hand to that same heart that missed him too, thinking about how he'd wished her Happy Anniversary.

Like it still mattered.

Like it was still true.

Chapter 22

Elizabeth was pretty much humming up a storm the next morning. Being with Terrance again made her nervous in some ways, but her body was purring like a satisfied feline. My God that man knew how to make love.

Last night they'd reached a whole new level of intimacy, and she didn't regret any of it.

Sure, she'd felt a little awkward waking up with him, but the way he'd kissed her and kept right on kissing her had squashed that "morning after" bug.

Someone knocked on her door, and she set aside her third cup of coffee to answer it. She had a good idea who it was.

Her BFF for life stood there, all cocky attitude. "I didn't want to come *too* early."

"Smart move," she replied and let her inside. Noticing the bag in her hand, she said, "You brought lunch. Good. I'm starving."

"I had to help a girlfriend out. After a night of passionate lovemaking with Matt, I'm ravenous the next day."

Then Jane leaned in close to her face, and Elizabeth

playfully pushed her back. “I don’t have anything left for you if you’re looking for cuddles.”

“Haha. I was checking your eyes. Definitely bloodshot. And your lips...swollen. Now about that beard burn...”

“Having fun?” Elizabeth asked smugly. “I did. Say whatever you want.”

“I don’t see any hickeys.”

“Oh, for crying out loud. Terrance doesn’t lunge and bite.”

“Good to know. That sounds like something a misbehaving dog would do, and I would think he’s more skilled than that.”

“The man does have skills,” she responded, snatching the take-out bag from Jane’s hand and walking toward the kitchen. “That was never in question.”

Jane followed her in, and as she took out the plates and silverware, her friend poured them two glasses of the sweet tea Elizabeth kept for Rhett—but secretly drank herself too.

“You don’t seem upset or flustered this morning,” Jane said, a question in her voice.

“I’m not. It was...intense. I won’t lie. Over dinner, I shut down on the whole Vixen thing, and Terrance got all stony silent and took me home. I thought it was over before it had even begun, and then I realized I had to trust him with everything if I wanted to be with him again. God, I’m such a girl.” And the tough girl part of her, who wanted no man to have a hold on her, kicked her under the ribs. *I know. Being human sometimes blows.*

They set up the kitchen table for their meal, and Jane fished out croissants stuffed with Brian’s signature chicken tarragon salad and served one to each of them, along with a cluster of grapes.

“Tell me everything. Okay, not *everything*. Keep it

interesting, but not explicit."

Elizabeth laughed. "Right."

Jane munched on her sandwich and grapes while Elizabeth talked, not touching her food. Her friend was so enraptured, she had to stop her from eating a stem.

"Wow," Jane said when she finished. "And I thought Matt and I were intense."

"Please, you two are way too small-town to ever be that intense. And I mean that in the nicest way possible."

Jane shrugged. "I know."

Someone knocked on the door.

"That would be Rhett," Jane told Elizabeth. "He texted me to ask if I thought you were okay."

"Seriously? He's never checked on me after a date."

"Not every man is Terrance." Jane fished out a third croissant sandwich, this one stuffed with paper-thin slices of French ham topped with brie.

"You got him a sandwich too?" Elizabeth asked as she left the room.

"I knew he was coming, and Rhett's always hungry," Jane yelled back.

When she opened the door, Rhett looked like a victim who was at the dentist's office for a cavity filling.

"What is this? A post-coital chat?" she asked.

He grimaced. "Please don't use that phrase. Whoever came up with the word 'coital' should be horse whipped. Now, I don't want any details. I just want to make sure you're all right."

"Rhett, her skin's as dewy as if she'd spent seven days at a mud spa," Jane said from the doorway to the kitchen. "Come on in. I brought you a sandwich from Brasserie Dare."

His whole face brightened. "You did? Janey, my darlin', I swear, you are the sweetest girl on the face of the earth."

"What about me?" Elizabeth asked, protruding her

lower lip in a pretend pout.

He chucked her under the chin as he headed to the kitchen. "Did you bring me a sandwich?"

"No," she said and followed him.

"Then I rest my case," Rhett said. He took a bite of the sandwich Jane offered to him without even sitting down.

"We have chairs in this house," Elizabeth said. "We even have plates and—"

"Elizabeth was just telling me how she let Terrance take her all the way home before rushing back in her car to have sex with him."

Plopping into a chair, Rhett scrunched up his face. "Jeez, Janey, I said I didn't want those kinds of details. He's one of my friends, and Elizabeth is like my sister."

"You're such a baby," Jane said, biting into her own sandwich.

Rhett took another bite, humming with pleasure now. "Okay, just tell me whether you told him about why you became Vixen."

She thought back to how their whole future had been poised to either crash and burn or blossom based on that one decision. "I did."

"Good," he muttered as he sipped Elizabeth's sweet tea.

Resigning herself, she got up and poured herself another glass.

"You can trust him, honey," Rhett told her between more bites of sandwich.

"He doesn't want any secrets between us," she admitted, and the thought still made her stomach wobble.

"That's the best way to establish a strong relationship," Rhett replied. "So you told him about Vince?"

"I told him most of it, but not who Vince is."

Rhett shoved his chair back so he could stretch out

his long legs. "I agree. You didn't tell me until recently because you were afraid I'd beat the guy to pieces, and you were right to be worried about that. If I hadn't mellowed..."

Yeah, Vince wouldn't have had a leg left to stand on.

"I'm not sure T has mellowed enough to handle it," Rhett told her.

Jane nodded. "Normally I would be all for full disclosure and all, but..."

The memory of Terrance's bloody knuckles flashed through her mind again. No, she couldn't be sure of what Terrance might do if he learned who Vince was. He hadn't asked, but there would come a time when he would, and she would have to tell him she wasn't prepared to share that information yet. It would take more time for her to trust he'd conquered his temper. They were so new together.

Would it be enough for him?

Well, it would have to be. He was supposed to be minding his Ps and Qs so his primetime TV show would go through. Beating Vince to smithereens would harm that—and it would cause unwanted attention to fall on her because of him. The very last thing she wanted was for that chapter of her life to be opened again. If Terrance went after Vince, then the man she feared most would know exactly where to find her. She couldn't risk that. Not even if it meant Vince would finally feel the same fear and anxiety he'd unleashed on her.

"You'll back me on keeping Vince's name out of it?" she asked Rhett.

"Yes." His sigh ruffled the napkin he was using to wipe his mouth.

"Me too," Jane responded. "If he asks."

"Terrance can be pretty tenacious. If he gets something in his mind, he'll..."

Move mountains, she realized. Intensity. Passion.

She'd traced those Chinese letters on his body over and over again last night.

"We'll take care of it," Rhett told her and grabbed her hand. "I just want you both to be happy, and if you can find that happiness together, I'll be over the moon."

"Me too," Jane said softly, but even Elizabeth caught the worry in her eyes. Her friend remembered all too well how scared she'd been the night of Terrance's fight.

"It'll be fine. We're just..." She stopped herself from making light of what they had. Her heart knew better.

They'd both admitted to thinking they'd been in love with each other before, but neither of them had gone the next step and said those words in present tense. Yes, Terrance had said she'd captured his heart, but that wasn't the same. They needed to get to know each other again. There was no rush.

"Don't fight falling in love, Liz," Rhett said, patting her hand. "Trust a good ol' boy on this. At first it might taste like the worst cough syrup on the planet, but after a few sips, you realize it's intoxicating."

"Yuck," Jane said with a laugh. "That has to be the worst description of love I have ever heard. I almost want to send Abbie a dozen red roses after hearing that."

"You impugning my comparison?" he asked Jane with a wicked gleam in his eyes.

The two of them knew what that look meant.

Jane scooted back her chair until she was perched on the edge of her seat, prepared to run for her life if Rhett followed through.

He lunged for her and scooped her up without even breathing hard, slinging her over his shoulder in a fireman's hold. She was laughing as she tickled his back, her feet dangling at his waist.

"Aren't you going to help me, Liz?" Jane asked, lifting her head as best she could.

"Nope. I don't have any desire to suffer the same

fate."

Rhett laughed as he said, "Smart move, Liz." Grabbing Jane by the waist, he shifted her and tossed her in the air.

Her friend squealed the moment before he caught her again.

"If only your fans could see you now," Elizabeth muttered.

Rhett set Jane back down in her chair, grinning like the school boy he was acting like. "Are you kidding? The men would envy the heck out of me. Not every guy gets to scoop two gorgeous women up and throw them in the air."

Jane smirked at Elizabeth, who shot off her chair and ran toward the bathroom for all she was worth. It was one sanctuary Rhett had never dared cross.

She didn't make it of course, and soon she was laughing as her hair hung to the floor when he threw her over his shoulder like a sack of flour.

Soaking up every minute of their fun, she didn't protest like Jane usually did. No one had played with her like this growing up, and she felt like she was making up for lost time.

This was her family, and family did funny, crazy things together.

She knew who had her back.

Chapter 23

Fortunately, Wednesday was a slow night at High Stakes, so Terrance left the kitchen in his sous chef's capable hands and changed out of his work clothes. His chef's jacket was dotted with sauce since he'd daydreamed about Elizabeth and let a sauce bubble over, a rarity. More embarrassing than his slip, his whole staff seemed to understand what was up with him.

Apparently his Latin dance antics at the beautiful Elizabeth Saunders' class were currently top tier gossip in town. It was his first taste of small town life. Terrance was used to his life being the fodder for the media, but somehow this was different.

Dare Valley was charming, but he didn't appreciate knowing his sex life was going to be discussed at Arthur Hale's Bingo night. Hadn't Jill chortled with glee when she'd told him about that? Dr. Evil was still wreaking havoc wherever she went. He'd sent up a chocolate soufflé, hoping to sway her from her sinister ways.

Time would tell if she could reform.

Even though he wanted to push his car over the limit to reach Elizabeth's house, he didn't speed. Was he acting like a good boy or what? His mother would never have believed it.

The lights were warm and welcoming when he arrived, and he jogged up her steps only to see the door open. Framed behind a sea of soft light, she stood there, naked as the day she was born, Venus come to life from a frothy pool, awaiting her pleasure.

His loins tightened at the sight of her.

"I knew you'd be early," she said as he reached her.

Yanking her to him, he lowered his mouth to hers, and like usual, they went from hot to combustible in that precious space of a second. He'd never mastered the art of making love to Elizabeth slowly the first time. Seemed like that pattern wasn't about to change anytime soon.

He shuffled them inside and slammed the door as she tore off his clothes. The bedroom was too far away, and she was so warm and ready, he ended up pressing her against the door and kissing his way down her body.

"I'm hungry," she said with enough sauce in her voice that he had to fight the urge to take her right then. "I thought you said you'd bring me something to eat."

He bit the inside of her thigh gently and then kissed the mark. "Later. God, I want you."

He continued his path of lush kisses inward, and she grew frantic and tense in his arms. She was panting, moaning, and he used everything he could remember about her body to drive her wild. When she came, the sight of her bucking against him was so erotic he had to lock his muscles to keep from entering her. He kissed her instead and nestled her against his chest when she descended back to him.

Those luminous blue eyes finally opened. "Hi."

Even though he was straining for his own release, he kept a leash on his desire. "Hi."

"I missed you today." She trailed her hand down until she wrapped her fingers around his hard length.

"Seems you missed me too."

"Ready for round two?"

Pushing him onto his back on the floor, she straddled him, and the sight of her curvy body with her long blond hair trailing over her shoulders stole his breath.

"Are you?" she breathed out as she took the condom he handed her and rolled it over him.

He didn't answer, simply rose up to a sitting position and took her mouth again before he finally entered her. Like always, their dance was instinctive. He knew just where to thrust, how deep and how fast, while she knew exactly when to circle her hips and drive him wild.

When their releases came, he felt that familiar pull of something more, something special—the same kind of sensation he had when he created a culinary masterpiece. The kind of emotion that went beyond the everyday and into a whole new realm.

Tucking her close, he didn't fight the moment, the pull, the feeling, whatever this was with her. She laid her head on his chest, her body soft against him.

"Do you ever wonder what it is between us?" he asked in a low voice.

Her muscles tensed for a moment, then relaxed. "Yes."

He waited, but she said no more. Neither did he. For both of them, it was enough.

Soon, he realized the hardwood floor was cold, and he needed to clean up, so he stood and extended his hand to her. They made it to the shower, where they enjoyed more fun and games.

Relaxed beyond words, he retrieved the groceries he'd bought from his car. He'd had the foresight to leave them behind before coming to her door, knowing he didn't want putting away groceries to be the first thing on the menu for them. When he returned, he lifted her onto the kitchen counter. She was wearing nothing but a cream silk robe. With that view, he began to sort through the contents of his well-stocked bags.

"You didn't have to bring groceries," she chided, but picked up the celery root the size of a pineapple with a puzzled look on her face, turning it over in her hands.

He'd bet a million bucks she didn't know what it was. Heck, most people wouldn't. "These ingredients are special. You can't get them in Dare right now."

Her look said it all. "So what are you going to make me?"

"A special ingredient arrived today that I want to try out. You up for something unusual?"

She eyed his bags with suspicion now. "You don't have bull testicles in there, do you?"

Like that would ever be his perfect ingredient. He was a man after all. No way serving up some poor male's balls would be his Holy Grail. "Fennel pollen."

Her eyelashes fluttered. "Excuse me. Did you say you're feeding me pollen? Terrance, I am *not* a bee."

"Could have fooled me. Earlier you sure were buzzing like one."

She socked him. "Those are sexy sounds, not...insect sounds."

"I'm not complaining," he said, taking out the container holding what could be his perfect ingredient.

He'd stared at it earlier after cracking the seal, hoping this would finally be the end of his quest. Inhaling the heady scent of fennel, he'd tasted a pinch. The licorice and citrus had saturated his tongue, and for a moment, it was like tasting the most perfect sunshine on a summer day, the promise of peace palatable. This might be the one.

"I'm going to add it to couscous, along with the most incredible olive oil you have ever tasted from Tuscany."

"Okay, I'll trust you."

Those words did something to him. Suddenly all he

could see was her, sitting there under the kitchen lights, her skin still warm and radiant from their lovemaking. Vixen had been so beautiful, but seeing Elizabeth all natural like this... Something shifted in his heart.

The container of fennel pollen fell from his hand onto the counter. He couldn't see anything but her, didn't want to see anything else, taste anything else, experience anything else.

"Hey!" she cried. "I'm hungry here, and while I want more sex too, I want to eat first."

He shook himself. She'd misunderstood his gaze. It hadn't been lust. It had been...hell, he didn't know what. Shoving his hand into the grocery bag, he drew out the couscous.

While she sipped the wine he'd brought, a buttery Chardonnay from one of his favorite vineyards in Napa, he cut and pan-fried the celery root chips. The couscous didn't take long, and as he drizzled olive oil on it, he knew it was the moment of truth.

When he added the fennel pollen, he would discover if it was the perfect ingredient.

Dusting the soft grains with the mustard-colored powder, he drew out a stainless steel spoon and prepared himself. Whatever it was—nirvana or mundane—he was ready to accept the truth.

Taking a delicate portion, he raised it to his lips, inhaled the fragrance of lemons and spice, and then opened his mouth. The couscous was perfectly al dente; the olive oil called to mind ancient and gnarled olive trees of Tuscany; and the fennel powder gave him the vision of a field of those tall green stalks swaying in a gentle breeze on a summer day.

The taste was marvelous.

There was enjoyment, yes, but not that moment where everything stood still. Not that feeling of home, of endless peace.

He set his spoon aside. It wasn't the perfect

ingredient.

Elizabeth jumped off the counter and rubbed his back. “Hey now. It can’t be that bad. I mean your food never sucks.” Taking his spoon, she took a portion and shoved it into her mouth. Her eyes widened. “Wow. I mean, that’s incredible. Why did you look so disappointed?”

“It’s not the perfect ingredient,” he told her. “I keep looking for it, but I haven’t found it yet.”

Somehow he ended up telling her, trusting she wouldn’t think he was crazy or the biggest food nerd on the planet.

“That’s a pretty tall order,” she said when he finished telling her. “Maybe that one thing doesn’t exist. For me, it’s like ice cream, I guess. I eat it when I’m upset, hoping it will fill the hole inside me, but it never does.”

She immediately busied herself with grabbing them plates and silverware, as though she’d revealed too much. Closing the container of fennel pollen, he set aside his hopes and dreams for the ingredient. No, it wasn’t the one, but it was incredible and deserved to be honored in his kitchen.

“I’ll have to make you my Italian gelato,” he told her as he brought the food to the table. Maybe the best ice cream would bring her peace. He wanted that for her more than anything.

“I’d love that,” she replied, watching him as she lit the candles. “But what I said about the ice cream...it’s a bit...heavy. I’m sorry.”

He turned his head and stared at her. “And my story about the perfect ingredient wasn’t? Elizabeth, I *want* you to tell me things like that. No secrets, remember? Come here.”

She crossed to him, and he simply opened his arms. The moment of vulnerability was ripe between them. He held her until he felt himself settle, heard her exhale deeply. He kissed her hair and let her go with a gentle squeeze.

"Okay. Speaking of transparency, I wanted to tell you I'm driving up to Denver in the morning to have lunch with Natalie Hale about business. Since you and Jane are tight, and Natalie is going to be her sister-in-law, I would appreciate it if you didn't mention the meeting until Natalie says something."

"Well...Jane and I—"

"Don't keep anything from each other," he finished. "I know, but I wanted you to know I'm having lunch with Natalie, and that it's professional, so there are no misunderstandings. It's up to you if you want me to tell you what it's about now or after I talk to her."

"I won't say anything."

He nodded and told her about his conversation with Mac. She was quiet throughout, just sipping her wine now and again. "I told you so you wouldn't think for a moment I was interested in her," he finally said, reaching for her free hand. "I know we never talked about being exclusive before, but we were that summer. At least I was, and I think you were too since we were together almost every night."

"I wasn't with anyone else."

"Good. I don't want to be with anyone else now either. Okay?" He'd never really had this conversation before, and he felt both queasy and excited.

Commitment. His first.

"And I'd like to...shit...make love to you without a condom if you're on the Pill. I can show you my latest tests. I'm clean."

He fished out a hundred to cover the awkwardness. He'd never made love to a woman without protection before.

"I'm on the Pill, and I'm clean too. I...ah...would like there to be no barriers between us. I've...never done that with a man."

He exhaled sharply. "Neither have I." Then embarrassment made him hunch his shoulders. "I mean with a woman."

"I knew what you meant." Her eyes lowered to the table, and her pulse beat strong in her neck. "We're getting pretty serious here."

A heaviness anchored in his gut. Wasn't commitment supposed to make you happy? "We were pretty serious before. Are you thinking about running again?"

"After I just told you what I did?" she whispered. "No. I just...sometimes it's really intense between us."

He reached for her arm and drew her to him again. Touching her always settled him, and he thought being close to him did the same thing for her. Lowering his head, he kissed her gently, caressing her bottom lip like he was tasting his first Chantilly cream.

"I know it's intense. But it's a good intense, right?"

She nodded and tucked her head into his neck, everything about her vulnerable now.

"I won't hurt you."

"You can't promise that, and you know it." She caressed his nape before returning to her seat.

"Hey," he said in a soft voice as she started to serve herself some couscous.

Her chest rose with a deep breath as she looked up to meet his eyes. He hated seeing the wariness there.

"I'm not him."

She jerked like he'd shot her, and he almost regretted it. But it had to be said.

"I know," she whispered.

The victory was sweet, and a little mind-blowing to a man who'd never really believed he wanted commitment.

The first time around, he'd taken their relationship for granted. Hid his delight at their exclusivity, trying not to make a big deal out of it. With this second chance, he was going to be more intentional. Spell things out. Somehow he knew it was the key to getting her to trust him all the way. Like he wanted to do with her.

He took over, serving her the celery root chips. Simple fare, but neither one of them liked to eat heavy this late at night.

Now wasn't the time to push for more information about the man who'd stalked her. The violence in Terrance scared her, and he would learn to control that. For both their sakes.

Her trust in him was enough for now, but as he poured them more wine, he knew the day would come when he'd ask for the man's name. Then he'd decide what to do about him.

Violence wasn't the only way to punish the bastard for what he'd done to her.

Chapter 24

Natalie had chosen Beast + Bottle for her lunch with Terrance not only because it was one of the best restaurants in Denver, but because the space had housed other great culinary giants like Aix, Olivéa, and Petit Louis. As far as Natalie was concerned, there was something magical about the location, and she knew Terrance would appreciate that.

Foodies believed in culinary magic—even supposedly cynical ones like The Tattooed Chef.

She loved the restaurant's honey-colored hardwood floor, simple white walls, and white-tiled bar punctuated with white posts. There was time to savor it since she'd arrived first by design. She was already sitting at their table when Terrance breezed through the front door, causing the staff to jolt to attention. Heads turned throughout the restaurant. A few women licked their chops at the sight of him in dark designer jeans, a cream Irish sweater, a suede brown jacket, and tan Italian boots.

Natalie knew the owners, and out of courtesy to them, she'd mentioned Terrance was dining with her when she made the reservation. It seemed only fair.

Terrance would have spotted her immediately given the restaurant's size, but the hostess brought him over with aplomb—like the distance between the front of the restaurant and their booth in the corner of the restaurant was akin to a trek across the Kalahari Desert.

When he sat down, Terrance planted his elbows on the table and leaned forward. "You gave them a heads-up, didn't you?"

She cocked a brow. "If you were the chef here, wouldn't you want to know?"

His smile reminded her of a silent movie actor preparing to swing from one pirate ship to another for treasure. "This is going to be fun. I like that kind of thinking. Only confirms why I drove up here today to meet with you."

"Yes, it *is* a bit of a drive, and I'd bet you aren't getting a lot of sleep these days." She batted her eyelashes playfully. "Now, are you going to tell me straight out why we're meeting or are you going to make me poison you?"

He chuckled. "Like any chef, I have a phobia of poison, so I guess I'd better tell you."

A server appeared at their table, all bright eyed and bushy tailed. "Chef T. It's an honor to have you eating with us today. Chef wanted me to tell you he has something special prepared for you both if you're willing. Of course, you can choose anything from the menu, but we wanted to make your visit to Beast + Bottle memorable."

Natalie had to bite her lip to keep herself from telling the server to buzz off. Her insides were jumping up and down like cheerleaders on the sidelines, eager to hear Terrance's news.

"I'm happy to enjoy what Chef has prepared. Please send him my thanks. Natalie?" His mouth quirked like he knew this interruption was driving her nuts.

"That would be lovely. Thank you."

She suffered through ordering drinks, but the instant their zealous server left them, she leaned forward. "Okay. Spill it. You're killing me."

He settled against the back of the booth, acting like he had all day. "At my request, Mac Maven would like to offer you the position of the onsite catering director of The Grand Mountain Hotel. You would also oversee the catering menus for all of the other Four Aces hotels, working closely with me to ensure the guests enjoy the type of culinary experience I have in mind."

This was...wow. Her mouth dropped open. "Shut the front door."

"No thanks. An elderly couple is walking in. I try to treat my elders with respect."

"Are you kidding me?" Matt might have put him up to this as a cruel escalation in their ongoing bumper sticker war.

"Nope. The job is yours if you want it. I can promise you that working with me is going to raise your profile nationally."

No kidding.

"How many hotels are we talking about?" she asked, slumping against the booth now.

"Four others besides The Grand right now, but a new one is being constructed in Vegas."

Vegas. She felt a swoon coming on. "That's six hotels," she breathed out.

"Good. You can count. I wasn't sure. It didn't say so on your resume on LinkedIn."

The banter snapped her out of la-la land. "Smart ass."

"Usually I would say you can't call me that if we're going to work together, but one of the first things I liked about you was your directness. Most people can't kiss my ass fast enough, and the women..."

She rolled her eyes. "Okay, so you're irresistible. Tell me more."

"You're not attracted to me," he continued. "That makes this work."

"It's not you," she said.

His hand went up, stopping her explanation. "I know. Our server is coming, beaming even more sunshine. Hold that thought about how attractive I am."

Six hotels was all Natalie could think as the server set down Terrance's sparkling water topped with a lime. And all of them catered to big-name clientele like Rye Crenshaw and his buddies...

"I'll have a glass of your finest champagne," she declared.

"Of course," Happy Server Girl immediately said. "Chef, would you care for a cocktail?"

"No, I have to drive back to Dare Valley." Left alone again, Terrance raised a brow. "Does that mean you've accepted?"

She could be coy with the best of them. "I'm celebrating the offer, which is undoubtedly an honor, but it's not a yes—yet. Tell me more."

"I knew you wouldn't be a pushover. Let me tell you what I'm thinking."

What he outlined was her dream job—a job she'd never thought possible. Running her own company and having clients like the Denver Raiders was one thing, but working with a chef like Terrance on catering menus for six hotels and a series of elite events...

She was in a whole new ballpark, like coming up from the farm team to the big leagues.

When he mentioned Mac was willing to talk about a joint venture, she took a healthy sip of her newly arrived champagne. "You're serious? I would have thought—"

"There's a reason he's open to it. One, because I asked. Two, because I want you to bring your bigger clients to the table."

Now she saw where this was going.

"You want the Raiders."

He shrugged. "Among other things. I told Mac that I want to cater special events in Denver and select other locations when the profile is high enough. It's good business for his hotels and for me. I plan to be my own Wolfgang Puck."

Aha. The big picture was emerging now. "Chef to the celebrities, catering big events like the Governors Ball at the Academy Awards. With his own kitchen line and food products, not to mention his own show." His willingness to come to Dare Valley finally made sense. Mac's high-class hotels broadened his reach, especially the one being built in Vegas. Tons of big-time chefs worked in Sin City.

"The kitchen line and *gourmet* products—"

"Pardon me for calling them 'food,'" she interrupted dryly.

"Those products are in play, and they're starting to be rolled out now that the financing is in place with one of the biggest investment banks in New York. Mac and I are planning an exclusive line of Four Aces products right now as well. Unlike some chefs on TV, I actually want to stay in the kitchen. Mac understands that and has given me carte blanche to hire anyone I want who can support my schedule."

"Because you being on primetime TV is also a good advertisement for Mac's hotels." Notwithstanding an exclusive line of gourmet products co-branded with the hotel chain. What would it be like to have your face on a food label? She wondered if he'd choose a drawing of himself like Paul Newman or a real photo like Emeril Lagasse?

"Bingo."

"Carte blanche, huh? That makes me feel like I need a crown."

"And who knows? If you're a good girl, I might have you on my TV show."

Now that made her sputter. "Seriously?"

"I can't make promises, but why not? You love food, and I bet you'd be a natural in front of the camera."

She signaled to the server for another glass of champagne. "Since lunch is most definitely on you."

"If you think Chef is going to charge us for anything, you're crazy. Having me here is good PR for his house. Trust me. There might be pictures later. I'll even tweet about our lunch here if the food's good enough. Their reservation list will go through the ceiling."

Yes, it would. "While we're talking about what we both like, I like that you know you're famous and have influence but aren't a jerk about it."

A reluctant laugh crested across his lips before he shook his head. "See. That's what I'm talking about. You're not afraid to call a spade a spade, and I sense I can delegate things to you and have you run with them. You're going to make my life a lot easier by bringing me catering menus in keeping with my brand for the hotels once we talk about what that is. Of course, you'll have to work with the onsite catering directors, but I expect you can play nice with others."

Being from a big family, she'd learned that lesson quick. "You're right. I'm very good at what I do, and I expect we'll work well together." Her sisters were going to scream when she told them this news.

And then she realized she would have to leave Denver.

"I'd have to move home." God, she would miss her sisters. Their weekly girls' nights were the most important part of her social life now that she was divorced.

"Don't you like Dare Valley?" he asked as the server headed their way with a tray of appetizers.

"Yes." Growing up there had been a dream, but she'd needed to move to the city and experience...more than Dare Valley had to offer.

Chef had gone all out with the apps, from lamb

sweetbreads dotted with crème fraiche and chives with a venison reduction laced with bourbon to pork belly roasted with figs on piping hot flatbread. When Natalie tried the guinea hen terrine, one of her favorite dishes on the menu, she groaned.

"Damn! Chef knows his shit." Terrance drew out two hundred dollar bills with a grimace and stuffed them into his pocket.

"Better put that money away or people will think you're buying my *services.*"

"You'd go for more than two Ben Franklins, and anyone who says otherwise, doesn't know his sh—. There I go again. Giving up cursing is harder than quitting smoking."

"When did you stop smoking?" she asked.

"When I started cooking food seriously in high school. It screwed with my taste buds, so it had to go."

"There's not much you won't sacrifice for your career, is there?"

"No, and I don't apologize for that. So tell me what you're thinking."

This time her smile could have outshone Mae West's. "I'm thinking I want to negotiate with Mac. But I have one condition for you. I want my key staff to come with me."

He nodded. "I understand that. You want to work with people you trust."

Whew. What a relief he understood that. But whether her staff would be willing to move to Dare Valley was another question altogether.

"I'd like to see you and your staff in action at the Raiders' dinner."

And just like that, she was thinking about Blake's voicemail again. She was going to see him—and soon. Was she prepared for that? Having Terrance there might be too complicated.

She crossed her arms. "You'll make my peeps

nervous, and it's a big night for me. For us."

"All the more reason to see you all in action. I promise I'll be nice. Besides, I'm not cursing out anyone in the kitchen anymore. I'm Mr. Nice Guy now."

"Sure you are." Though it did seem to be true. From what she had seen, the Tattooed Chef was reforming.

"So, you'll talk to Mac?" he asked, slicing a piece of the sweetbread and studying it.

"I'll talk to Mac," she agreed, thinking about what she wanted from this deal.

"He'll give you want you want," Terrance said like he'd read her mind. "Just don't beat around the bush. While the man likes poker, he prefers his business dealings to be more straightforward."

"I'll keep that in mind."

They sampled the entrees the server brought out. At one point, Chef appeared and took a few pictures like Terrance had predicted. While the guys were busy talking shop, Natalie texted her sisters about the offer. She would wait until she was finished with lunch to call her mom and text her brothers. That would need a different approach. Danny would be overjoyed to hear she was moving to Dare Valley, but until the deal was sealed to her satisfaction, she didn't want to raise her nephew's hopes.

"Are you ready for dessert?" the chef asked. It took her a moment to realize he was speaking to her.

"I'd love some," she responded. When the Beast + Bottle's chef was out of earshot, she picked up her conversation about Mac. "How about I call Mac from my office after we finish up here? You can come with me to meet my staff. Maybe it will ensure no one barfs or swoons when you come to the Raiders' dinner."

His brows knitted. "I've had women swoon but never barf."

"I was talking about the men. They might gag over how fashion-forward you are." She gestured to his clothes.

"You're a pain, but I like you. If you'll excuse me, I'm going to call Mac so he'll be ready for you. It wouldn't be fair to spring you on someone unsuspecting."

As he wandered off, a few women's gazes slid to his butt. Natalie was glad she was immune. No man had captured her attention since Blake.

Maybe moving to Dare Valley would give her the fresh start she needed.

But it couldn't touch the numbness that had taken root inside her two years ago.

Nothing but Blake could, and now she was moving even farther away from him.

Chapter 25

Elizabeth stood on her front porch basking in the sunshine beaming down on Dare Valley, clearing her mind from her poker research for Rhett's next tournament. May had finally produced spring weather, and with the temperature edging close to seventy today, she planned on soaking up every bit of the warmth.

When Terrance cruised down her driveway, her insides started to tingle. He'd rearranged his schedule to have lunch with her at Brasserie Dare, explaining that he wanted them to see each other in daylight hours too. For the past few nights, he'd come over after his shift at The Grand, making them a light meal before taking her to bed and reminding her no one had ever pleasured her like he could.

"Hey," he called as he emerged from the car and slammed the door behind him. "Nice day we dialed in."

Decked out casually in jeans, a white T-shirt with the words *Give Me Food or Give Me Death,* he looked good enough to eat.

"I know! The sun feels marvelous."

He jogged up the stairs, planted his hands on her waist, and kissed her until she was breathless. She trailed her hands through his hair, her nails lightly digging into his skull.

"Did you get everything done this morning?" she asked when he turned his attention to her neck.

"Yes. You have me for at least two hours. Then I have to get back to start dinner prep."

Even though they'd made love that morning, she pressed her hips to his. "Do you think we can eat fast?"

Edging back, he ran a finger down the center of the silver-threaded blouse she was wearing. "Why? Do you have something in mind?"

She let her hand trail down to his marvelous backside. "How about a nooner?"

His mouth flashed a wicked smile. "Before we eat? How uncivilized."

Then he picked her up Prince Charming style—something he'd never done—and carried her across the threshold. She had to tell herself not to get carried away, but it was dashing and romantic and made her heart feel like it had been filled up with a warm bubble bath.

As soon as he deposited her on the dining room table, she grabbed his shoulders, and he spread her legs. When his fingers found her bare under her denim skirt, she moaned.

"You planned this," he breathed out as he sent a forest fire raging across her skin.

"Oh, yes. You said you wanted us to do 'daylight' things. I figured this was one of them. We're not vampires, you know. We can make love when the sun is out."

"In that case," he said, picking her up again and heading out to the back. "Sunshine you shall have."

He opened the door to her deck and carried her to the Adirondack chairs, sitting down with her straddling him. Throwing her hair over her shoulders, she enjoyed the sensation of it trailing down her back, the sun's warm rays on her face.

"You look so beautiful," he whispered.

Coming out of her sunshine trance, she opened her eyes. He was staring at her like he was still getting used to seeing the real her. Like he was in awe.

Tracing his cheekbone, loving the feel of his stubble on the pads of her fingertips, she said, "So are you."

Those bottle-green eyes darkened, and all she could think was that this wasn't going to be a quickie after all. There was way too much connection here. Like always.

He took her mouth as his hands opened the buttons of her blouse, moving so slowly she thought about taking over. But she let him take his time and simply rocked her pelvis into him.

"You're driving me wild," he said in a hoarse voice.

"That's the idea."

Her hands slid under his T-shirt, and she stroked the hard muscles of his chest as he pushed her breasts up above her bra, playing with her nipples.

They kissed again, and the energy between them was like the promise of summer all around them. Taking their time, they loved each other slowly, him kissing her breasts while she stroked the long length of him.

When he pressed inside, she let her head fall back as she started to move. "Oh, Terrance."

Sometimes the feelings he evoked were so powerful, she simply didn't know what to do with them. But her body seemed to know. It went with the flow of them, making her moan as they increased the pace.

Their mouths fused again, and his hands cupped her hips, inviting her to take more of him. She did. She always could.

Soon she unraveled, crying out to the blue sky and the sun, which served as witnesses to all they were becoming. When he found his release moments later, he tucked his head into her neck, breathing hard, still gripping her tight against him.

"I could stay with you like this forever."

Now that he could stay inside her after they'd found their release, he often did. Her heart had made a funny jolt the other day when she'd awoken from sleep to realize they were still joined. It was like he wanted to remain a part of her for as long as possible.

She thought it unbearably sweet.

Kissing her neck, he finally laid his head back against the Adirondack, leaving her with no choice but to edge back a little to give them both more room.

His smile was a mere tilt of his mouth and so darn sexy it was criminal. "It just keeps getting better, doesn't it? I love being inside you."

This wasn't the first time he'd said it, and she cleared her voice over the emotion clogging it. "Me too. We should go if we're going to have lunch."

"In a bit. I can take as much time as I need. My staff will do fine without me."

"I thought you said you only had two hours."

His hand traced the ridges of her spine. "I can be flexible. Moments like these aren't meant to be rushed. Look! Isn't that a bald eagle?"

She tilted her head back, squinting in the sunlight. Sure enough, there was a white head and a yellow beak visible. "Yes. Aren't they majestic? I love it when they come around here. They seem so still when they rest in the branches of one of my trees."

His hand continued its hypnotic stroking of her back. "You'll have to call me when that happens. I'd love to see it. Being a city boy, I never saw much wildlife growing up except for an occasional hawk in Central Park."

"Have you seen a moose yet?" she asked.

"No. Are they common around here?"

"Ask Mac to tell you about his Porsche getting totaled by one. He was trying to protect Peggy from being chased by a moose that wanted her key lime pie."

He laughed. "You're kidding. I'll have to get the

recipe for that. If a moose wanted it..."

She joined in with his laughter, and a new peace settled inside her. Here they were, nestled together, sharing an appreciation for nature and telling funny stories. This ease between them had always been there, but they'd established the terms of their relationship now, and... Well, she found herself relaxing more. Almost like her heart had finally agreed to let the sentry guards defending it take a much-needed break.

"I like this," Terrance said, taking one of her hands and kissing the palm. "We need to have more daylight time together. I'll see what I can do."

Usually she held back from responding to sweet statements like that, uncomfortable with the vulnerability it entailed. But like the eagle circling above, she felt bold today.

"I like it too," she whispered and leaned in to kiss him.

His muscles jumped under her hands, like he was surprised by her response. Then he wrapped his arms around her and hugged her tight.

She let her eyes close and savored the feel of him. "I have something for you."

"More than you've already given me? This must be my lucky day."

Disengaging, she padded across the deck naked and retrieved the box she'd wrapped earlier. When she handed it to him moments later, he snatched her back onto his lap.

"A present?" he asked. "It's not my birthday."

Nerves pinged inside her as he tore the wrapping paper off and opened the box. His bark of laughter immediately soothed her.

"A crystal piggy bank for dollar bills," he said.

"I thought your Cuss Fund deserved its own place of honor."

"I adore it." His finger stroked her cheek. "I adore

you."

When their mouths met, the kiss felt like it was a testimony to everything transforming between them.

"If Brian didn't know we were coming, I'd stay right here," he whispered against her lips.

"I know, but we need to go. Besides, I'm starving."

They finally disengaged, and she felt a strange absence inside her. Okay, that was weird. And a little scary.

After they cleaned up, she told him she'd take a car so he could head straight back to The Grand. He agreed, and she followed him into town.

They'd told Brian they were coming, just as Natalie had done at the restaurant in Denver. Elizabeth had liked the idea, thought it was only fair. Checking her watch as she parked her car and left to join Terrance, she realized they were twenty minutes late for their reservation. Oh well. Nothing they could do about that now.

He was waiting for her outside the restaurant. "We're late. Hopefully Brian won't think I'm trying to mess with him."

She took a long look at him. "If I look anything like you do, they'll know exactly why we're late."

His brow quirked up. "You're right. With the way you're glowing, they'll know. I need sunglasses in the best way possible. Let's go."

When he held out his hand like they were sweethearts, she didn't hesitate. She took it and turned her face toward the sun.

Chapter 26

"Chef T," the hostess said with a bright smile. "Elizabeth. Welcome to Brasserie Dare."

Terrance hadn't been inside the restaurant before, and he was charmed by the quiet elegance of the place. The café scenes from Paris on the walls transported him to that magical food city. And if the smell of freshly baked baguettes was any indication, the food was going to be incredible.

"Sorry we're late," Elizabeth said immediately, something Terrance wouldn't have done. "We got held up."

Having fabulous sex. He wondered what the hostess would say if he added that out loud?

Terrance squeezed Elizabeth's hand, but she kept her gaze on the hostess, like she was afraid to look at him. There was a blush creeping across her cheeks. Well, now...wasn't that interesting? And really adorable. He wanted to kiss her right then and there, but he knew it would only make her more self-conscious.

"Let me show you to your table and get you something to drink. Chef Brian will be out shortly to greet you."

Once they were settled, the server brought them sparkling water with lime at their request. Chef Brian McConnell strode out of the back of the house, and Terrance rose to shake his hand.

"Chef T," Brian said. His handshake was strong and self-confident, attributes Terrance respected.

"Chef," Terrance responded.

"I was wondering when you were going to come to my house," Brian said, planting his hands on his hips. "Jill has been chewing my ear off with stories about teaching you her dance moves. If she asks you, tell her I said I was jealous of any man who sees her do those moves in private."

That sounded like Jill, so he laughed. "Absolutely. She's quite a pistol."

"Indeed. I'm a lucky man. Hey, Elizabeth. Good to see you."

"Hi, Brian," she said, tracing the condensation on her glass.

"I see the dance challenge had a happy ending," Chef Brian said. "Good for you two. Now, let's get down to business. Are you up for a private tasting?"

Was there any other kind when he went to a restaurant for the first time? Chefs always rolled out the red carpet. "Of course. What do you have in mind?"

"I was tempted to go Latin since you seem to like that sort of thing, but this is a French establishment."

Terrance laughed. Okay, now that Dr. Evil's lessons were behind him, he was starting to see the humor in the whole dance drama. "What were you planning? Turning on salsa music and having your server jimmy an aspic so it looks like it's shaking its hips?"

Brian chuckled, and a few customers leaned forward in their seats, straining to hear their conversation. Everyone had pretty much been staring at them since they'd arrived, taking discreet photos too.

"Does an aspic jimmy? I might have to try that one

out. No, I thought we could go for something else. How about we start you off with a charcuterie plate of some artisanal cheeses, meats, and my house-made venison pate?"

"Sounds excellent," Terrance replied. "I'm developing a new appreciation for venison."

"And since Elizabeth likes soufflés," Brian said, winking at her, "I made one with goat cheese. I also have seared beef tenderloin with a divine cognac peppercorn cream sauce, followed by a traditional walnut oil salad from the Périgord region."

Terrance was liking this more and more by the minute. The man knew his regional French cooking, something he appreciated.

"And for dessert?" Elizabeth asked.

"Yes, I know you and Jane love your desserts. I made a clafoutis with wild cherries, which I flambé with an aged French brandy."

"I like the variation," Terrance told him. "Thanks for putting this together."

They were going to be waddling out of here from the sounds of it, but he'd known better than to expect a rising chef would serve him a croque-monsieur sandwich and French fries and be done with it.

"It's my pleasure. Jill is really happy to be working with you. When the twins start sleeping more than two hours at a time, we want to have you guys and Mac and Peggy over for dinner."

You guys. He glanced at Elizabeth. The look in her eyes told him that she knew what he was thinking. Holding hands. Going to dinner parties together.

They were a couple, and while it was still new for them both, it felt *right*.

"What's your perfect ingredient?" he asked Brian, enjoying the shop talk. "The one you know you'll have in your pantry as long as you can cook because it settles down everything inside you."

"I know it's not very inventive, but it's herbs de Provence. When I receive my shipment from Paris and open the bottle, I just...it's like I'm there. Home. You know?"

When he was a punk kid working as a dishwasher and busboy in his first restaurant, Terrance had thought it unmanly the way the male chefs in the restaurant waxed poetic about spices and other ingredients. What self-respecting alpha male did that?

But over time, something had changed within Terrance. The making of each new dish had unleashed new aspects of him until he had a sacred appreciation for cooking and all it encompassed. Passion. Sustenance. Community. Pleasure. Beauty.

He'd succeeded in his craft because he believed in the magic and artistry of cooking. It sounded like Brian was a kindred spirit...even if he was married to Dr. Evil.

"Yes, I know."

"What's yours?" Brian asked him.

"Haven't found it yet, but I'm still looking."

With a clap on Terrance's back, Brian gestured to the server who'd just emerged from the kitchen door. "It's a great adventure. How about we bring out the first course?"

Terrance settled back into his chair. "We're looking forward to it."

When the venison pate arrived, Terrance spread a thin layer on a slice of the perfectly crisp baguette that was still warm in his hand. When it hit his tongue, he tasted game, spice, and a little cognac.

"Delicious. You should try it."

Elizabeth only buttered a slice of baguette. "I don't eat Bambi."

"Ah, come on. It's remarkable." He prepared a slice and nudged it toward her. "You didn't think you'd like snails either."

How he'd always delighted in exposing her to new

dishes, new tastes.

"It's the garlic and butter. Otherwise, they're still snails." But she took a bite of the pate and shrugged. "Not my favorite."

"Okay." He could respect that. Not everyone had the same tastes. "You'll have to excuse me then for eating it all."

"Eat away," she told him, and because her voice had turned sultry, reminding him of how hot and wet and tight she'd been making love with him in the sunshine, he slid his leg forward and caressed her calf.

She licked her upper lip and played with the top button on her blouse. Yeah, she'd always been able to give as good as she got when it came to this type of foreplay. He slid his leg away. Everyone was still watching them, although they'd resumed eating, and he didn't need that kind of moment captured on Twitter. After all, he was supposed to be acting like a good boy for Lane.

As the meal progressed, Terrance's admiration for Brian's talent only grew. The man had a way of bringing together typical French ingredients with his own personal flair. Every dish stayed with him after he finished eating it—the hallmark of a great chef.

When Chef Brian returned at the end of the meal, as they were finishing the cafloutis, Terrance said, "Are you sure you won't consider working with me at The Grand? I could use a chef like you to handle the day-to-day."

Brian's mouth might have parted a little in shock, but he quickly recovered. "Thanks, Chef T. Coming from you, that's a real honor, but I love running my own house even though working with you would be an incredible opportunity. I look forward to seeing your new menu at The Grand."

"You're welcome to come by as my guest any time. You can even bring my former dance instructor."

Chef Brian shook his hand. "She'd love that. Thankfully, we have lots of babysitting help, so we might be able to make it."

"Thank you for a wonderful meal," Terrance told him. "I wouldn't be surprised if you end up with a Michelin star here." And he meant it. He would even tweet about Brasserie Dare later to boost reservations. It wouldn't hurt his own list at The Grand. He'd never believed in cutthroat competition.

The chef's chest puffed out like a rooster. "That's what I'm working toward. Be nice to have one grace my house. It was good to see you again, Elizabeth. Tell Jane and Rhett 'hi' when you see them next." Again, he nodded to a server, who came forward with a white paper bag. He handed it to Elizabeth. "Since you and Jane like my croissants so much, these are on the house. A couple of chocolate and plain ones for you to enjoy."

She stood and kissed his cheek. "That's so sweet. Of course, I won't be hungry until tomorrow after all of that incredible food."

"I'm glad you enjoyed it. I'll see you both out."

After they said their goodbyes, Terrance walked to the sidewalk with Elizabeth. The sunshine was still pouring down on them, and all he wanted to do was go back to her place and make love some more. He put his hands on her shoulders.

"Go," she said, reading his mind. "You have a job and so do I. We can pick up where we left off later."

He leaned in to kiss her. "I'll text you when I'm heading out to your place."

"How about I meet you at yours?" she asked. "Just to mix it up."

Music to his ears. He thought about it for a second—only a second—and dug into his pocket. Fishing out the extra key to his house that he'd been carrying in anticipation of the right moment, he held it out.

"This is yours. Come whenever you'd like. Bring

some things over."

They both knew it was a big step, but it wasn't like their relationship was brand-new. Her eyes seemed to zero in on the key.

He held his breath, suddenly nervous. Was it too soon for her?

"Okay," she finally said and leaned up to kiss his cheek. "I'll see you tonight."

No key in return. Well, there was still time. At some point, she would trust him enough to give him one. He was counting on it.

As she walked away, she looked back, her blue eyes twinkling. "Maybe I'll cook you macaroni and cheese. From the box."

He knew he was grinning like a fool, but he was powerless to help it. "If you do, you'd better run for your life. I don't do 'box' anything."

"Snob," she called and then disappeared from view.

He was parked in the opposite direction, so he took off at a brisk pace. Checking his watch, he winced. It was three o'clock.

"Shit."

Great. He'd cursed. For a while there, he'd thought he would make it through the day without having to fish out a Ben Franklin.

When he reached his car, he drove down the side street to intersect with Main Street. Turning right, he spotted Elizabeth standing on the sidewalk, her face pale and stricken, talking to a man he didn't recognize.

He slowed his car. When the man's hand reached for her arm, she tried to pull away. He didn't let go of her, caging her in as he kept talking. Terrance's hands gripped the steering wheel. She was afraid of this guy. He could tell from the look on her face—the same look that had been there the night he came to her house and saw the baseball bat by the door.

Slamming to a halt in the street, he popped his

hazards on and ran toward them.

"Hey!" he shouted at the guy. "Get your hands off her."

There were a few people on the street, and a woman gasped. The man's head jerked around, and he froze in place.

"I was just trying to talk to her," he told Terrance when he reached them.

Elizabeth was trembling as she edged away from the man. Terrance pulled her close. Her skin was like ice.

"Are you okay? Is he bothering you?"

"He's..." She took a breath and shook herself. "It's okay. I'm handling it."

Clearly she wasn't. He turned back to the man.

"Leave her the fuck alone." He was too keyed up to care about cursing. Every protective instinct in him was raging.

"I was just talking to her," the guy said again, and Terrance even hated his voice.

"Well, she doesn't want to talk to you, so you'd better leave her the fuck alone."

He didn't have to flex his fists. As a kid, he'd known that his voice could be as intimidating as his body, and he'd learned to use both. The image of the other guy who'd laid hands on Elizabeth came to mind. Terrance forced himself to relax, knowing how much his violence scared her.

He could control this situation. He had to. For the sake of everything they were becoming.

The man took a few steps back and bumped into a lamppost. "I was just trying to see her again. We went out."

She'd dated this loser? "Well, she doesn't want to go out with you anymore. She's with me now, so leave her alone, or you'll answer to me."

He could say it. He didn't have to follow through.

The guy nodded and back peddled a few more steps

before turning and running down the street.

Terrance turned to Elizabeth and cupped her shoulder, rubbing the muscles there to bring her gaze to him. "Are you okay? Talk to me, babe."

Her body was still shivering with fear, and her blue eyes were troubled. "You shouldn't have done that...I was handling it...I need to go."

He hadn't even hit the guy, and she was still running?

She was halfway down the street by the time he caught up to her. "Elizabeth, I didn't hurt that guy even though I wanted to. Badly. Come on, babe, let's go talk. I can drive you home."

He would leave the dinner prep and any other business that came up to Jeremy tonight. She was too important to him to do otherwise.

She shook her head, making him want to grind his teeth. "No. I need...some time by myself. To think. Go to work, Terrance."

Then she took off, leaving him on the street as people wandered past him, whispering feverishly.

"Dammit!" he said under his breath.

Helpless, he stood there another minute, letting his blood cool. He was raring for a fight, but he'd restrained himself this time. He wasn't the pissed off street fighter he used to be, cruising the Big Apple, ready to use his mouth and fists to trample his way through life.

Terrance had curbed his impulse to beat the shit out of the guy who was bothering her. He had tried a different tack, but it hadn't mattered. Elizabeth was still scared of him.

He lowered his head, his heart heavy.

She hadn't told him about this asshole bothering her. That hurt. Just when he thought they were getting so close. Well, if anyone would know about this guy, Jane definitely would. Keeping Elizabeth safe was too important to put this matter to rest without any follow-up.

Even if she didn't like his tactics.

Chapter 27

After checking on the dinner prep, Terrance discovered his sous chef had everything running smoothly. Telling his staff he would be back by six, he ventured out again.

When he pulled into Jane's driveway, she was playing in her yard with the three dogs Elizabeth had told him comprised her new canine family post-Raven. Annie, her Chinese Crested, was dressed up in a pink doggie T-shirt, which made Terrance grimace. Why did people dress up their pets? He just didn't get it. While the golden Labrador, Henry, took off running for the car, the older chocolate lab, Rufus, stayed where he was, next to his owner like Mr. Chill himself.

As he got out of the car, Jane shielded her eyes and called out, "Terrance? Is everything okay?"

Yeah, she'd know he was supposed to be at The Grand.

"I need to talk to you about Elizabeth," he said as his feet ate up the distance between them, Henry jogging by his side. "There was a guy harassing her on the street today, and it sounded like it's happened before. She's upset, and I don't freaking know what to do for her right now."

Okay, so he'd managed not to drop the f-bomb in front of Jane. A minor victory.

"Oh no! Damn that Ryan James."

Now the jerk had a name. "He said they used to date...and he had his hands on her. I wanted to..."

"Kick him in the nuts?" Jane asked. "That's what I want to do."

Even though Jane was short and petite, Terrance didn't doubt for a second she could kick ass. And it made him feel better about how he'd reacted.

"Come on inside. I'll put the dogs in the play room."

She picked up Annie, who was prancing beside a goofy-looking Henry. The more stately Rufus looked like the indulgent grandparent to two youths from a younger generation.

He followed her into the house. While she was situating the dogs with water and a snack, he dug out his phone to check on whether Elizabeth had texted him. She hadn't, so he decided to text her.

Hey. Are you okay? I'm worried about you.

When there was no immediate response, his hands curled around the phone. Dammit.

"She's not responding to my texts," he told Jane when she finally came back into the den, two glasses of iced tea in her hands.

His publicist had left him a voicemail and followed up with a text.

Call me.

Ignoring her for the moment, he took the drink from Jane out of politeness, but didn't take a sip. "Tell me what's going on, Jane. This is the reason she had a baseball bat by the front door, right? Is this guy stalking her like the guy at Harvard?"

She looked away, like she was trying to decide what to say.

"Talk to me, Jane. I care about her, and I don't want

to see her get hurt."

Setting her tea on the dining room table, she took a seat. "What's happened with Ryan is nothing like what happened at Harvard. He's persistent, though, and it's triggered her. Triggered me." She held up her hands. "Even I'm shaking."

He'd known her for a while, not as long as Rhett, but he still considered her a friend. He took her hands for a moment. "I'm sorry. I don't mean to upset you."

"You're not the one to blame. It's men like Ryan who won't back off...and the ghost from the past Elizabeth has tried to put behind her."

And your ghost too, he almost said. Another man might have stalked Elizabeth, but Jane had been shaken to the core because of it. And who could blame her?

"I'll go talk to her," Jane said softly.

His frustration grew, and he had to curb his voice of its anger. "I appreciate that, and I know she'll want to see you, but I'm with her now. I care about her. I need to be able to help too, and I can't when she closes me out like this."

"I know. I've always liked you, Terrance. You're a good guy despite your rep. But I can't help you here. Elizabeth has to figure this out on her own. I know that's not what you want to hear, but I have to be honest with you. Why don't you tell me what happened earlier?"

Once he was finished, Jane stood up with her hands clenched by her side. "You're not the only one who sometimes doesn't know what to do. You did the best you could. You protected her. I know she's been trying to handle Ryan by herself, but he hasn't been listening. Part of me has to wonder if she's scared to be more assertive because of what happened at Harvard. She tried assertiveness before, and it backfired on her."

His mind spun tales of her standing up to the guy at Harvard only to be beaten down by a bully who scared her so badly she fled town and became Vixen.

"Will you tell me your account of what happened at Harvard?" he asked.

That time in Elizabeth's life was the key to understanding her.

Jane shook her head. "I know she's told you some things, but she needs to be the one to share the full story with you, Terrance."

He stood up, wanting to throw the chair across the room in frustration. "Then what do I do here?"

"Give her a little space. She knows she has to face these issues and overcome them."

"Not alone, she doesn't."

The first whisper of a smile crested across Jane's face. "No, she has us, but we can't fight her fear for her. That's something I realized a long time ago. She's gotta do that part herself. We can only love her while she tries."

He lowered his head, feeling the weight of helplessness. "Okay. I don't like it, but..."

Jane patted his back. "We have to trust that she can do it, you know? Elizabeth trusted me to find myself, and I need to do the same for her. She *will* overcome this. And hopefully you put the fear of God into Ryan James enough so he won't bother her anymore."

And if he hadn't this time, he would the next. No one was going to stalk the woman he loved.

Loved? Yes, he'd been scared to put what he felt for her in those terms again, but he *did* love her. No woman had ever made him feel what he did for her.

He'd loved Vixen.

Now he loved Elizabeth Saunders too.

"Does Rhett know about Ryan?" Terrance asked.

"Yes. But Elizabeth told him she was taking care of it. She was worried about what he might do to him."

Somehow it was a comfort to know she feared Rhett's reaction too. "If Rhett had warned him off before now, that incident on the street today would never have happened."

Jane picked up Annie when she appeared, snuffling at her owner's ankles. "I know this might be hard to understand, but sometimes we need to do things on our own."

He held up a hand. "I get it. I just don't see why another deterrent is a bad thing."

"It's not." She crossed the room to the side table by the couch and picked up her phone, juggling Annie. "I'll go see her if she's open to it. Why don't you get back to work and let things...unfold?"

He hated letting things unfold. Terrance Waters was the type of man who made things *happen*.

"If that's the only thing I can do right now." He shoved his hands in to his pants pockets. "Will you let me know if that changes?"

"Of course. Now go ahead and get back to work. She'll reach out when she's ready."

He would cook up a storm to keep his mind busy. The only other thing that would keep him distracted was if he went home to punch his bag some more, which wouldn't help anybody. Plus, he still had a job to honor, and he'd been away from High Stakes most of the day.

"Thanks, Jane." He kissed her on the cheek. "I'll talk to you later."

When he was at the door, Jane said, "Regardless of how she reacted, Terrance, I know my friend. She appreciates the way you stuck up for her."

When he reached the car, his phone buzzed again. Hoping it was Elizabeth, he dug it out, only to discover it was the biggest primetime network jerk of all time. Probably to poke at him more.

Then he wondered if this call was related to his publicist's messages. Something started to curdle in his stomach. He let it go to voicemail, not in any state of mind for a call with that asshole. Best hear what was going on before responding. He played the voicemail from Lane.

It's all over Twitter about you and that former poker slut, Vixen, and how you lost your cool with another guy. I told you not to be seen with bad girls, Terrance, and I can't say I like this press one bit. I don't care if she's put that bad girl persona behind her. This is not the kind of move that will get me to approve your TV show. You'd better dump her and tweet that this was nothing serious.

Oh shit! Their altercation on Main Street was on Twitter now? No wonder his publicist had been trying to reach him.

And as for Lane's comments about Elizabeth...Nothing serious? Dump her? Who did this asshole think he was?

Terrance pulled over to a scenic highway overlooking Dare Valley because all he wanted to do was race around the mountain's curves at one hundred miles an hour to exorcise his rage. But that was stupid. And he wasn't stupid anymore. His rage didn't control him. Earlier on the street, he'd been able to restrain the urge to punch Ryan in the face.

A lot of good that had done him.

He pulled up his Twitter account, and sure enough, he had a media blitz on his hands. Someone had tweeted a picture of Elizabeth, Ryan, and him on Main Street with the comment: *Chef T protecting his new lady love.*

His face was scrunched up, and he looked like he was going to kick some serious ass. Elizabeth looked scared, and Ryan whatever-his-name-was looked like a deflated bully.

Lady love, huh? Over ten thousand woman had commented on the tweet already, saying what a lucky lady Vixen or Elizabeth was. There were thousands of tweets by guys posting old pictures of Vixen, saying Chef

T had another hottie on his hands. Their lewd comments made him swear a blue streak. Other tweets were about him losing control of his reputed temper.

The media circus was a disaster.

He let out a string of curses. After today, his Cuss Fund would be pretty much bulging with Ben Franklins.

He was about to call his publicist back when her call popped up on his screen. Great minds...

"I've been trying to reach you," she said without a hello.

That's why he'd hired the no-nonsense New Yorker. After discussing possible statements with her, he decided to take the path of least resistance with Lane and not mess up his probation. They were going to say that Elizabeth was an old friend, and he was catching up with her in Dare Valley.

Until the two of them talked about officially announcing their relationship to the media, he didn't think any other response was fair.

Plus, he had to think more about Lane's comments. Was the man warning him that he wouldn't approve Terrance's show if he dated Elizabeth?

No one dictated his personal life, and Lane could stick a Ben Franklin up his butt if he thought otherwise.

Chapter 28

After talking to Jane, Elizabeth settled down on the couch with a Bond movie. Her heart wasn't feeling ripped at its seams anymore after hearing Terrance had visited her BFF out of concern. Jane told her Terrance was really upset and worried. While she hadn't told her to call Terrance, Elizabeth could read between the lines.

Her friend approved of Terrance, and that confirmation gave Elizabeth a sense of peace. Jane had never approved of any of the other men she'd dated, thinking they were shallow and not truly interested in loving her.

All true. Elizabeth had chosen guys like that on purpose.

Except for Terrance. At first she'd assumed he was like the others because of his badass rep.

But no.

He had hidden depth and a big heart. Yeah, he still was a street fighter, but even though he'd obviously wanted to hit Ryan, he'd held back after knowing what his fight at The Peacock had done to her. To them.

That meant something.

The whole incident had triggered all her repressed

anxiety again, and she hadn't been able to process anything until she was safely home with the door bolted behind her. Her mind had shut off, and the only thing she'd been concerned about was getting away.

Now she could step back and see Terrance had been able to control his temper this time. As she watched James Bond beat the bad guys and save the world, she decided to tell him the rest of the story about Vince. About everything.

She was just reaching for her phone when it buzzed. Rhett.

Had Jane told him what had happened? Or maybe Terrance?

"Hey, Rhett," she answered.

"Hey. Why didn't you tell me that Ryan guy was still bothering you?" The edge in his voice could have cut steel.

"Who told you?"

"Nobody did, and believe me, I will be talking to Jane and T about that. You'd better check out Twitter. Dustin just showed me over a hundred tweets about you and T. Our account is blowing up. There's a picture with you, T, and this Ryan jerk on the street, and it looks like he's about to kick the guy's ass, which I totally approve of. But the rest of it? Elizabeth, the Vixen stuff is all over Twitter again, and some of it's pretty ugly."

They were on Twitter? Fantastic. "Thanks, Rhett. I'll call you back."

She hung up, logged into Twitter, and started scrolling, her gut sinking as she read tweet after tweet after tweet. There were so many of them she finally went to Terrance's main Twitter page to see what he was saying. When she read his latest tweet, her heart stopped.

@elizabethsaunders formerly @vixen who works for @rhettbutlerblaylock and I are old friends. We were becoming reacquainted. Nothing more.

Old friends?

He'd used one hundred and thirty-seven characters out of the one hundred and forty Twitter allowed.

That's all it took to break her heart.

She read it again. *Nothing more?*

How could he say that after everything they'd been through? After he'd given her a key to his house today?

She threw her phone, and it bumped off the sofa's cushions. To think, she'd just decided to tell him *everything*.

She was a fool.

But she wasn't going to take this lying down. She deserved an explanation, and he was going to give it to her. They were *old friends* after all.

Grabbing her purse, she tossed the key he'd given her earlier inside it and zipped it shut. There had to be an explanation for his tweet. No man had ever looked at her the way he did.

Her mind was spinning out scenario after scenario on the way to his house. Dare Valley's lights cast a golden glow in the middle of the dark mountains surrounding it. Of all the places she'd thought she might reencounter Terrance, this hadn't been one of them.

For the moment, she didn't want to think about the ugly picture of them on Main Street. She looked like a victim in it, and she'd never wanted to look that way again.

Time to stop acting like one.

And that started with Terrance.

It was eleven, and his house was well lit, so she knew he was home. He opened the front door as she tore out of her car.

"Hey," he said as she came up the stairs to his porch.

"Hey," she said and then took a deep breath, choosing her words carefully. "Do you want to tell me what your tweet was all about?" Her voice rose as she asked him.

His expression was remote, and she couldn't read him for once. "We hadn't talked about releasing the news of our relationship to the media. I didn't want to do that without talking to you first, and since you needed some space...I did the best I could do after talking to my publicist."

The hurt around her heart started receding, replaced by the sudden urge to cry. "So you didn't mean anything by your *old friends and nothing more* comment?"

He rubbed the bridge of his nose, and she finally saw how tired he was. "Of course not. I was trying to herd Twitter cats, Elizabeth, not make a romantic proclamation. And we *are* old friends. Just a heck of a lot more than that. I love you, dammit, and I've never felt that way about a woman. When you pushed me away today—like you were scared of me—I thought I'd lost you all over again."

Her heart swelled. He loved her. Now. As Elizabeth. Even after today. "Oh, Terrance."

"Hey," he said softly, pulling her against him. "I'm sorry you thought I meant anything by that. I just...I didn't know how else to try and defuse the situation. I didn't mean to hurt you or scare you. God, Elizabeth. Tell me we're okay. I'm dying here."

He smelled like grill smoke and musk as she pressed her face into his chest. His arms were warm and comforting. While the night sounds surrounded them, she let herself settle into his embrace.

"I was scared I'd misread you again," she whispered. "I couldn't...think in that moment on the street. I just wanted to get away and be safe."

"I can understand that, but I won't lie—it hurt. God! I don't want you to be afraid of me. I'd never hurt you."

"I know that," she whispered.

His eyes lifted, and inside them she saw the vulnerability of a usually confident man plagued with doubt. "Do you?"

"Yes. And once I was able to process what happened, I realized how much you held back your temper."

He edged back and cradled her face in his hands. "It wasn't easy for me. Just like you were fighting years of wanting to be safe, I was fighting years of wanting to intimidate someone with my fists. Maybe we can keep working on our old patterns together. Just don't...shut me out like that. I thought I'd lost you."

"I'm still here, Terrance," she said, kissing his jaw, trying to soothe him through touch—something they'd always used to express these jagged emotions no words could capture.

"Elizabeth. I gave you a key to my house and told you to bring whatever you wanted here. I've never done that with another woman."

Her nod was perfunctory because her throat had closed with emotion. "I love you. I'm sorry I was too afraid to say it before."

There was a gleam in his eyes when he met her gaze, as if the moonlight was radiating from them.

"Thank God. I wasn't sure...you'd ever say it." Those quiet words sounded almost sacred, like he was speaking from the top of a great mountain or in an ancient cathedral in Europe.

Her hands clenched the rigid muscles of his back. "Terrance, other than Jane and Rhett, no one's ever loved me. And after everything with Vince and my parents...I didn't believe I could love anyone romantically. Trusting a man with myself seemed like the biggest mistake I could ever make."

His chest rose as he took a deep breath. "Vince? Is that his name?"

"Yes," she said, feeling a cold wind hurl through her now.

"You're shaking. Come inside with me."

Nestled against his chest, he led her into his house. "How about I make a fire?" he asked her, settling her on the couch, kneeling at her feet, and reaching for the Irish throw and covering her.

"That would be fine," she responded, her muscles locked in the shivering and tensing rhythm of fear.

"What about a glass of wine?"

She knew what he was doing. He was trying to make it easier for her to tell him more about events he knew were painful for her.

"Okay."

He kissed her cheek as he stood and prepared the fire. As the kindling started to catch, the wood popping and hissing now, she gazed into the flames. Orange and blue. So beautiful. Creation and destruction in the same element. Like life, it seemed. Her life. The image of the phoenix came to her again. Because of Vince, Liz Parenti had met Rhett and become Vixen. Everything she'd worked toward at Harvard had been destroyed. The journey she'd taken since hadn't been what she'd expected, but it had been what she needed. Now she needed to decide how the story was going to continue with Terrance in her life. And in her heart.

When Terrance returned with a glass of wine, she gripped the stem as he sipped what smelled like bourbon.

"Talk to me," he simply said and held out his hand.

She held it while she told him, sparing nothing this time. Every painful detail came out into that quiet firelight and was burned away, sealing the old wounds that needed healing.

A few tears rolled down her cheeks, and he set their drinks aside and squeezed her hand, never taking his gaze from hers.

From the hard line of his jaw, she knew he was becoming more and more upset as the words continued to tumble out of her raw throat. But he said nothing.

For that she was glad.

When she finished, she rubbed that delicate line of

flesh under her jaw, the one Vince had wrapped his hands around once, squeezing so hard she'd thought he was going to kill her.

"Oh, God," she said, overcome.

"Come here," Terrance whispered and pulled her onto his lap, rocking her back and forth as his touch finally forced the chill from her bones, something the fire hadn't been able to do alone.

"Have I ever told you how amazing you are?" he asked moments later. "To go through all that and survive? And not just survive, but triumph? I'm...overwhelmed by you. God, Elizabeth."

Her eyes squeezed shut. More tears spilled down her cheeks. "But I'm still so scared sometimes. I don't feel like I've...overcome it." Hadn't she run again today?

"You're being too hard on yourself. Things like that stay with you." His exhale had a jagged edge to it. "I still get sick to my stomach if I hear a baseball connect with a bat. Do you know why? Because a kid in my neighborhood took one to my friend's head one day when we were fourteen. He didn't die, but he was never the same again. Everyone has something they have a hard time getting over, Elizabeth."

Even Terrance. The thought soothed her. He seemed so much stronger than she was.

"Ryan has been bothering me," she said, returning to today's events. "We went out once, and I tried to be nice, but he's just one of those guys who keeps asking for another chance. I don't think he's violent, but he scares me. I've been afraid of what he might do if I'm too assertive."

His rocking motion turned more jerky, and she could feel the powerful emotion he was restraining. "You don't need to worry about him anymore. I promise."

She knew he was trying to be encouraging, but his vow to protect her scared her too. He was capable of hurting others if it meant protecting her. The thought turned her stomach.

"I know it's not fair to ask you this, but I don't want you to hurt anyone for me. Ever."

He leaned back to gaze at her. The fire lit his tense features. "I know you don't, and I understand that. Today was really hard for me, but I reined in my temper. The best I can promise you is to keep trying."

"Thank you."

His arms drew her closer, and he nestled his face into her neck. "Oh, Elizabeth. I'm dying here."

Now it was she who needed to soothe him, soothe all of the violent places that had been triggered for him today. She cupped his jaw and kissed him gently on the lips.

"Be with me."

His mouth was soft on hers as he lowered her to the couch, the fire warming them both. As they touched each other with a new reverence, the firelight flickered over them, pressing away the darkness. Her blood beat strong in her body with wanting of him. Her heart pounded with love for him.

When she took him into her core, the strong, muscular lines of him cresting over her like the powerful waves of the ocean, she surrendered. Laid herself bare.

And let him take her home.

Chapter 29

Terrance woke to the insidious chirping of a bird outside. Elizabeth was pressed against him, her backside nestled against his hips, her blond hair cascading across his chest.

The vulnerable line of her shoulder drew his gaze. All of that velvet white skin. He pressed a gentle kiss there, not wanting to wake her. Last night had been so emotional for both of them. Even now, hours later, Terrance wanted to take Vince apart with his hands. Hurt him like he'd hurt the woman he loved.

It was probably a good thing he didn't know the guy's last name yet. She hadn't shared it. All she'd said was that he was from a powerful family, and because her voice sounded hoarse and tear-clogged, he hadn't asked questions. Just listened. That's what she needed from him.

And if he were being honest, he'd needed to keep a lid on the raging emotions inside him. It had been a long time since he'd wanted to call up his old street pals and beat the shit out of someone. He'd wanted to punch Ryan.

Now Vince. Well, he deserved a beating.

Terrance knew the difference. He'd given and received both.

He was amazed Rhett had refrained from doling out his own brand of justice after finding out the truth. They would have to talk about that.

She stirred and stroked the arms he had around her, as attuned to him as he was to her. Something had happened last night. Saying *I love you* to another person changed everything. He wanted to fight her battles. He wanted to cheer her on. He wanted to talk with her and laugh with her every day. He wanted to lose himself in her arms.

"You're awake," she said, shifting in his arms so she could turn onto her side and face him.

"Hey," he said, cupping her nape and kissing her gently on the lips.

Sleep hadn't cleared from her eyes, and he could feel the hollowed out fatigue in her. They'd come together twice more after going to bed, each seeking the other as an anchor. Every touch had been filled with reassurance and acceptance, something words were too inadequate to convey.

As he leaned back and met her gaze, peace suffused him, almost like there was no beginning or end to the moment.

She was his.

And everything was well.

Then a new knowledge rolled through him, one he'd been waiting so many years for, one he'd searched the globe for.

Elizabeth was his perfect ingredient.

As she snuggled close to him, running her hand down his forearm, the awareness tore through his system. For a man whom cooking had saved, he'd figured it would be some exotic spice, some rare, hand-picked delicacy. Something like Manny and his grandmother had discovered.

Not a woman. Never a woman.

And yet it was *this* woman.

"Elizabeth."

As if sensing his mood, she pressed a kiss to the underside of his jaw and used her palms to push him onto his back.

"Let me love you," she breathed against his lips.

His eyes closed as he gave her his surrender. Let her trail her fingers in all of the spots she knew he loved. When she traced his tattoos, he could see them in his mind's eyes. The griffins that had given him the courage and wisdom to survive the streets and make something of himself. The Chinese letters that defined his credo.

Her mouth was warm and soft as she kissed his skin, not rushing. No, she was taking care with him, cementing all of these new emotions into his skin.

He groaned when she went lower, and his hips started to rise in anticipation. But he didn't want to come that way. Not without her.

"I want to be inside you," he said on a groan.

Edging away, she sat on his thighs to take him into her. As he slid deep, so deep, she took his hands in her own and brought them to her breasts. Even with his eyes still closed, he knew their shape and weight, how to touch and caress them so her head would fall back in pleasure. Everything in him was sensation mixed with love, and it was more potent than the best meal of his life, the one that had changed everything.

He'd been eighteen at the time. *Coquilles St-Jacques,* a traditional French recipe for poached scallops, was the most daring thing he'd ever made, and it had amazed him that he, a kid from nothing and nowhere, could make a gourmet dish like that. It was the first time he remembered feeling proud of himself. And it had filled him with hope that his life could be more, that *he* could be more.

Being with Elizabeth gave him a peace he'd never

before experienced, one that filled up the hollowness that had always been a part of him.

And something even more powerful—the hope for a future together.

He opened his eyes, needing to see her. The lush curves of her body fired his blood, but it was seeing the way that familiar blond hair trailed down her breasts, strands sticking to her full mouth, that filled his heart like an overstuffed pastry bag.

"I love you," he whispered, the words still so shockingly new and mind-blowing.

Her slender throat moved as she swallowed. Yes, the words were new to her too, both the giving and receiving of them.

She undulated in a motion that ripped his control to shreds, taking him deeper. "I love you too."

Their hands joined as she started to move in the exact way he needed, and he met her in a way designed to heighten her passion. After they came again together, he drew her onto his chest, keeping them joined, feeling the combined force of their heartbeats, an echo of the passion and love they'd shared.

Like they had the night before, they held each other, not needing words. Soon she rose onto her elbow. "You need to get to work."

That was the last thing he wanted to do right now, after everything that had passed between them. Still, he turned his head to glance at her clock on the nightstand like a responsible adult. "How about I make us breakfast before I leave?" It was only ten thirty.

"Sounds like a plan. Do you want to shower first?"

He raised a brow. "Any reason we can't shower together?"

That swollen mouth curved. "You can't seem to keep your hands off me."

His hand stroked the smooth round of her behind. "You're the same way with me, but I see your point. Let me grab a quick shower. You can start the coffee." There was reluctance in his voice, prompting an enticing smile from her.

"Deal." She pressed a kiss to his lips, and he had to admit he really liked the softness of the gesture.

Even kissing her had changed.

He slid out of bed and headed to the shower. When he reached the bathroom door, he turned to watch her snuggle against his pillow.

Should he tell her she was his perfect ingredient?

A part of him winced from embarrassment. He'd been pursuing his Holy Grail for nearly two decades. His chef friends all knew about his tireless pursuit. What would they say when they heard it was a woman? Manny wouldn't laugh at him, he knew. His friend and mentor would be elated to hear Terrance had finally found his own perfect ingredient.

The knowledge was still too new, so he decided to keep it to himself a little longer. Last night had been intense enough. There would be another occasion to share that with her, one filled with romance and light-heartedness. He didn't want to run off to work after making such a declaration.

"What?" she finally asked, those blue eyes aglow with the knowledge that he didn't want to leave, not even for a minute.

"Just thinking how beautiful you are," he replied and turned toward the bathroom.

He would wait for a special moment to say the words. For him, they were more important than *I love you.*

Chapter 30

Elizabeth slid out of bed finally and donned a gray silk robe, marveling at how so much had changed in such a short time.

He loved her. He'd actually said the words.

And the way they'd made love last night? It had felt as if their souls were speaking to each other.

They'd moved to a whole new level of sharing and intimacy, and for the first time, she understood what Jane had said about her relationship with Matt. Two people who'd admitted their love for each other could move the mountains. The way Terrance had listened and loved away the hurt had healed her somehow. Every cell felt lighter today, and for that she was grateful and more than a little humbled.

Humming, definitely another new action for her, she headed into the kitchen. Since he'd shown her how to operate his high-tech Italian coffee maker, she breezed through the process. Soon the smell of his pricy, special-made blend suffused the kitchen with its dark, exotic roast.

She detoured to the den to find her cell phone. Jane had called and then texted her, so she texted her back to say she was with Terrance and would call her later. Part of her didn't want to go on Twitter, but she did anyway. No more hiding. Problems could only be solved if they were faced head on.

There were still tweets pouring in, but nothing dire, thank God. Terrance's statement had done its job.

Her phone rang then, and although she didn't recognize the number, she decided to answer it. It might be the media, but she felt prepared to respond to their questions now. In the late part of the night, she and Terrance had agreed to tweet today that they were romantically involved. Since any stories about her impacted Rhett, she needed to start tackling the situation. She was his publicist, after all.

"Hello. This is Elizabeth Saunders."

"Hello, Liz."

A chill ran down her spine. No one called her Liz except Jane and Rhett, and there was something familiar about this man's voice.

Her solar plexus grew tight, like she'd been sucker punched. "Who is this?" she asked.

"I like your new name. It's so much more elegant than your old one. But it doesn't really fit with the slutty Vixen, does it? Didn't I tell you that I always knew what you were?"

Dear God, no. Recognition clicked. She broke out in a cold sweat, and her heart thundered in her chest.

"Hello, Vince," she managed to say in a raspy voice.

"So you remember me, do you, babe? I wasn't sure when I saw all of those pictures of Vixen with other men. I've missed you, Liz. You shouldn't have run away from me. We were so good together."

Her fingernails dug into her hand. *Stay calm. Don't let him get to you.* "Vince, I'm hanging up now, and I swear to you that I will call the police and report you if you ever call me back. Liz Parenti might not have been able to fight you, but Elizabeth Saunders can."

"But why would you want to fight me when we have a friend in common?"

Fear stole over her like ice water, and she clutched her robe tighter. "I don't know what you mean."

"Why, Terrance, of course. I saw you two on Twitter, and wasn't that a surprise? Your hair is different, but I recognized you right away. Terrance likes the bad girls, doesn't he? Did you tell him about me?"

Nausea choked her throat, and she had to sit down when her knees threatened to give out. No, Vince couldn't be his friend. He would never befriend such a monster. "What about him?"

"Answer me! Does he know about me, Liz?"

His old threats played in her mind. *I'll kill any man you're with. Do you hear me, Liz?* Would he try and hurt Terrance?

"He doesn't know who you are. He has nothing to do with this."

"Oh, but he does, Liz. You probably don't know who's financing his food empire. You know, his new venture into household goods and gourmet products."

Bile rose to the back of her throat. "No. It's impossible."

"He's with the best investment bank in New York, Liz. We started financing celebrity product lines ten years ago as a special niche. It's great advertising for the bank, and Terrance does like the best. But you know that. Except that he doesn't know you like I do."

Her skin was crawling now, like there was a swarm of flies covering her skin. Terrance's future was tied up with the man who had destroyed her life.

"I could cancel his new venture with one call, Liz, baby. Do you want me to do that?"

"No," she whispered, all her forced bravado gone. "Leave him out of this. Please, Vince."

"I like hearing you beg me. I've missed that. You'd better keep quiet about us, baby. I have a lot to lose now, and I don't need Terrance getting all upset. He's known for his temper. I'm afraid he might make a big mistake and come at me if you tell him who I am. You're going to make sure that doesn't happen, aren't you?"

How would Terrance react, knowing his banker was the same man who'd stalked and terrified her? Ryan was nothing compared to Vince, and Terrance had barely been able to restrain himself from punching him.

And if he did attack Vince, he'd lose everything. Not just the financial backing of his new venture, but his primetime TV show.

It would be all her fault.

"I won't tell him if you stay away from me and don't mess with his deal."

"I don't trust you. Just in case you're thinking about finding Terrance a new banker, let me assure you that I won't let him go. I know how you think, Liz. I'll ensure the production and distribution of his product line is halted. Permanently."

The thought of finding a new financier would have come to her at some point, but he'd already boxed her in...just like in the old days. "He'll sue you."

He laughed. "To what end? Our bank is one of the most reputable in the country. I'll say Terrance welshed on his contract with us. I might even say he...exhibited that volatile behavior he's so famous for, and we thought he was too great a capital risk. You know what that label does in business circles, Liz."

She did. If Harwick & Taylor thought Terrance was a business risk, everyone else would too. Their word was golden. "I don't understand why you won't let him go, Vince."

"Don't you? Before I wanted Terrance because of his fame, but that pales in comparison to having a renewed connection with you. Keep your mouth shut this time, Liz. What I did to you and Jane's lawyers last time will be a cake-walk compared to what I'll do to you and

Terrance if you don't play ball."

The key in the cell he'd fashioned for her turned in the lock, and she felt an all-too-familiar powerlessness steal over her. "We'll do it your way, Vince."

"Good. Then I'll look forward to seeing you at a few of the get-togethers Terrance usually attends in New York, assuming he brings you along. Make sure he does. I want to see you again. I like your hair, by the way. It suits you so much better than the dull brown hairdo you had at Harvard."

Stars appeared at the edges of her vision, and she felt herself on the brink of collapse. "I need to go, Vince." *She had to get away from him. Hide. Find a safe place again.*

"You'll go when I say so."

His words were hard like steel, and they cut through her flesh. No, this could not start again. She reached deep for any final strength, and like a life preserver in a vast ocean, she latched onto a thread.

"Terrance is here, Vince, and you don't want him to overhear us, do you?"

She jerked her head around to make sure he wasn't finished with his shower.

"You bitch. I don't like thinking of you with him. You were supposed to be mine." He was breathing hard now.

"You have a wife, Vince. I saw it in the news. You need to stop this."

"Don't talk about my wife. You don't deserve to speak her name, you slut."

Slut. Bitch. Whore. He'd called her all those things, not to mention how he'd slashed her tires and followed her, making her think she couldn't escape him.

"I'm going to go, Vince, before Terrance comes out. I won't say anything as long as you uphold your end. Don't call me again."

She punched the End button with a shaking finger.

The phone dropped into her lap.

He'd found her. He'd finally found her. And it wasn't over.

He was financing the dream of the man she loved and using that fact to threaten her all over again.

She wanted to weep, raise her fists to the sky. Scream. Life was so fucking unfair.

Shivering from the aftershocks of the call, she wrapped the Irish throw around her. She'd just made a deal with the devil.

To protect herself.

To protect Terrance.

Not just his financing and his primetime TV show, but his life. Who knew what Vince was capable of? He had enough money to hire people to hurt Terrance. She knew the violence he was capable of. Her mind flashed to the memory of him gripping her throat and threatening to kill her and any man who touched her.

Vince's voice held the same menace and craziness as it had at Harvard. She'd hoped time would tame him, but she'd read enough about stalkers over the years to know their brand of violence and intimidation didn't just disappear unless the person sought help.

Vince wasn't the kind to seek help. He was deeply disturbed, and his family was always there in the wings to conceal his mistakes. Like they had with her, branding her a gold-digging liar in court when she fought back.

"Elizabeth," Terrance called out.

She jumped in place, pressing a hand to her pounding heart. *Get control of yourself. He can't see that you're upset or he'll ask why.*

"I'm in here," she replied, hiding her hands under the blanket.

If he saw them...

"What do you feel like? French toast? Waffles? Oh, I know, how about eggs Benedict? You always loved...

What's wrong?" He strode across the room and put his steaming blue mug on the coffee table.

The lie was bitter on her tongue as she spoke it. "I shouldn't have read some of the tweets."

His mouth turned grim. "Dammit! I don't like seeing you like this." He rubbed her arms like he knew she was cold. "Forget them. Haters have to be the unhappiest people on the planet."

"People are going to say things," she responded, keeping her voice as even as possible.

"How about I tweet this? *Leave my girlfriend alone and fuck off.*"

Girlfriend. Any other time it would have been sweet, but she was too scared and cold for it to warm her now. "I think you're losing a fortune to the Cuss Fund."

"It's going to a good cause. The Children's Aid Society in New York is going to love me. I owe about two grand after yesterday." He inhaled deeply like he was trying to regain control of himself. "Seems I haven't started off any better today."

Hearing he was helping troubled kids—New York City kids who were struggling like he once had—undid her. He was such a good man, and he didn't deserve this mess she'd dragged him into. She leaned her head into his neck, inhaling the clean scent of him from his shower.

"You're not doing so bad, and as you said, the money is going to a good place. We just need to let these tweets roll off our backs."

"How are you supposed to do that when you're Rhett's publicist? I know you can't go radio silent on Twitter."

She'd loved handling Rhett's social media accounts. Now, she wanted to delete herself, and every sign of her, from the digital world. But that was impossible. "You're right. It's my job. I'll just need to grow a thicker skin."

And develop a better poker face with Terrance.

"Come here."

His arms wrapped around her, and she wanted to weep. She loved this man. There was no way she was going to let Vince hurt him and everything he'd worked so hard to accomplish.

"I love you, Terrance." The words burned her throat, laced with fear and desperation.

"Hey, I love you too. We're going to get through this, I promise. I'm going to have my publicist tweet about our relationship today and talk to my network boss. We just need to help everyone see the new you and not Vixen. Can we tweet about me going out with a Harvard grad? And then there's the whole thing about you having a higher IQ than me. I can joke about how you're slumming with me."

Hearing the undercurrent of shame in his voice, she pressed back. When she took his face in her hands and looked into his eyes, she could see the vulnerability from the street-smart kid he'd once been.

"Stop. No one is slumming here. We both have our pasts, but we both have value."

A part of her heart burst open as she realized it was true. Liz Parenti hadn't believed it, but she'd grown wiser as Elizabeth Saunders.

"You have value," she whispered. *And so do I, regardless of what Vince says.*

His eyes lowered, and for a moment, she could see him fighting his own demons. "How about we say we're a match made in heaven? I'm a food genius, and you're a poker genius?"

She traced his cheek, never wanting to leave this house. If they could stay here forever, they would be safe. "That's much better."

His nod told her his demons had been vanquished. Now she only needed to vanquish hers with Vince.

Chapter 31

When Terrance left her with a long, sweet kiss, Elizabeth broke down and cried, releasing all of the pent-up emotion crushing her chest.

Over a cup of chamomile tea, she told herself she'd done her best against Vince. Elizabeth was stronger than Liz. She would need that strength to keep this secret from Terrance.

But she couldn't keep it from Jane.

Twenty minutes later, she knocked on her best friend's door. Matt answered, which threw her for a loop. If he'd come home for "lunch," they were finished. He was dressed in tan dress slacks and a white shirt.

"Elizabeth! Hi! Come in. Jane and I have been thinking about you."

Jane and I. It was still weird, adjusting to the new tagline they used, but it was nice to have someone else who cared about her.

He gave her an impromptu hug. "You look like you needed that. Come on in. Jane's in the kitchen. I was just heading back to work."

Annie trotted up to her, and because Elizabeth needed the comfort of that sweet dog, she stooped to pick her up. Henry, who'd followed his smaller friend, immediately whined.

"He's still a little jealous when other people don't pet him first," Matt said. "We're working on that. Right, Henry?"

Matt held his hand out for a shake and the dog lifted his paw. Given how rambunctious Henry had been when Jane and Matt first met, the progress was remarkable. Rufus looked on like a proud papa from the corner where he lay sprawled.

Sure enough, her BFF was washing up a dishpan when Elizabeth walked into the kitchen.

"Look who's here, hon," Matt said, following her into the room. "I'll leave you two to your girl talk. This guy's gotta get back to work."

Walking over to her friend, he planted his hands on her waist. She leaned back and gave him a soft kiss. "Mayoral candidates can't be slackers—even if they sometimes eat lunch at home."

"I'll text you when I can meet you at the park to walk the dogs. I love you." He gave her another smacker and then turned away. "Bye, Elizabeth."

Stroking Annie's tuft of hair on her head above her yellow sweater with blue flowers, Elizabeth managed a smile. Barely.

"Are you okay?" Jane came over and hugged her immediately, dog and all. "I was so worried when Rhett told me about those tweets. You know me. I'm not on Twitter, despite all your prodding."

Since Jane was a rising poker star, the exposure would do her good, but that was the last thing she wanted to talk about.

"*Jane*."

Her friend must have heard the quiver in her voice because she pressed back instantly. "What is it? What's happened?"

Setting Annie on the floor, Elizabeth took Jane's

hands and squeezed them tight. "You have to promise me something. I won't ask you not to tell Matt, but you can't tell Rhett or anyone else what I have to tell you. Especially Terrance."

Only last month, she and Jane had finally blown the lid off their secret because of Jane's love for Matt. Now she was asking her friend to put it back on because of her love for Terrance.

"Okay," she said after a long moment. "What happened, Liz?"

She felt herself dissolve, the muscles in her face toppling like bricks in an earthquake. "Vince found me, and he's Terrance's banker."

Jane's face paled. "*No.*"

"Yes," she responded, nodding her head erratically, the shock rolling through her again.

Her friend's arms came around her and squeezed her tight, just like they had when she came home from her first run-in with Vince. "Tell me."

Through tears and a few sobs, she told Jane everything. By the time she finished, she was shivering again, and the dogs were whining, sensing her distress, nudging at her legs in comfort.

Jane finally stepped back, her hands on Elizabeth's shoulders. "You're safe. He can't touch you. I promise you, Liz. *He's not getting to you this time.*"

The worry that Vince might come for her in Dare Valley had crossed her mind, but she'd told herself he had too much to lose. "I'm afraid for Terrance. Jane, he all but threatened to destroy him. I can't let that happen."

"So you're going to keep quiet and not tell him? Liz, Terrance has a right to know he's doing business with the man who hurt you, who's *still* hurting you."

She should have guessed her friend would feel that way. "You don't know how much Terrance wants to be Wolfgang Puck with his kitchen items and gourmet food products, not to mention the primetime TV show. Everything he's worked for is just starting to come together."

"Not at the expense of you and your safety. That wouldn't be worth it to him. Dammit, he came to me to ask me what he could do after your run-in with Ryan on the street. He loves you, Liz."

She remembered the tender way he'd looked at her in bed a few hours ago. "I know it, and I love him, which is why I have to protect him from Vince."

"Let someone else finance Terrance. He's a hot enough commodity. I know it would be difficult from a business perspective since his products are just launching, but he'd do it for you."

"Vince already anticipated that." And she told her about the full threat concerning Terrance's business venture.

"Damn Vince!" Jane reached down to stroke Henry when he whined again. "It's okay, boy. I don't care what Vince is threatening. Liz, Terrance wouldn't want you to protect him, not like this. Tell him and let him decide what to do."

"Enough! Even without Vince's threats, you didn't see how close Terrance was to hitting Ryan yesterday. He'll tear Vince apart with both hands, and that will give Vince plenty of ammunition to do what he wants. He'll ruin him."

"You don't know for sure Terrance will react that way. He restrained himself yesterday."

She did know. She'd felt the caged tension in his body last night, which was his reaction to simply hearing about Vince. "This is totally different and you know it."

"I disagree. You need to give Terrance the choice. Just like I did when Matt was running for mayor."

"*Mayor?* I'm sorry, but Terrance is a *celebrity,* a national figure. That's nothing like running for mayor in a small town."

There was a stunned silence as Jane turned away.

Elizabeth reached for her. "I'm not saying this to hurt you or impugn Matt in any way. I'm only trying to explain why it needs to be this way, Jane. I don't want to deal with Vince ever again, and if this is the price, I'm willing to bear it."

"And what about those parties Vince mentioned Terrance bringing you to?" Jane asked, her voice rising now. "This isn't over. He wants to see you again, Liz. He's still obsessed with you. What are you going to do then?"

Visions of him finding her at a party and putting his hands on her again made her want to vomit. "I'll make up an excuse not to go. It will be fine."

It had to be.

Her friend remained cold and silent.

"Please, Jane! Support me in this." Tears coursed down her cheek. "I need you. When he called...I was so scared."

One tear trickled down Jane's face, and then another. They reached across the room for each other, crying, each reliving those horrible months at Harvard that had changed their lives.

"I'm sorry," Elizabeth cried. "This is the best I can do right now."

"I know," Jane whispered. "Just promise me you'll be open to another way if Vince doesn't keep this...I won't call what that bastard offered a truce."

The venom in her voice dried up Elizabeth's tears. "Okay. We'll see how it goes."

"I don't like keeping this from Rhett," Jane said, clutching her tight. "He'll be hurt if he finds out we didn't trust him."

Hadn't she thought of that and hoped there would be a way to confide in him? "I know, but you know what he'll do. He'll join forces with Terrance to beat the shit out of Vince. It would hurt both of their careers."

"Rhett wouldn't care," Jane responded, pulling back so she could grab some tissues from the counter.

But would Terrance? He would defend her. That she knew. But would he regret losing everything he'd worked for? How could he not? Cooking was everything to him, and they hadn't been together for that long. Even their love was new.

"This is how I want it to be."

After blowing her nose, Jane washed her hands and poured them two glasses of water. "Okay, but I don't like it. Any of it. I'll tell Matt, but only if he promises not to say anything. He won't like it, but he'll do it for me."

No, Future Mayor Boy wouldn't like it. The man was the All-American kind who kissed babies and shook hands with citizens because he liked it, because he wanted to better the community.

"Thank you."

Jane handed her one of the glasses, and Elizabeth took a big drink to soothe her aching throat.

"That's what best friends for life are for, right?" Jane had said the same thing to her when Vince first became a problem. Elizabeth had told her to find a new roommate and to avoid her until the danger passed.

Jane had refused.

"I love you, Jane," she whispered.

"I love you too, dammit," Jane said, picking up Annie and scratching her under the ears. "I don't like this. I want to see Vince get what he deserves."

"So do I, but perhaps that's not in the cards."

"We make our own luck," her friend said, eyes troubled.

"This is life, Jane, not poker, and the stakes are much higher."

You couldn't get much higher than someone's life. Their career.

"Promise me you'll tell me everything. I don't want

you hiding things from me too because you're afraid Vince might hurt me."

Her mind went blank for a second. It hadn't even occurred to her that her best friend was at risk too, but if Vince knew she was Vixen, he also knew Jane was Raven.

"Stop," Jane said, reading her mind. "I don't think he'll do anything to me."

But what if he did?

"If he does, we'll find another way," Elizabeth told her. "I won't let him touch you."

"Neither will I," her friend said, putting Annie on the ground. "We found a way to handle Vince before. We'll do it again."

But last time had involved running for their lives and leaving everything they knew and wanted behind.

"If it comes to that, we'll stand and fight this time," Elizabeth said, and the vow coursed through her veins like a powerful elixir.

"Yes. We're not the scared girls we were then. Vince better not mess with us."

Elizabeth nodded.

If he did, he was going to see just how much older and wiser they were.

CHAPTER 32

Tuning out Chef T was impossible. He was eroding her "zone," the one she needed to get into while catering the annual Raiders Spring Training dinner. Natalie finally walked the expanse of the kitchen, past yards of catering trays filled with prepared food, and stood her ground. Something she needed to do with her brother. She didn't know how he'd managed it, but she had a brand new bumper sticker on her Nissan SUV. *I LOVE SPAM!* Matt was a dead man, mayoral candidate or not.

"You're making my staff nervous," she said to the celebrity chef. She wouldn't admit he was the reason for her nerves. A bigger alpha was causing that problem, and he hadn't shown up yet.

But he would. It was only a matter of time.

Terrance said something under his breath, but since he didn't fish out a Benjamin Franklin, she knew it wasn't a cuss word.

"Can I help it that I'm this good looking?"

A reluctant laugh sputtered out—a feat since her mind and body were busy coping with the fact that she was going to see her sinfully hot ex-husband shortly. "I know you want to observe them, but I told you this wouldn't be fair. Poor Portia over there is covered in chocolate sauce because of you." She only hoped they would still have enough to serve with the raspberry cheesecake—the coach's favorite.

"I'll give you a hundred bucks if you can say 'poor Portia' three times," he teased, standing there casually in jeans and a short-sleeve T-shirt that showcased his famous griffin tattoos.

He deserved the fish eye for that.

"Hey! It's not my fault I walked in when she was pouring the chocolate sauce."

Portia had been star-struck until the ribbons of chocolate landed on her buxom chest and the floor. "And she didn't bring a change of clothes..." Poor Portia—okay it really was funny—looked liked she'd been attacked by a wild painter using chocolate brown for his live human artwork.

"Whoa, Portia!" a familiar voice said from the kitchen doorway. "What in the world happened to you, girl?"

Her long-time and usually unflappable assistant grinned at Blake, who didn't glance her way. No one frowned at Mr. Football Universe. Everyone liked him, and their divorce hadn't changed that with her staff. Traitors.

"I...got distracted," she said, an uncharacteristic blush staining her cheeks.

Who wouldn't blush in front of Blake Cunningham? He was wearing a charcoal Armani suit that hugged every muscular line of his body. His sandy brown hair was styled in the way she'd always liked—long enough for her to run her hands through it. And that jaw...it was perfectly chiseled and with just enough stubble to make her want to meow at the sheer sexiness of it all.

He still hadn't looked her way, and she knew he was biding his time until he could give her his undivided attention.

"Don't let my linebackers see you like this, Portia.

You look good enough to eat. They might tackle you and lick that chocolate right off. They're like hungry wolves around food. You know that."

Great. Now Portia looked like she was going to swoon, and who could blame her? The Raiders had some pretty hot linebackers.

"Did anybody see the new bumper sticker on Natalie's rig? You know, even though we were married, I had no idea she loved Spam. What a stocking stuffer that could have been."

Sure enough, everyone chuckled.

"Spam, huh?" Terrance asked softly, laughter in his voice, not disguising his interest in the scene.

She felt herself giving into a foodie blush. Between Terrance and Blake, she was losing complete control of her staff at the worst possible time. A few of the other women were spooning salad onto the counter instead of the gold-rimmed plates while another bobbled the sterno cans they were taking out of boxes.

"Okay, everybody. Back to work. The halftime show is over, and Blake needs to get back to the team."

Natalie steeled herself, waiting for Blake's glance to find her. Finally.

And then he turned his head.

That full bottom lip curved with wicked intent when their gazes clashed, and his brown eyes went dark with desire. Dammit. No wonder he'd waited to look at her. He needed to stop lusting after her. They weren't married anymore!

Of course her girl parts weren't acting any better, doing the Blake Cunningham cheer down below.

"Hello, Blake," she said in a professional tone, one she'd practiced for days.

"Hey, Nat," he replied, his voice husky.

Damn him for using her nickname. Everything slowed down inside her except the sound of her beating heart. All she could see was him, standing there with that infernal glow that always seemed to surround him—like he was backlit by the glory of being a superstar NFL quarterback.

Someone elbowed her, and she came out of her trance. "Aren't you going to introduce me?" Terrance asked.

Right. Chef T. In her kitchen. Meeting her ex. Life was so weird.

"Blake, this is—"

"I know who he is," Blake interrupted her with uncharacteristic rudeness, striding across the kitchen like it was the football field, and he was about to give a referee a piece of his mind for calling a flag on the play. "What's he doing here?"

"Observing the beautiful Natalie Hale in her element." Terrance crossed his arms, all cocky attitude and testosterone. "I'm a real admirer of her work."

Blake's head jerked back. "What the hell, Nat? Are you with this guy?"

Since Blake had never acted jealous for a single moment in their relationship, seeing the green horns appear figuratively on his head threw her for a loop.

"Are you lost?" Terrance asked Blake before she could respond, sliding his arm around Natalie.

She tensed at his touch, and he pinched her. She got the signal. Terrance was trying to put Blake in his place. The gesture was sweet beyond words.

"I didn't think players usually came back to the kitchen."

Blake's stormy face was like a clap of thunder in the now silent kitchen. "I can come back to the fucking kitchen any time I'd like, douche bag," Blake responded tersely. "Get your hands off her. She's my wife."

"Ex-wife," Terrance corrected in a soft voice laced with menace.

Natalie sucked in her breath. "What in the hell is wrong with you, Blake? You're acting like a child."

He grabbed her arm and pulled her away from Terrance. "What in the hell is wrong with *you?* That jerk has his hands all over you."

Blake rarely lost control of himself, but today he had. Completely. Since she didn't need anyone to overhear this conversation, which was bound to get her staff even more distracted, she let him lead her down the hall. When they were out of earshot, she yanked her hand back and then punched him in those rock-hard abs of his.

"Stop this."

He pointed his finger at her. "Me? What about you? You're one of the good girls, and that guy might be a great chef, but he uses up bad girls and tosses them aside faster than I throw a touchdown. Have you lost your self-respect?"

She drilled her finger into his chest. "Self-respect, huh? Maybe I just wanted some variety."

His jaw locked, and the storm inside him went from raging out of control to focused, determined. She'd seen him angry like this only once before—when the Raiders were down by five touchdowns to the worst team in the league at halftime. He'd rallied his team and crawled back to win the game with three seconds left.

"Besides, you're no monk." She took a deep, calming breath. "We're divorced, Blake."

"I didn't let you go so you could be with someone who'd treat you like shit. And no, I haven't been a monk, but sex isn't as good as it was with you. If you'd return my calls, you'd know that. I miss you, Nat. Dammit."

That salvo closed her throat. For a moment, she didn't know what to say or how they had gotten here.

"Blake, I need you to leave my kitchen and not come back again tonight. You know how important this evening is for my business. Would you want me to barge into your huddle on the field and talk to you and your teammates like this?"

He exhaled like an angry bull who'd decided to calm down and not ram the fence. "Honestly, I wish you would. That way I'd know you still care about me. About us."

His emotion was cracking her open in places she'd welded shut. "Don't. Don't do this. Not now." Not ever.

His large hands cradled her face gently. "When am I supposed to do this, Nat? You never call me back. You moved out of our house without talking to me and then wouldn't talk to me again except through our lawyers."

Not talking to him had been her only option. Otherwise she would have caved. "That was two years ago, Blake."

"It feels like yesterday to me."

He lowered his chin to rest on top of her head as he tucked her close. Her lip wobbled, and all of the hurt she'd hidden away began to break free in the warmth of his embrace. "Let me go."

Her plea was whisper-soft and agonized.

"No. I kept waiting for you to get over being mad and frozen so we could talk this out, but it's taking too damn long."

Even though his arms felt like the home she'd abandoned, she made herself press back. He'd been waiting for her? All this time? She had to have misunderstood him. "What are you talking about?"

His gaze burned into her. "I know you, Nat. I couldn't force you to talk to me or do anything with me when you left me. I gave you some breathing room, hoping you would...I don't know...calm down enough to talk to me. Talk things through, so we could get back together. Christ, I don't know. Move past what happened."

Why wouldn't he stop this?

"We need to talk about it, Nat. We need to talk about Kim."

This time she shoved away with all her might. "No!

No we don't."

When she tried to move past him, he blocked her way. "See this is what I'm talking about. You're so damn stubborn. It all goes back to Kim. Why won't you talk to me?"

She pushed against him, but he didn't move a muscle, being six four and two twenty. "Because it won't change anything."

"Won't change anything?" he asked, his face incredulous.

"Get out of my way, Blake."

His face fell. "I won't stop. You need this as much as I do. If we can't talk about what happened, neither one of us can move forward. All we do is work now. And I can't play football forever, so that's not an option for me. If you won't be with me again, at least give us the closure we both need. I need more in my life, and so do you."

She didn't want Blake to move on, she realized, and the thought made her feel like someone had walked over her grave. "Don't tell me what I need."

He lifted one of the dark strands of her hair and caressed it. "Babe, I always know what you need. You just won't always let me give it to you. Let me give it to you now."

Leaning down swiftly, he pressed his lips to hers. The warmth and texture was a shock for a moment until his mouth softened. His lips caressed hers like they had the first time she'd let him kiss her.

That kiss—and this one now—was soft and gentle, so filled with an appreciation for the preciousness of this rare delicate connection between them.

It was her complete undoing.

A tear ran down her face, and feeling it, she punched him hard in the gut again. This time he grunted and stepped away.

"This is the first time I've seen you cry in all the time

that I've known you, which shows me that I've made some progress. After seeing that chef with you, I'm done waiting you out. Expect to see more of me from now on. Good luck tonight, Nat. You'll do great, just like you always do."

And with that pronouncement, he turned around and left her standing in the hallway. She scrubbed at the face his hands had held so softly. Her mouth, which he'd kissed so sweetly. She was tempted to kick and punch the wall to release the crushing pressure in her chest.

When she wanted to cry, she lashed out.

No one knew that better than Blake.

He was the only one who could make her feel the dark, messy parts of herself—feel those horrible emotions about Kim—and he wasn't going to get the chance.

Not then.

And not now.

When she walked back into the kitchen, her bullshit armor was back in place. "Whew! Did you see Mr. Fancy Pants freak out like that? The Raiders better hope Blake takes a chill pill, or they're going to have a losing season this year. I'll have to talk to Coach. Portia, make sure to give Blake an extra slice of cheesecake to sweeten him up."

Everyone laughed and continued with their work.

Everyone but Terrance.

When she reached him, she held out her hand. She'd told Mac she would give his final offer an answer a couple of days after the Raiders' dinner. No reason to put it off now. "I'm accepting Mac's offer. It'll be great to work with you, Terrance."

Moving to Dare Valley would stop Blake in his tracks. Of that, she had no doubt.

For a moment, Terrance studied her like he was trying to unpack an unusual delicacy. Her hand fell to the side when he didn't shake it.

"I'm glad to hear that, but take another day or two before making your decision. Things got a little heated with your ex, and no one knows better than I do that moments like that aren't the best for a big decision."

"No need. This job is just what I need." Personally and professionally. She gave him a charming smile, the one she used to get men to eat out of her hands. "Besides, my family will be overjoyed to have me move back to Dare."

"Don't kid a kidder, Natalie," Terrance said and stepped around her to continue his study of her staff.

She must be losing it if Terrance could read between the lines.

Pulling herself together, she allowed the coldness she'd mastered to encircle her heart. The slight crack that had allowed that lone tear to break through frosted over nicely. She was back in control.

And no one was going to mess with that, least of all Blake.

CHAPTER 33

Even though Terrance wasn't spending his one night off alone with Elizabeth, he couldn't be happier. He and Elizabeth were heading to Jane's house for dinner with her, Matt, Rhett, and Abbie.

A couple's night.

The sensation of being in a couple—part of a *we*—was sometimes still awkward for a man who'd never wanted to be *attached* to anyone. Yet Elizabeth soothed away all the weirdness of being called her boyfriend in the media now that they'd gone public with their relationship.

His chef friends were having a field day, texting him pictures of bulls with rings in their noses or their nuts cut off. He ran with a rough crowd. Everyone in the restaurant biz knew divorce was high for a reason. They'd all thought they were being so much smarter by staying unattached. And the bitter ones who'd gone down that road only to be burned were seen as confirmation of that attitude.

But they didn't have Elizabeth, who'd helped him discover a new level of peace and happiness in his life. For that, for the enjoyment of his perfect ingredient, he could laugh off his friends' texts.

When he opened the door to Elizabeth's house with the bright, shiny brass key she'd given him a few days ago—so newly made the metal dust from the locksmith's cut was still evident—he could already smell her Chanel perfume.

She wasn't in the den, which was neatly arranged. She liked order, saying her mother had never cleaned their trailer growing up. It was another thing they had in common. He'd started to clean his mother's grimy studio apartment at the tender age of seven. The night Elizabeth had given him her key, he'd helped her clean up the house—something he'd never done with a woman.

It had felt a little weird—but cozy.

He was starting to like cozy, but he'd cut his balls off before admitting that to his buddies.

"Hey, is that you?" she called, her heels clicking on the hardwood as she came down the hall. "Well, don't you look nice."

He turned like a model so she could admire his jeans, white V-neck, and charcoal Hugo Boss jacket. "Thanks. *GQ* called. They want to run a piece on me. Have to dress the part."

"Get out! *GQ* called *you?* That's wonderful, Terrance."

When she flew across the room to press herself against him, he kissed her lightly on the lips, They were already lined in what he called Vixen red. He knew to keep it light.

When she gazed at him, her eyelids dusted with a soft white eyeshadow, her eyelashes black and curled with mascara, he saw both who she'd been and who she was now.

Vixen, who'd worn heavy stage makeup.

And Elizabeth, who wore so little makeup in comparison that he could see the tiny vein at her temple.

He loved them both.

Wrapping his arms around her, he said, "Since we trended on Twitter and all that jazz, I've had a few requests for interviews. I'm not doing all of them, but you can bet even I was thrilled about *GQ*."

"No shit," she said, and he took out a Ben Franklin and tucked it between her breasts, which were showcased in an emerald-green silk shirt, which made her skin glow like freshwater pearls.

"Of course, you could grace just about any fashion magazine too," he commented. "This hundred is for your charity of choice. I figure that we can both stop swearing."

"What if I like swearing?" she asked in a sensual tone.

"Being together is about supporting each other, right? I need your support if I'm going to ever stop swearing. I lost a fortune last week."

He didn't mention the reason by name. They were both being sensitive to each other, letting old wounds continue their healing.

"Come on," she said. "We need to go."

He opened the car door for her since he didn't want to start taking her for granted. She smiled, and as he watched her gorgeous legs slide onto the seat, he realized there was an upside to this whole gentleman thing.

Dare Valley was awash in blues and golds as he drove the short distance to Jane's house.

"I have to go to New York next week," he told her. "Some business has come up. I'll just be gone for a couple days. I'd love for you to come with me if you can. That way you can see my place. Meet some of my friends." *Get an idea what his life was there.* He left that unsaid.

When he glanced over, the hand holding her clutch

purse was clenched, her knuckles white.

"Is that too much too soon?" he asked, deciding to be direct and trying to keep any disappointment out of his voice. "I'm new at this whole being together thing, so I'm going to make some mistakes."

She cleared her throat. "No, it's okay. I just...didn't expect you to have to go to New York so soon. Who are you meeting with?"

Her body language told him there was more going on. Was she afraid he was going to party hard when he returned?

"You can trust me, Elizabeth. I know I run with a rough crowd, but I love you." Shit, he was sounding like some metrosexual, but he wanted to be honest with her, tell her how he felt. Even when it made him feel weird.

"I love you too, and I trust you."

He watched her relax her hand after she said that. "Good. Thank you. So would you want to come with me?"

She gazed out the window and not at him. "I'm not sure I can make it. I'm a little behind on my work for Rhett with...everything that's happened. But tell me more about who you're meeting. Did something happen business wise to prompt this trip?"

He wanted to persuade her, but he forced himself to hold back. "My agent thought I should have an in-person meeting with Lane about the TV show after the whole Twitter thing. My probation is up next month, you know." He'd been hoping Elizabeth would be there so she could show Lane she was more than just Vixen, but he didn't know how to phrase that. She might think he was using her, and that wasn't what he wanted.

"That sounds like a wise move," she commented, still not looking at him.

"I'm also going to meet up with my banker and talk about the new line of products Mac and I have planned for his hotel chain." After significant discussions, they both felt they had enough sketched out to seek financing.

Her fingers clenched the clutch again. "You and Mac are going to ask your banker to finance it?"

He'd told her about their plans, of course, but he hadn't mentioned the money side. "Yeah. Mac has his own banker, but I really like what my backer has done for me. I told Mac to let me approach them first to see if they would be interested. Like a right of first refusal of sorts."

"I see."

There was something in her voice, something not right, and for the life of him, he couldn't figure it out.

"What's the matter? I can tell you're upset, and I don't know why. We've been really attuned to each other lately, but this time I'm at a loss. I can't read your mind if you won't talk to me. It's just a business trip, which I thought might be fun for you. I want you to meet my friends—like we're doing tonight—see my place. Sleep in my bed."

Her hand squeezed the purse again, and he fought the urge to pull over on the side of the road. To get out and make her talk to him as the sun set around them.

"You make it sound like New York is still your home," she finally said.

Ah. Now he was starting to see things. "Dare Valley is my home away from home right now. I like working here and am excited to work with Mac to build his restaurants into award-winning places. But yes, I have a TV show in New York if Lane stops being a jerk and lets it go through after this two-month probation crap. I'll have to fly back and forth to shoot it."

More silence.

"I've lived in New York my whole life, and I love it there. I'm not saying I'm leaving Dare, okay?" He blew out a breath. "I want you in my life, so we'll have to talk about what this means for us if I decide not to stay here forever. You've probably wondered about whether I'm planning on moving to Mac's new Vegas hotel when it's finished, and to be honest, we've talked about it. I didn't bring it up with you before because everything was so new between us."

"Vegas would be a good venue for you," she finally said, and was that fatalism he detected in her tone now?

"I know your job is important. I'm not asking you to give anything up. But I don't plan on losing you either. We'll make it work no matter what happens."

Was that the right answer? Hell, didn't a woman want a man to say that sort of thing? He was so out of his element.

"I want you in my life too. The...enormity of things hadn't hit me until now."

Yeah, the possibility of staying in Dare Valley forever with her hadn't dawned on him either. He'd always seen the small town as another launching point. Sure, Rhett was making a home here, but did that mean Elizabeth wanted to live here forever too? Well, they didn't have a crystal ball right now, so there was no point in guessing the future.

He loved her.

She loved him.

That's all that mattered.

"Okay, then. Let's keep talking about this. I've found a way to make this new job work in little ol' Dare Valley while still pursuing part of my career in New York. We'll find a way to make our relationship work too as our careers keep growing and changing." If he knew one thing about life, it was not static.

"We'll take it as it comes," she breathed out, and again her hands relaxed on her purse. "Tell me more about the franchising. I had a special interest in that area at Harvard. Maybe I can help you figure out some other options."

While he'd already scoured the New York banking

industry to find the best bank, he didn't want to shut her down if she wanted to share her ideas.

"Well, I have the best investment bank in New York backing my efforts. Harwick & Taylor. Do you know of it?"

"Yes." Her voice was soft. "They have an esteemed reputation."

"Yes. So, here's what Mac and I are thinking," he said, hoping he would impress her a little with his business sense. He gave her a condensed version since they were nearing Jane's house. "I can give you more details after dinner."

"That sounds good," she said, but her voice still sounded remote. "I can do some research for you too."

"Elizabeth, you don't need to do work for me," he said in exasperation. "I have plenty of people doing that."

She turned her head quickly to glance at him—the first time since they'd started this conversation—and he read the fear and vulnerability in her eyes. Crap. He wasn't doing anything right.

"I didn't mean it like that. I only meant you have your own work, and I don't want to add to it. There are people I pay to do this sort of thing."

Her hands were clutched around that damn purse again.

"Of course. Oh, look, there's some deer."

He could give a flying f—caught himself there—about deer. She was changing the subject. When he finally pulled his rig in next to Rhett's SUV, he laid his hand on hers.

"I don't know what I've done, but I know you're upset."

She laid her head on his shoulder for a moment, and his heart settled a bit. She wasn't pulling away. The relief was tremendous.

"It's okay. You didn't do anything wrong. Let's head

inside."

Her door swung open before he could come around, and he fought his frustration. Something had changed between them, and he didn't like her sugarcoating it.

Matt opened the front door and came out onto the porch, Henry by his side. "Come on in. Rhett's making mint juleps with Jane."

Elizabeth kissed his cheek as they reached him, and Jane's fiancé hugged her a moment after giving her a look Terrance didn't understand. There was an undercurrent here. What in the hell?

Matt shook his hand and then led them into the kitchen.

Sure enough, Rhett was at it. He was moving his hips in a circle as he muddled the mint. Abbie and Jane were clutching their stomachs, doubled over in laughter.

"I see you're using your new Latin moves to make a mint julep," Terrance said as he approached the kitchen island, hoping to lighten the tension corded inside his gut. "Promise me you won't thrust your hips at my drink like that."

"You can use your own moves on your own drink, bubba," Rhett said with a wink.

"Okay, *bubba,* step back and let me show you how a real man muddles," Terrance joked, rolling up the sleeves of his jacket. "Hey, Jane. Hey, Abbie." And he kissed them both on the cheek as he passed them.

Elizabeth made the rounds as well, and it was good to see her shake off whatever that crap was in the car. He was going to have to pry it out of her later.

He and Rhett got into a muddling competition, of which Jane declared him the winner. Rhett claimed to have won in the Latin dance category, and Terrance was happy to give him that concession.

The dogs were told to stay in the family room, and while Henry looked like he was going to disobey, one stern look from Jane had him plopping his butt on the ground. It was still astonishing to see her transformation from Raven to a stone-cold poker player who could beat even Mac Maven and make ninety pound dogs do her bidding.

"I heard from Mac that you're rolling out the new menu at The Grand, Terrance," Jane said as she served them a wine-glazed leg of lamb, garlic mashed potatoes, and white asparagus—the latter a nice touch, he thought. "Matt and I will have to try it out. And since it has to be said, Terrance, I know you can cook much better than this, but I hope you enjoy it."

It was hardly the first time he'd heard this line. Few people had the guts to cook for a chef. Yet even when they did, most felt the need to throw in some caveat. He could only reply as graciously as possible to reassure her.

"Jane. Please don't apologize for your food. I'm honored to be a guest in your home, and I know I'll enjoy what you've made. Thank you for cooking for me. It doesn't happen very often."

Her smile was soft, and Matt nodded his approval at the politic answer.

"He's right about the cooking part," Elizabeth said. "I'd be afraid to even scramble an egg for him."

So Elizabeth was afraid to cook for him? "What am I, the Culinary Ogre?" he asked and made a monster face.

Everyone laughed.

"I'd stick with The Tattooed Chef, man," Rhett told him, serving himself a mountain of mashed potatoes. "Little kids would run in the other direction if you made that face at them."

"Well, you do have a rep for yelling at people in the kitchen on your show," Elizabeth said.

True. But not on his new show. He was moving past that image. "It's never personal. Plus, it was good for ratings."

Even he'd been astonished by how far he could push things on air. The more shade he threw, the higher their ratings had been. Now it was time to strike a new balance on primetime.

"You should make him your Beef Wellington, Elizabeth," Jane said. "It's wonderful."

"I'll second that," Matt replied, lifting his glass. "To good friends."

"To good friends," they all echoed and tapped their glasses together.

The burgundy wine was velvety smooth, had a long finish, and was redolent with the flavor of black cherries and loamy soil followed by rose. "The wine is excellent, Jane."

"Thanks, Terrance. Domaine Romanée Conti never disappoints."

"Jane has finally persuaded me that beer can't stand up to wine," Matt said with a laugh. "We've gone head to head, and I keep losing."

"Now, that's just tragic," Rhett drawled. "Beer is the national drink of this fine country."

A lively discussion ensued on that topic, and as Terrance gave his two cents on the matter, he reached under the table to gently rest his hand Elizabeth's thigh. When she glanced over at him with a smile, he felt something turn over in his chest.

Whatever had happened in the car was behind her now, and he was happy to relax into this sensation of having dinner and conversation with old and new friends, Elizabeth by his side.

When Jane brought out dessert, a multi-layered chocolate dacquoise, she announced, "I was fresh out of ideas, so I decided to ask Brian to make something for us. I hope you enjoy this baby. It's one of my faves from Brasserie Dare."

The meringue had the perfect crunch, and the crushed hazelnuts he detected in the chocolate ganache added an extra texture he appreciated. "Marvelous, Jane. I really enjoyed my meal at Brasserie Dare. Brian's a talented chef."

Abbie's eyelashes fluttered as she took a bite. "Jill says she has the best life in the world. She gets to eat your food during the day, Terrance, and Brian's for breakfast and dinner. I have to agree with her. Of course she also says she has to keep coming to your dance classes, Elizabeth, so she won't weigh a ton."

"Do you want me to take a cooking class, sugar?" Rhett asked, rubbing some chocolate off the corner of her mouth.

"Stop that," she said, slapping his hands away. "If you take a class, please bring Dustin along. I swear, Rhett and Dustin would starve if I didn't feed them."

Rhett kicked back, wiping up the crumbs on his plate with his index finger—something only he could pull off at a fancy dinner party. "No, we'd eat out all the time or only eat hog dogs and hamburgers. And steak. I can cook a mean steak."

"I stand corrected," Abbie said. "They would have plenty of meat."

"So, T, how's your cooking show coming along? Maybe if Dustin and I watch it we'll become better cooks. What do you think of that, Abbie?"

"I think it's a brilliant idea. Has that unpleasant man decided to give the go-ahead?"

Terrance wasn't surprised Rhett had shared that tidbit with Abbie—he'd griped about Lance to all of his friends—and he wasn't worried they would speak out of turn. "I'm going to New York next week to meet with the network guy to see if we can move things forward." Best scenario. He could charm that jerk into canceling his probation period. Worst case. He'd finish it without a blip. Either way, he *was* going to have his show.

Jane tensed and shared a look with Elizabeth, who stilled beside him again like she had in the car. His frustration returned. What in the hell was wrong with him going to New York?

"You and Mac are franchising some new products for his hotel chain, right?" Rhett said. "Mac's tickled pink about it, showing me the kinds of products you two have in mind. I suggested bread and butter pickles, but he vetoed that. I guess you're going to talk to your fancy banker man in New York."

"I have to admit I'm really excited about this venture," Abbie said, reaching for the cup of tea Jane had brewed for her. "Your joint product line is really going to help put our hotel chain on the map for something beyond poker."

"The hotel chain is already on the map. I'm just going to throw my name in more publicly."

"That's a nice thing to say, Terrance," Abbie said with a smile. "I'll keep my fingers crossed for your trip."

Terrance reached for his coffee, covertly watching Elizabeth and her friend. When Jane looked at Matt, Terrance followed his gaze. They shared a significant look too.

He'd always been able to detect trouble, ever since he was a loner kid in a rough neighborhood. His gut churned. Something was wrong here, and he wasn't in the know.

"Thanks, Abbie. I'm sure everything will fall into place," Terrance said, hiding his hand for the present.

"Did the lamb not sit well with you, Elizabeth?" Rhett asked. "You look as pale as a possum in the moonlight."

Her chuckle was as forced as they come. "A possum, Rhett? How unflattering. Must be the wine. Perhaps I had too much."

She hadn't.

Terrance turned his head to study her. She wouldn't look at him now.

As he was reaching under the table to touch her

thigh again, to establish that precious connection between them, he noticed her hands were clutching her napkin, the knuckles white, just like how she'd been gripping her purse in the car.

What the f–

"How about we take our drinks out back," Matt suggested, standing. "It's not too cool tonight, and our new fire pit is waiting to be christened."

"Have you decided which house you're going to live in when you two get hitched?" Rhett asked, pushing back and helping Abbie with her chair as she rose.

Terrance did the same with Elizabeth, almost in slow motion.

Something was terribly wrong, and he couldn't think about anything else.

"We're staying here even though technically Matt's not living here," Jane told them. "Shh... Dare Valley doesn't like their mayoral candidates living in sin."

"Oh for heaven's sake, Jane," Matt said in exasperation.

"Well, it's true. We chose my place since it has a couple more bedrooms for when we decide to have kids. Of course, we're planning to get married first."

Rhett nudged Abbie, and she shook her head. He leaned closer and whispered something in her ear. She whispered back. By the time they turned their attention to the others, he was grinning.

"Jane?" he said. "Do you mind if I ask Mac and Peg to swing up here for a bit? Keith's soccer game should be over by now, and they're picking Dustin up for us from his soccer practice."

"Sure thing," Jane said, standing now. "It was too bad we couldn't find a night when everyone could make it."

"With the kids' activities after school, it can be a challenge," Abbie said as they went outside.

The night was cool, and the stars above would have

captured Terrance's complete attention if not for the rigidness of Elizabeth by his side. When Rhett called her over to point out one of the constellations to her, Terrance gripped the railing.

Rhett seemed clueless, but Jane and Matt undoubtedly knew something he didn't.

Should he ask Jane about it if Elizabeth refused to talk to him? But she'd made it pretty clear she wouldn't tell him anything Elizabeth wouldn't.

When Mac and Peggy finally arrived on the back porch with Keith and Dustin, Matt brought the newcomers drinks.

"Good to see you again, Private Dancer," Peggy said to Terrance by way of hello.

She wasn't the kiss and hug type, so he only rolled his eyes. Keith ran over to Rhett, who slung him upside down, making the young boy squeal with laughter. The moment he put Keith down, Rhett took Abbie's hand. Dustin took his mother's hand with a grin.

"We didn't think we could get everyone together at the same time," Rhett said, "so we decided to share our news with y'all first. Honey..."

Abbie's smile was radiant as she said, "We're having a baby."

Keith let out a whoop of pure pleasure, and Jane rushed forward to hug them all.

Elizabeth's mouth dropped open, but her expression soon turned into a grin. "Oh my God!" she said, dashing toward them. "Congratulations, Rhett, Abbie, Dustin. That's wonderful."

Lifting her off the ground in a bear hug, Rhett said, "I figure that between the two of us, we're going to make an artsy poker player."

"Do you think the baby's going to grow as tall as you, Uncle Rhett?" Keith asked.

"Only if he's a boy," Rhett said, taking Mac's hand and giving him a man bump. "How about that, Maven?"

"Couldn't happen to better people. I'm going to be an uncle again." When Mac and Abbie embraced, she pressed her face into her brother's neck. "I'm so happy for you, Abbie."

She wiped a tear away. "We figured it wouldn't be fair to Dustin if we waited until he was in college to have a baby, so Rhett convinced me to accelerate the timetable. At least he'll have a little time to enjoy his brother or sister."

"I'll be coming home for college, Mom," Dustin said as Mac grabbed him in a bear hug.

"You'd better," Mac said. "This kid is going to need an older brother."

Peggy hugged Abbie, and the others offered their congratulations one at a time. Terrance was the last one to give Rhett a man hug.

"Congratulations. Seems some cooking classes might be in order for another reason now. You'll have another mouth to feed."

Rhett pounded him on the back. "Yep. I need to take a cooking class on baby food once Abbie's job is finished. It's going to be fun. I've never been so happy."

But even his friends' uplifting mood following the happy announcement couldn't shake off Terrance's sour one. Elizabeth was on the other side of the deck now, talking to Jane and Abbie.

He had never felt so alienated from her, not since finding a Dear John note and the lingering smell of her Chanel perfume on his pillow.

Chapter 34

Terrance was stewing. Even from across the porch, Elizabeth could see how angry he was. She couldn't blame him. His impending trip to New York had sent her into a tailspin.

All she'd been able to do was sit in her seat, her purse clutched in her hands, wondering if Vince had called him and asked for the meeting. A taunt like that would be just like him.

When Terrance explained the purpose of the trip, she'd tried to relax. Until he started talking about how he and Mac wanted to discuss their new franchising venture with Vince, something she should have anticipated. Her mind was in turmoil, the pressure giving her a headache. Terrance and Mac could not give Vince another business venture.

Even Jane's famous poker face hadn't been up to scratch when the trip came up at dinner. The way she'd looked at her and then Matt had made it that much harder to breathe like normal.

Especially when Terrance laid his hand on her thigh, his desire to reestablish connection evident.

Now they were drinking out on the porch, and

Elizabeth was doing her best to reestablish her severely compromised poker face.

"Can you help me in the kitchen?" Jane asked, taking her elbow and steering her away before she could reply.

Girlfriend was not taking no for an answer.

"Does anyone want anything?" Elizabeth asked as she let Jane pull her to the patio door.

"How about you get some of that fancy champagne for a toast?" Rhett called.

"Rhett, I can't drink," Abbie reminded him.

"The doc said you could have a sip, but if you don't want any, sugar, that's just fine. What else would you like?"

"Water would be great," Abbie replied.

Elizabeth tried to smile when she met Terrance's stony gaze, but it was of no use. She yanked open the door, eager to escape the questions she could see in his eyes.

Jane strode to her wine cooler and pulled out a bottle of Dom. Turning, she pointed the pricy bottle at Elizabeth.

"Remember when you agreed you would revisit our discussion about telling Terrance? Well, now's the time."

"Shh. Do you want someone to overhear?" She scanned the various entry points in the kitchen to make sure no one had followed them inside.

"Elizabeth! We need to talk about this."

"Not now, Jane," she said, grabbing champagne glasses from the cabinet.

Jane popped the cork and started to pour, her motions choppy. "Matt doesn't like this whole thing one bit, and I know he's even more upset now that he knows Mac's involved through this new franchising venture. Elizabeth, it can't go forward."

She darted a glance at the doorway again. "I know,

Jane. I'll think of something."

"*Tell him.* He deserves to know. You're not protecting him...you're hurting him."

She picked up four glasses, balancing the stems between her fingers. "I'll send someone else in to help you," she said and walked back out without another word.

What should have been a night filled with laughter and happiness was instead rife with worry and despair. The champagne tasted flat in her mouth after Rhett gave a toast that brought tears to her eyes.

To our baby. May he or she know how much all of these people here tonight already love him or her.

Rhett teased her and Jane about being aunts for the first time, but Terrance kept his distance, staying on the edge of the group, sipping his champagne with narrowed eyes.

When everyone said their goodbyes, they walked to his car without speaking or holding hands. He didn't even open the door for her. Only slammed his own.

They drove back to her house in silence, her heart thudding in her chest. Still intent on keeping her secret, she searched for plausible excuses that would pacify him given how important his life in New York clearly was to him . He was being featured in *GQ,* and his star was rising even higher now. There was no way she could hurt his career.

When they reached her house, he cut the engine, but made no move to open his door. "Do you want me to go? Because the way you acted tonight sure as hell makes me want to leave."

If he did, they would be in tatters again, and she wasn't sure she could patch them together a third time.

She laid a hand on his arm. The muscles were locked beneath two layers of fabric, his griffins poised to fight.

"Please come inside."

"Give me one good reason why I should after

tonight."

Oh, God. "Because I love you, and I'm scared." That was the truth at least. "And I don't always know what to say or how to handle what's between us either."

He turned in his seat to face her. "What is it about New York that bothers you so much? It's not just this trip, because I saw the way Jane and Matt acted when I mentioned it tonight. Whatever you told them, it couldn't have been about the trip. I only told you on the way over there."

His logic wasn't wrong, and she decided she could only share her feelings. Not the cause of them. She hoped it would be enough for now.

"I'm afraid I'm going to lose you," she whispered. "Everything you've ever had or wanted is in New York. All your friends. Your hangouts. The show. I can't compete with that."

"Oh, Christ," he muttered and shoved open the car door.

He stalked around the front and circled to her side. She pushed open her door, and they both stood in the cool night air, gazing at each other.

"Do you have any idea how much you mean to me?" He thrust his hand up to the stars. "I love you. *I. Love. You.* If I haven't yet conveyed what a big deal that is for me, then I'm sorry. You don't ever need to be afraid of competing with my life in New York, Elizabeth."

Her lip quivered in the cool night, and she wrapped her arms around herself in a futile attempt to control the emotions raging inside her.

He kicked the ground and strode off two steps before coming back to stand in front of her. "You're my perfect ingredient. You! Okay? I've scoured the world for something—a spice, a condiment, a rarity—thinking food was the answer to filling up this hole inside me. I never thought it would be a woman. Cooking saved me. It's been the best part of my life...until you."

Her hand reached out to clutch his jacket. Her heart was thudding in her chest, pushing against the confines of the old lies she'd internalized, the ones that said she couldn't be anyone's everything.

"Do you understand now?" he asked. "New York is *nothing* compared to you. Nothing."

"Oh, Terrance," she whispered, pressing her face into his chest, hanging on as wave after wave of emotion rolled through her.

Reaching for his face, she raised on her tiptoes to press her mouth to his. He yanked her to him and ravaged her mouth, pouring out all his anger and frustration. She welcomed it, soothing him with soft kisses while his fingers dug into her waist, as if searching for an anchor.

He swung her up finally into his arms and jogged the short distance to the front door. After she managed to unlock it, he kicked it shut and carried her to the bedroom. Setting her down by the bed, he tore off her shirt, sending buttons flying in every direction.

"I can't wait," he told her in a hoarse voice, all finesse gone.

She didn't answer. Only undid the lone button on his jacket and helped him shrug it off and then his shirt. He peeled off the rest of her shirt too and then swept away her black skirt, hose, and heels in one pass. Kicking them free, she reached for his belt, and soon they were both naked.

Falling back onto the mattress, she gazed up at him and opened her legs. His hot stare sent shivers across her body. When he slid over her, covering her, she stroked his face.

"I love you."

"I love you too, dammit, and don't forget it."

Her hands clenched his backside, any mention of his Cuss Fund forgotten now, and he pressed deep into her with one thrust. She was more than ready for him, and even though he'd been swept away by emotion earlier, he found his tenderness as he started stroking into her.

"You destroy me," he uttered in a hoarse voice.

She understood. She felt the same way. As she rose to meet his thrusts, she could only try and communicate through her body what he most needed to know.

That he was her perfect ingredient too.

His hands grabbed hers, and together they rode out the storm. When they found their release—panting, skin flushed with sweat, their bodies pulsing—he rolled onto his back with her on top, staying inside her.

"Will you come to New York with me now?" he asked her in the quiet aftermath.

She loved him. If going to the city meant running into Vince, then she would meet her demon face to face. Terrance didn't have to know anything unless Vince made the wrong move.

If he did, she would tell Terrance everything.

Chapter 35

Girls' Night was Natalie's favorite part of her week. As she let herself out of her building to walk to the Irish pub she and her sisters loved for its peppy music, she felt a piercing sadness. Her sisters were over the moon about her new job, but they all knew what it meant. There would be no more nights like tonight or lunches or impromptu hangouts.

She loved her brothers, but Matt and Andy weren't girls.

Talking to them was just different.

Of course, there were upsides. She would be able to spend more time with her brothers and her mom and Danny, of course. Oh, and the rest of the Hale clan. Jill couldn't wait to work with her at The Grand.

Plus her ongoing bumper sticker war with Matt would be so much easier. Since he'd already won the primary and it looked like he was going to run uncontested, she was planning to slap a new one on his SUV the next time she saw him: *Honk If You Like Hotties*. That would put his boxers in a knot, all right.

Maybe she could start a Girls' Night in Dare with Jill, Meredith, Jane, and Elizabeth. Oh, and they could invite Peggy and Abbie, whom she didn't know well, but already liked.

Nothing said she couldn't have fun with other people. She just wouldn't be able to see Moira and Caroline during the week.

Turning her maudlin thoughts down to low, she lifted her face to the sky. The spring weather was glorious, and the warm breeze ruffled her silk jersey dress in cobalt blue. She'd wanted to go bold tonight. A new job awaited her, and her spirits were high. Mostly.

A dog barked behind her in rapid bursts, and she turned to look when it kept on barking.

Her heart dropped in her chest.

Touchdown was racing toward her on the sidewalk, his brown eyes alight with joy at seeing his best friend again.

Blake.

Damn him.

She knelt down as the six-year-old Beagle reached her. He licked off the makeup she'd just reapplied, but she didn't care. She'd missed this little fella. Leaving him behind had been so hard. Blake had offered to share the dog with her, but Touchdown had been his before she and Blake met.

Besides, she couldn't be in the same room with Blake—something he clearly didn't understand.

While giving Touchdown kisses—yes, he'd named his dog Touchdown—she glanced up at Blake. He was walking along the sidewalk with the leash in hand in total disregard for the city ordinance.

Like usual, he made her belly grip with lust. He was enjoying the warmer weather too, wearing only a fitted T-shirt and navy and black shorts showcasing his fabulous legs.

Anyone who said women had better legs than men hadn't seen Blake's. He had more defined muscles than should be legal. Her mouth watered, and she wanted to lick her way up his calves.

Her libido was an idiot. Always had been around him.

"You're not playing fair," she told him when he towered over her, his scent like hot sex and spice washing over her.

He knew how much she loved his legs, so he undoubtedly knew she was enjoying the view.

"Babe, I told you I'm done playing fair. Besides, nothing says Touchdown and I can't go for a run by your place."

"You're not running," she replied with some sauce in her voice, still petting Touchdown, who had rolled onto his back for more loving.

"We were. We just slowed down as we came to your building. We come by here every once in a while."

Her head darted back. "You what? But you live thirty minutes away."

That was the whole reason she'd picked this area.

He shrugged. "What can I say? We miss you."

She stood up this time, forcing her eyes not to take a happy stroll up his body. "Stop this. I mean it, Blake. We're divorced. It's over. Please leave me alone."

Those brown eyes flickered down, then met hers with a fiery punch that rocked her back on her toes.

"I love you, and it doesn't matter if we're divorced. It's been two years since you left me, but I still feel the same way."

He hadn't said those three little words to her since she left him.

"Why are you so surprised, Nat? Do you think it's easy to keep taking all the hits you dish out? If my heart could get a concussion, I would have so many I'd be forced to retire. Hell, I'd be a vegetable."

For a moment, she felt guilty. "Then stop coming around and pushing me."

"I told you. I can't." He shrugged again, ducking his

head to his shoulder like he was embarrassed. "I love you too much. And I'm worried about you. The fact that you're living in this place only makes me worried." He gestured to the brown brick three-story building. "This place isn't you. I thought it the minute you moved in."

No, it wasn't. She'd chosen a place without any charm or color—a reminder that all could be lost in an instant.

"God knows you wouldn't let me give you any money in the divorce, which pissed me off plenty, but you make good money with your business. You could afford something better."

Her family had said the same thing. "Maybe I like the neighborhood."

"Maybe you're full of shit."

That was Blake for you. He would always call her on things, just as she had with him from the beginning.

Touchdown nuzzled her fingers, and she stroked his soft fur. "This isn't fair to him, you know."

His brown eyes turned all business, like he was about ready to make a big play on third and long. She braced herself.

"No, it's not fair. He misses you." The breeze caught his sandy brown hair. "You probably think you packed up all your clothes, but I had one of your T-shirts in my dresser as a keepsake. The one you wore the night I proposed to you."

The yellow one. It had always reminded her of sunshine. He'd never told her, not even when she thought she'd lost it somewhere.

"When I...took it out...Jesus...to remind myself of how you smelled, Touchdown snapped it out of my hands and claimed it for his bed. Something I was going to do."

Oh, God.

"But I couldn't fight my own dog like that, so it's his blanket now."

Her mouth grew dry.

"Take him for part of the week, Nat. You know he's lonely when I'm on the road during the season. He'll keep you company. I know you're not happy, babe."

Her happiness or the lack of it wasn't something they were going to discuss. "I can't share Touchdown, Blake. I'm moving back to Dare Valley."

His face contorted with shock. "You're what? But your sisters are here. Your business is here."

"My business is expanding, and I can see my sisters on the weekends." No surprise Blake would list them first. He knew what they meant to her.

His hands latched onto her shoulders. "But you can't leave. *I'm here.*"

She had to steel herself not to feel any of the emotion in his voice. "I told you to let me go, Blake. Now you don't have a choice."

He blew air out of his nostrils like a bull, something he did when he was about ready to rush up the middle of the field against a three hundred pound lineman who wanted to kill him.

"Don't tell me what I have to do. Oh, and by the way, I know you're not with that Tattooed Chef guy. It was all over Twitter that he's with someone else. You're a real bitch for trying to make me jealous, but then I realized you wouldn't have done it if you didn't care about me."

That's what he'd concluded? Then her inner voice schooled her. He was partially right, of course. "Maybe I just wanted you to leave me alone."

"No, babe. If you didn't care, you wouldn't have fought with me. You certainly wouldn't have cried."

Like she needed to be reminded of that momentary weakness. She shoved at his chest. "Stop saying all these things."

"No," he said, yanking her against his hard chest.

His mouth pressed hard against hers, hot and filled with the promise of more lust than she could take. The edge of his anger was there when he bit her bottom lip, and even as she pushed against the rock hard muscles of his abdomen, her mouth was opening to let him inside.

He tore away her defenses again with just one kiss, stroking her tongue just like she remembered, like she wanted. She bit him lightly too, wanting more contact, and he understood because his mouth slanted across hers as they danced on the warm sidewalk. His hands settled on her hips, and he rocked the hard length of his body against her. She moaned, coming alive again, unable to stop it, and tilted her head to the side for an even deeper, wetter kiss.

A car honked in a staccato beat, breaking her trance. Good God, she was kissing Blake on the street like she was out of control.

She *was* out of control.

She jerked her head back and had to force herself to ignore the magical press of his hand on the small of her back, one of her biggest arousal points. And he knew it, of course.

"We're on the street," she said and realized she was panting.

"I don't give a damn," he breathed, pressing his face into her hair. "God, I've missed your smell. I would wake up and still smell you on the pillow next to me—even when I was sleeping in a hotel on the road. I almost hated you for that."

She understood. She'd had her own memories to combat.

"Let me go."

"No," he whispered, kissing her neck. "Let's go inside. I want to make love to you so bad it's killing me."

With Blake, it had never been anything else but making love. "I'm not having sex with you again, Blake."

"It was never just sex, and you know it." His breath hissed out when she remained aloof. "Fine. Let's talk then. Dammit, how many more times are you going to make me beg?"

He *was* begging, and it couldn't be easy for him. She knew he had his pride.

Touchdown whined, but Blake didn't let go of her. "It's okay, boy. Mommy's being stubborn, but she knows we love her."

How many times had he said that when the two of them would get into a little tiff over something like him not loading the dishwasher or cleaning up the sink after he'd shaved? The little things she sometimes missed about being married.

Even though she wanted his hands on her, craved them and all they could do to her body, she forced them away from her. This time, he didn't fight her.

"Blake, I'm moving to Dare Valley. You've just started training for another football season. This is over." Squatting down, she hugged Touchdown to her chest, and dammit if she didn't feel tears pop into her eyes. "Bye, boy," she whispered. "I love you."

When she stood, Blake's eyes were narrowed and his mouth was pinched. It was the same expression he'd had when the team lost the Super Bowl a few years back. Like everything in the world hurt right now and might never be right again.

"Goodbye, Blake."

Before she turned, she saw the thick chords of his throat move. Touchdown barked once, but she didn't look back.

Then the beagle started barking like crazy, and Blake didn't stop him.

Tears ran down her face as she started to run, but she still didn't look back.

If she did, what remained of her resolve would crumble, and she would fly straight into his arms.

CHAPTER 36

Being in New York City with a local would have been enjoyable if Elizabeth wasn't so freaking nervous twenty-four seven. Terrance fortunately attributed her nerves to some residual disbelief that she was his perfect ingredient.

And the usual nerves about meeting his friends.

In his lofty penthouse apartment with its impressive view of Central Park, he did his utmost to set her mind at ease, making love to her as his bottle-green eyes stared into hers, then introducing her to his favorite restaurants and gourmet markets. He even showed her the rough neighborhood where he had been born, then brought her to the Hell's Kitchen restaurant that had changed his life.

His old friend and mentor, Manny Caruthers, the tough chef who'd kicked Terrance's butt into shape was older now, but he still looked like he belonged in a biker gang.

"Manny, this is Elizabeth. It turns out my perfect ingredient isn't an ingredient at all...it's her."

Manny hugged her like a teddy bear, and said, "Your quest has ended at last, T, and with an angel no less.

Elizabeth, it's wonderful to meet you." Then he grabbed Terrance in a hearty embrace after releasing her. "I'm so happy for you, kid."

Elizabeth's heart had almost burst with love in that moment.

After their restaurant shifts, she met Terrance's chef friends, and they drank late into the night. Everyone was nice to her, but he was right. They were a rough crowd and the lot of them cursed like sailors. She'd thought poker players were mouthy, but they had nothing on the people in the restaurant business. Terrance only lost four hundred dollars to the Cuss Fund that night, and his buddies teased him unmercifully about it. His pronounced New York accent returned as he spoke to his friends, and it caused lust to simmer in her belly.

The next day he fed her Zabar's famous chocolate babka bread. Tried to teach her to whistle like a native to call a cab. Held her hand and pointed out his favorite landmarks in Central Park.

She stayed in his apartment while he met Lane about the primetime network show. His meeting with Vince was set for the next day. So far he hadn't mentioned having dinner with the man he only called Junior.

She dreaded it.

She feared it.

She wasn't sure she could stomach it now that she was actually in New York. Every time she thought of seeing Vince again, feeling his eyes crawl over her in that possessive way of his, she started to sweat and grow nauseous. She decided that if Terrance suggested meeting his banker for dinner, she could use her physical symptoms as an excuse. She wouldn't be faking them.

Jane hadn't been over the moon about her going to New York with Terrance, but she'd asked for frequent text updates. Keeping her best friend in the loop was a lifeline.

Even if the only update Jane really wanted concerned Vince.

When Terrance came home from the network meeting, he was all smiles. He had a bouquet of tulips in shades of cream and magenta in one hand and a bottle of Dom Perignon in the other.

"Lane called off my probation and approved the show," he announced. "Said he's finally convinced I'm serious about watching my temper and my mouth. I told him about the Cuss Fund and the money going to charity."

Even though the knots in her stomach were so tight they couldn't be loosened by his news, she was able to smile. Finally. "Oh, Terrance. I'm so happy for you!"

"Oh, and he was impressed to hear you graduated from Harvard. He went to Yale."

She'd told Terrance he should talk up their relationship and provide any nuggets of information about her background that would help his case. "Poor man," she said in her most stodgy New England accent.

"Are you ready to celebrate?"

"Does a poker player pray for a royal flush?" she asked.

Setting the champagne aside, he grabbed her with one arm and kissed her long and deep. "Now all I need is for Harwick to agree to do the franchising for Mac and me. You're my lucky charm, babe."

Even sated from his lovemaking an hour later, she didn't feel like a lucky charm. She felt like a fraud.

Easing out of bed, she watched him sleep. He would only take a catnap, she knew, but it was enough time to do what she knew she must, no matter how hard.

She grabbed her phone from the kitchen counter and went into Terrance's guest bathroom, locking the door behind her. Mac picked up on the third ring.

"Elizabeth. How lovely to hear from you. How's New York?"

"Wonderful. How are things there?"

"Great. I just ordered my new niece or nephew their first present. I couldn't help it. It's a onesie with The Grand's logo on it."

Mac Maven might be a World Series of Poker champion, but he'd helped raise Abbie's first child like his own. Seems he was just as happy to be involved this time around.

"Mac, I need to tell you something, but you can't ask me how I know it or why I couldn't tell Terrance."

His silence made her clutch the bathroom vanity. She looked away from her reflection in the mirror, the shame too great to bear.

"All right. We've known each other long enough for me to know you must have a good reason for asking."

"I do." She took a breath. "You need to find another investment bank for your joint franchising deal with Terrance."

"Is Harwick & Taylor in some trouble financially?"

She worried her lip. "No, it's more of the ethical variety. I'd be happy to recommend some others to you."

"I understand. No need to make any recommendations. We can try my bank. It doesn't have the reputation of Harwick & Taylor, but it's one of the country's top five investment banks for this sort of thing. I'll tell Terrance."

"He's meeting with them tomorrow," she told him, acid churning in her stomach.

"I know. I'll call him tonight."

"Thank you for not asking any questions, Mac."

"You're welcome...because I do have plenty of questions, Elizabeth. It seems the mysteries didn't end when Vixen retired. I'll let you go."

No, this subterfuge was worse than any Vixen had

ever staged.

She thought again about telling Terrance the truth, which she'd wanted to do at least a million times since coming to New York. But it wouldn't work. She knew he wouldn't be able to control himself this time, not after knowing everything Vince had done to her.

"Bye, Mac."

When their call ended, she pressed the phone to her chest. It was done. Mac would be kept out of Vince's clutches and so would another professional venture of Terrance's. He would move to primetime now that his show had finally been given the green light, adding to his growing culinary stature as the next Wolfgang Puck. Vince's bank would continue to finance his other products without interruption.

She and her stalker wouldn't ever meet in person. She would make sure of that.

Everything was going to be fine.

Maybe if she kept repeating it, she'd start to believe it.

CHAPTER 37

As Terrance rode the glass elevator to the top floor of Harwick & Taylor, he smiled at a few of the women staring at him. More than once since being back in town, he'd been stopped for an autograph or to take a picture.

The street rat he'd once been had creds now.

He wondered what his mother would have thought of that.

The bank's executive offices hummed with power and money, from the elegant gold nameplate of the bank to the diamond-studded logo shimmering under discreet lighting on the walls.

When he arrived, he was immediately greeted and asked if he wanted anything to drink. Since he'd already had an espresso at his favorite breakfast place with Elizabeth, he asked for sparkling water. He could have asked for a mango lassi, and they would have jumped to make the unusual drink appear in under ten minutes. That's how good this bank's service was purported to be, although he'd never tested that.

"The Mr. Harwicks will see you now," the well-dressed assistant said, pausing politely before leading the way to the corner office.

Referring to two people like that always amused Terrance. Upper crust manners. So pretentious. Why not say, "Senior and Junior will see you?"

It didn't bother him that they were stuffed shirts. He was thrilled to have gotten financing from the best investment bank in the country. Him. The kid from the neighborhood across town where kids got shot dead in gang wars and teenage girls hooked on the street to make rent when they ran away or were kicked out. Where garbage wasn't picked up because the trash guys were too scared to come regularly. Where even the cops walked around with bulletproof vests on.

He ran through the items on his agenda, minus the franchising deal with Mac. His boss' call had surprised him last night, and he'd been left with more questions than answers. Mac had said he wanted to keep their venture separate—that he'd rather use his own bank. There had been something off about the whole thing, but since he trusted Mac, he let it go. They could talk more about it when he returned to Dare Valley tomorrow with Elizabeth.

There were only four enormous offices on the top floor, two for Harwick and son, one for Taylor, and one for their chief financial advisor.

Harwick Senior and Harwick Junior stood when he arrived in the conference room. The room held a long mahogany table used for the bank's mega-conservative board meetings, the wood so shiny a person could use it to check if their poker face was working properly. His sparkling water was already there at the end of the table, to the right of Senior, who rose immediately. Junior, who was seated next to his father, stood as well and shook Terrance's hand when he reached them.

"Good to see you, Terrance," the younger man said, with what looked like a tight smile on his face.

Usually the man was oozing charm, calling him Chef

T, but he was always more formal in the presence of his father. Harwick Junior liked to party with the celebrities, which is how Terrance had first met him. Both of them had been dinner guests at a friend's house in the Hamptons, and Terrance had hit him up casually about the new line of products he was creating. Harwick Junior had played coy, but Terrance could always tell when he had someone hooked. They'd signed the deal soon after, with Harwick Senior present.

He'd never cared much for the younger man—but he didn't have to like the people he did business with so long as they were the best at what they did. And they were.

"Good to see you both as well. Harrison, how's the golf game these days?"

The older man loved to talk about his frequent trips to the green. Terrance had polished up on his knowledge of golf so he could small talk with the best of them, but he'd been able to wiggle out of Harrison's invitations to play at his club so far.

Terrance hated golf. Didn't see why some men could work so hard to get one small ball into one small hole. But he had his own eccentricities, of course. He'd been obsessed with finding his perfect ingredient up until a week ago, so he wasn't going to point fingers.

Their meeting went as he'd hoped. Mostly small talk, with some discussion of the strong sales the initial kitchen and gourmet products were showing. Harwick Senior always dropped in to give his august touch before leaving the details to his son.

"Any news on the new TV show?" Harrison asked. "I expect you had meetings with them while you're in town."

He leaned back, happy to see the cufflinks he'd bought at Tiffany's wink out from under his Fendi jacket. He might not be wearing a banker suit, but he looked like he had money—in his own kind of way. Not the stuffed-shirt, matching belt, matching shoes combo so common in New York's financial district.

"All I can say is that there will be more positive news soon." His smile was wicked sharp. Until the network's official statement was released, he was keeping his mouth shut. Anything else would be unprofessional of him.

"Good. I'm glad to hear it. Lane has a reputation for being a bit more conservative than his predecessor, but he's a proven executive."

All Terrance cared about was that the man continued to support his show.

"Vincent is going to run through more of your numbers while I move along to another meeting. It was good to see you again. We look forward to supporting more of your success."

Yeah, Harwick knew the TV show was going to make them all richer—not that the old geezer needed more money. But that's not what banking was about. That Terrance understood.

He rose when the gray-haired man did and shook his hand. "Thank you for making time to see me."

"Next time you're in town, we'll have dinner. I'm sorry I was already booked."

"No worries. This trip came together fast." No one mentioned the Twitter event, thank God.

"Business always keeps us on our toes. Vincent, I'll see you later."

"Yes, sir," the younger man said. "Shall we go to my office?" he asked, turning his mega watt smile on Terrance. "I can pull up more detailed numbers there."

"That would be great."

They walked down the hall to the massive double doors of Junior's office. The interior boasted an impressive view of the city, a couple of landscape paintings Terrance would estimate at over twenty million each, and Harwick's framed and embossed

Harvard degree, which Terrance had always found too pretentious for words.

Who cared where someone went to school? He'd been to the school of hard knocks and landed on his feet. And no one besides him needed to see his degree from the Culinary Institute of America. It had given him the keys to open new doors, sure, but it wasn't what made him a sought-after chef. No, that came from somewhere inside himself.

He wondered if Harwick had crossed paths with Jane and Elizabeth at Harvard, but surely she would have mentioned it. The man seemed a bit younger than him, but he'd never been a good judge of age.

"As we said, your early sales figures are looking good, Chef T," Harwick said, returning to their usual informality. "The product line is rolling out nicely, but I don't have to tell you that the new TV show will give you a huge jump in sales. We've estimated an additional thirty percent conservatively."

Conservatively. Every bank's motto.

"I think we can count on more," Terrance said. "I certainly plan to do my part to push the products."

Harwick steepled his hands on his shiny mahogany desk. Not a sheet of paper was out of place, and Terrance found himself wondering how much time the guy spent nitpicking over it.

"My father wasn't going to mention it, but your recent trending on Twitter gave you a lot of publicity—although it might not be the kind of publicity you had in mind."

Leave it to Harwick Junior to mention it. Either that, or Harwick Senior had agreed Junior should be the one to broach the topic.

Terrance shrugged. "We live in a digital age. These things happen."

"It's a good thing your new girlfriend was comfortable with tweeting about your relationship. It seems to have turned the negative press around."

There was an edge to the guy's voice, and Terrance's back went ramrod straight. Was this guy insulting Elizabeth? If so, he wouldn't take it. Harwick had a reputation with the ladies even though he was married, a fact that had never bothered Terrance until now.

"Elizabeth is wonderful," he said in a flat tone. "I'm lucky to have her. Speaking of which, I promised to take her to Tiffany's, so I need to head out soon. Is there anything else you wanted to discuss? It sounds like everything is exceeding our projections."

He wasn't on a schedule, but he didn't like the turn of this conversation. The man was his banker. Not his friend.

"Are you two picking out an engagement ring?" the man asked, his mouth a tight line now.

Rings? Whoa! He hadn't thought that far down the line, but he realized the relationship might go there in the future. He loved her and wanted to spend his life with her. Marriage had never held an allure, but with her, he liked the idea of it. They could make that leap whenever they wanted.

"I'll decline to comment since you never know how things get tweeted," he joked and rose.
"And now I really do need to go. Thanks again for meeting with me."

"Are you two free for dinner tonight? My wife and I would be happy to host you. The scheduler only consulted my father's schedule when you called for a meeting. Not mine. She was new, and we didn't retain her after her mistake."

No one could mistake the jealousy in his tone. He'd fired someone for mixing up dinner plans with Daddy?

"Unfortunately we've made other arrangements tonight with an old friend. Perhaps the next time we come back to New York."

"I'll look forward to it."

They shook hands and Terrance walked to the door.

As he was opening it, Harwick called, "Please give Liz my best."

Terrance turned around for a moment and forced himself to smile back pleasantly. "I will." He hated people who shortened other people's names, trying to be more familiar with them.

As he walked down the hall, he tried to shrug it off. Harwick had been more of a dick than usual. They'd never talked about women before, so perhaps that had been the difference. Terrance wouldn't allow him to bring up Elizabeth in the future. Now that he thought of it, he didn't like the idea of ever bringing her to dinner with Harwick, especially if he was as lascivious as his reputation implied.

A woman was waiting at the executive assistant's desk as he was leaving. She had on at least a hundred thousand dollars worth of jewelry and looked like the jet set type.

"Can you tell Vince I'm here?" the woman breathed out.

Vince. He hoped the nickname pissed that degree-flaunting jackass off.

Calling her Liz like that.

As the elevator dropped down from the one hundred and eleventh floor to the lobby, so did his stomach.

Harvard.

Vince.

Liz.

Elizabeth's name had been Liz when she was at Harvard. That much she'd told him. Had Harwick known her? Was that why he'd asked all those personal questions today—something he'd never done before?

When the doors opened, he strode across the lobby to the street. His gut was burning now, searing from the inside out. The Vince who'd stalked Liz at Harvard came from a powerful family. Few families were as powerful as Harwick's.

The image of her strained and pale face this morning rose up in his mind.

His head exploded. Jesus.

Was Vincent Harwick the Vince who'd stalked her?

He stopped in the center of the street, oblivious to the people bumping into him and swearing under their breath. His fingers dug out his phone.

"Hey," she answered, and there it was, that thready edge in her voice he'd been trying to soothe for days. Since his first mention of the meeting with Harwick, to be exact.

"Is Vincent Harwick the man who stalked you?" he asked her straight out. He could apologize later if he was wrong.

Her sharp intake was all the confirmation he needed. His other hand balled into a fist. He wanted to smash something.

"Tell me, goddammit." He needed to hear her say it.

"Terrance, please listen—"

"I want an answer," he growled as car horns sounded on the street.

"Did he say something?" she asked, her voice hoarse now.

"*I want to hear you say it!*"

"Yes! But please don't do anything. I don't want everything you've worked for to—"

He silenced the phone. Silenced her.

She'd lied.

She'd knowingly let him walk into that meeting with the man who'd stalked her.

A chauffeur bumped into him as he came around the long sleek black limousine he'd just parked by the curb. The hair on the back of Terrance's neck bristled, and he turned around. Harwick was walking toward him, the blond from the reception area hanging onto his arm like he was her sugar daddy.

"Terrance," he called out as the couple waded around the ever-present stream of people on the street.

"You son of a bitch," Terrance ground out, every muscle locked in place.

The man's head jerked back. The blond moved away, her eyes wide.

"Excuse me? What did you just say?"

Terrance got into Harwick's face, just like he used to do to the guys who got on his bad side in his old neighborhood. He could see the whites of the man's eyes now, like a frightened horse who knew he was about to be broken.

"You stalked my girlfriend."

"Sir," the chauffeur said, appearing beside them. "Do you want me to call security?"

"No," Harwick—Vince—said, tugging on his tie now. "We're fine. Aren't we, Chef T?"

"You called her Liz."

"I don't know what you're talking about," the man said, throwing a tight smile at the blond he was with, who was watching the scene with keen interest.

He told himself to keep his cool even as he grabbed Harwick by the lapels of his ten-thousand dollar suit. "Don't fucking lie to me. I know what you did to her."

"I didn't do anything," Harwick said in a violent whisper, shoving Terrance's hands away. "Liz was a slut back then and a liar, and she's clearly no better now. I told her we'd dump your contract if she didn't keep her mouth shut. And now she'll find out how much I meant it."

Camera flashes were blinding him now that he'd drawn attention to himself.

Slut.

Liar.

His control snapped. No one was allowed to call Elizabeth those names. The street kid broke through and punched Harwick squarely in the belly.

People gasped.

Adrenaline racing, he fought with his old instincts. It took a moment, but Terrance was able to pull back from giving the man the full, thorough beating he deserved.

Harwick was bent over, his breath heaving out, clutching his belly. It would have to be enough.

More flashes blinded Terrance's eyes. Strong arms came around him then, and he jerked against them.

"Calm down," the chauffeur said as security guards swarmed out of the Harwick & Taylor building.

Men in security uniforms surrounded him, and he heard police sirens in the distance. He struggled against the arms restraining him.

"Let me go, goddammit!"

Harwick finally straightened and marched over, his eyes hard as marbles now. Terrance had grown up around killers, and he knew what a man's looked like when he wanted to hurt someone for fun. Harwick had that look.

"I'm going to destroy you for that and that bitch Liz too."

Then he punched Terrance in the gut and stormed back into his family's building, the blond running after him in her four-inch designer heels.

The blow didn't make him flinch. Or cough. Or even spit. As a youth, he'd become a master at keeping his cool when bigger kids beat him up.

The police elbowed their way through the crowd that had clustered around the scene, some of the onlookers still taking photos. Videos. Hell, he'd just given them an eyeful. It would already be hitting Twitter.

But it didn't matter.

None of it mattered.

The chauffeur released him into the police's custody, and he was taken to sit in the closest vehicle after he showed them his ID. His ID! Like they didn't know who he was. The people on the street were shouting his name.

Harwick had refused to allow the police to bring him inside, away from the media-frenzied crowd, likely hoping to add to Terrance's disgrace.

When the cop asked him for a statement, he shrugged and said he didn't have one to make. The cop left him alone with a guard by the car, telling him not to leave until they sorted the situation out. People continued to take photos of him, and he lowered his head.

Elizabeth had known all along and hadn't told him.

She'd talked to Vince about him and hadn't said a word.

Everything they'd promised each other had been a lie.

Chapter 38

By the time Elizabeth had hailed a cab to head downtown to Harwick & Taylor, Twitter was exploding with tweets about the violent altercation between Terrance and Vincent Harwick, the scion of financial giant Harwick & Taylor. Terrance wouldn't answer her calls or texts, and she had no idea whether he could. All she could do was click on links to pictures of them fighting in front of the bank on the street in front of hundreds of witnesses.

It was her worst nightmare come true.

Terrance's face looked like cut steel, so hard and angry she shivered in her seat. Vince looked the same. Menacing. Triumphant. Especially in the picture where his chauffeur was restraining a struggling Terrance on the street.

The only silver lining were the pictures of Vince's cloying mistress hanging onto him as he rushed back into the building. People were speculating on the identity of the woman since she wasn't Mrs. Harwick.

Reporters were already on site, and cops seemed to be everywhere, judging from the live photos taken at the scene. An assault on a senior bank executive like

Vincent Harwick was big news. Even bigger since the perpetrator was a celebrity chef.

And since the photographic evidence of Terrance's recent altercation with Ryan had made the rounds, that story was woven into the one with Vince. Each media sound bite, each tweet was building a picture of a troubled man who'd snapped.

Based on what she could see online, no statements had been made by either Vince or Terrance. Her phone rang, and she saw that it was Mac. Dread circling in her belly, she answered.

"Mac," she said simply, chafing at the monotonous crawl of traffic.

"Elizabeth. I assume whatever it was that you didn't want Terrance to know about Harwick & Taylor has come to light. My publicist just called to fill me in on the events out there. Where are you?"

His hotel chain would be affected by this, she suddenly realized, since he employed Terrance. Her nightmare grew.

"In a cab trying to get to the bank."

"Go home. If you show up, it will only make things worse. You need to start thinking like a publicist. Terrance is going to need our help now."

Help. Yes, he would need that and more. "You're right."

She told the cab to take her back to the apartment, frustration making her sit on the edge of the seat. Terrance would come home sometime. Then he'd have to talk to her.

"Are you going to tell me now what your reservations were about Harwick & Taylor?" She'd known Mac for too long to miss the edge in his voice.

"Vince Harwick stalked me when I attended Harvard." She glanced at the cab driver. With the TV screen blaring on the divider between the front and the back, she didn't think he could hear her. Still, she wanted to err on the side of caution.

"Oh, Elizabeth," Mac said, his voice whisper soft.

She hung her head.

"And you didn't tell Terrance that?"

"I was trying to prevent this from happening. Look I'm not in a place to talk now."

"Okay. We'll do what we can with Terrance's people. For the moment, I suggest you say nothing."

Nothing. She'd been good at that of late. "Agreed. I'll talk to you later."

She realized there might be reporters camping out on the doorstep of Terrance's building, so she dialed up his building's phone number and asked if there was a private entrance she could use. After paying the cab driver a block away, she followed the directions to the underground entrance.

Inside Terrance's apartment, she turned on the TV, dialed up her computer, and watched her phone. The story continued to spread. Reporters speculated the business deal between Harwick and Terrance must have gone bad. Others discussed Terrance's reputation for violence, and how it seemed to have escalated in recent days.

No one said anything negative about Harwick & Taylor. Their esteemed reputation would keep them looking lily white through all this.

Soon, a new story broke, and it had her sinking to her knees in the middle of his penthouse. His primetime TV network had announced they were dropping his new reality TV cooking show.

Terrance was losing everything.

And it was all her fault.

The tears started. Her phone rang, and she grabbed it, hoping it was Terrance. It was her best friend instead.

"Jane," she whispered, her throat raw.

"Liz. Oh, Liz. What happened?"

She told her what she knew, which wasn't much.

"Jane. I need you."

"I know. I've just rented a private plane in Denver."

God, she was so lucky. She hadn't even needed to ask her to come. "Terrance is so angry, Jane. And now he's lost the TV show because of this. Because of me."

"Stop. This is *not* your fault."

Her gaze swept around the penthouse to where her things were mingled with his. Everything had felt so right between them. Now she couldn't imagine how they would ever reclaim that.

"I should have told him." Maybe if she'd done things differently...

She should never have trusted Vince. He must have said something to Terrance. Nothing else made sense.

"Terrance might have taken a swing at Vince anyway. Matt said he would have, if that makes you feel any better. Liz, Rhett and Abbie are coming with Matt and me."

Her family was circling the wagons. She'd always been able to count on them. "How mad is Rhett?"

"He loves you, Liz, but he was hurt. And mad. I've never seen him so mad. He wanted to take Vince to the woodshed. But it doesn't change how he feels about you."

Her guilt grew. Rhett had been her brother, friend, boss, and savior. God she hoped he could forgive her.

"Mac is trying to decide if he should come with us to New York or stay in Dare," Jane continued "He's being inundated with phone calls."

Yes, the press would want to know if the hotel tycoon was going to dump his violent celebrity chef like the primetime network had done. There was already speculation about what Mac would do in the media, and reading the speculation made her gut churn.

"Has anyone heard from Terrance?" she asked Jane, wishing he would call back, if only to tell her he was okay.

If the police charged him with assault...

Since people had tweeted that Vince had hit Terrance too she was hoping it would even things out. Harrison Harwick wouldn't want to charge Terrance with assault if his own beloved son could be implicated for anything—like stalking Elizabeth. He'd remember Liz Parenti once Vince clued him in on the situation.

The Harwick men would find other ways to punish Terrance. First up would be reneging on their business contract for Terrance's culinary product line. Then they would turn their attention on her, she'd bet.

"He's briefly talked to Mac," Jane told her. "He's waiting to hear if he's going to be charged."

Then her friend paused, and she knew she was about to hear something that would hurt her.

"He told Mac he's going to say it was a business misunderstanding if they press him."

"He's protecting me?" she breathed out. "Even now? But he'll lose everything if he says it's a business misunderstanding. No one will want to work with him again."

"I know."

She covered her mouth with her hand, trying to hold back the sobs that wanted to break free. Terrance might be angry with her, but he was trying to save her too, just like she had done for him.

"I need to go to him."

"You know you can't. You have to trust him—and Mac. His team is on this now."

She heaved herself off the floor, wishing she was the kind of person who threw things. It might make her feel better. "I hate the waiting."

"Just hold on. We'll probably get in late, but we'll be there as soon as we can. Liz, we're going to get through this—just like we did last time."

Last time they'd run for their lives—or she had. Jane had come along for her own reasons.

"Oh, Jane. Thanks for being the best friend...a girl could ever have." Her throat constricted, making her words drop to a whisper.

"You know it," her friend said, her voice breaking too. "I love you, Liz. It's going to be okay."

But was that really true?

"I need to call Rhett. I can't wait until he gets here."

"Good idea. Just remember. We have a lot more resources than we did when we were at Harvard, and a lot more people to root for us too."

But how did that help Terrance unless he revealed the real reason for the fight?

"Thanks, Jane. I mean it."

"No need to say it. It's what sisters do."

Once they signed off, she called Rhett.

"Hey, sugar," he said, his voice heavy with emotion. "How are you holding up?"

"Rhett, I'm so sorry I didn't tell you. I...was afraid you'd tell Terrance and—"

"Let's leave that for another time. Jane told me why you did what you did. I don't like it, but I love you. Now we just need to sort through this load of shit and help T. He's gonna need it."

She grabbed a tissue and blew her nose. God, she was a mess. "I know he does. It's bad, Rhett. He's lost the TV show."

"I heard that," he said with a sigh. "We're just going to have to help him not lose anything else. I don't know how much Abbie and I can do to help, but we're coming to New York with Jane and Matt to be with you two. That's what family does."

You two. Them. Together... She loved the sound of that, but she wasn't sure Terrance wanted her anymore, not after the way his voice had sounded on the phone. Part of her couldn't blame him. Tears plopped onto her leggings.

"Thanks, Rhett. I'll see you soon."

"Hang in there, sugar. We'll find a way to make things right."

Unable to bear the silence when she hung up, she called Terrance again. When he didn't pick up, she decided to leave a message.

It's me. I don't know what to say except...I'm so sorry. I just...don't know what to do. I'm worried about you. I know you're mad at me and you have every right...but I love you. Please call me or text me and tell me you're okay.

As she ended the call, her mouth tasted bitter. *Okay?* What in the hell was okay in this kind of situation?

The media continued to spin the story. When pictures of Terrance getting into a black sedan with dark-tinted windows were posted, she felt light headed. He hadn't been charged...yet.

Her phone lay in her lap. He didn't call. He didn't text.

She felt like she was being buried alive in a coffin of her own making. The darkness pressed in on her as the hours passed, but she made no move to turn on the lights. She didn't want to see any evidence of this place where they'd been so happy. She didn't deserve it.

When the front door clicked open hours later, she jumped up. The hallway light came on as Terrance appeared in the doorway, his face rigid, his eyes hard.

He'd never looked at her with such anger, such vehemence.

"Terrance, I'm so sorry," she said, starting to walk toward him.

"Don't." His voice was harsh, and he held up a hand. "I almost had one of my people come pack me a bag so I wouldn't have to see you, but I'm not a coward."

Pack his bag? Oh, God, he was leaving.

"Please—"

"Enough, Elizabeth. You *lied* to me. After I told you

how important honesty was to me. You let me walk into the office of the man who'd stalked you, and you said nothing to me. Nothing! You fucking talked to him behind my back. How could you make a deal with that man?"

She clenched her hands, rocking in place. "He called when the story about Ryan broke on Twitter." Even now she could hear Vince's menacing voice in her ears, a sound from so many nightmares. "He recognized me. I never thought something like this could happen! That you could be in business with him. When he found out you didn't know who he was, he said I'd better keep it that way."

Terrance stared at her with hard eyes, and she could see she wasn't reaching him. She took another step toward him.

"Don't make me say it again."

"I was afraid he was going to hurt you."

He thumped his chest with his fist. "Hurt me? Are you fucking kidding me? I can take care of myself. I have since I was a kid. A guy like Harwick doesn't scare me."

"Well, he should. Not only could he destroy your business deal, but he could hire guys to hurt you. I was protecting you!"

He shook his head. "No, you were protecting yourself. If you'd believed in me, you would have trusted me to handle this."

This time, he strode across the room. She almost backed away from him and the anger pouring out of him.

"You thought I'd beat the shit out of him if I knew, didn't you?"

Her bottom lip quivered.

"Didn't you?" he yelled.

"Yes! I was afraid of what you might do. Of what he might do to you! And me!"

He tore away from her.

"What else was I supposed to think? You almost knocked Ryan out for hassling me. And you knocked the guy at The Peacock flat for calling me names and putting his hands on me."

His mouth twisted. "Right. And Vince did a hell of a lot more than both of those guys put together. All I could think of was what he'd done to you. Then he baited me about you. Called you names. How else was I supposed to handle that? It wasn't my best moment, and God knows, I'll have to apologize, but I don't regret a thing. He deserves a hell of a lot more than what he got for what he did to you. I stopped myself from giving him the beating he deserved."

She extended her hands to touch him, her whole heart breaking. "Terrance, please."

"Don't touch me, Elizabeth. Don't ever touch me again."

His flat, unemotional tone had her hands fisting at her sides. "How many times will you make me say I'm sorry? I love you. Terrance, please don't throw away what we have because of this."

His head shook slowly, oh so slowly, like he was seeing parts of her for the first time that he didn't like. "What we had were some good times, a hell of a lot of intense shit I don't ever want to go through again, and enough mistrust for a lifetime. We're done."

"Don't say that!"

"Why not? It's the truth," he said and spun around, heading to his bedroom, the bedroom they'd shared. "You even talked to Mac about this, right? That's why he changed his mind at the last minute about using my bank."

She followed him, her chest tight with tension. "I didn't want Vince to have yet another thing to hold over you if he decided to hurt you because of me. And Mac didn't deserve that."

"So you were protecting Mac too?" He flung a few pairs of shoes from the walk-in closet into a black duffel bag. "You went behind my back on business. *My business*. Did you tell Mac why?"

He wanted to know if she trusted Mac more than she did him. "No! I didn't even tell Rhett about this."

His laugh was bitter. "Were you afraid he might tell me, or that we'd both beat the shit out of Vince?"

"Both!"

"Well, at least you can be honest about that."

"Why won't you understand?" she asked him. "Why can't you forgive me? This wasn't easy for me either. I didn't see another way out."

"If you don't understand," he said, shoving clothes into the duffel bag, "then I can't help you."

She followed him into his massive bathroom and watched him load up toiletries and his shaver. "What do you want me to do? I'll do anything to make it up to you. *Anything,"* she said quietly.

His bottle-green eyes met hers in the mirror, and for a minute, every muscle in his body seemed to tremble. A moment later he was in control again.

"Reporters are going to call you since they *think* you're my girlfriend. Don't say anything."

Her heart bled at that. "The calls and emails have already come pouring in. I haven't answered any of them."

"My team and I are going to dig our way out of this. Mac's going to support me, but I need to talk to him about that. It might be in his best interest to sever ties with me too. I won't be the cause of any trouble to his business."

His martyrdom almost brought her to her knees. "But I'm the one who caused this. If—"

"You didn't cause anything. I hit the guy on a public street in downtown Manhattan. That's on me. Now it's time to pay the piper."

"But if I'd told you about him..."

"I probably would have decked him anyway, Elizabeth." He slung the duffel over his shoulder and walked over to her. "I had to admit that to myself when I was sitting in the back of a cop car—something I hadn't done since I was fifteen."

She drank in his features. Curled her hands into fists so she wouldn't touch him.

"You were right to fear what I'd do to him," Terrance told her in a low voice. "You just can't take the street out of the rat."

Her heart broke. "Don't say that."

He strode past her. "It's the truth, and I always promised you the truth."

The arrow found its way into her gut. "What if I tell the media why you did it?" she asked. The very mention of it was enough to cause a sudden constriction in her throat.

She'd thought it through over and over again since Vince's call. The very idea scared the bejesus out of her. Talking about all of it again, bringing back the hurt and pain. No one had believed her before. Why would they this time? And Vince would come at her with everything he had.

"What? You're going to say Vincent Harwick of Harwick & Taylor stalked you when you were at Harvard? Elizabeth, no one believed you then, and according to what you told me, his lawyer painted you as a fortune hunter and a slut. All of that's going to get dragged out, and nothing good will come of it. Throw in the Vixen pictures...and...well, you're going to look like the slut they accused you of being."

Shame burned in her. He was only confirming her conclusions. Everything Vixen had been and done would be misrepresented. At least Liz Parenti had looked like a normal girl. Vixen was another matter all together.

His hand lifted, almost as though he was going to touch her face, before falling to his side. He moved away from her, widening the gap between them. "I'm pretty sure Harwick senior and son will sue you for defamation or worse if you try."

Everything she loved would be tarnished if she tried to fight Vince again. Defeat knocked her down for the last time.

"Elizabeth."

Terrance called her back from the darkness. She looked over at him. He held up a key and placed it on the side table.

She knew what it went to. It was her key. The symbol of her trust in him. The invitation into her heart.

The darkness enveloped her completely again.

"You can leave my key when you leave the apartment. I'll have the things you left at my place in Dare Valley sent to you when I get back. You can stay here as long as you need. Just know there are reporters crawling outside. My property manager told me that you already called him about the private entrance. Use it when you leave."

Unable to speak, she nodded.

"Promise me you won't say anything. I know guys like Vince. Don't tangle with him again. You should head back to Dare Valley as soon as possible."

She had to swallow the lump in her throat. It was over. Everything between them was gone. He was speaking to her like someone checking off the boxes on a list.

House key returned. Check.

Proper breakup speech concluded. Check.

Was he going to wish her well now too?

"Terrance?"

"Goodbye, Elizabeth." His eyes scanned her once more. Then he turned around and walked out of the apartment.

She wrapped her arms around herself and started to cry when the door shut. A horrible, messy, loud cry that came from her belly—because her heart was lying in pieces, and there was nothing she could do to put it back together.

When someone knocked on the door a while later, she was still sitting in darkness. The effort it took to push off the floor and walk to the door exhausted her. When she opened it, her family stood waiting in the hall.

Jane rushed forward and wrapped her arms around her. She pressed her face into her neck and held on. Then large arms wrapped around them both, and she knew it was Rhett.

Taking deep breaths so she wouldn't start bawling again, she absorbed their comfort and their strength. When she pressed back, she grabbed Jane's hand.

"I'm all packed and ready to go. I hope you made reservations somewhere." Even now, she could smell Terrance's cologne. If she didn't get out of here, she'd go mad.

"We're at the Plaza," Jane said. "Was Terrance—"

"He was here," she said flatly. "He left."

She couldn't talk about it.

Turning away, she headed back to the den and grabbed her luggage, but Matt took it from her and wheeled it past Rhett and Abbie, who were holding hands, frowns on their faces.

"Just give me a moment."

Her family left her, and her eyes went to the key she'd taken off her keychain—the one to his house in Dare Valley. It lay on the same side table where he'd put hers.

But she left her key there.

She hoped Terrance understood her message.

Chapter 39

The bourbon in Terrance's hand felt like it weighed as much as one of his five-gallon stock pots. His friend's restaurant was as silent as a tomb. Without any distractions, all he could think about was Elizabeth.

After meeting with his publicist and the rest of his team, he'd called his chef friend and asked if he could stay with him for a while. And go to his restaurant in the dead of night.

Being in a restaurant had healed him before. He hoped to God it would again, especially now that he feared he might have lost his place in one for good.

His phone rang, and he saw it was Mac. His boss.

"Where are you?" Mac asked the minute he picked up.

Terrance gave him directions, and when a discreet knock sounded on the front door of the Michelin-star restaurant, he pushed off the bar stool to open it.

His friend looked about as exhausted as he was.

"Bad day?" Terrance joked.

"Not my best." He closed the door and scanned the restaurant. "You're alone?"

"Yeah," he said. "My friend understood why I

wanted to come here. Mac, I need to apologize to you."

His boss waved his hand. "I know why you did it. Elizabeth told me today when I called her."

Terrance's body felt like it had aged thirty years as he strode back to his bar stool to pick up his bourbon. He threw it back. "I couldn't stop myself when he said those things about her." Vile things. Things that still made him want to wrap his hands around Vince's throat.

"I'm not surprised. Peggy told me stalkers like to taunt. She said you should have kicked him in the nuts."

His laugh was hoarse. "I like your wife. Could have used her help with the cops today."

"Was it bad?"

Other than being looked at like he was nothing again, just vermin on the street, it had been a walk in the park. "It got better when Harwick refused to charge me. He said it was a misunderstanding." But he knew that wouldn't be the end of it. Not with a monster like Harwick.

This time Mac laughed, but there was an edge to it. "That's rich. I'm sorry about the TV show, Terrance. But who knows? Given what you've said about the network guy, you might have dodged a bullet with that prick."

He poured Mac a drink. "That's what I've been trying to tell myself." Otherwise, he couldn't take it.

In one day, he'd lost everything.

Including the woman he loved—by her own actions.

Now it was time to go a step further and do the right thing. "Mac, I think you need to find yourself another chef. I'm damaged goods right now, and I couldn't live with myself if I hurt your business."

Mac threw back his bourbon. "I had a feeling you were going to say that. Now let me tell you what I think. Poker players are rough around the edges. They don't call me The Maverick for nothing. We'll handle it. I assume you and your publicist worked out a statement that has you humbly eating crow."

So much so that he feared he would choke on it. "Yeah. I say I'm sorry, that it was a serious business misunderstanding, and that I'm seeking the help I need."

"Then we'll be fine. You can cook and keep a low profile. Not too many big-shot reporters are going to hole up in Dare Valley to keep tabs on you like they would here. This will blow over."

But he knew how to get lost here, and he couldn't do that in Dare Valley. Not with Elizabeth around. "I can't go back there, Mac. Not now." He didn't give a reason, but it was implied.

His boss fished out his phone and texted something. "I thought you might say that. Think on it. If you can't come back to Dare, you can head up the kitchen at another one of the hotels. I have four more to choose from until the Vegas one is finished."

For years, Terrance had felt like there was no one in his life he could count on. Slowly, as he'd turned himself around, that group had grown. And for that, even in the midst of this mess his life had become, he was grateful.

"You're a good friend."

"Shit. You might make me cry."

His laughter bubbled out roughly, and he thought about giving his boss a Ben Franklin as a joke to start his own Cuss Fund. But he couldn't manage it. The Cuss Fund didn't matter anymore. The show was over.

"Are we having a moment?" he asked.

"Probably. If not, we will when Rhett arrives."

His body tensed at that. Rhett was supposed to be with Elizabeth. "If you're going to hang around, have another drink."

They sipped their bourbons in silence, Terrance growing edgier as he wondered if Rhett was going to tell him to forgive Elizabeth and take her back.

God, he couldn't handle that right now.

Not when he missed her like this. The hole he'd lived with all his life was back, and it was larger than it had ever been. The one person who could fill it was lost to him.

When the knock on the front door sounded a half hour later, Terrance pushed through his dread and rose to open it. His friend hugged him and stepped inside.

"You look like someone took you to the woodshed but good, T."

He shrugged, waiting to hear what Rhett would say.

"You done good," Rhett said, slapping him on the back. "If I'd been there, I would have kicked him in the nuts, guy rule or not. Repeatedly."

Yeah, most guys didn't kick other guys in the nuts. It was an unspoken rule on the streets.

"That's what Peggy said," Mac told him when Terrance remained silent.

"She's a smart woman," Rhett said, dropping onto a bar stool and helping himself to the bourbon. "That's why she married you."

"Indeed."

"How is she?" Terrance made himself ask Rhett. Elizabeth's tear-ravaged face and pained gaze haunted him.

"Jane's with her. They were still talking when I left. We have a suite at the Plaza."

Good. The hotel knew how to protect famous—and infamous—people. "I'm glad you guys are there for her."

"We're here for you too, T." Rhett downed the bourbon. "Or are you planning on fighting your way out of this alone like some macho asshole?"

"I got myself into this, and I'll get myself out of it. This doesn't have to affect anyone else."

"Bullshit. What the hell are friends for?"

Okay, now his throat was raw, and not from the bourbon. "I'm going down, man, and everybody around me needs to step back, or they'll go down with me too."

"So, you're just going to take the hit and not fight back?" Rhett asked. "You're going to let that asshole win?"

"That asshole has already won. He was the victor seven years ago when Elizabeth and Jane ran. Now, he's got me by the balls too. The best we can hope for is to protect Elizabeth from him. I told her not to say a goddamn word."

He paused then. The cussing was just a reminder of the backward direction his life was taking. Rhett was right. It had to stop. He had to be the change he wanted to see. Even though it hurt to remember all the reasons he'd started the Cuss Fund, he reached into his wallet and drew out a hundred dollar bill because it was something he could do—for himself. His friend glanced at the Ben Franklin he shoved into his pocket, but said nothing.

Rhett knocked back his bourbon. "What's your plan?" he finally asked.

He told him what he'd told Mac, and Rhett said nothing, which only made Terrance nervous. When Rhett got stony silent, it meant trouble.

"We're not even twenty four hours into this here circus," Rhett finally said. "Let's see how things play out. Maybe we'll be surprised."

Terrance knew how they would play out. He would deliver a shitty apology he didn't mean in front of dozens of reporters in the wrinkled suit he'd stuffed into his duffel bag. His products would disappear from the shelves. He'd seek professional help because he'd need his head shrunk if he ever fell for a woman again. Somewhere he'd cook.

He had to, or he'd die.

"Don't get your hopes up," Terrance said, shoving back his sleeves and staring at his tattoos. "People like me are never branded the good guy."

He'd never admitted it to anyone, but he'd put those

griffins on his arms not only as a symbol of rising above his circumstances—that was the nice answer—but also as a f-you to all of the people who'd already judged him a street rat, a nothing. If he said it first, maybe it wouldn't hurt as bad.

But God, it still hurt.

He was back to being nothing again.

Chapter 40

The waiting room to one of New York's biggest morning shows was filled with flowers, bright colors, and plenty of people checking Elizabeth's makeup and asking if she wanted another cup of coffee.

Jane sat beside her, holding her hand. "You're gonna be great, Liz."

Waking up at the Plaza without Terrance beside her for the first time since they'd come together had helped her find the inner strength to face her greatest fear.

Vince was going to pay for what he did.

Even if he told the world she was gold-digging whore.

She was going to make her story public so everyone knew why Terrance had attacked Vince.

He wasn't going to lose everything he'd worked so hard for because of her.

"I'm so afraid I'm going to forget what we wrote," she told Jane.

"Come on. You can keep track of the cards of famous poker players without batting an eyelash. This is a walk in the park."

It wasn't, and they both knew it. She was going to be

sick again, violently sick. The poor girl who'd done her makeup had rubbed her arm in comfort when she'd returned from bolting to the bathroom. A breath mint and reapplied makeup had helped her look and feel slightly better, but sweating profusely and puking were hell on Chanel.

Her lawyer was standing by as well, knowing that heads were going to roll once she gave her public statement about Vince Harwick of the esteemed Harwick financial empire.

Including her own. Vince would make sure she graced his chopping block.

Matt had even helped her by reading over her lawyer-approved statement, adding his two cents on how she could humanize herself and the story more so Vixen wouldn't be the center of attention. His advice was to keep it on Liz Parenti. Show the audience pictures of that young, innocent girl at Harvard.

With Jane's help, she'd pulled together a series of photos of them from Harvard. They'd poured all their energy into creating a media package to curry viewers' sympathy, and she'd asked Mac's publicist to go over it as well since she respected her opinion.

"You're going to break their hearts, Elizabeth," the woman had said.

If so, their hearts would be just be like hers.

Shattered.

News of her exclusive interview had spread across the airways, and Terrance had been calling her nonstop. She hadn't answered, fearing he would try and talk her out of it. Worse, fearing she would break down and curl into a ball at the sound of his voice.

Rhett was in charge of keeping Terrance from showing up today, and so far, he'd succeeded.

Mac and Terrance's publicists were over the moon about her telling the truth, Mac had told her, and both camps were going to release a statement right after her interview saying that Terrance had been protecting Elizabeth from a deeply violent man.

Mac had never backed down from a fight, and he wasn't going to start now.

Jane was betting she wasn't the only one Vince had stalked, but Elizabeth couldn't think about that now. If others came forward, they would band together. Heal together if need be.

And take that bastard down.

"Ms. Saunders?" the woman assigned to her said. "It's time."

Elizabeth hugged Jane tight.

"You're going to do great," her best friend whispered. "I'm so proud of you."

One more squeeze, and she stepped back. She could only nod jerkily. Her voice wouldn't work.

It *had* to work.

She was led to the set. Numbly shook hands with the show's hosts.

There was small talk, and then the female host touched her arm gently. "Just remember you're doing this for every woman who's ever been threatened by a man."

The cameraman cued them. The host introduced her.

She looked into the camera. And found her voice.

"Hello. My name is Elizabeth Saunders, and I was stalked by my college boyfriend."

Chapter 41

Terrance watched Elizabeth's interview from his chef friend's apartment. His heart beat painful and fast in his chest as he watched her pale features, listened to her thready voice tell the story she'd once told him in tears.

Rhett had forcibly stopped him from going to her and trying to talk her out of it. His friend had threatened to knock him out, and he'd meant it. *She has to do this, T, and I'm not going to let you or anyone else stop her.*

Now he realized it was true. She had to do it—not just to save him, which he knew was her primary motivation, but for herself.

He'd never been more proud of anyone in his life.

Elizabeth had done what she had to do. Just like he had.

Now all he could do was support her.

After her interview, his publicist's phone rang off the hook with more requests for interviews. For the next couple of days, he made the rounds to all the major shows, telling the story about the innocent Liz Parenti and her stalker boyfriend, Vince Harwick.

His business deal with Harwick & Taylor had been bought by Mac's investment bank with Mac's assistance after Terrance's lawyers had reached out to his former business partner. He was glad to be done with the Harwicks professionally.

But it wasn't over for Elizabeth.

No, the Harwicks had immediately launched their own campaign to paint her as a fortune hunter and a slut, but it didn't stick. Her vulnerability and raspy voice on camera, backed up by other Harvard students who remembered Vince's possessiveness, turned public opinion against them. As did the teachers from the Ivy League university who'd touted her genius and Harwick's entitled attitude.

Two more women came forward to say Vincent Harwick had stalked them while they'd worked at the bank. Then the tide turned even more. Vince's wife released her own statement about her husband's philandering and possessiveness, filing for what would become a very public divorce. She even publicly apologized to Elizabeth and the other students for her soon to be ex-husband's behavior.

Immediately, Mr. Taylor of Harwick & Taylor issued a brief statement to the press that the junior Mr. Harwick had resigned to see to his personal life.

No lawsuit had been launched yet by the Harwick family against Elizabeth, and Terrance hoped to God it wouldn't come to that.

Elizabeth deserved peace after all she'd been through, and he hoped she would find it.

He texted her only once after the interview. Wrote three or four different phrases until he settled on something simple.

Thank you for what you did.

Her answer was equally brief.

I did it for both of us.

Nothing more. Well, what more was there to say?

None of this changed the facts. Elizabeth had lied to him and hadn't trusted him. Had believed the worst in him. And it was on him that he'd validated her fears.

He couldn't live his life with someone like that.

But by God, he missed her, and the pain was almost too much to bear.

After further conversation, he and Mac had decided to move forward with putting Terrance in charge of another one of the Four Aces' hotel restaurants until Mac's new hotel in Vegas was open for business. He wouldn't get the chance to work with Natalie, of course, and the call she'd given him a couple of days ago—offering her support and making increasingly inappropriate jokes in an effort to cheer him up—had made him realize it would be a loss. But Dare Valley just wouldn't work. He was still mulling over which hotel location to choose that would in the meantime.

Being back in the city, he still felt the urge to hide in its anonymity. He started cooking in his buddy's kitchen because he felt like a salamander left on land too long, craving water.

But it wouldn't be enough. He'd have to cook professionally and soon.

He'd have to go back to his life—whatever that life was now.

The only thing he knew was that it didn't include Elizabeth.

Now it was time to put one foot in front of the other. And that meant returning to his apartment. He was a jumble of nerves on the way there, fearing her Chanel perfume would still linger in the air. He steeled himself to face it like a man.

His phone rang as he was opening the door to his apartment, and he dug it out of his jeans. It was his agent.

"Hey, Nadine."

"Terrance, I have someone on the line who wants to

speak with you." Her excitement was infectious. "I think you're going to want to talk to him."

"Okay. Put him on."

"Mr. Waters, this is Howard Farnsworth of CST Television."

Terrance's body felt like it was sinking into the floor. Howard was the primetime network executive of Lane's rival network. "Mr. Farnsworth."

"I understand you don't currently have an offer for a primetime television show."

His heart started beating hard in his chest. "No, sir. I'm in between jobs right now."

The man laughed, and the sound was booming and genuine. Terrance found himself liking the guy right away. "I'd like to change that. I've been following you, and I think you can do great things on my network. I was raised in the south side of Boston, so I like people who stick up for women and can still cook the pants off the competition."

Now he could hear a trace of the rough neighborhood in the man's voice. "Is that so?"

"I would have clocked that guy good too, if I were in your place. My wife thinks you're a hero. We'd like to have you over for dinner while you're still in town to talk things over. What would work for you?"

He'd planned to stay in the city for a few more days, finishing up business, and then he was going to prescribe himself some therapy: a beach and a hammock and a bottle of rum, with loads of quiet. No press allowed.

"How about tomorrow night?" he suggested.

"Wonderful. My wife will be having it catered, lest you worry. I've been married to that woman forty-two years now, and she still can't cook an egg worth hell, but since I can't either, it works for us."

He felt a smile come and go on his face, a rarity lately. Yes, he already liked Howard a lot. This felt like a much better fit than Lane ever had.

"Great. I'll see you then."

"I'll send my car for you at seven."

Wow, a dinner invitation and a private car. The man was serious. It looked like he was going to get his primetime TV show after all.

And all because of Elizabeth.

He was frowning as he moved into the family room. Dropping the duffel, he closed his eyes briefly, letting her perfume tickle his nose. Her scent lingered here just like he'd feared.

Elizabeth wasn't a woman who was easily forgotten.

He braced himself to cook his way out of all of these god-awful feelings. Then he noticed two keys resting on the side table.

Crossing to them, he picked them both up. They were cold in his hands. He remembered telling her to leave his key when she left.

His key was there all right.

But she hadn't taken hers back.

His heart thundered in his chest. She was trying to tell him something.

It was time to find out what.

Chapter 42

Natalie had gotten up late after staring at the ceiling for two solid hours before finally falling asleep. Blake was interrupting her sleep patterns again with vivid dreams of their life together.

Tears streamed down her face each time she awoke.

After getting dressed, she brushed her teeth in furious strokes, wincing when she rubbed her lower gum too hard. Her phone rang. It was Moira. She hit speaker.

"Hey, Mo! What's up?"

"Where are you?" her sister asked, her voice urgent.

"At home. I'm running late. Why? What's going on?"

"Turn on your TV. You aren't going to believe this. My whole office has stopped working. Everyone is in shock."

Her stomach chilled. God, please don't let it be another school shooting or a terrorist attack. "What's the matter?"

"Just turn on a local station. Any station. My God, Nat, I just can't believe it."

Her phone beeped, and Caroline's name appeared on the screen. Then Andy sent her a text.

What the hell?

"I'll call you back, Mo."

She ran into her front room and hit the remote, searching for her favorite local station. The first thing she registered was Blake standing at the microphone, dressed in a somber gray suit, camera flashes punctuating the air around him like starbursts.

The news banner at the bottom hit her like a Mack truck, and she sunk to her knees in front of the TV.

BREAKING NEWS: DENVER RAIDERS QUARTERBACK RETIRING

No, she thought. He wouldn't. *He couldn't.*

She had to turn up the volume to hear him over the buzzing in her ears.

"I've talked to Coach Kilpatrick and the team about my decision. They weren't exactly thrilled, but they know why I have to do this. I hope the fans can understand that sometimes our personal lives take precedence over our careers, and this time, I've decided I have to put that first."

His personal life? Oh, no. No, no, no, no, no. He couldn't retire from football because of her. Football was his reason for living.

A memory wormed its way into her mind. She'd told him that once after they were married, and he'd kissed her and said *she* was his reason for living now. Football came in at a close second.

"This team..." He broke off, and her heart bled for him, knowing how much this was hurting him. "This team has been my family, and we've been through a lot. I will always be grateful to them for letting me lead them. And I want to thank the fans, who made my Sundays...just awesome. Well, except when I didn't play well. Then they pretty much tanned my hide, which I deserved."

A few reporters laughed, and Blake had to cough to clear his voice.

"That's all I have to say right now. Thank you."

And with that bombshell, he left the podium, reporters shouting questions after him.

She broke out in a cold sweat.

He couldn't do this. Not because of her.

Maybe it was something else. It *had* to be something else. Had something happened to his parents or his sister?

She couldn't live with herself if he'd done this for her.

Her phone alerted her to an incoming text. Rising, she barely felt her body. It was like all of the life had been sucked out of her.

She picked up the phone. Looked at the screen.

Blake had texted her just seconds ago.

I told you we're not done.

She fell back against the door, bumping her head. Oh, God.

Another call sounded. Her mom. Then another text. Matt this time.

She couldn't answer. Couldn't speak.

What had he done?

Chapter 43

Elizabeth stood under the shower in her bathroom and let the water wash off her trip from New York along with the tears that hadn't stopped flowing.

It was done.

Vince was known for what he was. She'd spoken with the two other women who'd come forward with stories like her own. They'd cried together as they shared their all-too-similar tales, including how Vince's family had used their money and power to silence and intimidate his victims.

Other women were safe from him now—the three of them included.

She could only hope the extensive coverage would help even more women stand up to their stalkers. It had only taken her seven years to come forward, to stop being a victim.

Liz Parenti had no regrets.

As for Elizabeth Saunders...that was another matter.

She wasn't sure she'd ever get over the regret of losing Terrance.

Based on what she'd heard from her friends, he was planning to work at another one of Mac's hotels. Maybe it was for the best. Coming back to Dare Valley would be hard on both of them.

Part of her hoped he would go.

The other part longed to see him one last time.

Their brief text exchange hadn't been enough.

She feared nothing ever would be.

Shutting off the shower, she dried herself off with a plush towel and wrapped herself in a white terrycloth robe. Having hand-dried her hair, she looked in the mirror and tried to love what she saw.

A woman who'd done the hardest thing imaginable.

A woman who was alone again after discovering the joys of being with a wonderful man.

She didn't know if she could love again, but she was different now. Her heart was more open, and the fear that had controlled her life was easing. No, it wasn't completely gone, but she felt braver and stronger with each day that passed now that she'd faced down her demons.

With each new sunrise and each bold step, she was becoming more accustomed to being in the crosshairs of danger. Now she knew how to navigate it. And she had no need for masks anymore.

That was something to celebrate—as were the tweets and emails pouring in from other women, women who told her how inspirational it was to see her stand up to a bully like Vince.

She was inspiring others, and she could be proud of that too.

Now it was time to make a cup of tea, call Jane, and try and relax into what her life was becoming now. She was more than Vixen, more than Rhett's publicist.

She was a survivor.

Heading to the kitchen, she came up short when she saw Terrance in her family room, standing by the sofa, running his hand over the cashmere throw with the same gentleness he'd used to caress her skin.

The shock of seeing him had her clutching her robe. "Terrance! What are you doing here?"

He was wearing jeans and a navy T-shirt pulled up to the elbows, revealing his griffin tattoos. They seemed to take flight when he lifted one hand and held up something she couldn't make out.

"You left your key."

Her heart sank back into place. For a moment there, she'd thought he had forgiven her.

"I didn't forget it, but since you came over to return it, you can leave it on the table."

His bottle-green eyes had dark circles under them. "How are you?"

So they were going to have some small talk after all. "Okay." What did he expect her to say? Bawling three times a day over him?

"I'm proud of you—for what you did about Vince."

Oh, how her throat grew thick at that. "Me too."

He shoved away from the couch, her key still in his palm—almost like he couldn't bear to set it down. That would mean the final parting between them.

"Thank you," he said in a quiet voice. "For what you did for me."

It took her a moment to answer. "It's like I said in my text. I didn't just do it for you, but I'm glad it helped you. I didn't want you to lose anything because of me."

He kicked at her floor with his Italian shoes. "Right. I seem to have everything back and more now that you've painted me as a hero. So why do I feel like I've lost everything that matters?"

The trembling started at her knees and worked its way up to her bottom lip. "What are you trying to say?"

Finally, he crossed the room to stand in front of her, his eyes scanning her face. "I don't want to live without my perfect ingredient."

"Maybe you'll find another." She forced herself to say the words.

"I don't think so."

"Then..."

"I thought you might like to come to dinner with me."

Dinner? Was he saying he wanted them to get back together? "When?"

"Tomorrow night." He looked down and kicked at the floor again. "The only problem is that you'll have to come back to New York with me."

Her mind put up a protective shield. They'd lost everything there.

"I thought we might start over," he went on. "Go together to New York like we were seeing it for the first time."

Her heart started to spin in her chest, but cold hard logic wrapped its icy coils around it, halting the celebration. Now that she'd stopped hiding from her past with Vince, she couldn't bury the hurt between Terrance and her.

"We can't erase what happened between us, as much as I'd like to."

"What if I told you that I forgive you and sincerely want you to forgive me?"

Then he looked directly into her eyes, and she saw the hurt and fear and vulnerability he'd shown only to her. Hope rose up inside her, something she'd thought permanently dead.

"I love you, Elizabeth. And that's never going to change. Despite what happened in New York. I've spent the last five days trying to run away from that fact, which scares the sh—heck out of me, but I can't."

She cupped her hand to her mouth to quell the sobs clamoring to be released.

"Talk to me," he said harshly. "I'm...dammit...I'm scared too, okay?"

When he fished out a Ben Franklin and stuck it in his pocket, she said in shock, "You're still doing the Cuss

Fund?"

He shrugged. "I realized self improvement should never be driven by fame. I've asked to be on the board for The Children's Aid Society in New York because it will help kids who are struggling...kids like I used to be. It's time for me to stop running from my past. I want to be a better man. One who deserves a woman like you."

Unable to hold herself back anymore, she bridged the distance between them and wrapped her arms around him. His hands clamped around her back, and he pressed his face into her neck.

"Oh, God, Elizabeth."

The raw sound of his voice made her rub his rigid back in comfort. "I'm sorry, Terrance. I'm so sorry."

"I know, babe. *I know*. I am too. You were right to think I would hurt Vince. It was hard for me to admit that."

"It doesn't mean I don't love you," she whispered. "I know you wanted to...protect me."

He sighed. "I always will, but this street kid needs to stop seeing violence as one of his tools. I'm going to see someone about that."

Pressing back, she cupped his face. "So am I. For my stuff. We both have more healing to do."

His forehead rubbed against hers then. "I want to do it together."

A tear leaked out of the corner of her eye. "I do too."

"I love you," he whispered. "So much."

She kissed his tense jaw. "I love you too."

His head lowered slowly, giving her time. She met him halfway. Their lips reunited, and as he made love to her mouth, her heart settled back into place. She basked in that warmth as he undid her robe and cupped her breasts, cherishing her. Her hands caressed his back, cherishing the feel of him in turn.

He swept her up into his arms and carried her to the bedroom. Lowering them to the soft mattress, she opened her legs for him to settle his weight on her. She'd missed this, his solid presence, the urgency of his mouth, the hard press of his body. The gentleness of his touch. It called up the fire in her, unleashed a new feeling of security.

They were together again—with no secrets.

And nothing was ever going to separate them again.

He loved her slowly, sliding his mouth down her body, to kiss and caress the places that inflamed her—the ones only he knew—the crook of her elbow, the top of her hipbone, the back of her knee. She trailed her fingers to his own hidden places—the underside of his ear, the place where arm and shoulder met, and the middle of his thigh.

Every hidden place was brought into the light for healing, and when he glided inside her, she felt a new sense of completeness. As they moved together, her body sensed they were moving to a special place—one built by the pure pleasure of trust and commitment.

She fell into that place with him, and he joined her, each of them calling out. In the quiet of the room, they rested there, stroking each other, whispering loving words, reclaiming the miracle of their connection.

Finally, she nuzzled his chest. "So when do you want to leave for New York?" Right now all she wanted was to stay in bed with him for the next few days and shut out the world.

He kissed the top of her head. "Tomorrow morning I forgot to tell you that we're having dinner with some special people."

"Who?" she murmured, tracing his Chinese letter tattoos.

"The head of CST Television and his wife have invited me to dinner at their home to discuss a new TV show."

Now that *was* news. She pushed onto to her elbow. "Oh, Terrance! I'm so happy for you."

"His wife was really moved by our story, and Howard doesn't much like Lane, who's his chief competitor. You know, I think this is going to work out for the best."

She'd never really believed in that, but now she was starting to see life anew. "I think so too. You're going to do great."

"We're going to do great." He rolled onto his side and traced her waist. "If the show goes through, I'm going to be traveling to New York more. I'd like you to come with me when I do."

Her smile stretched the muscles in her face in the best way possible. "I'd like that." Then she lowered her eyes and traced his chest. "Are you staying here then?"

"Yes," he said, tipping up her chin. "If you'll have me."

"Oh, I'll have you."

This time he lifted her hand and kissed her knuckles. "I pretty much mean all the way here, Elizabeth, although I promise you a more romantic proposal."

She wasn't sure what dropped first. Her mouth or her hand from his. "You want to get *married?"*

His smile was lopsided but oh so sweet. "I know. I never thought it would happen for someone like me. But with you...Elizabeth, I...like the idea of...well hell...belonging to you."

She had to lay her head against his chest as the tears came. "I want to belong to you too," she whispered, raising her head to look into his eyes.

"Oh, babe," he said, his voice hoarse now. "You kill me in the best way possible."

She knew what he meant. He did the same to her.

"I have something for you," he said and rolled out of bed.

Before she could miss him, he slid in beside her and handed her a present wrapped in black and white striped paper. She eyed it. It was too large for a ring, and he raised his brow as if he knew she was thinking just that.

When she opened it, her heart simply soared. Resting on a bed of white satin was the most beautiful crystal Phoenix she'd ever seen. "Oh my goodness...it's so beautiful."

"I thought about getting another tattoo, but I'm moving past that. This present seemed more appropriate. You've risen from the ashes to become more beautiful yet again. It's no wonder you're my perfect ingredient."

"Terrance," she said softly, touching her hand to his cheek. "You're my perfect ingredient too."

"That's what I'm planning to call my TV show, by the way. In honor of you."

His mouth curved, and his face transformed with the same joy she was feeling rise in her heart.

Both of them knew finding the perfect ingredient only happened once in a lifetime.

Dear Reader,

I hope you loved Elizabeth and Terrance's story as much as I did writing it. Food has always been a passion for me, as many of you know by now. The art of cooking and sharing it with people was something my grandmother taught me, and it was a delight to experience the culinary arts through Terrance's eyes. I can tell you he inspired me to buy new ingredients and try new dishes more than any chef I've written about so far. As for Elizabeth, her journey to recover her sense of safety and stand up to her stalker had me cheering since I know many women experience violence at the hands of men every day. Her transformation melted my heart, and I wish the same triumph for any woman who's experienced something similar.

If you enjoyed this book, I would love for you to post a review since it helps more readers want to read my story. When you post one, kindly let me know at readavamiles@gmail.com so I can personally thank you. Please also consider recommending this book to your book clubs and friends. Thank you in advance!

To keep up with my new releases and any book sales I have, please sign up for my newsletter and connect with me on Facebook. I love to post about food and other fun stuff, so come and join the party.

Now, let's talk Natalie and Blake. Aren't they simply scrumptious together? They have been in my head for a long while now, and I can't wait to share their story, A BRIDGE TO A BETTER LIFE, this Spring 2015. In the meantime, if you haven't already, come check out Rye Crenshaw in COUNTRY HEAVEN and John Parker in THE CHOCOLATE GARDEN in my Dare River series (a connected series to Dare Valley where our favorite characters go back and forth). Rye, John Parker, and Clayton from THE PERFECT INGREDIENT have proved tantalizing heroes in their own right (if not terrible Latin dancers ☺). Clayton and Amelia Ann's story (that's Rye's sister fyi), FIREFLIES AND MAGNOLIAS, will be out Winter 2015. If you liked their antics with the Rhett and Company, you'll love Dare River.

Thanks again for cherishing Dare Valley as much as I do. You all rock my world in the best way possible. And because you *love* for me to include recipes, I have one for you: Bananas Foster. My own special recipe. Keep reading!

Lots of light and joy,
Ava

The next Dare Valley book, A BRIDGE TO A BETTER LIFE (Natalie & Blake), will be released Spring 2015.

And watch for the next Dare River story, FIREFLIES AND MAGNOLIAS (Amelia Ann & Clayton), out Winter 2015!

Sign up for my newsletter on my website so you don't miss any news!

AND NOW FOR THE RECIPE FROM THE PERFECT INGREDIENT...

Bananas Foster

Bananas
Butter
Honey
Cinnamon
Bourbon (optional)

Slice a handful of bananas length-wise and in half. Melt some butter in a pan, careful not to have it turn brown from high heat. Add the bananas, a dollop of honey to taste, and cinnamon.

Sauté until golden brown. The honey will bubble and create a gorgeous caramel-looking sauce. Now you can serve this just as it is or move onto an advanced step: the flambé. If you have never flambéed, I would research it to make sure you are doing it correctly. My first time involved singed bangs and a wall of fire, but you know...like Terrance, I was all that more determined to get it right. If you don't want to deal with the fire part (and after hearing about my singed bangs, who can blame you?), simply take the pan off the stove and add a little bourbon. The alcohol does cook off, albeit not completely, with the heat. Pour over ice cream and serve. Voila. One of the simplest and most satisfying desserts around.

About the Author

USA Today Bestselling Author Ava Miles burst onto the contemporary romance scene after receiving Nora Roberts' blessing for her use of Ms. Roberts' name in her debut novel, the #1 National Bestseller NORA ROBERTS LAND, which kicked off her small town series, Dare Valley, and brought praise from reviewers and readers alike. Ava's books have reached the #1 spot at Barnes & Noble, ranked in Amazon's Top 20, and been in the Top 10 at iBooks. A two-time Reward of Novel Excellence Nominee by InD'tale Magazine for NORA ROBERTS LAND and FRENCH ROAST, Ava has also released a connected series called Dare River, set outside the country music capital of Nashville. She's fast becoming a favorite author in light contemporary romance (Tome Tender) and is known for funny, emotional stories about family and empowerment. Ava's background is as diverse as her characters. She's a former chef, worked as a long-time conflict expert rebuilding warzones, and now writes full-time from her own small town community.

If you'd like to connect with Ava Miles or hear more about her upcoming books, visit www.avamiles.com or find Ava on Facebook, Twitter, or Pinterest.

14467156R00198

Printed in Great Britain
by Amazon.co.uk, Ltd.,
Marston Gate.